# Fireball

Tyler Keevil was raised in Vancouver, Canada. He first came to the UK in 1999 to study English and Lancaster University. Since immigrating to Wales to marry his wife Naomi and live in Llanidloes, he has won several awards for his short fiction, and his work has appeared in a variety of magazines and anthologies. He recently started lecturing in Creative Writing at the University of Gloucestershire. Tyler enjoys winter sports, including ice-hockey and snowboarding, but since coming to Wales he has also discovered the wonders of hiking and camping – particularly along the Pembrokeshire coast.

# Fireball

Tyler Keevil

Parthian
The Old Surgery
Napier Street
Cardigan
SA43 1ED

www.parthianbooks.com

First published in 2010
© Tyler Keevil 2010
All Rights Reserved
This edition published in 2012

ISBN 978-1-908069-78-8

Editor: Lucy Llewellyn

Cover design by Marc Jennings
Typeset by Claire Houguez
Printed and bound by Gwasg Gomer, Llandysul, Wales

The publisher acknowledges the financial support of the Welsh Books
Council.

*for all the Cove kids*

# 1

Chris knew it was coming to an end. He didn't say anything, but he didn't have to. I could just tell. We'd gone down to the beach at Cates Park to drink a few beers and throw away those stupid medals. That's where it happened. They said I helped him, which is complete crap. Chris didn't need my help. He could have done it blindfolded, with one hand. Of course, nobody wanted to believe that. Bates claimed we did it together, and that's how the papers wrote it up. If it weren't for my dad, I probably would have ended up in jail.

But basically, Chris did it alone.

'Shit,' I said. 'Did you kill him?'

'Beats me.'

We were standing on either side of him, looking down. His face was a mess. Drops of blood lay scattered all over the sand, like bright red bugs.

I leaned in closer, listening. 'I think I can hear him breathing.'

It wasn't much – just this gentle gurgling sound.

'I guess he's alive, then,' Chris said. 'Not that it matters either way.'

I didn't know what he meant at the time.

After he stole the squad car, they tried to stop him by setting up this shitty little roadblock. For most people it might have worked. Not Chris. He just drove straight through it at a hundred miles an hour. Almost instantly, the car became this blazing fireball, bright as the sun. Even that didn't stop him. He kept going, off a cliff and into the ocean. At first, it was impossible to tell what killed him: the impact or the fire or the water – or the guns. Apparently they shot him a bunch of times, too. Afterwards they handed the body over to some expert – this forensics expert in thick glasses and a huge turtleneck. When I saw him on the news, I flipped out and tried to kick over our television. No joke. My dad had to hold me back. I mean, Chris would have hated that guy.

He hated turtlenecks.

The sun glittered off the sand and scattered light across the bay. A sticky film of sweat coated my face. I couldn't stop trembling. In that kind of situation, I'm pretty much useless. I just freeze up. But Chris knew exactly what to do. He crouched in the sand and patted Bates down. They said we stole his wallet, which was another lie. We threw his wallet in the ocean. The only thing we took was his keys. And his car, of course. That turned out to be a big deal, but at the time it just kind of happened.

'Maybe we should get some help.'

That was me. I was shitting myself, for obvious reasons.

'Whatever. Let's just go.'

Chris walked over and opened the door. I picked up our bag of weed and followed, like always. From as far back as I can remember he'd been leading and I'd been following. That's just how it was between us. He got behind the wheel, taking his time. He was still sucking wind from the fight but his face was calm, the calmest I'd seen it since we saved the old lady. He shut the door, then rolled down the window and adjusted the mirror. His knuckles were bloody and swollen, as if he'd been punching a brick wall.

He looked over at me.

'You coming?' he asked.


# 2


When I got to my new school, a lot of people freaked out. Everybody in Vancouver had heard about Chris by then, and as soon as the other kids discovered that I was the friend – the unnamed friend always referred to in the news reports – they totally wet the bed. Hardly any of them would talk to me, and the ones that did always acted way too friendly, as if they wanted to get on my good side just in case I had a hit list. The parents took it even worse. A few banded together and started this feeble protest. Seriously. Not that I cared. Nothing ever came of it, and once the uproar died down I was pretty much left alone – which was fine by me. These days, I'm not too stoked on people in general. The problem is that they're always making assumptions, and I just can't handle having to deal with that shit any more.

'You knew that Chris guy, right?'

I was asked that by some kid at school – this little weirdo with a blue mohawk.

'Yeah. So?'

'So was he like, you know, a total nutcase?'

I just stared at him until he left.

That's what everybody thinks, and it harsh pisses me off.

They go around assuming he was a nutcase and they never even met him. They just heard about him, or read about him, or saw his picture on the news. And it's the same with me. They all just assume I'm as tough as Chris because I knew him. I'm not, of course. I'm not half as tough as him. At my old school, people found it weird that we could even be friends. That's pretty weak, though. I mean, it's not like Chris was fighting constantly. He only fought when he had to. The rest of the time we just hung out. We went swimming, or got stoned, or watched movies. We watched pretty much every kind of movie you can imagine, but what we really liked was anything about a giant shark or mutant snake or radioactive spider. We couldn't get enough of that stuff. Every other weekend we'd pile over to Julian's and watch a creature feature on his dad's widescreen TV. Of course, all that changed once she came along.

'Do you think I'm too skinny?'

That was exactly the kind of thing she liked to ask him. It wasn't insecurity. She knew she wasn't 'too' anything. She was perfect. She just wanted to draw attention to how perfect she was.

'You're okay.'

'Just okay?'

'Better than okay.'

Chris took a swig of beer. The three of us were sitting in Julian's jacuzzi while he mixed drinks inside. She had her arms stretched above her head, examining her body like it belonged to somebody else. I could see the lines of her ribs pressing through her skin. She was pretty thin, actually. Not super thin. Not anorexic thin. Just slender.

'How's your hand?' she asked.

Chris held it up. He'd broken a knuckle on some clown's face at the Avalon. He tested it experimentally, clenching all five fingers before flexing them straight.

'Getting better.'

'That guy was such an asshole.'

'Everybody's an asshole. Except Razor.'

Her lips curled into a smile – this very ironic smile. Secretly she loved it when he talked like that. Hardly anybody can talk tough and get away with it. If I tried, I'd look like a treat. But Chris could do it, because with him it wasn't an act. That's just how he was.

'Don't be so negative,' she said.

Beneath the water, beneath the cover of all that foam, she put her hand on his thigh and started stroking it like you might pet a puppy. I guess she thought I wouldn't notice. Chris looked away, pretending to ignore her. The more he did that, though, the more she wanted him. That's the way it works. He wanted her too, of course. We all did. You just had to look at her and you couldn't help wanting her.

'What's up?' she asked him.

Chris shrugged, took a sip of his beer. Totally casual.

The thing is, when it came to that kind of stuff, Chris wasn't super experienced or anything. None of us were. I'd only ever made out with one chick before – in a closet, back in grade eight. After that I hit a pretty long dry spell. Jules claimed he'd gotten gummers from some girl at a West Van party, but he wouldn't tell us her name and I'm pretty sure he was lying. Chris did a little better than either of us, for obvious reasons. He'd never hooked up with anybody like Karen, though. It wasn't just the fact that she was super hot. It was in the way she acted, the way she carried herself.

Before Chris, she'd only dated older guys.

We met her a few days after we got our medals. We were down at Cates Park, hacking a dart, when she came out of the water and walked right over – as if she'd spotted us from a long way off. Most of the chicks down there are bleached blonde, fake and bake clones. Not Karen. She had dark brown hair that hung down her back in wet little snarls, and as she crossed the sand her body glistened all over with saltwater. Totally cinematic. At the beach she always wore the same thing: this blue bikini, super skimpy, with tiny gems in the pattern of three waves on her hip. She didn't look like any girl I'd ever seen. She looked more like some kind of mythical sea creature sent to seduce us.

'You guys are the heroes, right?'

Julian said, 'That's us.'

'I'm Karen.' She showed us her teeth. 'I saw your picture in the paper.'

We didn't know what to say. We were still pretty messed up over the whole thing, and Chris hated talking about it. I was surprised he didn't tell her to fuck off. Instead he made room for her in the sand. She stretched out next to us, her body burnt to butternut from weeks of tanning. Every time she moved – even if it was just to flick her hair or shield her eyes from the sun – we were aware of it. We lay like that, with all three of us feeling her presence, for about six or seven minutes.

'What are you guys doing later?' Karen asked.

'I don't know,' Julian said. 'Just hanging out.'

'Can I come?'

Me and Julian kept quiet. It was up to Chris.

'If you want,' he said.

For the next few weeks, until everything fell apart, that's

what the four of us did: we hung out. We'd laze around the beach all day, then go find a runner to pick up some booze. We drank at Julian's house, since his parents were always on vacation, or we went to the Avalon. Some nights we just cruised up and down Lonsdale in Julian's car. Chris got in a few fights, a few more than usual, and Bates started causing us trouble. Other than that, there was nothing extraordinary about it. That's what I tried to explain to the cops, and the press. But everybody just assumed we were out doing all kinds of crazy shit – beating people up and taking drugs and starting riots – and Chris was made out to look like the ringleader.

That's another problem with people. They need things to be simple – especially in news articles. Hardly any of the papers mentioned our medals. If they did, it was in a super snide sort of way. The headline in the *Province* read: *'Hero' Loses Control*. The fact that they put 'hero' in quotation marks harsh pissed me off. It was like they were trying to say he'd never really been a hero at all. Not that he wanted to be one in the first place. He hated that crap. So did I. Julian was the only one who liked it. But basically, nobody wanted to hear about the decent things he'd done. That's way too complicated. In their eyes, you're either a good guy or a bad guy. Chris had beaten up a cop and stolen his car, so he had to be a bad guy. The fact that he'd saved an old lady's life didn't mean shit. The funny part is, he would have agreed. It didn't mean anything. We shouldn't have bothered to haul her out of there in the first place. We should have stood around like everybody else and watched her drown.

Maybe that way Chris would still be alive.

If it weren't for my dad, I'd probably think all the adults in the world are insane. At least he knew Chris. He liked

him, too. That's why he saw through the bullshit. He didn't
believe the cops or the press – not for a second. He could
see that they just made up a story – the usual kind of news
story – that everybody wanted to hear. The worst part was
how Julian went along with their version. So did Karen,
actually. They rolled over together like a pair of well-trained
poodles and let people tell them what happened. Not me. I
know what happened. I was there for most of it and Chris
told me some of it and the rest I can imagine.

However much they lie, they can't change what I know.


## 3


'I told her about the fireball.'

I looked at him. He'd never told anybody about the fireball,
except me. I was a little bit annoyed, actually. The two of us
were sitting by Julian's pool, cutting up a garden hose. For a
long time we'd been trying to figure out a way to breathe
underwater. It was like an ongoing, fairly casual hobby of ours.

'Why did you do that?'

He shrugged. 'She asked me about the trippiest thing I'd
ever seen.'

'And you said the fireball?'

'Pretty much.'

Apparently they were at the lookout on Mount Seymour, in
the back of her dad's Jeep. I've been up there tons of times,
and even during the summer the air is thin and cool. At night
they would have been able to see rows of shaggy pines dropping
down towards the Cove, and the city lights glittering like stars
that had crashed to earth. And off to the side, if it's clear, you

get a wicked view of Burrard Inlet. The whole situation must have been pretty romantic. I guess, under those circumstances, I could forgive him for telling her about the fireball. Besides, it didn't change the fact that he'd told me first.

After it happened, he called me as soon as he got home – in the middle of the night.

'I was biking along Fairway – the bit just off the Parkway. It was totally dark. Then the sky lit up and on the horizon I saw this ball of fire. Fucking huge. Orange and purple and red – every colour you can imagine. Falling from the sky. It lasted for five or six seconds.'

'Holy shit,' I said. I knew right away that this was serious. 'Were you baked?'

'Not even, man. A little bit drunk, but not baked.'

'Maybe it was the Northern Lights again.'

'It wasn't anything like the Northern Lights.'

He knew exactly what the Northern Lights looked like because we'd both seen them when we were super stoned on nutmeg this one time.

'I guess you could have imagined it. Like an acid flashback.'

'No. I know what I saw.'

He was still breathing pretty heavy. From biking home, I guess.

'What was it, Razor?'

I felt like I had to give him an answer. Chris trusted me when it came to explaining that kind of thing – even when there was no real explanation.

'It could have been a meteor. An extremely large meteor.'

'Yeah?'

'Yeah. Don't worry. I'll look into it.'

The next day I phoned all the papers and weather stations, but nobody had reported seeing a fireball. That didn't mean anything, though. If Chris said he'd seen it, he'd seen it.


'What did she say when you told her?'

Chris had shoved the hose over the top of his snorkel, and was tightening a little metal clamp to hold it in place. He was super good at putting weird shit like that together.

He shrugged. 'She sort of laughed.'

'She laughed?'

'I don't think she really believed me. Come on. Let's try this thing.'

We'd attached the other end of the hose to a foot pump – the kind you use to inflate airbeds. Chris put the snorkel in his mouth and went underwater while I pumped air down to him. It worked, too. For a while. Then he started to get a bit of backwash and felt dizzy, so he came up. I was still thinking about it.

'I can't believe she laughed at your fireball.'

'Whatever. She probably thought I was talking shit to impress her.'

That was one thing she didn't understand about Chris. He never lied or talked shit to make himself look good. Most guys do – including me – but Chris didn't have it in him.


## 4


Up until all of this started, our summer vacation had been fairly casual. Mostly we went cliff jumping at Pool 99. We'd take Julian's car, or a bus to Riverside Drive, then hike in past the 'No Trespassing' sign and follow a trail down to this stony, sun-baked beach by Seymour River. Technically, we weren't supposed to be there. Pool 99 isn't as sketchy as Lynn Canyon, but over the years a bunch of kids have still died there. They died hitting bottom, or landing wrong in the water, or being held under by currents. They died all sorts of ways, but none of them had been worth anything. Then a kid died who was rich and smart and played tennis, and it became this huge tragedy. The papers wrote it up and his parents tried to sue, so the district put this shitty wooden fence around the area and closed it down.

That never kept us away, or anybody else, either. Come summer, Pool 99 is always overrun by about eight hundred sweaty, noisy teenagers. If we got there early, before the crowds, it was all right. Otherwise there could be problems. Chris and crowds didn't mix. If you put him in a group of people, a little pocket would immediately form around him. Like on those soap commercials – when all the grease sort of moves away from the detergent.

If he felt like it, Chris could huck huge gainers and front flips and suicides. He was stoked on cliff jumping, but he couldn't stand being around all those treats, talking shit to each other and showing off for their girlfriends. So when it was packed, he never jumped. He just chilled. The three of us had our own spot, near the base of the cliffs, that people knew to leave for us. We'd throw down our towels and spark up a bowl and check out the girls through our sunglasses. Julian always wore this pricey Hawaiian shirt that he'd bought at a store in Park Royal, just in case any chicks came over to talk to us. Sometimes they did, too. He thought it was because of the shirt, but I'm pretty sure it was because of Chris.

'What do you think? Should we jump one of those mothers?'

'Fuck off, Jules.'

Julian loved talking about cliff jumping, but he hardly ever did it. Heights terrified him. Also, he didn't like taking off his shirt. Not because he was fat – he had huge muscles from all the protein powder he gobbled – but because of his birthmark. He had this weird, fist-sized birthmark in the middle of his chest, right over his heart. It was bizarre. It freaked people out, including me, and Jules knew it. He kept that birthmark under wraps.

'Come on. It'll be sweet.'

I said, 'Go ahead, man.'

He didn't, of course. None of us did. We just sat there. Chris lit a smoke. The sun coated the canyon with a thick yellow glare and the rocks beneath our towels felt hot as a grill. Above us and to the right, clumps of people had gathered on the cliffs, waiting their turn. They went in one by one, like lemmings, and after each jump there was always a lot of hooting and cheering and applause. Some were jumping Superfly. That's nothing. Even Julian had jumped Superfly. A few others were jumping Logs. It's twice as high and pretty sketchy, but not too bad. I never go higher than Logs. Actually, hardly anybody goes higher than Logs. To jump Cooks, you have to climb onto this stump and leap blind through all these tree branches. Then you still have sixty feet to go before you hit water. Even if you land perfectly, you always touch bottom jumping Cooks. That's what Chris told me, anyway. And if you land wrong, you just straight up die – which is how it got its name. People started calling it Cooks because that was the name of this kid who got killed doing it. Not the rich kid. Some other kid.

12

That afternoon, a couple of guys were jumping Cooks.

'Look at these clowns,' Julian said.

They were older than us and had those fake, doughy muscles that the guys from West Van develop by pumping tons of weights without actually doing anything else. One wore a pair of shiny Diesel swim trunks that probably cost about five hundred bucks. The other had on this raunchy little Speedo, so tight you could practically see his balls popping out the sides. I glanced over at Chris, just to see what he thought. He sat and watched them, the smoke dangling from his lips, his face totally blank.

In the shallows across from us these Barbie-doll blondes were cheering them on.

'That's wicked, guys!'

'Come on, just one more!'

It wouldn't have been so bad, except you could tell they were only shouting to get everybody else's attention. So their boyfriends were jumping Cooks. So fucking what? It wasn't like they were the first people to ever jump it. Then, as if that wasn't enough, the girls pulled a camcorder out of their beach bag, to record this great event. Every time the guys swaggered out of the water following a jump, they'd give each other a high-five and say something stupid into the camera, something like, 'How about another one, babe?' It was like watching two guys masturbate in public. Seriously. There was no stopping them.

Finally, Chris decided to put an end to it.

He stood up. He didn't look like those guys at all. He was almost scrawny, his skin pulled tight over hard knots of muscle. Without saying anything, he flicked his smoke in the water and made his way up the cliffs. Everybody was already looking that way. Now the audience was all his. The steroid monkeys and their girlfriends stopped goofing around to watch. When he reached Cooks, he climbed up onto the stump. There was a moment – this moment when everybody sensed that something insane was going to happen – and then it did.

'Holy shit!'

He jumped stomach first, his arms and legs spreadeagled like a skydiver. He hung in that position as he dropped through the air. At the last possible second, he bent at the waist and pulled his arms and legs in, pointing them straight down at the water. That was how he hit: jacknifing through the surface without making any splash at all. When he surfaced, there was no hooting or cheering or applauding. The canyon suddenly went all quiet, like a funeral parlour – just the way Chris liked it. He'd pulled a suicide off Cooks. Nobody did that. Superfly, sure. Logs, maybe. But Cooks? You'd have to be insane to try it. That's what all those people were thinking as they watched Chris slosh over to the bank. The thing is, Chris didn't give a shit about impressing them. Like I said, he hated show-offs almost as much as he hated turtlenecks. He was just sick of those guys and their screeching girlfriends.

One of them said, 'That was pretty slick, man.'

Chris looked at him, in that way of his, and the guy shut up. After that they put their camera away.

The rest of the afternoon was perfect. By 'perfect' I mean that nothing spectacular happened at all. We burned a fat one and joked around – totally mellow. A couple of girls came over, wanting to get high. They were pretty cute, actually, but they turned out to be harsh gnats. Eventually we gave up talking to them and just made fun of them until they left. Then we munched out on this giant bag of nachos. Also, I think we went to get some pop from the gas station on the way home. I don't really know. But basically, that's the last time I can remember feeling normal. The next day we went down to the beach at Cates Park instead of the river. We did that sometimes, for a change. Now I wish we hadn't, of course.

But there's no use thinking like that.

# 5

After everything that had happened to us, there was no way Chris was going to let Bates arrest him. Fuck that. It all seems sort of inevitable now, but it wasn't like we planned it or anything. We didn't know Bates was going to turn up at the beach – and we definitely weren't looking for him. We'd spent most of our summer trying to avoid him. Nobody believed that, of course. All the articles said that we jumped him, and people just assumed it was true. The thing is, Vancouver really only has two newspapers. There's a few other little papers, but the *Sun* and the *Province* are the main ones – and they're both equally shitty. The *Sun* described Chris as 'a cruel adolescent with a penchant for violence'. Whoever wrote that is a total fucking idiot. Cruel? Cruel is about the last word I'd use to describe Chris.

Take that camp trip. We went on this camp trip with all the kids in our grade. The first night, some dickheads managed to snare a raccoon that had been digging in the food bin. Everybody heard the commotion and came out to watch. The guys strung the thing from a tree and started spearing it with sticks. It was pretty sickening. The campsite was lit up with tiki torches, and the circle of flickering faces reminded me of that film we'd watched in English class – the one about kids killing pigs on a desert island. Their spears punched in and out of the raccoon's belly, making these wet, meaty sounds. You could smell the blood. It was everywhere: all over the raccoon, all over the forest floor. That was bad enough, but the screaming was even worse. I'd never heard an animal scream before. It was fucked. After a while, the guys wore themselves out. They stood around, holding their spears and talking about how tough they all were. Meanwhile, the animal just hung there, mewling like a kitten.

'You better kill it,' Chris told them.

'Huh?'

'You can't leave it like that. Finish it.'

The guys looked at the raccoon, twisting and turning on the rope. They shuffled their feet and glanced at each other, hoping somebody else would want to do it. Nobody did.

Chris pulled out his pocket knife, the one his dad had given him, and walked over to the animal. Holding it behind the head he pointed its nose towards the sky. Then he slashed it across the throat. Blood spurted out, black and shiny in the torchlight, and coated his hand. The raccoon stopped moving and didn't make a sound. Of course, after that everybody in the grade was talking about how Chris had killed a raccoon.

When his old man died, Chris lived with us for a while. His mom had always been a bit of a booze-hound and it only got worse after that. She was too messed up to look after him so he stayed at our house. My dad was cool about it. He rented us restricted movies, played street hockey with us in the driveway, and even took us paintballing a few times. I mean, my dad's not actually cool, but he at least tried to think of cool stuff for us to do. Eventually things settled down at Chris's house and he went home. For a few months, though, it had been like my dad was a dad to the both of us.

Chris's death hit him pretty hard, too.

'I don't know how he could just punch a cop like that.'

'It didn't happen like they say.'

But he knew that – I'd told him already.

'Did he punch the cop?'

'Sure, a bunch of times.'

We were sitting in the living room. My dad was holding the *Province* up close to his face, staring at the article as if it was written in some kind of secret code. He had a tall-boy of German beer in one hand. I'm pretty sure he was hammered. He hardly ever gets hammered in front of me but the day after Chris's death was an exception.

'You can't just hit a cop.'

'Bates started it.'

'That doesn't matter,' he said. 'As soon as you do that, you're crossing a line.'

It really bothered him. He couldn't get over it. The way he talked, you'd think knocking out a cop had killed Chris – not driving into a blockade at a hundred miles an hour. I guess it's because my dad's got this enormous respect for the law. He's a lawyer, after all. I know what most people think about that. They think it means we're rich, and that my dad's an asshole. But here's what they don't understand. He's not a typical lawyer. To be a typical lawyer you need to join a firm and work in a giant skyscraper downtown, on the top floor so your clients have to climb about thirty flights of stairs to reach your

17

office. And then, when they finally make it up there, you charge them a grand just for saying hello. But my dad couldn't do that. He tried it and he hated it. He hated all the other lawyers in the firm, too. So he rented an office above a bakery and started a private practice way the hell out in Ladner, where he does commercial work and land claims for the Natives. He cuts his clients pretty sweet deals, and in exchange they give him tons of smoked cod and sockeye salmon. I'm not complaining – it's great salmon. But basically, my dad isn't an asshole. He can act like a bit of an asshole sometimes, but that's different from being one. And we're not rich. I mean, we get by. I can't deny that. But we're not rich like people in West Van are rich, or like Julian's family is rich. Jules is crazy rich. His dad's a sports agent and his mom's into some kind of pyramid scheme and every time I turn around they've got a new car – a Porsche or a Beamer or a Lexus. It's like they're planning on starting an auto mall in their garage.

Occasionally, my dad's obsession with the law can be a pain – like when he made me turn myself in. I understand now, of course. Doing that was probably the only thing that saved me from going to jail, or juvie, or whatever. I mean, Bates knew us both. We'd been arrested together earlier that week. It was only a matter of time before they came looking for me. When it happened, though, I felt like my dad was selling me out. He'd turned me over to the enemy.

'Officer Bates claims you attacked him together.'

'What?'

'Did you hit Officer Bates?'

I shook my head.

Two cops took me into this room with metal chairs and a

metal desk, and kept me there. Totally alone. My dad warned me ahead of time about what to expect, but all their questions still caught me off guard. I felt like Alice when she comes face to face with those two fat guys. You know – the ones in the bow ties and beanie hats. Tweedledee and Tweedledum.

'Are you saying Officer Bates is lying?'

'Is that what you're saying?'

I can't pretend I wasn't scared. The two of them stood on either side of my chair, looming over me. I kept my arms crossed and my head down. It was obvious how much they hated me. I couldn't stop shaking – as if I'd suddenly come down with hypothermia.

'I... didn't... hit him.'

'Don't bullshit us, bud.'

I gritted my teeth. Their faces blurred in front of me, and I had to sort of wipe at my eyes to keep from crying. I tried to think of what Chris would do. He wouldn't let these cops push him around. Fuck that. He'd stare them down and tell it to them straight up.

'Bates made a grab for Chris,' I said. 'Chris hit him. He kept hitting him and Bates went down. That's what happened. I don't care if you believe me or not.'

It would have been awesome, but my voice cracked a little when I said, 'or not'. Still, those cops were surprised. They drew back, blinking like I'd shined a flashlight in their eyes. Up until then they'd been putting words in my mouth, coaxing my story out of me – like they did with Karen and Julian. Now I knew how to handle them. After that, I stuck to my story.

They can only push you around if you don't push back.

## 6

The cop stood there, shouting to us from shore.

'Break a window! See if you can break one of the windows!'

We didn't know what the hell we were doing. It was like trying to stop a boat from sinking. Except, in this case, the boat was a big black Cadillac with an old lady inside. And we weren't really trying to stop it from sinking – we were trying to get her out of there.

In other words, it was nuts.

Julian hung off the driver's door, yanking on the handle like a wild man. It wouldn't budge. I'd scrambled onto the roof. The shiny paint felt hot and slippery beneath my knees. I tried bashing the windscreen with my fists, but from that angle I didn't have the strength to break it. My eyes stung with salt and sweat and my vision was blurred to shit. When I looked at the shore, all I could see was this mass of bodies in bathing suits, with a cop standing at the front. There was a lot of yelling and screaming going on. None of it meant anything to me. We were all alone out there. Shielding my eyes, I leaned forward and peered through the windscreen. I could see the driver slumped against the steering wheel, half-submerged in water. There wasn't much time. Actually, there was no time. If it wasn't for Chris, we would have lost her for sure. While Jules and I struggled away, he dove down to the bottom and came up with that rock. It glittered in the glare of the sun, jagged and covered with barnacles and twice as big as his fist.

'Give me some room, man.'

Jules backed off as Chris paddled around to the driver's side. Grabbing the handle for leverage, he smashed the rock through the window. It didn't shatter like regular glass. It cracked into all these tiny pieces, like diamonds. Chris cleared the leftovers away with his hand. I think that was when he must have cut himself. It wasn't a little cut, either. There was a gash on his wrist and streaks of blood all along his forearm. Chris didn't even notice. He just reached through, unlocked the door, and yanked it open. As soon as he did, water rushed in and the car started sinking faster.

'Come on!'

I slid off the hood and splashed over to him. He propped the driver up, getting her head above water. At the time, we didn't pay much attention to her. I mean, we were too busy saving her to notice much about her. I only remember seeing the white ringlets of hair plastered to her scalp, and the way her pink dress billowed up in the water like a parachute.

Chris struggled among all that fabric.

'This goddamn seatbelt's stuck!'

Most of the cab had gone under. Julian and I moved in to help. The two of us wrenched on the belt while Chris ducked beneath the surface to work the buckle. It was jammed, all right. Maybe from the water, maybe from the crash. I don't know. But we pried it loose.

Somebody shouted: 'Get her out of there!'

It was that cop again. He was full of great advice.

Chris took her by the shoulders, Julian got hold of an arm, and I grabbed fistfuls of pink dress. We tugged and pulled. Somehow, we managed to drag her free of the car. This cry went up on shore. People were cheering for us. But she was a dead weight, limp and lifeless in our arms. It took all three of us to swim her back. As we drew close, the cop waded out to meet us, full of encouragement. We didn't know him then, but it was Bates.

21

'Great job, guys – now bring her up here.'

According to the *Sun*, we 'helped Officer Bates perform a water rescue'. I laughed pretty hard when I read that.


# 7


People think I'm exaggerating when I talk about his fights. I mean, he wasn't even fully grown. How tough can a sixteen year old be, right? They only say that because they never saw it happen. Chris didn't swing and flail and throw haymakers like all those treats you see in internet videos. His punches sort of exploded out of him – these little bombs that blew up right in your face. Also, it was almost impossible to knock him out. I guess his skull was extra hard or something, because he could take tons of punishment without going down. It was like a special ability or a super power. Even when he should have lost, he usually won.

'Hey Razor – what's up?'

'Not much, Kristofferson.'

He'd called me from Lonsdale. We biked over there once in a while, to play games at the Hippo Club Arcade – back before it burned down.

'You want to come meet me?' he asked.

'I'll come and beat you, all right.'

'The old beat and greet, huh?'

On the other end of the line, I heard somebody swearing. The voice sounded tinny but clear, as if they were shouting at him from nearby.

Chris said, 'Can you hold on a minute?'

'Yeah. Who's that?'

But he was already gone. I heard more shouting, then some scuffling and this cracking sound, like a broom handle being smacked against concrete.

Chris's voice came to me faintly: 'Are we done? Huh?'

A moment later he was back on the line, panting.

'So,' he said, as if it was nothing, 'where should we meet?'

'What's going on?'

'Some guy just lipped me off.'

That kind of thing happened all the time. Fighting was as natural to him as eating, sleeping and breathing. And dying, I guess.

He never started fights. He didn't have to. Fights found him. The thing about Chris was that he didn't look tough. He wasn't super built or anything, and he had a young face – smooth and almost pretty. It was the kind of face other guys wanted to hit. Only he hit back. Harder. He didn't train. He never took boxing or martial arts or anything. I did. I got it into my head that I wanted to be tough like him, so I enrolled in kung fu classes for about three years. I worked pretty hard at it, too. Twice a week I would go down there, learning these moves and training with a bunch of other wimps. They taught us how to kick and punch and block. Eventually I even got a brown belt. I learned some stuff, I guess, but the thing about kung fu is that it doesn't make you tough. Toughness is just something you're born with.

Or without, in my case.

I didn't try to hide it, at least. You know – I wasn't one of those guys who pretends to be super tough. I guess that's why Chris started calling me Razor. He nicknamed me after this wrestler, this tough-as-shit Mexican who always had a toothpick in his mouth and talked a lot of trash to his opponents. Basically, he was the exact opposite of me. Whenever Chris saw me walking in the halls, he would start singing Razor's theme song – one of those super lame wrestling themes – and I'd raise my arms over my head as if I'd just won a big match.

He'd say something like, 'Who'd you scrap yesterday, Razor?'

And I'd say, 'Oh, six or seven guys.'

'At once?'

'You know it.'

Eventually the nickname got around and everybody started calling me that. It was the kind of thing Julian would never have put up with – not even as a joke. It would have harsh offended him. Jules had this image of himself in his head, and he didn't like anything getting in the way of that image. One time he even told me that he thought he could take Chris in a fight. I didn't say anything. I was too shocked to say anything. Jules? He had about as much chance against Chris as a cow fighting a panther. He wasn't just bragging, either. He was dead serious. He'd actually tricked himself into believing he was tougher than Chris.

Julian had a few issues, I guess.


'Looks like we got a couple of high rollers, here.'

Me and Chris were on our way out of the Avalon – this raunchy bar right on the border of North and West Van – when some treat said that to us.

'Don't worry about it, man,' Chris told him. 'It's casual.'

'What's casual?'

'Your turtleneck. It's totally fucking casual.'

When I said Chris never started fights, what I meant was that he hardly ever started fights. He might have started a fight if, say, somebody made the mistake of lipping him off.

Especially if the guy was wearing a turtleneck that threatened to swallow his head.

'Oh, a tough guy, huh?'

We'd already walked ten yards past him. Chris stopped and turned around.

'Yeah, I'm a fucking tough guy, buddy.'

He went back to meet him. The guy had a fake tan and dark, well-oiled hair that matched his stupid shirt. Chris grabbed him by his turtleneck and shouted in his face.

'You want to go? Huh? You and your fucking turtleneck?'

The guy started shoving him back, but he had three friends with him who stepped in. They held the turtleneck while I grabbed Chris. One of them was a monster. He had huge pipes and those weird shoulder muscles you only see on roid monkeys. He stood between Chris and the turtleneck and spread out his palms, playing up his role as this big pacifier.

'Take it easy, pal, or I'll have to pop you one.'

He thought he had the right to say that, since he outweighed Chris by at least fifty pounds. In his mind, it wasn't even a contest. That's because he didn't know Chris. I had an arm over his shoulder, but he was tearing at it like a horse against a harness.

'Take it easy? Fuck you, man. Fuck you. Your buddy's wearing a fucking turtleneck and I'm going to fucking kill you.'

It was such a bizarre thing to say that they didn't know what to do. The four of them started blinking at the same time, like a herd of deer about to get ploughed by a truck. I think they'd realised he was ready to take them all on together. He would have, too, if I hadn't been there to hold him back. He was still ranting as the guys got into their car.

'I bet that's the last time you wear a fucking turtleneck, buddy!'

There wasn't much they could say to that – for obvious reasons.

After the crash, the press interviewed all these people – all these nobodies – and every single one seemed to have some idiotic story to tell about Chris getting in a fight. Half of them weren't even true, but that didn't matter. They printed them anyways and tried to convince everybody that he was super volatile. That's the word they used: volatile. Fuck that. I mean, sure, he had a bit of an issue with turtlenecks, but that's not the same as being volatile. It was just another one of their stupid assumptions. Like they assumed his temper had to do with what happened to his dad. Maybe it did, too. But none of them understood how much the whole thing with Mrs Reever had messed him up. She was the old lady we saved. I would have explained all that to the press, if anybody had bothered to listen. They didn't, though.

They never listened.

'I'm sorry, man. I'm sorry.'

We were on the bus, heading home from the Avalon that night. Usually we made Julian drive us around, but I think he was at tennis practice, or maybe a family dinner. I can't really remember. Either way, we had to take the bus. For most of the ride, Chris sat hunched forward, staring at the floor, with his hair hanging in his eyes. He had brown hair – sort of sandy – that he didn't really bother to comb or cut properly.

'It was nothing,' I told him. I meant it, too. I was used to his fights. What I wasn't used to was him getting all distraught like this. 'Those guys were clowns, anyway.'

'I'm sorry,' he said again, as if he hadn't even heard me. Chris hardly ever apologised for anything. 'I just can't stop thinking about it. It's fucked.'

'I know.'

'I see her face, sometimes.'

I waited.

'I dream about it, too.'

'What kind of dreams?'

'Weird dreams.' He looked up, finally. 'It trips me out, you know?'

I knew. He'd always been kind of angry and shit, but after she died it kept getting worse. It was like there was an elastic band inside him, winding itself tighter and tighter and tighter.

## 8

They went on and on about his home life. Since he beat up a cop they just assumed his house was filled with gas-huffing junkies. That's not the truth at all. Nobody huffed gas in Chris's house. There was a shitload of drinking, and some funny business that one time, but no gas huffing. And no abuse, either. His dad never laid a hand on him. Neither did his mom. That didn't stop the reporters, though. They ran lame little headlines like: *Violent Teen's Troubled Background*. They used that term all the time. Troubled. Don't ask me why. As far as I can tell, 'troubled' is just another one of those words – those meaningless words – that people throw around to explain things they don't understand. It's like 'volatile'. Chris was volatile and his home life was troubled. So what? He didn't care about that shit so I don't see why anybody else should, either.

'Give me another,' Chris said.

'That's it. We're bone-dry.'

'Dry as a couple of boners, huh?'

'Drier than Sonny Bono.'

We'd polished off an eight-pack of Wildcat, just the two of us. It was a Friday night, I think. Or maybe a Saturday. I don't really know. This was a few years ago, back when we'd first started drinking. We were in the Cove – the row of tourist shops and food joints by the marina. During the day, it can get pretty annoying down there. People come from all over the place to eat ice cream and go kayaking and act like complete idiots. There's always tons of super ignorant American tourists, too. You know – like entire families that think Canada is just another state. But at night all the idiots go home. That's when it became ours again. The only thing that stays open late is the pizza place. The guys who work there are pretty awesome, actually. They don't mind if you hang around, so long as you buy a piece of pizza. Sometimes you don't even have to buy it – you can just trade them a joint or a pinch of weed and they'll hook you up with any slice you want.

But basically, we were in the Cove. Also, we were out of beer.

'Shit,' Chris said. 'I guess we'll have to hit up my house.'

That was the only reason we ever went over to his place: to steal liquor. His mom had stockpiles of booze, crammed in cupboards and cabinets and closets and drawers. Mostly she drank vodka or wine, but she had tons of other stuff, too – whiskey, beer, rum, whatever. Their condo was like a giant liquor store without a cash register or security guard. We stole from her constantly – not that she ever noticed. She had so much booze lying around that she could barely keep track of what she drank, let alone what we drank.

When we got there, Chris asked, 'What do you want?'

'I don't know. White wine?'

'White wine tastes like piss, man.'

'I like the taste of piss.'

'You little piss-pot.'

After he said that, we couldn't stop giggling. Stealing liquor usually made us a bit giddy. We'd done it so much we were practically professionals. Our plan was always the same. I'd run interference on his mom while Chris grabbed what we wanted.

'Forget the piss,' he said. 'I'll get the good stuff.'

'Yeah. The good stuff sounds good.'

He opened the door. 'Ready?'

'Ready.'

Chris lived in this housing complex just off the Parkway. There were three floors, but each floor only had one or two tiny rooms. The basement, where you came in, was used for storage. A lot of his dad's things were still down there: old leg traps, a lobster cage, fishing nets, pieces of driftwood. His mom never cleared them out. Come to think of it, she didn't go down there much. Mostly she stayed on the second floor, in the kitchen. That was where we went to find her: sitting and sipping and smoking at their dinner table.

'Hey Mom.'

'Why, hello there.'

At one time, his mom had been hot. You could tell by the way she held herself. She sort of sprawled in her chair, slinky and sultry as a cat. A very drunk cat. One strap of her dress had fallen off her shoulder. She didn't bother to push it back up or anything, either.

'How are my favourite boys?'

'We're good, Mom,' Chris said. 'We just came in to warm up for a minute.'

'Is it cold out?'

'Pretty cold, I guess.' Chris yawned. 'Anyways, I got to take a leak.'

That was my cue. He left and I stayed with her in the kitchen. I walked across to the sink, then rested my elbows on the counter and leaned back. Totally casual. I was still pretty plastered from the Wildcat, which made me act all cocky. She watched me, smiling in this shrewd sort of way. When she smiled, she still looked half-decent. I guess that was because she had nice teeth – just like Chris. The booze had ruined her face but not her teeth.

'So what are you boys up to this evening?' she asked.

'Not much. Just hanging out.'

'Sounds like trouble.'

I laughed, a little too loudly. I thought I could hear Chris opening the hall closet.

'What about you?' I asked. 'What are you doing tonight?'

She held up her glass. 'Trying to relax.'

Tipping her head back, she downed the rest in one gulp. Afterwards she got up and oozed over to the fridge next to me, then yanked open the freezer door. That's where she kept her Smirnoff. As she poured herself a refill, a bit of vodka spilled onto the counter.

She asked, 'What about girls? Any girls on the agenda for tonight?'

'Uh, no. Not really.'

'I don't know what I'm going to do with you two. Don't you like girls?'

'Sure.' I edged away, because her face was hovering too

close to mine. 'Now that you mention it, we'll probably be seeing some girls later on. I think so, anyways.'

'You can't avoid them forever. You've got to learn sometime.'

I laughed again. 'Oh yeah?'

That was when it happened. She took my hand and held it against her tit – her left tit – then sort of made me squeeze. I stood there, frozen, with my hand on her tit and this stupid smile on my face, like one of those psychotic dummies that ventriloquists use.

'I could teach you a thing or two,' she said.

I jerked my hand away as if I'd burned it. Then I sort of stammered and babbled and tried to laugh it off. I think I said something like, 'Come on, now. That's enough of that.'

'Relax, honey.' She patted my cheek, acting all motherly. 'I was only joking.'

Maybe she was. How should I know? I just knew I didn't want her to make me feel her left tit again. A second later Chris came back, grinning. He gave me the thumbs up.

'We better get going, man.'

'You boys be good, now.'

He left. I rushed after him like the kitchen was on fire. Once we were outside I asked, 'Did you get any?'

'Yeah. I got some Wiser's.'

'Give it here.'

I took the bottle and slammed it back. I couldn't shake the feeling of her tit beneath my hand. I was freaked out, but also a little turned on. I mean, his mom wasn't totally butt or anything. But she was still his mom, and that made me feel kind of ill – like when you're looking at porn on the internet and accidentally stumble across one of those messed up websites. You know – the kind that show people

31

doing weird shit to each other.

'What's up, man?' Chris asked.

I couldn't lie to him. I never lied to him.

'Your mom made me touch her tit.'

We sort of looked at each other.

'Which one?'

'The left one. She said she was only joking, though.'

'Oh.' He took the bottle and drank. 'Don't mind her. She's just a drunk bitch.'

'Sure man. It's casual.'

Neither of us knew how to react. I almost felt like apologising, even though I knew it didn't make any sense. But then, me touching his mom's tit didn't make much sense, either.

Anyways, we didn't see his mom very often.

We didn't see his dad very often, either.

He lived way out on the far coast of Vancouver Island. He didn't have a house or apartment or anything like that. He didn't even have a phone line. He just lived on this old fishing boat that he'd fixed up, and made money by selling salmon and crabs and geoduck to the local restaurants in Tofino. I don't know if he had a licence, but he got by all right. That's what Chris told me, anyways. His mom didn't think so. She used to say, 'He lives like a wild animal over there.' She said it in a snide way, but he actually reminded me of an animal. He was big and shaggy as a bear and had these crushing paws for hands. A couple of times a year Chris took the ferry over to the Island and went fishing with him. Sometimes I got to tag along. At night we'd sleep below deck in the bunks, and each morning we'd chug out past the surf, with his dad at the wheel and me and Chris watching the rods in the stern.

'Hey – that one's jerking.'

'We got a bit of jerky, all right.'

Sometimes we'd trawl, and other times he'd cut the engine and we'd sit around casting and jigging. That's when I first started noticing his hands. It sounds bizarre, but his hands were something else. The palms were all cracked, like old soap, and the fingers were thick and muscular. They looked tough enough to crush coal, but he could tie off fishing lines, or bait hooks, as delicately as a granny knitting wool. He could do anything with those hands.

One thing he did with them was give us beer.

'You boys want a brew?'

'Sure.'

The fridge on the boat didn't really work, so near the stern he kept a little cooler – one of those blue coolers with a white, flip-up lid. There was always a motley selection of beers inside, covered in brine to keep them cold. He felt around and pulled out two cans of Kokanee and a bottle of Molson Dry. We got the Kokanees.

'Watch this.'

Chris's dad leaned back and whipped his rod forward, one-handed. Line whizzed out, chasing the lure across the water in a high, perfect arc. It landed with a satisfying splash about forty yards away. He grunted and began reeling in. That was another thing he could do with his hands. I'd never be able to cast like that. I have to swing the rod over my head with both arms, like an axe. Half the time I nearly snag myself or the person sitting next to me. I'm a pretty shitty fisherman, actually.

'You boys getting any pussy these days?'

We laughed. His dad always said stuff like that, just to mess with us.

Chris said, 'Yeah. Every night.'

'What about you, buddy?'

That's what he called me. He called Chris 'son' and he called me 'buddy.'

'Yessir. Lots of pussy.'

'More than you know what to do with, I bet.'

'Yep. I got pussy coming out my ears.'

That got him laughing. He had this huge, booming laugh that reminded me of Santa Claus. Come to think of it, with his red plaid shirts and that hoary beard, he almost looked like Santa. Almost, but not quite. He was more like Santa after a three-week drinking binge.

Nobody really knew what happened with his dad – not even Chris. When his dad didn't pick him up at the ferry terminal one weekend, Chris just assumed their fishing trip had been cancelled. He was used to that. But his dad didn't call that week, or the next. There was no way to reach him so a family friend went down to the marina to check on him. The berth was empty, and his boat was gone. For a while, everybody assumed he'd taken off.

Then some kayakers found his boat – anchored near Ucluelet.

Apparently there'd been some sort of accident. He'd been putting out his crab traps, got tangled in the lines, and fallen overboard. The weights had held him under, and there wasn't much left when the coastguard hauled him back up. Chris didn't like to read the articles so I read them for him. They all said the same thing. The investigators had found a bunch of empties in the boat and ruled it an 'accident due to negligence'. The articles were always accompanied by statistics about alcohol and water-related deaths.

The day Chris heard, I was on my way over to his house.

'How's it going, man?' I said, totally oblivious.

'Not so good. They found my dad's boat. He's dead.'

Neither of us knew what to say for a bit. We just stood there, fidgeting.

'Do you want to be alone?'

'No. But don't treat me any different, okay?'

'Yeah. Okay.'

We got out our bikes and went for a little ride. It was a clear, spring morning and his dad's death didn't seem real. It was more like something I'd heard about on the radio.

Halfway to Cates, Chris said, 'It wasn't like I knew him super well, anyways.'

That was it. He never mentioned it again, and I didn't either. He lived with us for a while, and after a few months it was like his dad had never existed. I mean, we were pretty young at the time and I just didn't have any reason to think about it. But now, after all the shit that's happened, I've been thinking about it more and more. There's been a hell of a lot of drowning going on lately, and I figure you could do worse than going out that way. It would be the same as taking a long drink. Nice and cool and thirst-quenching.

Not that I'd like to try it or anything.

9

You could see everything from up there. The ground dropped straight down in front of us, as if we were standing at the top of the longest slide I'd ever seen. Except the slide was covered with trees and rocks and patches of dirt. And at the bottom, instead of a playground, there was an entire city smothered by layers of smoke and smog and heat.

'What does it remind you of?' Karen asked.

We stood and stared. Totally seared.

'Paradise,' Julian said. 'A city in the clouds.'

In a way, he was right. The haze and the light were almost magical.

'No,' Chris said. 'It looks like ruins. Like a bomb wiped everything out.'

I could see that, too. Not much was left in the vapour – only a husk of a city. I kept looking, trying to decide who was right. But the longer I stared, the less certain I became. I could see skyscrapers and warehouses and bridges and cranes, but they seemed to shimmer and shift in the heat. None of it was real. I didn't even know what I was looking at any more.

'It's one of those things dying people see in the desert,' I said finally. 'A mirage. It's a fucking mirage for sure. As soon as you get too close, it vanishes.'

'All at once?'

'All at once.'

Chris's dad had told him about this cabin – a little emergency shelter hidden in the mountains behind Seymour. Hardly anybody knew about it. The cabin was on a lake, and there was only one way to get to the lake. You followed a secret trail that kept going higher and higher. Then, when you couldn't go any higher, you stopped to burn a fat one. That's what we did, at least, and I can't imagine doing it any other way. It was probably the best time the four of us spent together – except maybe for when we all went swimming and pretended to be starfish. At that point, she hadn't chosen Chris, yet. It was like

36

we were standing on a four-way seesaw. Perfectly balanced.

'You're all wrong,' Karen said. 'It's a cocoon, can't you see?' She cupped her hands in front of her, tracing the cocoon's shape. 'One day it'll split open.'

I squinted my eyes. Then I saw it. I saw that the layers of smog were really layers of silk, and that the buildings buried within were actually part of a single, massive creature.

'But what's inside?' I asked. 'What's going to come out?'

She smiled at me – this very knowing smile. 'Something better.'

I'll never understand girls.

We kept climbing. We passed the first ridge and wound our way into the coolness of the next valley. The air down there was rich and earthy. With each step the ridge we'd crossed rose higher behind us, blocking out the city. After that there was nothing but shaggy pines, jagged rocks, and cliffs that loomed at wonky angles, like big grey waves about to crash over us. Every so often we stopped to smoke a bowl or hack a dart. That was when we talked. We had these super deep conversations, just like the one we'd had on the ridge, about everything and nothing at all.

Chris took the lead. He picked his way along the path, casual and comfortable as a cat. He'd worn his beige cargos and carried a duffel bag slung over one shoulder. He loved the woods. Not because he was a nature fanatic, but because nobody lived there. He would have loved the city just as much if it was empty. His favourite movie was this low-budget science fiction flick where everybody in the world dies at once. Or maybe they get sucked away to another planet or something. I can't really remember. But basically, three get left behind. Most of the movie is about these two guys and this one girl, hanging out together in abandoned cities. Chris loved that. He wanted to be one of those people. He told me so.

'Man, what a great day!'

Julian kept saying stuff like that. He'd worn his favourite hiking outfit: shorts and sandals, with a white tank top and this huge, ten-gallon cowboy hat. I don't know what he thought about the woods. I doubt he thought about them at all, actually. Knowing Jules, he was probably thinking about her, walking right behind him. Keeping his back straight and his chest puffed out, he swaggered along like a pimp hopped up on goofballs. Every so often he'd stop to stretch his arms, flexing all the muscles and taking these deep, dramatic breaths.

'Don't you just love this?'

'It's beautiful,' she'd say.

She was always polite like that. She had great manners. She was rich, too. Later on she admitted it, but I suspected right from the start. She just smelled rich. Rich people smell different. They smell newer and cleaner, somehow. But it's a fake smell, like apple air freshener in a dirty car. Come to think of it, Julian smelled like that, too.

'Listen.'

We stopped and listened. When Chris told you to do something, you did it. I could hear our ragged breathing, and the soft zip of flies, and birds chattering in the trees. Behind it all was this gentle breeze, nuzzling the pine needles and whispering in my ear like a ghost.

Chris said, 'That's the sound of forever.'

Stuff like that makes perfect sense when you're baked.

In the next valley, the trees gave way to piles of rocks and boulders. There'd been a landslide. Half the mountain had crumbled away, pouring into the basin like cereal into a bowl. It took some acrobatics to hike over the rubble. Being at the back was agonising. Not because it was any harder, but because Karen had taken her shirt off for the hike. She scrambled along in front of me, stretching and leaping in nothing but a bikini top and these scruffy jean shorts. I didn't know where to look. I mean, it was impossible not to stare at her, but I didn't want to act all sleazy. So I stared at her backpack. She'd brought along one of those little kid backpacks, just big enough to hold a sleeping bag and a twixer of vodka. She wore it pretty low, hanging down near her waist. There was a tiny white flower stitched into the canvas, along with the words: York House Academy. Super classy. Karen went to this all-girls private school across town. It's the kind of school where a year's tuition costs more than a new car. No joke. It's like twelve or fifteen grand or something.

Julian asked, 'How much further to the lake, man?'

'About three hours.'

I had to stare at that shitty backpack for three hours. I'll admit I didn't stare at it all the time, just most of the time. Once in a while, I couldn't help peeking at other parts of her. And I don't mean her ass, either. What I mean is her pointy little ears, or the spot between her shoulder blades where all the sweat gathered, or the curve of her hip just below the waist. That's the problem with staring at a girl's ass. You miss everything else. There's about six hundred body parts that are way hotter than a girl's ass. Like eyebrows, or elbows. Elbows are so hot it's insane. Some elbows, anyways. Like hers.

At the lake, there was a lot of flirting going on.

Julian was an expert. I don't know how he did it. He'd pinch her arms, or poke her belly, and once he had her giggling he'd tickle her until she screamed. She seemed to like it, too. That was the weirdest part. If I tried something like that, it wouldn't go over so well. I'm not loud enough, I guess. With Jules, acting loud was part of the routine. It made him seem harmless, like an overgrown kid. Come to think of it, he was pretty harmless.

'Look at these chicken wings.'

That was what he called her arms. Don't ask me why.

'They're so delicious.'

He took her bicep into his mouth, biting it like a dog.

'Julian!'

It went on and on and on. It started to harsh piss me off, actually. I would have given anything to flirt with her like that. Not Chris. He had his own methods, which were even better. He flirted with her by completely ignoring her. Julian fawned all over her, and Chris treated her like an unwanted dog that had tagged along.

'What are you guys doing?' she asked him.

'Blowing up the dinghy.'

'Can I help?'

'No.'

She made a face – this pouty face – and went back to Julian. Chris didn't even notice. Once we'd finished inflating the raft, me and him paddled out into the middle of the lake. It was cramped and cosy in there. Our legs were all folded up and sort of entangled, like Siamese twins. After a while, we let the paddles rest and spiralled in slow circles. Just chilling. Near the valley rim, the smouldering sun looked impossibly large, like a giant tangerine. It squirted orange and red light across the water, staining the surface. We floated like that for maybe ten minutes among the oozing streams of colour.

Karen and Julian's voices reached us clearly over the water.

'Now you're asking for it.'

'No – Julian!'

She started squealing and giggling at the same time. Totally immature. I looked towards shore. I saw the reeds in the shallows, the pebbled beach, and the rickety A-frame emergency hut. Julian had picked her up and was carrying her over his shoulder in a fireman lift. She kicked her legs and beat on his back with her fists, still laughing.

Chris caught me staring.

'You want a piece of that, Razor?'

I shrugged. 'She's definitely a bit of a fox.'

'A petit renard, huh?'

I sat back, closing my eyes. 'She's not really my type, though.'

I was lying, of course. Me and Chris never lied to each other, but sometimes if a girl's involved you have to make an exception. It's like when you're little, and you both want to play with the same toy. One of you has to let go or there'll be trouble. So I lied to him. Up until then, they hadn't done anything. He would have told me if they had, but he'd been holding back on account of me. Now I'd given him the green light.

I didn't have much chance with her, anyways.


'Come on – get in here you little tramp.'

'Why should I?'

'Because you want to.'

She laughed and came over. Like I said, she loved it when he talked tough. She took my place in the dinghy and they paddled out. Me and Jules sat on the porch, watching them float away, both of us wishing we were the one with her. The sun had set, leaving the lake cool and still as a slab of stone. We could hear the murmur of their voices but it was impossible to make out what they were saying. Jules passed me the mickey of Canadian Club he'd been drinking with her.

He asked, 'Do you think she likes me?'

'I don't know, man.'

Neither of us spoke for a bit. I could feel the whiskey heating up my belly.

Then he said, 'Remember when Pat Shaw beat you up?'

Of course I remembered. It had only happened in October. He scuffed his heel on the dirt. 'Sorry I ran off like that.'

'It's okay, man. I don't blame you.'

That made him feel better.

'You want to cook some of that food?'

'Sure.'

I ducked into the cabin. It was more of a hut, really – with a single room where we'd laid out our sleeping bags. I carried all our supplies onto the porch, and we cooked Pot Noodle on my camp stove while getting absolutely hammered. My stove harsh sucks. It runs on canned heat and takes about three hours just to boil a cup of water. By the time Chris and Karen paddled in, the whiskey was gone and we could barely stand up, but the noodles still weren't ready. Chris broke out a twixer of his mom's vodka, and the four of us huddled around the stove, waiting for those shitty noodles to soften. Julian loved it. He kept stirring the water with his spoon. Every so often he'd scoop out a noodle and take a little bite. Then he'd say something super optimistic, something like, 'Only a few more minutes, guys.' That harsh cracked me up. Jules wasn't such a bad guy, really. Just a little confused.

## 10

Last Halloween, I hit this guy in the eye with a bottle rocket. No joke. Right in the eye. It was a total fluke. I could have shot six hundred more bottle rockets, aiming for his eye, and I wouldn't have been able to do it again. I wasn't even trying to hit him in the first place, let alone in the eye. I was just sort of shooting in his general direction.

'Who the fuck did that?' he shouted.

We were down at Myrtle Park, this park by my house where we went every Halloween to have bottle rocket wars. Kids come from all over the North Shore, carrying bags loaded up with Roman candles, bottle rockets, sonic booms – whatever. You never know who you'll meet down there. That's what makes it so awesome.

'Did what?'

'Shot me in the fucking eye!'

There were two of them. One pointed in my direction.

'That kid. It was that kid.'

I don't know how the hell he knew it was me. I mean, it was like a war zone down there. Firecrackers were going off all over the place: hissing and whining and spitting and popping. Flashes of light and streaks of flame and the stench of sulphur smoke filled the air. Somehow, in the middle of all that chaos, this guy had spotted me. I was alone, too. Well, almost alone. Julian was with me, but that's even worse than being alone.

'What are we going to do?' he asked.

'Act real casual,' I said.

I was drunk and feeling cocky, or else I would have taken off. Instead I just stood there, in this really lame Spiderman costume that was way too tight and made me look about six years old. The two guys trudged across the battleground towards us. The first was short and fat and mean-looking, like a bulldog. I didn't recognise him. The other guy – the one I'd hit – had thin, bony cheeks, a crooked nose, and teeth that looked too tiny, like a ferret's.

It was Pat Shaw.

'You nearly took my eye out, bitch.'

'Sorry, man. It was an accident.'

My voice sounded all high and squeaky, like I'd inhaled helium. Julian didn't say anything. We both knew about Pat Shaw. He'd gone to jail for taking a baseball bat to the back of this guy's head. The guy had looked at him wrong or something.

'I don't give a fuck,' he said.

'Listen, Pat,' Julian said, lifting up his mask. He was wearing a Jason hockey mask. Don't ask me why. Horror movies scared the shit out of him. 'It wasn't me, okay? I didn't shoot it. I know you have a beef with this guy. But I'm not part of it. Right?'

I couldn't believe it. I'd known him for ten years and suddenly I'd become 'this guy'. Unfortunately for Jules, Pat wasn't buying it.

'You're both dead,' he said.

Then he grabbed me and punched me two or three times – super fast. Right in the stomach. I doubled over, clutching my gut and gagging for breath. He must have hit me again, or kicked me, because I ended up on the ground. I remember seeing Julian sprinting away through the haze, but my vision was all screwy – like in a movie when the camera's tilted at a weird angle. I heard him shrieking, 'It's Pat Shaw. Pat Shaw!' He was in a real panic. That caused all the other guys to panic. They started running with him.

44

'You like that, huh?' Pat shouted down at me. 'You want some more?'

After that it gets harder to remember. Something cracked against my temple. Then I felt these blows on my lower back – right in the spine and kidneys. That was when I did something pretty embarrassing. I screamed. I screamed and covered my head with both arms, curling up into a ball like a baby porcupine.

Then someone said: 'Leave him alone.'

It was Chris. While everybody else had been running away, he'd been running towards me. There was the hot, salty taste of blood in my mouth and my ears were ringing as if a tuning fork had been struck against my skull. I still couldn't breathe, but somehow I managed to roll over. Pat was standing right there, ready to kick me again.

He said, 'Who the fuck are you?'

'Just leave him alone.'

Chris was dressed as a zombie – a fairly old-school zombie. He'd slashed up his jeans and hoody and painted his face green. I'd helped him put fake blood all over his cheeks and forehead. He looked pretty nuts. I wouldn't have wanted to mess with him, anyway.

Pat said, 'Fat fucking chance.'

He turned on Chris, took a step, and followed through with the biggest haymaker I've ever seen. It smashed into Chris's jaw, knocking him backwards and down, right down to the ground. One punch. Pat had one-punched him. I'd never seen anybody do that to Chris.

'You fucker,' I said. I think I was crying. Not a lot, but a little. 'I hate you, fucker.'

Pat laughed. So did his friend. If they'd been smart, they

would have gone over to finish Chris off. Instead they stood there laughing like jackasses. I guess they thought he was all done. So did I, for that matter. They only stopped laughing when Chris moved. He got a hand beneath him, then a knee, and sort of peeled himself off the ground. Real blood dribbled from his mouth, smearing his make-up and covering his chin. All of a sudden he actually did look like a zombie, like something you couldn't kill.

Pat said, 'You're kidding me, right?'

In answer, Chris took off his hoody and tossed it aside, almost casually. He raised his fists and spread his feet slightly apart. I knew that stance.

'Okay,' Chris said. 'Let's go.'

They asked me – a bunch of times – why I got in the car with him that day.

That's why.


When they took our photo for the paper, Chris wore that same outfit. Not the make-up, obviously, but the jeans and hoody. It wasn't like he had tons of clothes or anything. Besides, having the jeans all cut up like that looked pretty sweet, even if he wasn't trying to be a zombie. I still have a copy of the picture. I've handled it so much the clipping is getting tattered, and you can't really make out our faces any more. Julian's dressed in a suit. The medal is hanging from his neck and he's beaming at the camera like a real champ. I've got mine around my neck, too. But I look uncomfortable and sort of confused about the whole thing. Then there's Chris. He's holding his medal at his side and looking off frame. The expression on his face is distracted, as if he's seen something the rest of us haven't. As if he already knows what's coming.

## 11

Surreal. That's the word for it.

It was just like that Hayden song. You know – the one about the woman who locked her kids in their station wagon and drove it straight into a lake, killing them all.

*The car is rolling down to water...*

*Why are we strapped in our seats...*

Except, in this case, it was the lady – not the kids. And she'd strapped herself in there. Plus, it was an accident. Or everybody thought it was. But basically, whenever I hear that song, I can't help thinking about it.

The beach at Cates used to be pretty sweet. It was never that crowded or anything, and the only people who went there were potheaded hippies and a few grimy beachcombers. But over the last few years it's suddenly become the place to be, and all these treats have started turning up. I don't even know where they come from. Probably Sentinel or Handsworth or one of the other shitty schools in West Van. It's getting almost as bad as Kits Beach. The girls just lie there, oiled up with suntan lotion and trying to look like models. The guys are even worse. They've all got waxed chests, stiff limbs, and orange skin from popping too many tanning pills. They kind of look like department store mannequins, actually. The only difference is that mannequins can't move. These guys are always moving. They prance around the beach, hucking frisbees and smacking volleyballs and laughing these super fake laughs. I don't know why they drive halfway across the North Shore to show off at our beach, but watching them isn't exactly an enjoyable experience. It wasn't for Chris, anyways.

Julian saw things a bit differently.

'What do you think, guys? Want to toss the frisbee?'

He started bringing this beach bag to Cates, filled with power bars and bottled water and at least four kinds of sunscreen. He even carried a frisbee in there, hoping that one day Chris and I would change our minds and play with him. Or maybe he secretly wanted somebody else to ask him. Maybe he was planning on becoming a mannequin all along.

I said, 'I don't think so, man.'

'Come on.'

'Fuck off, Jules.'

Chris hated frisbee. He harsh sucked at it, too. He threw like a girl, with this very limp wrist. That's because he never played. You can't be good at something you hate. If he wanted to, he could have practised frisbee for a week and he'd have been better than anybody. He didn't bother, though. Just looking at a frisbee made him want to fight somebody. So what we did at the beach was the same as what we did at the river: we lazed around. We'd find a sunny spot on the grass and put on our shades and light up.

'Man, what a scorcher.' Jules took off his hat to wipe his forehead. Underneath his hair was all wet and spiky, like a baby chicken's. 'How's that bowl coming, Chris?'

'It's coming in your mouth.'

The sun had stopped dead, directly overhead, like a white-hot nail pounded into the sky. Light smashed down against the water, shattering into these blinding shards. Stepping onto the sand was like sticking your foot into a pit of coals. That's how hot it was – too hot to move, too hot to doze, too hot to do anything but lie there and get ridiculously stoned.

'Hit this, Razor. It's blazing.'

Chris handed me his pipe – one of those glass pipes with psychedelic patterns in it. I sucked hard on the mouthpiece. Smoke scalded along my throat and filled my lungs. I didn't exhale. I just sat there with a tingling tightness in my chest as the pipe passed from me to Julian to Chris. When it came back to me, I coughed up smoke and took another hoot, and another, holding it in longer each time. After the next one my head rush didn't wear off. I knew what that meant.

'Razor?'

Chris offered me the pipe. It had come full circle again. I shook my head. 'I'm good, man.'

My skull had gone all light, like a balloon. At any second it was going to lift clear of my shoulders and float straight up, leaving the grass and sand and surf miles below. Chris and Julian kept smoking. I ran a hand through my hair, feeling the strands all damp and stringy with sweat. I began to notice things. I noticed the seaweed smell of low tide and the reek of food frying at the concession. I noticed the lazy burr of mosquitoes and the lap of sea on sand. I noticed the total stillness of the day – the way the heat seemed to stifle everything.

And I noticed that car.

It was long and low and ancient – some kind of old-school sedan. It cruised along like a glossy-black landshark, coming down the road that connects Dollarton to the parking lot. Sunlight flashed off the chrome and windshield, as if the whole cab was glowing.

At that point, you couldn't see the driver.

'Hey,' I said.

Chris and Julian looked at me.

'They're going too fast.'

We were sitting next to the boat launch so we saw exactly

how it happened. There was no wild swerving or braking or honking. That's what some people said but they were lying. When I'm baked I remember things way better so I'm sure about this. The car just kept going, picking up speed. It flew past the parking lot and headed straight towards the boat launch. There was this moment when I thought to myself, *It's not going to stop.* And it didn't. It rolled down the ramp and slipped into the ocean, smooth as a submarine.

Chris said, 'Shit.'

The three of us stood up together to watch. The car cleared the ramp and floated about ten feet further. Bubbles boiled up around the doors and bumpers and steam started hissing out from under the hood. Now we could see the driver at the wheel, just sitting there.

Someone on the beach screamed, 'Oh my God!'

Then everybody started shouting and running around. It reminded me of that saying: like a chicken with its head cut off. There were about six hundred chickens on the beach that day and they'd all had their heads cut off. I guess one of them had the sense to call for help, since Bates turned up a little bit later, but other than that they were pretty much useless. They were great at tossing frisbees around or rubbing each other down with suntan oil, but when it came to something like this their mechanical limbs short-circuited and their robot brains blew a fuse. The thing is, I wasn't much better. I was so fried I might have stood and stared with the rest of them, hoping somebody else would know what to do.

Somebody did.

Chris said, 'Fucking come on.'

Then he sprinted down the boat ramp and dove in.

I followed.

She'd had a stroke. That's what the doctors said, and I believed them. There was no other explanation for why an old lady would drive her car into the ocean like that. She'd felt it coming on and turned off Dollarton highway. Then she'd lost control – of her body, of the vehicle – and ended up in the drink.

Everybody agreed on that.

Of course, there's no way to be sure. I mean, did she actually have the stroke while she was driving, or did she have it after she'd sucked back a few litres of seawater? Nobody asked that question. They just assumed it was an accident – like with Chris's dad. I guess they didn't want to think about the alternative. I thought about it, though. I thought about it before we ran into that guy at the funeral, and after what he said I thought about it even more.

I still do.

The cop was older than us, but only by a few years. His face was round and fleshy, like he'd never lost his baby fat. Also, his uniform looked one size too small. I don't know if he'd just grown too chubby for it, or if they were cutting costs at the police department, but either way he didn't fit that thing. He looked more like a kid who'd dressed up as a cop for Halloween.

Basically, that was Bates. That's what was waiting for us on shore. He waded into the water up to his knees, but he didn't actually help carry her. He just ordered us around.

'Great job, guys – now bring her up here. That's it.'

I could barely walk. My legs felt like strips of liquorice and I was quivering all over. We managed to pulled her up the boat ramp. Soaking wet and limp as a doll, she must have weighed about five hundred pounds. Her dress dragged and slithered across the concrete, and left streaks of water where it touched. The beach mannequins gathered around us, pressing in and pushing against our backs. They wouldn't shut up, either. They kept whispering and chattering like the whole thing was part of some reality TV show.

'Back the hell up!' Chris yelled.

'Let's remain calm, here,' Bates said. 'Everybody just remain calm.'

We ignored him. Even then, we knew he was full of shit.

'Over there, man,' Julian said. 'Not on the cement.'

We stretched the woman out on the grass beside the boat ramp. She looked awful. Actually, she looked worse than that. She looked dead. The skin on her face was grey and puckered. Both eyes showed white except for a sliver of iris just below the lids. Her lips had gone all blue and her mouth was parted as if she'd just seen something really, really, horrible.

Bates said, 'Oh, shit.'

Then somebody screamed. It wasn't a girl, either. One of those big, beefy guys let out a little shriek, like a baboon.

'She's dead!'

'She's not breathing!'

'What happened?'

Chris shouted, 'Shut up! Just shut the fuck up!'

By that point, there must have been nearly fifty people surrounding us, all of them useless. Bates was useless, too. He stared at the lady with this frozen expression on his face, as if seeing her had turned him into stone. When I asked him if an ambulance was coming, he couldn't even answer. He just stood there, like a total fucking pylon. In movies, cops are always the ones in charge. Not Bates. They printed it differently in the papers but the sight of Mrs Reever completely threw him. He didn't know what the hell to do.

We didn't know what to do, either, but at least we did something. Chris started it. He knelt in the grass and pressed his ear to her chest, trying to listen.

After a few seconds he said, 'She's not breathing.'

I can't remember whose idea it was. I mean, it wasn't like one of us came out and said, 'Let's try to resuscitate her.' We'd taken this stupid lifesaving course in gym class, and it all kind of happened automatically. We pulled it off, too. I don't know how. In class, we screwed up every single time, but that day we were like this team of trained professionals. Jules held her shoulders, ready to flip her over if she choked. I knelt beside her and worked her heart with the heel of my hand. Chris was the one who breathed for her. He slipped a finger under her chin and tilted her head back, then pinched her nose with his other hand. It was pretty sick. There were little wispy hairs all over her chin, and yellow slime leaking from her nostrils. I couldn't have done it. Not a chance. But Chris didn't flinch. He leaned forward and put his mouth over hers – gently, as if he were kissing her.

## 12

The medals they gave us looked expensive. They were gold-plated, with a wreath etched all around the edges. Hero of the Week. That's what it said on the front. Our names were engraved on the back. I guess the medals were kind of impressive and shit, but I wish they hadn't made such a big deal out of it. We had to go downtown, to a conference room in City Hall. The air was rotten and dusty, like in the basement of a library. A bunch of people gave speeches and said how great we'd been. Then the old lady's daughter got up and thanked us, all teary-eyed. Even Bates was there, getting a few words in on our behalf.

'Every so often,' he said, 'kids can surprise you.'

I bet he regrets saying that, now.

They saved the worst part for the end. Everybody piled out onto the steps, where the press was waiting. There were reporters from the papers and a camera crew from City-TV, this local station. Nobody came from the CBC, though. We weren't big enough news. Yet.

The mayor made a lame speech and hung those medals around our necks, like a hangman preparing the noose. All these flashes went off, right in our faces. The mayor shook hands with each of us, smiling this super fake smile at the cameras. I don't think he said anything to us. He said stuff about us, but not to us.

He said, 'If only we had more citizens like these young men.'

After the photo session, the reporters asked us a bunch of questions, but they didn't want to sit down and actually hear our version of things. They just needed a couple of easy quotes to put in their article. My dad told me how it works. They've got a quota for all the different sections in the paper: sports, news, politics, human interest. We were the human interest. The TV networks are the same. Nothing else had happened that week so we became this huge deal. Thanks a lot, dickheads. The guy from City-TV was pushier than all the others. He shoved his microphone right in Chris's face.

'How does it feel to be a hero?'

Chris swatted the mic away. 'I don't know. All right, I guess.'

They didn't print that, for obvious reasons. I think they printed Julian's answer instead. He said something very polite, something like: 'We were just glad to be of assistance.' That harsh cracked me up. But I don't blame Jules. Not really. It was easy to get caught up in all that, and think we actually were the heroes they made us out to be. The press can make you believe anything. We'd pulled her out of there and revived her and got those medals so we had to be heroes.

Two days later she died anyways.


## 13


They called him a dropout, which was another lie.

Chris didn't drop out of a single school. He got kicked out of at least six, but he never dropped out. That didn't stop them, of course. They chased down all his old teachers, and each one said the same thing: that Chris had a history of bad behaviour. By 'bad behaviour' they meant that he didn't do every single thing they said. He smoked weed. He skipped classes. He got in fights. It was like the reporters had a little list they needed to tick off so Chris would fit their shitty profile. All the staff they interviewed hated Chris, anyways – except maybe our principal, Mr Green. And Mrs Oldham. She was the band teacher. Me and Chris both joined band in grade eight. I think it was my dad's idea. He had these clarinets stashed in the attic from when he played as a kid, and he gave them to us. We used to get super baked and meet in the music room at three o'clock with all the other band geeks. Neither of us could play worth shit. We'd just sit there, making these shrill sounds on broken reeds and laughing our asses off. Mrs Oldham didn't seem to mind. She was about eighty-nine years old and deaf as a skeleton. She always said she liked our enthusiasm. After Chris got kicked out, Mrs Oldham would sometimes ask me about him – even when I stopped going to band. She'd accost me in the halls, or catch me at my locker.

'How's your friend Chris doing these days?'

'Oh. Okay, I guess.'

She'd nod – sort of sagely – and keep walking. She was pretty cool, in a weird way. And she was the only teacher who didn't say anything bad about Chris. If everybody else is saying something bad about a guy, most people will try and get in on the action. But Mrs Oldham kept it pretty real. She just told them Chris was a music enthusiast. That harsh cracked me up. It also made me cry, actually. I mean, when your friend dies, you expect to miss all the obvious things about him. But what you don't really expect is to miss all the little things, too. Like the way he played the clarinet. Chris played his kind of backwards, with his right hand above his left instead of the other way around. He only knew about five notes, and they were never the right ones. That didn't bother him, though. In the middle of a recital, you would hear Chris blaring away, making up his own music as he went along. I didn't have the guts to do that. Maybe in practice, but not during a performance.

I always just sort of faked it.

Our old school, Seycove, used to be pretty rad. Since I left apparently they've fucked it up and made it like all the others, but when we first arrived in grade eight it was just this giant chunk of concrete, painted blue and grey, with dirty linoleum floors and battered steel lockers. There was never enough space. They kept having to add portable classrooms and extensions to accommodate all the students. Our sports teams always got their asses kicked, and when it came to exams and academic standings and shit like that the teachers at Seycove kept things fairly casual – which was fine by me.

It meant that some of the wealthier kids commuted across the North Shore to Sentinel or West Van High or wherever. Supposedly, those places have better facilities. There's this one private school, Collingwood, that has a super good athletics programme and tennis team. They even get to use graphite sticks when they play floor hockey. All we had were these raunchy little plastic ones. But whatever. As far as I can tell, it doesn't matter if you go to a good school or a fairly shitty one. It's still school. Nobody actually learns anything there – except maybe how to dress and act and talk and think like all the other mannequins.

Chris lasted about five months at Seycove.

He wasn't the greatest student ever. He didn't do his homework, or his classwork. Now that I think about it, he didn't really do any work – except in tech class. That was the only course he liked. He spent a whole month building a miniature boat almost exactly like his dad's. It had a furnace that worked and everything. You could stuff weed in the boiler, light up, and inhale through the smokestack. It was awesome. He got the highest mark in the class for that boat. The rest of us could barely hammer a nail into a wall and Chris could build a whole boat without even trying. I still have it, actually. I went and stole it from his house after he died. I would have asked his mom, but she was asleep at the time. I doubt she'll miss it, anyways.

Tech class was kind of an exception, though. Chris couldn't handle history or English or science or geography. He had a tendency to wander in and out of classrooms whenever he felt like it. Not because he was stupid or anything. He just hated people telling him what to do. When you think about it, high school is nothing but people telling you what to do. So obviously there were going to be problems. During the first few months of grade eight, I did my best to help him. I let him copy my homework, and cheat off me during tests. My dad helped, too. He gave us those clarinets, and paid for us both to go on that shitty camp trip. He told me it would be good if Chris 'got involved'. For a while it worked, too. He didn't exactly make the honour roll or anything, but he scraped by.

That was before Kevin showed up.

Kevin was this two hundred pound roid monkey who spent most of his time pumping weights. He thought he was pretty hot shit because he came from East Van and was two years older than the other kids in our grade. He'd been kicked out of every school in his district, and so he had to come to ours. As soon as I saw him in the halls, swaggering around and glaring like a psychopath, I knew that Chris would have to fight him. Everybody else knew it, too. They wanted it to happen. A bunch of clowns latched onto Kevin, so he had his own shitty little entourage. I'm pretty sure they were the ones who started all the rumours. Within a week everybody was talking about it. Kevin wanted to fight Chris. Chris was saying shit about Kevin. Total bullshit. Chris didn't give a fuck about his reputation, or what anybody said. He just wanted to do his own thing, like always. But that was too much to ask.

Finally, Kevin worked himself into a frenzy.

'What the fuck is up, punk?'

He'd come over to Chris's locker, wearing huge shitcatchers, a Raiders Jersey, and a cross on a silver chain. Totally thugged out. Totally butt. He had his entourage with him.

Chris didn't even bother looking at him. 'Not much, there funky bunch.'

'You're supposed to be pretty tough, huh?'

Kevin wasn't super smart or anything. He had a hard time picking a fight.

Chris said, 'I like a bit of the old rough and tumble, all right.'

'So maybe I'm tougher.'

'So maybe you are.'

That stopped him. He wasn't really prepared for that.

'Well – I'm going to fucking fight you.'

'Okay. When?'

'After school, bitch. Lacrosse box. You and me.'

It didn't bother Chris at all. He took the whole thing pretty casually. He took it so casually that he completely forgot about the fight. We smoked a bowl during lunch and cut class to go biking. It was only later, when we were watching a movie, that he remembered.

'Shit – I was supposed to fight Kevin today.'

'Really?'

'Yeah.'

Stuff like that kept happening. Kevin would arrange a time and a place for them to fight, but Chris never bothered to go. I mean, for him, a fight wasn't like a date that could be planned out ahead of time. It was just something that happened. Of course, because of this, everybody started assuming Chris had turned into a pussy. They thought he'd lost his edge. He'd been tough in elementary school, but high school was a different story. Julian decided that it was a big deal. This was back when he was still a little runt and even more insecure than he is now. His mom always gave him two lunches, trying to bulk him up. I think she might have been the one who got him started on the protein powder, actually.

'They're saying you're a pussy, man.'

It's always the pussies who worry about being called a pussy.

'That's too bad,' Chris said.

'Are you just going to take it?'

'I don't know. I'll fight him sometime.'

It might have gone on like that forever, if some dickhead hadn't told Kevin about Chris's dad. I never found out who it was. Most of the kids from our elementary school knew because Chris had taken a month off school, so it could have been anyone. Looking back, I guess it doesn't really matter who told him. Somebody told him. Me and Chris were sitting in the library when Kevin stormed in, all riled up and ready to play his wild card.

'Hey bitch,' he said. 'What kind of faggot catches himself in his own crab trap?'

That got Chris going, all right.

High school kids are worse than reporters when it comes to talking shit. There were tons of witnesses to the fight – pretty much everybody who was in the library – but none of them could agree on anything, not even who'd won. Some said it was Kevin, because he'd thrown Chris into a bookshelf. Others said it was Chris, because he'd gotten in the most punches. The only thing they could agree on was that it was the biggest fight anybody had ever seen. It was, too. I saw it all. They fought up and down the aisles, knocking over desks and chairs and scattering books everywhere. A whole row of shelves fell down, like dominoes, and nearly killed this one girl who'd been sitting there reading. It took three teachers and the principal to pull them apart. In the end, whatever anybody else claimed, it was pretty much a draw. That's what I thought and that's what Chris said, too. If it had happened a year or two later, he would have destroyed Kevin. But back in grade eight Chris didn't have much muscle mass. He was fast, and tough, but still scrawny. Kevin was practically full-grown. So it was a draw. They were both pretty messed up, and they both got expelled. The other kids talked about that fight for the rest of the year. Like so much else involving Chris, it became sort of an urban legend. The day Chris fought Kevin.

Those shitheads are probably still talking about it.

After that, Chris made a circuit of the North Van schools. He got kicked out of Windsor and Argyle and Sutherland and a couple of others, usually for fighting. He ended up at Keith Lynn, which is kind of a school and also kind of a prison. It's nearly impossible to get expelled from Keith Lynn. You're only allowed to attend if you've already been banned from every other school in the district. Basically all the craziest guys on the North Shore go there. When Chris told me, I just assumed there'd be a lot of trouble. In my mind, life at Keith Lynn was sort of like those real-life prison dramas you see on TV. You know – where everybody's shanking each other with weapons they've smuggled in past the guards.

'What do you think, Razor?'

'I don't know, man. It sounds pretty nuts.'

Chris had a plan. Rather than worry about who wanted to scrap him, or which guys were going to jump him after school, he decided to get all the trouble out of the way at once. It was the kind of plan only Chris could have come up with. On his first day, he borrowed my dad's old ghetto blaster. It was this huge paint-spattered steel box with massive black speakers. It didn't play CDs or MP3s or anything. Just tapes. Chris biked all the way up to Keith Lynn with that ghetto blaster strapped to his back. He was wearing flip flops and a tank top and huge fluorescent jams that hung past his knees. Nothing else. He pedalled right up to the front doors of Keith Lynn, got off his bike, and propped the ghetto blaster on his shoulder. He put in this tape – the only tape he had – and cranked the volume to the max. Then he walked through the halls, staring people down. If it had been any other tape – like rap or death metal or anything – I'm pretty sure he would have got in about a hundred fights. But it was his mom's tape, this collection of eighties classics. And the song that happened to be on was that one that goes: *I'm walking on sunshine, whoah-oh, I'm walking on sunshine...* It was nuts. It scared the shit out of all those thugs and posers and dealers and wannabes.

After that, for obvious reasons, nobody fucked with him.

I went a bit weird when he started going to Keith Lynn. I thought that he might make all these new friends – these super tough friends – and then he wouldn't need me any more. That's pretty weak, I know. But people were drawn to Chris – mostly losers and loners, like the junkies at Opium Park – and I was worried that the same thing would happen there.

'Hey man – what's up?'

I always called him after school, just to check in with him. I had to wait until he got home since he didn't have a cellphone. He hated them. He hated the thought of people calling him all the time. I didn't have one, either. My dad bought me one for my birthday but I kept dropping it and breaking it and crap, and after a while the company refused to replace it. Me and Chris both kept it pretty real in that way. Pretty old-school.

'Not much, Razor. Just got back.'

'Oh,' I said. 'What are you doing now?'

'Hanging out with some guys. Want to come?'

'No. I'm gonna chill. I'll catch you later.'

I hung up the phone and flopped down on the floor of my basement, totally depressed. I tried to imagine what my life would be like without him. I couldn't. It just seemed sort of pointless and lonely. I was still lying there when he showed up, about an hour later.

'What's shaking, buddy?'

I sat up, trying not to look surprised. 'Nothing much. Just baking.'

'The old shake and bake, huh?'

'You got it.'

He sprawled out beside me and put his hands behind his head.

'What did you guys do?'

'Not much. They wanted me to join their gang.'

'Oh.' I thought about that for a bit. 'Are you going to?'

He looked at me like I'd asked him what two plus two equals.

'I'd rather go play ultimate frisbee.'

I started laughing – a little too loudly. I was just so relieved, you know?

'Hey,' I said. 'How long we been friends?'

'Beats me. Since we were babies, I guess.'

I almost said something super lame, something like: 'And we'll be friends until the day we die, right?' But I stopped myself just in time. Chris didn't need to hear that shit.


# 14


'He's a pervert. All he wants to talk about is masturbation.'

I didn't believe Chris when he told me that. I thought he was messing with me. The three of us had to go see a police counsellor – this trauma counsellor – in the week leading up to Mrs Reever's funeral. We didn't have any say in the matter. I guess they just assumed her death would screw us up. Each of us got an appointment. Chris went first, then Julian. The next day it was my turn. I bussed over to the police station on Lonsdale, the same station they locked us up in after the riot. I'd never been there before. I was asked to wait in this office that smelled like old cheese. The counsellor didn't show up for a while. When he finally did arrive, he turned out to be a young guy with thick, wet lips and these massive man-breasts that jiggled around beneath his shirt like overfilled water balloons.

He also turned out to be a pervert – just like Chris had told me.

'Have you tried masturbation?'

He said 'masturbation' like it was some kind of new drug. As in, all I needed was a small dose of masturbation and I'd be fine.

'Uh, no,' I told him.

'That's unusual for a young man like yourself.'

'Is it?'

It's not like I have anything against masturbation. I pull my goalie once in a while, like everybody else. But I didn't see what my masturbating had to do with some old lady's death. I doubt he knew, either. That's the thing about counsellors. They're not even real shrinks. Most of them are students or volunteers or wash-ups. I didn't find that out until I went to a real shrink and she told me.

It didn't surprise me, though.

'Masturbation is very healthy, you know. It relieves tension.'

'Oh?'

'Our society has a strange view of self-love. We don't often talk about it, but everybody masturbates.' He leaned forward, deadly serious. 'I masturbate.'

I opened my mouth, then closed it again. I couldn't help imagining this fat guy with his hands down his pants, grunting and gasping like an overgrown ape. My face started going totally red, as if I was having an allergic reaction.

'Your friend, Chris, told me that he masturbates.'

He was totally lying. I asked Chris later and he didn't say that. Not a chance.

'Maybe you ought to try it,' he suggested.

'Uh, maybe.'

He leaned back, with this pleased expression on his face – as if we'd really established something. In a way, we had. We'd established that he was a pervert.

'Do you want to talk about what happened with Mrs Reever?'

I shrugged. Anything was better than masturbation.

'How do you feel about it?'

'Well, it was pretty shitty I guess.'

'Do you think about her often?'

In truth, I thought about her all the time. I dreamt about her, too. I dreamt about her wet, withered face and the cold feeling of her flesh beneath my hands, like putty. But I didn't want to tell all that to the counsellor, and he didn't really want to hear it. He was more interested in talking. He rambled on about life and death, and how Mrs Reever had lived longer than a lot of people. I zoned out for most of his little speech. I just sat there and did what I always do when I want to convince adults I agree with them: I smiled and nodded.

At one point, he asked me if I went to church.

'No.'

'Never?'

'Not that I can remember.'

My dad's about the biggest atheist you've ever met. He's not quiet about it, either. When those guys come to the door – those religious guys wearing suits and carrying Bibles – he invites them in and tries to convince them they're wrong about everything. He's got this dinosaur vertebra he used as an ashtray back when he was a hippy. No joke. He stole it from some dinosaur park. Drumheller, I think. He loves to bust out that backbone and show it to the religious fanatics. You know – just to prove there was evolution and shit.

The counsellor asked, 'So you don't believe in God?'

'I guess not.'

'You don't sound very sure.'

'Well, it would be nice if there was a heaven or something.'

'That would be nice, wouldn't it?' He picked up a pen and smiled – this totally patronising smile. I think somebody forgot to tell him that I wasn't six years old. 'Of course, we can't be sure what happens when we die. That doesn't change the importance of what you did. I'm sure Mrs Reever, wherever she is, appreciates how bravely you acted.'

I smiled and nodded, wanting to scream.

The thing is, I actually did want to talk about it. That counsellor was useless. My dad wasn't much better. I mean, my dad's pretty rad as far as parents go. But he's not the type of guy who likes to talk about awkward shit – and that includes dead old ladies.

'Hey pops.'

'Hey big guy.'

Every day after work, my dad throws on this raggedy bathrobe, plants himself in front of the TV, and cracks open a few of his cheap German tall-boys. That's the best time to talk to him, when he's sucking back beer and watching wildlife shows on the nature channel.

'Are those eggs?'

'Larvae. Insect larvae.'

I sat and watched with him for about ten minutes, slowly working myself up to it. I figured he'd know more about death than anybody. I mean, I don't really remember my mom but he still thinks about her. I know he does. That doesn't mean he likes talking about it, though. I found that out pretty quick when I finally got around to asking him.

'People die,' he told me. 'That's life.'

'Sure, but...'

'But what?'

I kicked my legs up onto the footstool. What I really wanted was a can of beer, but I couldn't tell him that. My dad would have kicked my ass if he found out how much I drank.

'But what the hell's the point?' I said finally.

My dad picked up the remote control. He turned off the television. We sat like that, with me waiting and him thinking. These were really tricky questions, even for him.

Eventually he said, 'There is no point.'

That was it. Then he turned the TV back on. In the nature programme, the larvae were beginning to hatch. They must have been filming with some kind of microscopic camera, because the insects filled the entire screen. They looked like something out of those creature features we always watched: massive and slimy and hideous as they wriggled into existence.

I found the whole thing pretty traumatising, actually.

We don't keep photos of her around the house. My mom, I mean. It's not like my dad doesn't have any, either. He's got tons and tons of photos from this trip they took down to South America the year before I was born. They bought a Volkswagen camper and ran away without telling anybody, and when they came back she was pregnant and they were married. It was like an elopement and a honeymoon all rolled into one. On the way they took about nine hundred photos. I know because my dad showed me the ones he turned into slides. He would never have done it when he was sober, but he came home absolutely hammered one night and woke me up at one in the morning. He'd been out to dinner with a client or something. First he wanted to arm wrestle – he loves whipping me at arm wrestling when he's drunk – and afterwards he decided to show me those slides.

It was a super big ordeal. We had to haul the projector and slides out of the attic, then set up the projection screen on a rickety old tripod. Lastly my dad made me wipe down the slides while he changed the lamp on the machine. By the time we got started it was nearly two o'clock, but it was worth it. Up until then, I'd only seen my mom in tiny photos and portraits and crap like that. The slides were ten times better. She looked young and real and alive – this skinny, dark-haired woman in a straw hat and huge sunglasses. My dad looked pretty much like he does now, only thinner and with more hair. Also, he had a goatee – this hippy goatee. There were shots of them hanging out at beaches, and lounging by their van, and hiking around Mayan ruins, and partying in rundown villages with all these natives. Wherever they were, it always looked way too hot: trees dry as kindling, roads parched and cracked, ramshackle clay buildings sagging in the sun like melted plastic. The heat never seemed to faze them, though. They were just happy to be together, surviving on tortillas and pop. They only drank pop because you can't trust the water down there.

That's what my dad said, anyhow.

My favourite slides were all in one sequence. It started with the two of them standing on the beach beneath a palm tree. In the second shot, my mom had climbed onto my dad's shoulders, and by the third one she'd shinnied halfway up the tree. Then, in the last slide, they were holding this coconut between them, cracked in half and dripping milk. Something in their expressions really got to me. They'd completely forgotten about the camera and whoever was taking the photos. They were both gazing into the coconut like it was this rare treasure they'd found in the middle of the desert – a treasure that held all the secrets they needed to live happily ever after. It didn't, of course. It was just a coconut.

I mean, she died pretty soon after that.


## 15


'You feel anything?'

'No, nothing yet. You?'

'No.'

We only tried it once. Once was enough. It was back when we were too young to get booze or weed or anything good. I think we were twelve. Or maybe eleven. I can't really remember. But we'd read on the internet that nutmeg could get you high, so we boiled half a cup and rented The Lion King. Chris loved that movie. He couldn't get enough of it. He was convinced it would be ten times better if we were stoned – especially the part where Simba's dad comes out of the sky in the shape of stars. As soon as our brew was ready, we each shotgunned a mug of nutmeg. It didn't taste like much – kind of like weak soap mixed with cinnamon.

It didn't do much, either.

'How about now?'

'No.'

Neither of us could sit still. Our rec room is filled with a bunch of crap my dad bought at garage sales: old reclining chairs, this water-stained coffee table, and a threadbare two-seater sofa. Chris was pacing back and forth in front of the TV, playing with my kung fu sash. First he tied it around his head. Then he draped it over his shoulders, like a scarf. I sat on the sofa and picked at the armrest. There was a hole in the cover and all this loose stuffing sprouted from it like a bizarre, spongy fungus.

'This blows, man.'

'Yeah.' Chris threw the sash on the floor. 'Nutmeg blows goats.'

'I'd rather be blowing a goat.'

We weren't high at all. We were just bored. After a while we got sick of waiting and put on the film. Our favourite part was the bit where Simba goes to live in the jungle with that pig and the little squirrel. Usually, those guys harsh cracked us up. That night, though, I don't remember laughing once. I was exhausted. I couldn't figure out why. Chris kept dozing off, too. When the movie ended he mumbled something about going home. I yawned and nodded and shuffled to my room and passed out.

Then I woke up.

Somebody was banging on my window – the little window above my bed. It freaked me out. I managed to sit up, but couldn't really stand. My head was reeling and my limbs felt as if they'd been dipped in cement. Also, I started gagging: these weird, dry gags. Somehow, I batted aside the curtains. Chris was out there, his face pressed to the glass.

I unlatched the window.

'Get out here, Razor,' he said. 'You can see the fucking Northern Lights.'

I had no idea what was happening. I staggered to my back door, then crawled over the fence and met him in the front yard. The nutmeg had smashed me into this pulpy, unthinking mass – I was a blob of human jello. Chris slapped me playfully across the head, pawing at me with

his palms. The impact bounced around inside my skull –
this super weird sound hallucination. His eyes were wild
and his face had gone all sweaty and pale.

'You feeling it?'

'I'm feeling sick, all right.'

'Sick as a dog, huh?'

'Sicker than Snoop Dogg.'

I was trying to laugh about it, but only because I didn't
want to look like a bed-wetter. Secretly, I thought I might
be dying or something. No joke. If Chris hadn't been
around, I probably would have called an ambulance to come
get me. That's how screwed up I felt.

Chris threw himself down on the grass.

'Look, man.'

I looked. I saw a black sky and these bright clusters of
stars.

'Yeah. Cool.'

'No, asshole. Look!'

I looked again. After staring for a minute, I saw it. There
were ribbons of colour – pink and red and purple – rippling
against the blackness. I let out this little squeak and stumbled
back, falling to the ground beside him. The grass felt wet and
prickly against my bare skin. I hadn't even bothered to dress
myself. I was only wearing a pair of boxer shorts.

'What is it?' I whispered.

'The Northern Lights, man.'

'You can't see them this far South.'

Chris snorted. 'Oh, yeah?'

We lay like that, spreadeagled on the grass like gingerbread
men. I started feeling a little better. It was just me and him and
those waves of light washing over the sky. The city was silent.

The world was silent. Everybody had died and left us alone.

'What makes them do that?' Chris asked.

'I heard it's the earth's magnetic field or something.'

He thought for a while, then said, 'You know what I think?'

'What?'

'It's dead people. Dead people are hanging out in the sky.'

'Like ghosts?'

'No – not the normal kind. They wouldn't be allowed.' He gestured towards the flickering colours. 'It's more like the energy of dead warriors. Vikings and shit like that.'

I didn't say anything. If I'd tried to say anything, I would have cried. I'm serious. For some reason, ripped as I was, his version sounded better than any afterlife I'd ever heard of – better than heaven, and way better than reincarnation. Reincarnation is the worst of all, no matter what Karen said. I mean, who'd want to live all over again?

'How do we get up there?' I whispered.

'You just got to make sure you go out with a bang.'

'That's all?'

'That's all.'

I don't think he really believed that, but it sounded pretty sweet at the time.

## 16

We were driving back from the Avalon – that same bar where Chris almost fought the turtleneck – when we got pulled over. It was the four of us, like always. Julian had his dad's new car, this super nice Mercedes with crazy rims and huge tyres.

Karen rode shotgun. Chris and I sat in the back. What I remember most is the smell of the perfume she always wore. I don't know the brand name or anything, but it smelled sort of like oranges and lemons and a bunch of citrus fruits rolled into one. It might not sound like much, but that perfume drove us completely insane. I would have jumped out the window just to get her attention – that's how great she smelled.

We took turns shouting shit at the pedestrians we drove by, trying to impress her. Julian tore up and down all these little side streets. At every corner he'd gun it and pull a huge fishtail. Then we hit Marine and saw the lights – blue and red in the rearview.

'Shit.'

'Pull over, man.'

Julian did. For whatever reason, he'd headed back towards Taylor Way to get on the Upper Levels, which meant we were in West Van – and everybody knows that West Van cops are the most insane fascists you'll ever meet. No joke. They're always shooting poor people for carrying pellet guns or cap guns around. Their mission is to keep the district rich and white and crime-free. They even shot this one teenager for answering the door with a remote control in his hand. The cop who did it claimed he thought the remote was a gun, which was a total lie. He just wanted to get rid of that kid. Those jokers shoot more kids than almost any other police force, except maybe the corrupt ones in third world countries.

'Ditch that booze, Razor.'

I had a mickey of rum in my hand that I'd completely forgotten about. I looked at it stupidly, like the guy in a movie who's picked up the murder weapon just as the detective comes in. I was pretty hammered, actually. We all were, except

Julian. That was one thing about Jules. When it came to drinking and driving, he happened to be extremely responsible.

'Here,' Karen said.

Snatching the mickey from me, she leaned forward and tucked it into the back of her jeans. Then she pulled her shirt down to cover it and the rum disappeared, like a magic trick.

'Everybody be quiet.'

The cop got out of his car, leaving the emergency lights on. All we could see was this spooky silhouette marching towards us through the red and blue beams.

Then I saw his face as he passed my window.

'Hey,' I said. 'It's Bates.'

Karen asked, 'Who's Bates?'

We didn't have time to explain. Bates was right there. I don't know what a North Van cop was doing in West Van. Maybe he was already bucking for a transfer. He had a flashlight in his hands – one of those heavy duty Maglites that doubles as a nightstick. He used it to rap on the driver's side window. Julian pressed a button by his armrest and the glass whirred down. Just before he opened his mouth, I had the feeling Jules was about to say something super stupid.

And he did.

'What's the problem, Batesy?'

Batesy. No joke. That's what he said. Bates did a little double take, and there was this moment when you could tell he'd recognised us but didn't really know how to react.

Then he said, 'Licence and registration, please.'

That was it. He had this super severe expression on his face, too. Before then, I'd just thought he was a bit of a treat. That was the moment I realised he was a total marzipan.

Jules handed over all that junk and Bates flipped through it.

'This isn't your car.'

'No, it's my dad's.'

Bates smiled, as if establishing that Jules didn't own the car was a major personal victory. Then he rested his hand on his holster and peered around the car. Mostly he looked at Karen. He looked her up and down in this really sick way – totally perving out.

'Do you know how fast you were going?'

He said that to Jules, but he was still eyeballing Karen.

'About fifty?'

'That's what you should have been doing. You topped eighty back there.'

'Sorry about that, officer.'

'You kids been drinking tonight?'

'No, sir.'

'Then you won't mind breathing into this, will you?'

Bates whipped out his breathalyser, super fast, and shoved it right in Julian's face.

'What do I do?'

'Just breathe.'

Jules opened up and blew. We waited while Bates checked the reading.

'Stay right here.'

It was total crap. Jules had been drinking pop all night. But Bates wanted to jerk us around a little. He went back to his car and sat inside it for about three hours. I could see him fiddling with the radio and poking at his computer screen.

'What's he doing in there?'

'Pulling his goalie,' Chris said.

Julian laughed, but it was a fake laugh. He had both hands clenched tight on the wheel and he kept glancing anxiously in the rearview mirror. Totally wetting the bed.

Eventually, Bates came strutting back.

'You passed your breath test,' he said. 'Doing eighty in a fifty zone still counts as excessive speeding – but I cut you some slack and charged the minimum fine.'

He held out a slip of paper. Julian stared at it, sort of bewildered.

'You're giving me a ticket?'

'That's right.'

'Oh, this is great,' Jules said, getting all flustered. 'Just great. Last week you gave me a medal and now you're giving me a ticket. Thanks a lot, officer. Thanks a lot.' His voice trembled a little, as if he was having a hard time keeping it from breaking.

'You're lucky it's only a hundred, hero.'

'You know what this is?' Julian muttered. 'It's bullshit.'

That surprised me, actually. I didn't think Jules had it in him.

'What did you say?'

Jules kept his head down, his hands on the wheel. 'Nothing.'

Bates smirked. 'That's what I thought.'

He hitched up his pants, like a cartoon cop. You could tell he really thought he'd taught us a lesson. Then, just as he turned to go, those words came out of Chris's mouth.

'Let's remain calm, here,' he said – sounding exactly like Bates when we'd dragged Mrs Reever out of the water. 'Everybody just remain calm.'

Bates froze, as if he'd been stabbed in the spine. Then Chris started laughing. So did Karen. She didn't even know why it was so funny but she laughed anyway. That got me going, too. We were all cracking up. The only one who didn't laugh was Jules. And Bates, of course. He just stood there, looking like he wanted to pull out his gun and shoot us.

He probably would have if he'd thought he could get away with it.

The weirdest part of all is how Bates ended up being the hero. After Chris kicked his ass, Bates got the same treatment as us: interviews, talkshows, the whole deal. They probably even gave him a medal. If they haven't given him one yet, they should. Seriously. They should give him a medal for being the biggest dickhead on the entire planet, and the biggest liar in history. He's told his story so many times he probably even believes it by now. I bet he actually thinks that he helped save Mrs Reever, instead of standing around like a crash test dummy. And you know what? I couldn't care less. Not any more.

My dad wrote a letter for me, and mailed it to all the papers and networks. He loaded it with complicated references and legal terminology, so it sounded totally professional. Then he got his secretary to type it on official letterhead, just to scare the shit out of them. The letter said he was working on my behalf, and if they printed any more bullshit we'd sue their asses off. It was pretty sweet. He also filed a formal complaint with the police department, questioning Bates's actions. Nothing happened to Bates, of course. Actually, something did happen to him – he got promoted, and transferred to West Van. He got all of that, and he got away with what he'd started by giving Julian a ticket: he punished us for doing what he couldn't that day at the beach.

After Bates left, Jules drove along Marine Drive at about thirty clicks. He gnawed on his lip and wouldn't look anywhere but directly ahead, at a fixed spot on the windscreen.

'What a total asshole,' Karen said.

Nobody answered.

Then it happened. Julian emitted a little, choking sob – like a child. We all sat there, frozen. I don't think I've ever been more embarassed for a guy in my life. Part of me knew exactly how he felt. It was pretty shitty and hypocritical for Bates to turn around and do that. At the same time, one thing I wouldn't recommend is crying in front of girls. It doesn't go over so well. I mean, sure, we all have to cry sometimes. I still cry myself to sleep thinking about Chris. That's not the same, though. Nobody ever sees me cry – especially girls.

Karen reached over and patted him on the knee. 'It's okay, Julian.'

You could tell she was a little disgusted, though. That's the thing about girls. They hate cry-babies. They might say they like sensitive guys, but that's a lie. What they really want is somebody who wouldn't think twice about fighting six people at once, or staring down a guy with a gun, or beating a cop half to death.

That's what she wanted, anyways.


## 17


When we were younger, another thing we did was make movies.

We used my dad's video camera – this bulky old camcorder he'd picked up at a garage sale. I must have been about two or three when he bought it. I can't really remember. It was a little while after my mom died and I guess he wanted to capture a few memories. He took some footage of us at the wading pool and me riding my tricycle around the yard and a bunch of other typical things, but the best stuff he shot was during my fifth birthday party.

In the video, we're getting ready to eat my cake. My dad must have baked it himself, since the icing is all lumpy and messy. But he made up for that by covering the cake with army men – those green army men that stand on plastic bases. When the lights get turned off, everybody starts singing happy birthday. In the darkness, you can see the faces of my friends gathered around the table, watching as I blow out the candles. Jules was super thin and pale back then. He keeps poking his finger in the icing and licking it off. Chris is sitting beside him. I don't think he had many birthday parties of his own. He's got this extremely solemn expression on his face, as if blowing out candles is the most important thing ever.

I loved to bug him about that.

The novelty of the camcorder wore off pretty quick. It disappeared until Julian, Chris and I dug it out of the attic, a bunch of years later. At first we just screwed around with it. We'd put on my boxing gloves and pretend to be heavyweight champions, or film ourselves belly-flopping into Julian's pool. Eventually we started making skits and little scenes. The skits were always about cops who wore huge sunglasses and busted Mexican drug dealers.

'What's in the bag, Pedro?'

We thought all Mexicans were named Pedro.

'Just some clothes, hombré.'

'Clothes, huh? We'll see about that.'

'Back off, gringo – or I'll pop a cap in your ass!'

'He's packing heat!'

It always ended in a gun battle that nobody survived.

Later on we began stringing scenes together. We'd copy our favourite creature features and make our own versions. The best one we did was called *The Worm*. It's about this giant worm – obviously – that goes around eating people. Jules was the worm. We stuffed him in a mouldy sleeping bag and shot him up with his dad's paintball gun. It was pretty awesome, until Jules started crying. We also made this film called *Bloodlines*, about a were-chicken. It was basically an hour-long rip-off of every werewolf movie we'd ever seen. Except with one of those rubber chickens you get at novelty stores. Come to think of it, I don't think we even finished that one. We sort of skipped to the finale, where the chicken gets killed. We jammed a brick of Black Cat firecrackers down its throat and blew it up in slow motion.

Most of the time I ended up filming. Chris and Julian were no good at it. Also, they only wanted to be in front of the camera, and thought anything else was boring. Not me. I liked it. I really got into it. I'd plan out the shots and tell them where to stand. My dad showed me how to record from the camera onto our computer, so I could cut out the stuff we screwed up. Eventually I learned to keep track of all the scenes in my head. We'd even shoot them out of order, just like they do for real movies. At first it felt weird to start with the ending then go on to the beginning and finish with the middle. I got used to it pretty quick, though. Sometimes I'd decide to cut the scenes together in a way we hadn't even planned. I mean, going from start to finish isn't the only way to tell a story.

There's at least sixty different ways.

## 18

'Promise. Promise me you won't get in any fights tonight.'

'What if somebody starts shit?'

Karen put her hands on Chris's waist and looked him in the eyes. The three of us were standing in front of my house, sharing a beer, waiting for Julian to come pick us up.

'Just promise. Please?'

'Okay. I promise.'

She had no idea how big a favour she was asking of him. Neither did we at the time. We just knew that we were going to some party near Caulfield, in West Van. Somehow, Jules had roped us into it. This was a few days after he'd cried in front of Karen on the way home from the Avalon, and I think he was trying to compensate for it. He wanted to be the big slick for a night, and me and Chris were forced to come along for the ride. Karen didn't make it any easier on us. Her and her promises. To Chris, promises were sacred. He never broke a promise in his life.

'How do I look?'

Karen twirled around, balancing on her toe like a ballerina.

'Good,' I said.

'Yeah. You look hot.'

She did, too. She'd picked out a black skirt, low heels, and this burgundy top. Sexy, but classy. Jules had told us all to dress up. For Karen, that wasn't a problem. For us, on the other hand, it was a huge problem. In the end I borrowed a pair of old cords and this V-neck sweater from my dad, which made me look like a cop from some seventies TV show. Chris didn't even bother. He just wore his jeans – the ones he'd sliced up for Halloween – and a t-shirt with the faded picture of a wildcat on the front. It was supposed to look like Native art but you could tell it had been painted by some shitty white person. Neither of us was going to win any kind of best dressed award for the evening.

'There he is!' Karen shouted.

She ran onto the street, waving her hand like somebody trying to hail a cab. Julian was driving his dad's Lexus, not the Mercedes. It was twice as big as a normal car and only got about three miles to the gallon – but it looked awesome. He pulled up onto the curb, just to show he could, and we piled in. Karen took the front. The interior reeked of leather polish and Julian's cologne. He'd really dolled himself up. He'd lathered gel in his hair and worn this Calvin Klein polo shirt, unbuttoned at the top so you could see his silver chain. I had to admit he looked pretty good. He knew it, too.

'You guys ready to lock and load?'

'You got it, Richard Gere.'

'Yeah – put it in gear, gearbox.'

I could tell that pissed him off, because he floored it before we'd even shut the door. Straight away, he cranked up his dance music and started careening around corners. The beat was so loud it felt as if the speakers were actually inside my skull. He was doing it on purpose, too. Chris and I couldn't hear shit, which meant he had Karen all to himself in the front. Only snatches of the conversation reached me.

'... super nice house...'

'... cool guy...'

'... think I know him...'

I leaned forward and shouted, 'Hey!'

'What's up?'

'Whose party is this, anyways?'

Jules turned down the music to answer. 'Tim Williams. He goes to Collingwood.'

That's the school with the graphite hockey sticks and super good tennis team.

'Sweet,' Chris said, making it pretty obvious that it wasn't sweet at all.

Julian pretended not to notice. 'Yeah – it should be.'

Then he turned his music back up and kept talking to Karen. The two of them were ridiculously excited. Meanwhile, me and Chris brooded in the back, in the dark, nursing a mickey of his mom's Smirnoff. We didn't even have anything to chase with.

I started feeling a bit sick.

The thing is, it's not like I hate everybody in West Van. I've got some relatives out there who are pretty sweet. But they've never really liked it much, either. The problem with West Van is that it tends to be super excessive – and this party we went to was no different.

We came off the Upper Levels at the Caulfield exit, and wound our way through this endless maze of monster mansions. Each one was the size of three normal houses. That area of West Van is unreal. There's no poor people left. They've all been shot or run out of town. Realtors charge you five grand just to look at a house, let alone make an offer. Some of the lots were so big you couldn't even see how far back they went. Most of them had gates, too.

'Here. This must be it.'

The street out front was crammed with all kinds of super sweet cars: Beamers and Audis and monster SUVs. There was even some kind of limited edition Porsche. It was nuts. We parked further down and walked up the drive, which was about five miles long. The house looked crowded, but also pretty sedate – not at all like the toga party Julian had later. To begin with, there was some kind of professional bouncer at the door. He actually had a little clipboard with a guest list and everything.

'You got an invitation?' he asked.

'Tim invited me. I'm Julian.'

The guy checked his list.

'What about your friends here?'

'Uh ...they're with me.'

'Hold on a sec.'

The guy pulled out his cellphone, which was so small you could hardly see it. 'Tim – I got a Julian here. Brought three friends with him. Can you confirm?'

Me and Chris looked at each other. We were both trying not to laugh. I leaned over and whispered, 'Yeah – I can confirm that this is officially the shittiest party of all time.'

The guy didn't hear. He was listening and nodding into his phone.

'Uh-huh. Gotcha. Okay.'

He stepped aside.

'Go on in,' he said.

It was like we'd arrived on another planet.

The first thing I noticed was the space. Every room was massive, with super high ceilings and yawning archways. Even a little room, like the foyer or the bathroom, was at least twice as big as you'd expect. The next thing I noticed were the people filling the space. It was as if somebody had dressed up all the beach mannequins in ridiculously nice clothes – Diesel, Armani, Banana Republic, whatever – then carefully arranged them around the house in various positions. They stood there sipping cocktails and chatting, totally stiff and fake.

'This is fucked, man,' Chris whispered.

'I know. It's nuts.'

We stuck close to Julian as he made his way through the hallway, the lounge, the dining room, another lounge, and into this entertainment room with a huge TV hanging on the wall. Every so often he'd stop and say hello to somebody. He knew a bunch of the people from tennis lessons or the winter club or whatever. Karen did too, actually. We didn't. We just trailed along in their wake. We'd get introduced to somebody and then end up standing there as Karen or Julian talked with them. Conversations were always the same.

'It's so good to see you!'

'How do you know Tim?'

'That outfit is amazing!'

Everybody looked incredible in exactly the same way. It was like they all had the same personal stylist. The only ones who stood out were me and Chris. People noticed us wherever we went. I mean, it was obvious we didn't belong within a hundred miles of that house. Eventually we got sick of everybody staring at us. We left Julian and Karen to their mingling and headed off on our own.

'Let's check out the balcony.'

'Lead the way, Chubby Checker.'

It was my idea. I was hoping that we might find some normal people out there. We did, too. Well, Chris did. I didn't have much luck. We split up and I approached this group of guys standing around one of the tables. There were tons of tables on the balcony – these fancy wooden tables decorated with fresh flowers and Chinese candle lanterns. The guys had cleared everything off their table except for a bunch of coins and buttons and a couple lines of coke. I had no idea what they were doing, but I walked over anyways.

'We could feed it out here, to the wing.'

'Not if they're man-marking.'

'Well, if they're man-marking it's a different story.'

They all talked pretty fast, bobbing their heads and chewing their lips. Totally coked up. One of the guys bent down and snorted a line through a bill, then stood up and pawed at the powder beneath his nostrils. He started moving buttons around, arranging and rearranging them like a general making a battle plan.

'If they're man-marking, we should go inside-outside.'

'Like a basketball-style pick play?'

'Exactly!'

I nodded along with the others. 'Then you could take a shot from the point.'

They all looked at me, then at each other.

'From the point?'

'Yeah. You know – just throw the puck towards the net.'

'We're talking about ultimate, buddy.'

'Oh. I thought you were talking about hockey.'

After that they all turned their backs on me and closed ranks. Like I cared. I mean, what kind of treats get ripped on coke and plan frisbee strategy at a house party? I hate coke. Me and Chris could never afford it. This one time we crushed a bunch of caffeine pills and tried snorting them instead. We thought it would be like poor man's coke. It wasn't. It just burned our nostrils and tripled our anxiety levels. Next to acid, that was probably the worst narcotics experience of my entire life.

'Razor!'

Chris called to me from across the balcony. He was standing by the railing with this dark-haired girl. She was kind of pudgy, but not bad pudgy. Not fat. Just soft. She had a nice smile, too. Chris waved me over and I went to join them.

'Linda wants to smoke a joint.'

'Sweet.'

Me and Linda stood together while Chris got out his stash.

'Where are you guys from?' she asked.

'The Cove.'

'I knew you weren't from around here.'

Chris lit up and handed the joint to Linda. We smoked it sort of furtively, taking big, fast tokes. It got us baked pretty quick – especially Linda. I don't think she'd smoked a lot of pot before. After two or three rounds, it was like a switch had flipped in her brain. All of a sudden, she couldn't stop talking. It was nuts.

'Do you guys like West Van?' she asked.

'It's okay, I guess.'

'That's only because you don't live here. I go to Handsworth, and some days it makes me so crazy I want to scream. I can't wait to graduate. I'm going to move to Korea and teach English. Oh my God!' She put her hand to her mouth, eyes wide. 'I have to tell you about what happened on the weekend. My little cousin's cat got eaten by a cougar.'

'Holy shit!'

'That's crazy.'

Me and Chris were both smiling. She was pretty fried.

'Uh-huh. And get this: it was her birthday. How awful is that? She's only five years old. And apparently, she was sitting by the window, watching the cat play around in the yard, when this humongous cougar came out of nowhere and gobbled it up.'

I started giggling. It just seemed too bizarre. 'In one gulp?'

'In one gulp!'

She laughed, too. We couldn't help it.

Chris said, 'How's that for a birthday present?'

'Instead of getting a cat, your cat gets eaten.'

'Happy birthday!'

We laughed about that for at least five minutes. Then, when we finally calmed down, I started feeling a bit guilty. Linda did, too. You could tell. I mean, it was her cousin after all.

She sighed. 'What would you tell a five-year-old if that happened?'

We didn't answer at first. Chris flicked our joint off the balcony. It landed on the perfectly cut lawn and smouldered for a few seconds before fading away. For some reason, I started thinking of Mrs Reever.

Chris said, 'You tell her that life's fucked, and everything dies.'

## 19

The old lady started choking. Chris jerked back as yellow bile burbled out of her mouth. Me and Jules got her on her side. That was one of the things they'd taught us in first aid: get them on their side. It worked, too. This mixture of lung fluid and seawater spurted all over the grass. I couldn't believe how much came out of her. Later they said it was about a litre. At the time, though, it looked like way more. And the smell was harsh nasty. I couldn't take it. I turned away and started dry-heaving. It was pretty embarrassing, actually.

Jules shouted: 'She's breathing!'

She was – if you could call it that. It was weak and raspy and shallow, like a sick dog. That didn't stop everybody from cheering. A few guys patted me on the back, as if we were all on the same team and I'd just scored a game-winning goal. Chris didn't move. He knelt there the whole time, staring down at her. His face was completely white, like an egg. He had some of that bile on his lips and chin. I remember thinking: *He tasted it*. The smell made me gag but he had to taste it.

A few minutes later the ambulance arrived.

Everything went haywire after that. I guess that's what happens if you save somebody's life, but I still wish we'd refused to accept those medals, or go on the Crazy Dan show, or talk to any of the newspapers. I wish we'd just hauled her out of there and left it at that. We didn't want any of the attention. They forced it on us. At first, we didn't mind. But after she died, well, then we minded.

They put her on life support for a few days.

At that time, nobody knew she was a vegetable. Physically, she was in pretty good condition. The doctors assumed she'd pull through. Everybody loved us. For a little while, at least, it felt like we'd really done some good. They printed our picture on the front page of the North Shore News, and pretty soon people were writing in to say how inspirational we were and shit like that. No joke. Mostly it was other old ladies and senior citizens. That's the thing about elderly people. From reading the headlines they just assume the world is full of insane kids who want to throw phone books at them and egg their houses. So when they saw the article about us they thought we were really something.

One of them wrote: 'These young men are pillars of society.'

Another said: 'Knowing what they did warms my heart.'

Those old ladies couldn't get enough of us. They weren't the only ones, either. People recognised us on the streets and around the neighbourhood and all over the place. The shop-keeper down in the Cove, who usually threatened to beat the hell out of us with a broomstick, gave Julian a bunch of cigars for free. Only a week before, my next door neighbour had accused me and Chris of slashing his tyres. Now he was all smiles and handshakes, Mr Hypocrite, pretending like we were best friends. Everybody treated us differently. Doing one good thing – just one – had somehow transformed us in their eyes.

It must have been even trippier for Chris, who typically took way more shit than me or Julian. He took shit all the time from parents and teachers and cops and everyone, because of his reputation. Whenever a kid got jumped or a car got stolen or a house got vandalised, the police came looking for Chris. It was just like in Casablanca when the guy says 'Round up the usual suspects.' Chris had been a usual suspect most of his life. Now, all of a sudden, he was a saint. I'm not saying he let it go to his head. I'm just saying it must have been weird not to be treated like scum for a change.

Then they went and pulled the plug on her.

Apparently she'd inhaled too much seawater. We'd brought her body back to life but her brain was completely wiped, like a broken hard drive. They could have kept her on life support forever and she would have stayed like that. There was nothing left. So her family gave them permission to let her die. The papers didn't publicise that so much. It would have ruined their story. But it still got around. Then there was a weird period, when people didn't know what to make of us. Were we heroes or weren't we? Did it still count for anything if the old lady had died anyway?

I don't blame them. Not really. I didn't know what the hell to make of it, either. Her dying didn't change our actions, but it made them sort of pointless. I mean, we'd done our best, but we hadn't actually accomplished anything. It was like this movie I saw – where some guy rushes into a burning building and lifts a lady out on his shoulders. He thinks he's saved her life, and can't figure out why all the other firemen are cracking up.

Then he realises he's carrying a dummy.

## 20

They were totally alone, in the quiet of that cabin, surrounded by all these flickering candles. Well, technically they weren't totally alone – me and Jules had puked and passed out in the corner, like a couple of dead marmots. Drinking all that whiskey and vodka, and eating nothing but Pot Noodles, wasn't the greatest idea we'd ever had. And in that state, we didn't really count for much – so it was as if they were alone. Obviously something was going to happen, and it did: Karen took off her shirt. I mean, when it came to hooking up Karen didn't mess around. She pulled it off, tossed it aside, and stood right in front of Chris with her hands on her hips.

That's what he said, anyhow.

'Was she wearing a bra?'

'No. No bra.'

He told me about it down at the Hippo Club – this super shitty arcade on Lonsdale. It's not there any more. Somebody burned it down. Right to the ground. Actually, now that I think about it, it was the kind of place that deserved to be burned to the ground. Most of the games just ate your quarters and the controls always felt greasy and sticky. The only people who went there were losers and loners and half-assed wannabe drug dealers.

And us, of course.

'Did you feel her up?'

'Not at first,' Chris said. 'She just wanted me to look.'

'That's potent, man.'

We were standing side by side, playing Space Invaders – that old-school game where the aliens march back and forth in little rows, dropping lower and lower, coming down to get you. I could see Chris's reflection in the screen. Totally intense. He always got intense when we played Space Invaders. They had new games at the Hippo Club, too, but we both hated that stuff. We only liked games where the graphics harsh sucked – like where you can hardly even tell what's happening half the time since everything is just blocky and weird.

'So were they pretty sweet looking?'

Chris patted his fire button. 'What?'

'You know. Her tits.'

He said they were super pale. The rest of her was tanned but her breasts were almost white. Except for her nipples, obviously. Her nipples were dark. I guess because of her complexion or something. I don't know. But he said they were sort of brown. Like little acorns poking out of her chest.

'Watch out for that guy.'

Only one alien was left. He'd turned red and started moving super fast. That's what the aliens do when you kill off all their friends – they get ridiculously angry.

'I got him covered.'

I lined up my ship and kept firing until I hit him. Then we took a little breather, loosening up for the next level. Chris shook out his wrists and rolled his shoulders.

'But you touched them eventually, right?'

He shrugged. 'Sure.'

Chris wasn't one of those guys who liked to brag about all the shit he did with chicks. Trying to get it out of him was pretty frustrating, actually.

'Well, what did they feel like?'

'I don't know. They felt like tits, man. Soft and squishy and warm.'

'Like fresh play dough?'

'Yeah, sure. Like that.'

A new batch of aliens started crunching down the screen, and we picked them off one by one. We were on a roll. Neither of us had even lost a life yet.

'Was that it? Or did you guys do some other stuff?'

'I kissed her. She told me to kiss her so I did.'

He didn't say so, but I bet he kissed her pretty hard – almost like he was smothering her with his mouth, sucking all the breath out of her. Super passionate. He'd tasted death and kissing her must have been like the exact opposite.

'Here comes the blimp,' Chris said. 'Shoot that fucking blimp, Razor!'

The blimp is this thing that floats above the aliens, right at the top of the screen. I moved my ship over to the right and squeezed off a shot. I nailed it, too. Afterwards Chris told me what they did next. It was like my reward for hitting the blimp.

'You know that desk, in the corner of the hut?'

'Yeah,' I said. It was an old work desk. 'What about it?'

He said Karen got up on it and stretched out, like a patient on an operating table. Only, in this case, she was more like the doctor. She told him exactly what to do. She told him to kiss her neck and throat and shoulders, and she told him to kiss her belly and ribs and hips, right down to the edge of her jeans. She even told him to kiss her on the nipples.

'You're shitting me,' I said.

'No. Hey – look out.'

But the aliens had got me. My ship made a little groaning sound and disintegrated. After that our game went downhill. I just couldn't concentrate. I kept thinking about them, hoping he'd tell me more. But apparently that was as far as it went. They both crawled into separate sleeping bags and drifted off, innocent as mice. Maybe it would have gone further if me and Jules hadn't been lying there. It's hard to say, really.


## 21


Days during last summer always started the same. I'd sleep until noon. Then I'd get up and eat some cereal and sleep a little bit more. After that, I'd call Chris or he'd call me, unless one of us was working. Now and again, I cut lawns and raked leaves for old people in our neighbourhood, and Chris sometimes did a bit of casual labour for his mom's ex-boyfriend who was a carpentry and construction contractor.

Otherwise, we were home free.

'What do you want to do, man?'

'I don't know,' I said. 'Did you talk to Jules?'

'Yeah. I told him we were riding our Beamers to Lonsdale.' That was the best way to ditch Jules. The day he got his driver's licence, he stopped riding his BMX forever. He wouldn't even ride one for the sake of riding one. He thought biking was kid's stuff. He didn't want to be seen pedalling up and down Lonsdale, especially by his pals from the winter club. That was fine by us. Julian was our buddy and everything, but we had stuff we did without him, and he had stuff he did without us. Like play tennis.

'What's Karen doing?' I asked.

'She's out shopping.'

Karen was obsessed with shopping. So was Julian, actually. Come to think of it, the two of them had a lot in common. They were both rich, they were both shopaholics, and they both turned out to be fairly treacherous.

'Screw it, man,' I said. 'Let's bike to Lonsdale, then.' I figured we might as well, since he'd already told Jules that's what we were doing. 'We can hit up the Hippo Club.'

'Yeah. We could put the hippo in the tub.'

'I'm feeling pretty tubby today.'

'You're sounding like a bit of a tub-thumper, all right.'

That was how we talked when we were alone. Don't ask me why.

'I'll be there in ten.'

'Okay, tenpin.'

It was another scorcher. That summer just kept getting hotter and hotter. They talked about it on the news and everything. There was nearly a drought. That hardly ever happens in Vancouver. There's about nine hundred rivers and lakes all over the Lower Mainland so having a drought is a pretty huge deal. Not to mention uncomfortable. Usually I love biking but that day it was murderous. I started sweating before we'd gone more than a few blocks.

'Do you think you guys will do it?'

'I told you I don't know.'

We took a break at the corner store just before the bridge. There was shade there, and pop. We drank the pop and sat in the shade and lit this super tiny joint, thin as a needle.

'But she wants to do it, right?'

'I think so. She talks about it a lot.'

I took a quick toke and washed it down with some pop.

'Yeah? What does she say?'

'You know. Weird stuff. "I want your first time to be with me." Stuff like that. And how she thinks about giving me gummers.'

I choked up smoke and glanced at him, just to make sure he wasn't messing with me.

'She's a pretty potent chick, huh?'

'Yeah. Come on – let's keep going.'

I didn't want to keep going, but Chris was already getting on his BMX. He rode this silver Mongoose that he'd bought at a garage sale and totally fixed up. He'd done the same for me, actually. I had a Huffy – this fairly old-school Huffy with rainbow spoke beads.

We pedalled along the low road, down by the train tracks. Just as we came off onto Esplanade, we heard this sharp blaring sound – like the squawk of an extremely fat goose. I knew that sound. By then it was as familiar and annoying as the school bell, or an alarm clock. We pulled over, still kind of hoping that the squad car might cruise past us.

It didn't, of course.

After the speeding ticket fiasco, we just kept running into him. We'd be down at the beach, hanging out, and all of a sudden he'd be there – checking our pockets and rooting through our bags. Or we'd be chilling in the Cove and we'd spot him prowling around in his patrol car. He was all over the place, like there was more than one of him. He'd pop out of bushes, or appear behind you, or be waiting for you as you came around a corner. It reminded me of this movie we saw one time, about a psycho cop that starts killing people who break any little law: speeding or jaywalking or littering or anything. He pulls up to them and shines his flashlight right in their face and then blows them away.

It's pretty nuts, actually.

And this thing with Bates was almost that nuts. We became his favourite hobby. Some guys collect stamps, other guys buy porn mags. Bates hassled us. He really got off on it, too. I wouldn't be surprised if he drove down to the Cove specifically to hassle us – that's how much he hated our guts. Don't ask me why. I doubt he even knew why. It started after Chris lipped him off that night he gave us the speeding ticket, and just kind of snowballed from there. It was like he wanted to see how far he could push us. His favourite thing to do was confiscate our beer. He loved pouring the cans out one by one, as slowly as possible, making sure we watched. And if we didn't have any beer, he'd think of something else. He'd think of something super lame and stupid, and hassle us about that instead.

'Hey heroes,' he said. 'Where are your helmets?'

No joke. He wanted to know where our fucking helmets were.

'We don't have any,' I said.

'It's illegal to ride bikes without helmets.'

Maybe it is. But nobody had ever told us before.

Chris said, 'So?'

Bates swaggered over to him. He hated Chris most of all. He could push me around, and make Jules cry, but against Chris he was powerless – which drove him absolutely insane.

'So maybe I'll give you a ticket. How's that sound, hero?'

'It sounds pretty sweet,' Chris said.

He wasn't being lippy, either. He just happened to be in this extremely good mood. I mean, he'd already hooked up with Karen and pretty soon they'd be doing it. Even Bates couldn't rile him under those circumstances.

'Yeah,' I said. 'We love tickets. They're awesome.'

'Me giving you a ticket is awesome?'

'That's right.' Chris patted me on the back. 'Super awesome.'

Bates sort of laughed. It was short and loud, like a fart coming out his mouth. 'We got a couple of comedians, here,' he said. 'What a great combination.'

He was trying to play it cool, but you could tell he didn't know what the hell to make of us. I bet he thought we were high on some super harsh drug, like crack cocaine or crystal meth. When his radio started making noise, he looked almost relieved. He walked over to the car and picked up the receiver, keeping one eye on us as if he thought we might hop on our bikes and ride away. And as soon as his back was turned, that's exactly what we did.

'Hey Razor,' Chris whispered, 'let's jet.'

We eased away from the curb and started pedalling. Totally casual.

'Hey! Get back here!'

'Bite me, Batesy!'

He had his car, but we had a pretty solid head start. Plus, we knew all the shortcuts around Lonsdale. We turned up behind the abandoned car wash, hung a right, and cut across this overgrown park filled with rusty hubcaps and old tyres. Then we zigzagged through a bunch of alleys and side streets. Bates hounded us the entire way. Sometimes his siren was close, other times it was far off, like an air raid warning in those old war movies.

Then, pretty soon, there were two sirens.

'Damn, man.'

'This is getting heaty.'

'Let's ditch the Beamers,' Chris said. 'We'll come back for them, later.'

We hopped off and threw our bikes over a fence. Then we started walking. We walked back towards Lonsdale and ducked into this pizza joint on the corner – one of those places that sells pizza by the slice and nothing else. There were no tables or chairs. Just pizza.

'I'll have a ham and pineapple.'

'Me too. Two ham and pineapple.'

The guy working behind the counter gave us pizza. It was terrible. The temperature in there was about five hundred degrees, and the pizza had been sitting in the heat for hours. The crust had gone all soggy and the cheese was soaked through with oil. I took one bite and that was enough. I mean, when it's that hot and you've been running from the cops the last thing you want is a mushy, melting piece of pizza. What I really needed was a pop.

'Hey – you got any pop?'

'What pop you want?'

The guy was foreign or something. He didn't look foreign but he talked foreign.

'Root beer.'

He gave me the root beer, but it wasn't even cold. It was warm, and a little flat – like hot syrup. I've been to some pretty bad pizza joints, but that was the worst one ever. And we were stuck in it. We stood around in the stifling heat, pretending to eat soggy pizza and drink warm pop. After about five minutes, a cop car cruised past. Then it turned around and came back, going slower. It rolled to a stop right in front of the pizza place, which had these big glass windows. We could see the driver staring at us, squinting a little.

'Come on, Razor!'

We started running. We'd only run about ten yards when another car pulled out of the alley, blocking our escape. There were cop cars all over the place: behind us and in front of us and on both sides of us. Bates had called out half the North Van police force. I think there might have even a been a few cops from West Van. When he saw that, Chris just started laughing. I did, too. I mean, obviously I was wetting the bed a little, but at the same time I'd never seen so many squad cars in one place. Pedestrians stopped to stare, as if they were expecting some kind of huge drug bust. It was a total shitshow.

Bates was the last to arrive.

'Yeah. That's them. Those are the guys.'

He walked over with three other patrolmen. They grabbed us, in case we tried to run again. There was one tall guy with a moustache and grey hair who looked a little wiser than all the rest. For that reason, I'm pretty sure he was a North Van cop. They're part of the RCMP or the Mounties or whatever, which makes them a little more professional than the killer cops from West Van. They hardly ever shoot anybody, at least.

'Why'd you run?' he asked.

'We didn't want a ticket.'

That was me. Chris didn't answer. He was still trying to catch his breath.

'What do you mean? A ticket for what?'

'For not having helmets.'

The old cop looked at Bates, as if he'd just admitted to wearing diapers.

'That's what this is about?'

'Well, they ran, didn't they?'

The old cop just sighed and shook his head. Then he turned back to me.

'You two caused us a lot of trouble.'

'Yessir. Sorry about that, officer.'

I actually was sorry, too. I mean, I didn't mind apologising to this guy. He seemed like a real cop. Not like Bates at all. For one thing, his moustache was huge – nearly as big as his entire face. Also, he looked pretty washed-up. The best cops are always the wash-ups.

'Well, give them the ticket, then.'

The other officers waited while Bates wrote out the ticket. By that point, he knew he'd really screwed up. He could barely write the ticket properly. Then, when he ripped it out of his little book, he tore the paper right down the middle. One of the cops – the one holding Chris – snickered and tried to hide it behind his hand. That got his buddy going. Pretty soon, most of the cops were chuckling. Pretty soon, most of the cops were chuckling – except for Officer Moustache. He stood there with his arms crossed, looking completely pissed off.

Of course, all this just made Bates hate us even more.

**22**

One drug I wouldn't suggest trying is acid.

None of us knew what the hell to expect, but it was worse than they say. Way worse. In school they're always telling you: 'Don't do drugs.' That's bullshit. Some drugs are okay. Weed, for instance. And nutmeg. But acid? I'd rather break a bottle on my head than do acid again. I mean, it didn't even get us high. It just completely screwed our brains up.

'Jesus it's hot out tonight.'

Karen wouldn't stop saying that, even though it wasn't hot at all. It was just a regular night. We were sitting on the cliff at Greyrocks – this tiny island down in the Cove – and the air felt cool and fresh and clean. To me, at least. Not to Karen. She looked like she'd been locked in a sauna for about three weeks. Her face had gone all blotchy, like a rotten plum, and her hair was this mess of sweaty, tangled strands. At one point, she peeled off her shirt and sat there in her jeans and bra and nothing else. Then she screamed. Don't ask me why. I wasn't paying much attention to Karen or her screaming.

I had problems of my own.

'Hey,' I said. 'What the hell?'

On my forearm, right above my wrist, I have these two moles. Normally they're just regular moles: small and brown and harmless. But the acid changed them completely. They started pulsating as if they were alive. Then they turned into the heads of little worms, burrowing out of my skin. I swatted at them, trying to catch them. It was pretty fucked.

Jules had it even worse. He was huddled up by himself, crying.

'I'm so weak,' he sobbed. 'I hate it.'

Julian had been a runt up until grade nine: skinny and frail and almost anaemic. Then one summer he grew about a foot and started eating protein powder and taking tennis lessons. After that he wasn't such a weakling. The problem was, he'd been a runt for those important years of his life, the years when everything matters, and the acid brought it all back to him.

Somebody shook me by the shoulder. Chris.

'Are you feeling it?' he asked.

He was sitting on an old tree stump, with his legs crossed beneath him. His face was half-covered in shadows that looked almost like fur. As I watched, the fur spread over his cheeks and chin, and seemed to rise in a mane around his shoulders. He grimaced, showing teeth that were white and sharp and wet. He'd turned into some sort of wolf man.

The wolf man said, 'I don't feel anything.'

I tried to answer him, but I couldn't. I was just too messed up.

'I'm going for a walk.'

The wolf man hopped down from his stump and prowled off without glancing back. I followed him. That island isn't very big. There's the cliff, some trees, and a little beach. You'd have to be a total marzipan to get lost, but as soon as we stepped into those woods, that's exactly what happened. I felt as if I'd stumbled into a shadowy maze filled with all kinds of bizarre booby traps. Branches poked at my eyes, twigs clawed at my hair, and little thorns stuck in my arms like fishhooks. I kept falling over stumps and roots and shit like that. It was a living nightmare. Every so often, I'd catch a glimpse of this hairy silhouette, but the wolf man always vanished before I could catch up. I must have staggered around in there for about six hours. At one point I even started snivelling, like a lost little orphan from a fairy tale – a fairy tale about how children shouldn't drop acid because it's the worst drug ever invented. Then, just when I'd given up all hope, I found the beach.

The wolf man had got there first.

He was padding back and forth along the shore and making this strange sound – this whimpering sound. It reminded me of the noise a dog makes when it's standing at the edge of a swimming pool, and it wants to jump in because it can see people splashing around and having fun. Except, in this case, there weren't any people. There was just this stretch of water, black and still as oil. When I stepped onto the sand, he stopped pacing and turned around. The hair covering his face had disappeared. So had the mane and teeth. It was Chris again. I crossed over to him. He watched me approach as if he didn't quite recognise me.

'Did you see her?' he asked.

'Who?'

He pointed at a spot about twenty yards from shore.

'Out there.'

I peered into the watery murk. All I could see was the opposite shore and the public dock and the lights of the houses, but I didn't want to admit that to Chris.

'Sure, man. I think so.'

He knew I was lying, though. It was like being with somebody when they spot a shooting star and you don't. It's not your fault, but you still feel like you've let them down.

## 23

'You've put in me a tricky predicament, young man.'

'I know, Mr Green. Sorry about that.'

I kept apologising, over and over. I didn't know what else to do. It would have been different if I'd hated our principal. But other than Mrs Oldham he was the only staff member at Seycove I actually liked. He had a square jaw, sort of like a comic book character, and this deep baritone voice. Back before Chris got expelled, Mr Green busted us both for smoking up in the woods behind the school. Don't ask me how. Some loser must have ratted us out. Chris got called to his office first, and after lunch it was my turn.

There was no use arguing with Mr Green. He was pretty savvy.

'I know you weren't smoking cigarettes out there. I can smell it on you.'

I opened my mouth, but he held out a palm to stop me.

'Don't say anything. Don't admit to it. I don't want to hear it.'

He got up and went to stand at the window, clasping his hands behind his back.

'I had a chat with your friend Chris, earlier.'

He knew Chris and I were tight. We'd been in his office together a bunch of times.

'Oh, yeah?' I said, trying to sound positive.

'He was stoned, too. What's worse, you were both smoking it on school property.'

He came to stand over me, and I sort of wilted back into my chair.

'Do you know how long I've been doing this?'

'No, sir. I don't.'

'Twenty-two years. Twelve as a teacher. Ten as a principal.' He stroked his jaw, getting super thoughtful. 'If you've done something as long as I have, certain patterns start to emerge. Certain things repeat themselves. Do you understand me?'

'I think so.'

'Like your friend, Chris. He must seem like a pretty hip guy to you.' One thing that cracks me up is when a teacher uses some word that's about forty years old. 'But I've seen kids like him before. Kids with his attitude. His problem with authority.' He sat back down. It was weird. If he'd been lecturing me, it would have pissed me off a lot more. But he actually looked pretty sad about the whole thing. 'Back in my day we all wanted to act like James Dean. We all wanted to have the leather jacket and be the rebel without a cause. But that's a limited philosophy, son. A one-way street. Right now, Chris is heading down it. And as far as I can see, you're content to go along with him. Isn't that right?'

'Sure. I guess so.'

'Well, you can only be a follower for so long. You can't be a sheep your whole life. Chris has to make his choices. You have to make yours. Understand?'

I nodded. I was still seared and found his whole speech pretty confusing.

'I sent Chris home,' he said, 'and I'm going to do the same to you. You look a little under the weather, understand? You're feeling sick, and need the rest of the day off. And you're not going to come back until you're feeling better. Are we absolutely clear on that?'

'Yes sir. One hundred per cent.'

I practically ran out of there. He didn't even phone my dad. It was fucking rad. Me and Chris had the whole day off. When I got home, he was already waiting in the basement.

'Hey stoner,' he said.

'What's up, boner?'

'Mr Green busted me and sent me home.'

'Me, too.' I grabbed him in a headlock and we started shoving each other around. 'He gave me a huge speech about you.'

'What'd he say?'

'I can't really remember. I was blitzed. But he said you look like James Dean.'

'That's awesome.'

We smoked another bowl and biked up to the movie store. When we asked the lady if she had any James Dean movies, she told us to try the library. It was right next door. We found one, too. *Rebel Without a Cause*. It was harsh old-school, and some of the other actors were pretty shitty, but James Dean was awesome. He didn't really look like Chris, but he acted like him. We hadn't made one of our movies for ages – we kind of gave up all that stuff when we hit high school – but after watching *Rebel* we busted out my camera and threw together a few scenes. Mostly it was just the two of us standing around in my dad's blazers, smoking our faces off. The annoying part was that I felt too much like the little sidekick. You know – the scrawny kid who acts kind of gay and doesn't get the girl.

That harsh depressed me, actually.

## 24

He hit the ground like a sack of cement. Wham. I'd seen Chris give it to a lot of guys, but none got it as bad as Bates. Chris put everything into those punches: all the hate and rage and frustration that had been twisting his insides for weeks.

The elastic had finally snapped.

Bates lay there, half-conscious, making these little groans. There was blood everywhere. It streamed from his nose and mouth and cuts on his cheek and forehead. His face was a red, pulpy mass – like a squashed tomato. Chris started kicking the tomato. He kicked it across the jaw, and two or three times in the gut. After the first kick Bates went still. After the fourth kick, or maybe the fifth, I grabbed Chris in a half-nelson.

'That's it, man. That's it.'

He fought against me, still kicking. I didn't let go until he stopped resisting and tapped me on the forearm to let me know he was calm.

We stood over Bates, panting like dogs.

'Shit. Did you kill him?'

At that point, the whole situation felt fairly surreal. Only fifty yards away, hidden by trees, dozens of people were enjoying a regular day at the beach. I couldn't see them but I could hear them, shouting and laughing and splashing. Overhead, all these seagulls circled around and around, like scraps of paper caught in a whirlwind.

'You coming?' Chris asked.

He was sitting in the squad car, his face half-hidden by shade, and I was standing by the driver's side door. The sun slapped down on my scalp and the back of my neck. I glanced over at Bates. He lay completely still, like a fat blue slug squashed in the sand. Beyond him I could see the flicker and flare of sunlight off water. Then there was the beach, with its coal-hot sand and constantly breaking surf. That was the world, as far as I could tell: just an unbearable mix of heat and noise and light.

I couldn't let him go alone.

I walked around the front of the car and slipped into the passenger's seat. Chris popped the handbrake, backed up, and shifted into drive. We cruised past the boat ramp and through the Cates parking lot. There were people all over the place: lounging on the grass, unpacking beach gear, waiting for parking spots. None of them noticed us. When a cop drives past, people don't pay much attention to the driver – they only see the car. It's a lot like a hearse in that way. Chris turned his hearse onto Dollarton Highway and accelerated. He hadn't driven much but the squad car was an automatic, which made it easy. Things began to feel more normal. It was a beautiful day and here we were, driving along. I rolled down my window and rested my elbow on the door, mimicking Chris.

'Check it out,' he said.

He pointed at a pack of smokes on the dashboard. I lit one for both of us and started fiddling with the radio. I don't know if it was broken or what, but I couldn't find any FM. Eventually I just gave up and left it tuned in to this Chinese radio station. All the music and ads were in Chinese. Even the DJ spoke Chinese. Mandarin, I guess. It was pretty awesome, actually.

'Sweet, man. Turn it up.'

I did. This funky rift filled the cab, trilling along our spines, and a lady started singing at the top of her lungs. It was like we were in the opening sequence of a movie – one of those gritty Hong Kong action movies where everybody's always sweating and smoking and driving super fast, and nobody gives a shit whether they live or die.

**25**

They invited us to the funeral. Don't ask me why. We were a little surprised to receive the invitations. I guess they thought we had a right to be there. Maybe they assumed we wanted to pay our last respects to this lady we'd never even met, whose life we had almost saved.

But basically, we decided to go.

Jules drove us to this church across town. It was the first time I'd been to a funeral, except for my mom's and that doesn't really count because I was still a baby. I won't ever go to another one, either. I'd rather drop acid again than go to another funeral. We parked on the street across from the church – a tiny building covered in white stucco.

'Ready to roll?'

'Roll out the red carpet.'

'Yeah,' Jules said. He never really got our jokes. 'Ready or not, here we roll.'

The church was hot and cramped as a kiln. Not many people came – maybe thirty or forty – but there wasn't even enough room for everybody to sit. The late arrivals had to stand against the walls. We got the last three seats in the back. I was dressed in a cheap suit that my dad had bought me for my cousin's Christening. When I was twelve it might have fit me. Not any more. I felt like I'd squeezed myself into a straitjacket. The sleeves were way too short, and every

111

time I moved I expected the shoulders to rip apart. That was bad enough, but I was also sweating my balls off. Streaks of morning sun smashed through the plate glass windows, setting the church ablaze with orange and red and yellow light. Outside you could see waves of heat squiggling in the air, and the whole place stunk of perfume, cologne and body odour. At one point it got so bad I covered my face with my shirt and started breathing through my mouth. It was nuts.

Things began to happen.

A minister waddled up to the altar. Behind him hung this wooden cross with a life-size Jesus stretched out on it. Even Jesus looked hot. His sad old eyes stared straight down, towards the coffin at his feet. The casket was open but from where we sat I couldn't see inside. After mumbling a few words of welcome, the minister started preaching. I felt awful for him. He was wearing these huge robes that looked thick and heavy as blankets. A glaze of sweat glistened on his face, and he kept having to wipe his forehead with his handkerchief. I don't remember much of what he said. It was impossible to concentrate in all that heat, and the minister didn't have the stamina to speak with conviction. He started strong but by the end his words were coming out in short, wheezy phrases – like an asthmatic.

Finally, he gasped, 'Let us pray.'

One by one all the heads in front of us dropped down. Jules did the same – lacing his hands together before his face. He went to church every Sunday so he knew exactly what to do. Chris didn't. Neither did I. I've never said a prayer in my life. It seemed kind of stupid to start for no reason, so I kept my head up and my eyes open. All I could see was row after row of sweaty scalps, as if the whole congregation had ducked down to hide. The minister mumbled a few words about Mrs Reever being up in heaven and at peace.

Then he said, 'Amen.'

And everybody else said, 'Amen.'

Speeches came next – too many speeches to count. First the family gave speeches. Her husband was dead so he didn't give one but her daughter did, and both her sons, and even a bunch of her grandchildren. Then came her friends from the apartment block. All of them had something nice to say about her. She loved cats. She enjoyed playing bridge. She drank single malt whiskey. She had a collection of silent films. She baked cherry tarts. Meanwhile noon was approaching. The temperature rose about a hundred degrees and I started getting dizzy. Each heartbeat sounded like a gong going off in my head. It got harder and harder to see. The people up at the altar became these colourless, blurry shapes. I could hear them talking but none of them actually said anything. The meaning of the words evaporated in the heat. Between speeches, I imagined standing up and putting an end to it.

I wanted to shout, 'She's dead, okay? Let's leave it at that.'

I didn't have the guts, though. Plus, what was the point? They needed their little speeches, to connect with her in some way. And part of me understood why they were trying so hard. On the other hand, she was dead and we were alive. Where's the connection in that? The only thing we had in common with her was that, one day, we'd all be just as dead.

Some of us sooner than others.

At the end the minister asked us to rise. That was the weirdest part of all. We stood up and formed a line and passed in front of the casket one by one. It was time to say goodbye to Mrs Reever. By that point it must have been mid-afternoon. The heat kept up its slow torture. Sweat had soaked through the back of my shirt and my collar felt tight as a choker. The air was too thick and cloying to breathe. You had to drink it in big gulps, like perfumed water. The stench caught in my throat, and I was terrified I'd puke. I'd puke on the flower display or down the front of somebody's suit or all over the glistening coffin. It wasn't just the smell that made me nauseous. It was the thought of seeing her again.

But she looked different than I expected.

The line moved forward, smooth and steady as a conveyer belt, and when our turn came the three of us stood side by side, looking down. Her face wasn't all grey and pasty like I remembered. They'd dusted her cheeks with rouge and lined her mouth with dark lipstick. Silver hair curled around her head in an old-fashioned perm. In a lot of ways, she looked more alive than she had on the day we'd saved her.

Jules got all teary-eyed.

'She's so pretty,' he sobbed.

I didn't have it in me to cry. Neither did Chris. We just stood there, dazed, until the momentum of the line moved us along. Afterwards there was a reception, with crackers and drinks and people talking in small, solemn voices. We headed straight for the bar. It wasn't really a bar – it was just a table they'd set up with a dozen bottles of wine and some cheap styrofoam cups. We hung around that table and got completely hammered. That's the only good thing about funerals – when it comes to the booze it's pretty much a free-for-all. We couldn't figure out why everybody else wasn't pounding the stuff back. I mean, a few people had a glass or two, but only one other guy was interested in getting really tanked. At first he'd swing by, pour himself a drink, and then make a slow tour of the room before circling back for more. Later on he stopped pretending and just stood there drinking with us.

'Say,' he said, 'this wine is quite good, don't you think?'

'Yeah, it's pretty tasty.'

He was scrawny and pot-bellied, and had combed his hair in a weird little twist over his bald spot. He kind of reminded me of the guy in this play we'd gone to see for drama class – *Death of a Salesman*. He looked exactly like the actor who played the old man, the one who has an affair and then dies in the end. You know – the salesman.

'You boys related to the old girl?' he asked.

Chris and I didn't know what to say. We stared into our wine cups, and let Jules explain how we'd dragged her out of the water. He didn't mind. He liked talking about it in a way that Chris and I didn't. The only problem was that he tended to get all choked up. By the end of the story his eyes were watering and he was having trouble finding the right words.

'If... if only we'd gotten there sooner...'

It was a little embarrassing, actually.

'Don't feel too bad about it, kid.' The guy selected a bottle and topped all our glasses up with white wine. He was pretty awesome. 'Old Mrs Reever was getting on. She hadn't been the same since her husband died. You understand what I'm saying?'

We didn't. We just stared at him.

'She had problems.' He leaned towards us, lowering his voice. 'Mental problems. I handled her accounts so I ought to know. They put her on drugs, which helped some. But every so often she'd stop taking them, like old people tend to do. And she'd get a bit...' He tapped his temple and whistled, making the cuckoo clock sound. Then he laughed. Also, he slapped Jules on the back, a little too hard, like a football coach breaking the huddle. 'So I wouldn't beat myself up over it, kid. Between you and me, she's better off like this. If she'd had her choice, well, it wasn't such a bad way to go. I wouldn't be surprised if...'

He trailed off, staring into his wine like she might be swimming around down there.

'If what?' I said.

The guy looked up, startled. Until then, I hadn't realised how absolutely plastered he'd gotten. It was almost as if he didn't know who I was, or who he'd been talking to.

'Huh?' he asked.

'You wouldn't be surprised if what?'

'Oh, sure.' He drained his glass and wiped absently at his forehead. 'That's right. I wouldn't be surprised at all. Anyways, boys, you take care of yourselves. It's been a slice.'

He wandered off, cruising around the room like a plane with a broken wing.

'Jesus,' Chris said. 'Let's get out of here.'

We each took a bottle and tucked it under our jacket. Then we marched straight through the doors and down the steps. There was no way in hell Jules could drive us home. He could barely walk. Dressed in our suits and carrying our bottles of wine, we stumbled across the street to this park. There was a playground in one corner, and the whole area was covered in kids. They were everywhere: dangling from the monkey bars, bobbing up and down on the seesaw, chasing each other across the grass. The sunlight flashed off their hair, their clothes, their gap-toothed faces. There was an old dead lady in that church and all these kids out here, alive and happy and oblivious. It was completely screwed up.

'Damn,' Jules said.

'What?'

'No bottle opener.'

We used Chris's pocket knife instead – the same one he'd killed that raccoon with. We sort of stabbed at the corks until they crumbled into pieces. For the rest of the afternoon, we sat in the shade sucking back warm wine filled with bits of cork. Somehow, later, we got back to the Cove. I think we took the bus, or maybe we even walked. It's hard to say. I don't remember much after about three o'clock.

## 26

'Very few people accept the reality of death. For the most part, they simply forget about it. Life is so much simpler that way. But occasionally death makes a startling appearance, like an unwanted guest at our private party. Then he can no longer be ignored.'

After the funeral and all that wine, the three of us decided to break bottles on our heads. It was enough to convince my dad I should go see a shrink. He thought I was on the verge of a nervous breakdown or something. That's just like him. Since I don't have a mom he can't only be my dad. He has to be my dad and my mom – which makes him a bit neurotic at times. So he made an appointment and took me to this lady downtown.

I didn't know what to make of her.

'Do you mind if I smoke?' she asked.

I shook my head. She reached for the purse on her desk and pulled out a pack of Players. I shifted around in my chair – this oversized leather recliner that kept trying to swallow me whole.

I'd expected a sofa, like shrinks always have in movies, but there was only this chair. She sat directly across from me, right near the window. It was hard to see her because of the light coming in from outside, but I had the impression of sleek black hair and a sort of haggard face. The main thing I noticed were her ankles. She had great ankles. The rest of her body was okay, too, but her ankles were her best feature by a mile. She wore a long skirt – sort of a reddish brown colour – and beneath the hem her ankles looked smooth and pale as fresh plaster.

She lit a cigarette, pursing it between her lips like an expert. She caught me kind of eyeing up the pack and offered it to me. 'You're old enough, right?'

'Sure.'

I rose out of my chair, took one, and leaned down to let her light it. It was pretty cool, actually. I'd expected a real grilling and instead here we were, hacking darts together.

She said, 'I'm going to tell you something I probably shouldn't.'

I waited, sucking on my cigarette.

'I had a daughter. A beautiful little girl. Six months ago, her father decided to take her white water rafting. During the trip, she was tossed from the boat and drowned – like that.' She snapped her fingers. 'She was my everything. Now she's nothing. She's gone.'

I coughed up smoke. I mean, of all the things I expected to come out of her mouth, that would have been pretty far down the list – maybe second or third from the bottom.

'That's terrible,' I said, choking on the words.

'It's worse than terrible. But this is what I'm trying to tell you: it's okay to get worked up over what happened. You and Chris and – what's that other boy's name?'

'Julian.'

'That's it. You and Chris and Julian. You wouldn't be normal if you could just walk away from something like this and not think twice about it. Death is a horrible truth. People might tell you otherwise but you're better off believing me on this: death is a horrible truth.'

She sighed and gazed out the window. She had a corner office overlooking Pacific Centre. All the surrounding buildings were super modern skyscrapers. The metal and glass structures blazed in the sun like heaps of molten slag. Her office was different. It was cool and dark and strangely intimate. I felt safe in there – safe and protected from the heat.

Without looking at me she asked, 'What happened to your ear?'

She must have noticed the bandage. I mean, it was pretty obvious. The doctor had just stitched me up and slapped some gauze over my ear with big strips of medical tape.

'I broke a bottle on my head.'

'On your ear?'

'On the back of my head. The follow-through cut my ear.' I laughed. 'That's the only reason I'm here, you know. When my dad saw what I'd done he harsh freaked out.'

'Why did you break a bottle on your head?'

'We were out drinking. Chris did it and then I did it and then Jules tried. He couldn't do it, though. He tried five or six times and nearly knocked himself out.'

She smiled. 'Chris went into the water first, and Chris broke the bottle on his head first. Does Chris do everything first?'

I thought about that. 'Pretty much.'

'What's so special about Chris?'

'I guess you'd have to meet him.' I leaned forward and

tapped my cigarette into the ashtray on her desk. 'He's a scrapper, for one. He never backs down.'

'And you admire that?'

'Sure.' I hesitated. 'I mean, he's not scared of anybody. Or anything.'

'What's there to be scared of?'

'You know. Getting beaten up. Or looking stupid. Or not knowing what to do. He always knows what to do. Ever since we were little it's been like that. No hesitation.'

She mashed her cigarette into the ashtray, twisting it back and forth like somebody turning a screw. After a moment she said, 'My daughter was the same, in a way. That confident.'

I nodded. All that nicotine was harsh giving me a head rush.

'Do you want to see a photo of her?'

I did. I said I did and I wasn't just being polite. She stood up, took a picture frame off her desk and brought it over to me. I cradled it in my hands. The photo showed a girl who looked about eight years old. She was grinning at the camera and sitting on this pink bike with a big white banana seat. Blue and red streamers hung from the handlebars.

'She looks happy,' I said.

She took the photo back and placed it in the same position on her desk.

'I don't tell everybody about her, in case you're wondering. But I thought it would save us time. Death is something I know about. Even if you're only here because of your father, that doesn't mean we can't talk it over. Is there something in particular that's been bothering you, that you don't feel comfortable discussing with anybody else?'

I stared at the carpet in front of her, avoiding her gaze. From where I sat, I had a great view of her ankles. They were so white and pure they seemed almost saintly. A woman with ankles like that had to be trustworthy. Otherwise there was no point to anything.

'Well, there's the dream,' I said.

It was always the same.

The four of us would be sitting at the government dock, dangling our legs over the edge. The surface of the water was white with sunlight and shimmered like the scaly body of a giant fish. It should have been hot but in the dream I never felt hot. Don't ask me why. After a bit, Chris and Jules would tell us they were going to get ice cream from the Cove. Other times they didn't say anything – they just sort of faded away or disappeared. Poof.

That left me and Karen, sitting side by side.

'Want to go swimming?' she asked.

'We don't have our bathing suits.'

'We don't need them.'

Then she took off her shirt, peeling it over her head in one clean motion. She wasn't wearing a bra, either. I saw the swell of her breasts and the dark flash of her nipples. None of it seemed strange. It didn't even seem strange when she stepped out of her shorts. I mean, I could see everything and I took it all in stride. Totally casual. Somehow my clothes came off – almost magically – and then we were in the water, which was thick and sticky as glue.

'Let's see how far we can swim,' she said.

We kicked and stroked through the ooze, pulling ourselves along. I had my head down so I couldn't tell how far we'd come or how far we had to go, but at one point Karen stopped and so did I. We were in open water, far away from land – far away from Chris and Julian and anything except each other.

Karen splashed me in a friendly way.

'You're funny,' she said. 'I like that.'

I splashed her back. 'Chicks are all the same.'

In the dream, I always talked a bit tougher than usual. You know – like Chris. I didn't say much but whatever I said, it was tough. Karen loved it, too. She paddled over to me and draped her arms around my neck. I stopped treading water and held her waist, feeling a little thrill at the smoothness of her hips. We hung together like that, somehow staying afloat.

'There's something I have to tell you,' she said.

I never found out what it was. We always started kissing. Her mouth was sweet and smoky and wet. I felt her belly against mine. She wrapped both legs around me and I sunk into her slick, stinging warmth. This was it. We were doing it. Karen and I were doing it.

I pulled back to see her face, to see her expression while I moved inside her. Her eyes were closed and her mouth was parted in a silent moan. For some reason her hair was perfectly dry. It was dry and in the bright glare of the sun it looked almost gray. Gray and permed. Her features looked strange, too. Her cheeks were dusted with too much blush and her lips were smeared with burgundy. It was Karen and it wasn't. I knew who it really was, under that mask of make-up, but I didn't care. That was the craziest part of all, actually.

I wanted her anyways.

I didn't plan on telling my shrink about the entire dream, but it sort of all came out. Afterwards, I regretted it immediately.

We sat there in complete silence, listening to the steady thrum of her air conditioner. Obviously, she'd decided I was a harsh nutcase. If it hadn't been for the nicotine, and those ankles of hers, I would never have spilled my guts to her. Not a chance. But she'd tricked me. I could feel her eyes on me and I started getting all hot and uncomfortable. Why didn't she say something? She could at least say something. I mean, my dad wasn't paying her to sit there and stare at me like I was some kind of alien.

'Do you know what the French call an orgasm?'

'Uh, no,' I said.

If there's one thing I can say about my shrink, it's that she was full of surprises.

'La petite mort. The little death.'

I wasn't sure if that made me feel better, or worse.


## 27


'Dude – are you okay?'

When I asked him that, I don't think Chris recognised me. Not at first. It was like he'd breathed all his life into her and that was it. He had nothing left. He was kneeling on the grass, with Mrs Reever stretched out in front of him and mannequins pressing in from all sides. I had to help him to his feet. By that point she'd started breathing again. People gathered around to congratulate him, but just then I could tell he didn't want anybody touching him – even me. I let him go and he shoved his way through the crowd, through the mass of mannequin faces. As soon as he broke clear he started wiping at his mouth and spitting again and again and again.

'What did it taste like?'

'What did what taste like?'

We were pretty wasted, obviously – or I wouldn't have had the guts to ask him. I mean, I may as well have asked him about his dad or something super personal like that.

'You know. When you gave her mouth-to-mouth.'

Chris picked up a stick and poked at the fire. Me and him sometimes went camping at this place on Mount Seymour. We called it Julian's Birthmark. Don't ask me why. I guess because the spot was all mottled and muddy and sort of hidden. It was in the woods near a little stream. There was a clearing for our tent – a beat-up canvas tent my folks had used in South America – and this log that jutted out like a pirate plank over the nearby ravine. That was our toilet. If you had to piss, you pissed off the plank. The rest of the time we would sit around the campfire wearing my dad's old ponchos and getting absolutely hammered.

Chris said, 'It didn't taste like anything. It was one of those tastes that reminds you of a smell.'

'Yeah?'

'Yeah. Like the smell of sour milk.'

'Not even.'

'Or like meat you've left out too long. Or like fish guts rotting on the beach.' He didn't look at me as he spoke. He was staring into the woods and talking sort of quietly, almost to himself. I had to lean closer to hear. 'Like the inside of a compost. Like a raccoon flattened at the roadside. Like the time me and you found that nest of maggots.'

He tapered off, still staring. I took a slug of rum. It was pretty fucking creepy, hearing him say that shit. 'Seriously, man?' I said. 'Or are you just messing with me?'

'I don't know.' He shrugged. 'It tasted like all those things, and none of them.'

Then he poked at the fire again, turning over one of the logs without looking directly at the flames. Chris never looked directly at the flames. You know – so he didn't lose his night vision completely. His dad had taught him all about surviving in the wild. It wasn't like he was paranoid, though. He just liked to be ready, in case a bear attacked us or something.

'Sometimes I can still taste it,' he said.

'Shit, man. Here.' I offered him our mickey. 'See if this helps. Captain's orders.'

I'd cut a few lawns that day and we'd used the money to buy some Captain Morgan. The label showed this guy in an old-school naval costume, standing with his hands on his hips and looking like a total marzipan.

'A dose of the captain's special sauce, eh?'

'He's getting pretty saucy, all right.'

Chris tossed back what was left, his throat pulsing in the firelight as he swallowed. I reached over and sort of patted his knee. I almost said something like, 'It's okay, buddy.' But luckily I didn't. I mean, it obviously wasn't okay, so saying stupid shit like that wasn't going to make any difference.

When Chris finished he stuck the bottle in the fire. It cracked and started to melt. We sat and watched the glass as it heated up, glowing orange like blobs of lava.

I went back there last week, to camp by myself. It wasn't the same, though. To start with, somebody had cut down all the bushes and turned Julian's Birthmark into a bike track. Then, almost as soon as I set up my tent, this fucking guy appeared with a big black dog and told me he'd bought the land and that I had to leave.

'You can't just buy the woods, dickhead. Nobody owns the woods.'

'Do you want to see my deed, kid?'

'No I don't want to see your fucking deed!'

I freaked out a little. I think I even threatened to kill his dog. I wouldn't have done it, obviously. I'd never kill a dog – unless it attacked me first. But this one seemed okay. It started rolling around in the dirt, trying to cool off, panting and grinning at us.

The owner took my threat the wrong way, though.

'I'm gonna report you,' he said. 'You mountain bikers are all the same!'

'I'm not a fucking mountain biker!'

We shouted at each other like that until eventually we established that I'd never ridden a mountain bike in my entire life. I only owned a BMX. After that the guy seemed to calm down, and I did, too.

'It's the mountain bikers that are the problem,' the guy said. 'They come up here and destroy the woods and shit in my stream.'

'They shit in your stream?'

'Uh-huh. It's my only water supply, too. They shit in it because they hate me. I think they're trying to give me cholera.'

'That sucks, man.'

He bitched about the mountain bikers for a little longer, but I wasn't really listening. I'd come up there to be alone, and remember Chris, not to hang out with this joker. Eventually he got the hint. Then he walked in a circle around the campsite, inspecting everything – like he thought maybe I'd hidden a mountain bike in my tent, or behind a log.

'Well, I guess if you're just camping you can stay the night.'

'Thanks a lot, man.'

I said it pretty sarcastically, though. Then, because the whole situation was starting to piss me off – especially him thinking he could tell me whether it was okay to camp at our campsite, the one me and Chris had found way before this fucking guy had bought the woods – I stood up and started taking down my tent. And the whole time, I kept thanking him and telling him how great a guy he was. He stood and watched, getting more and more confused.

Eventually he asked, 'What are you doing?'

'Thanks for your support. You're super generous, you know that?'

I packed up my stove and my beer, too, and stuffed it all in my pack.

'I thought you wanted to camp here.'

'For sure, dude. It's going to be awesome.'

I was still saying shit like that as I walked away.

## 28

'Try this one, man.'

'Not bad. It needs more booze, though.'

At the party in West Van, after we got that Linda chick baked, me and Chris went hunting for some liquor. It took us a super long time to find the bar, which was hidden in the basement. But it was worth it. We were expecting a little table with the usual selection of twixers, and maybe a few cases of beer. It turned out to be ten times better than that. They had an actual bar, with barstools and brass taps and every kind of booze imaginable: Grey Goose vodka, Drambuie, Grand Marnier, Glenfiddich, and a bunch of other shit neither of us had ever heard of before. They had all that, and there wasn't even a bartender to look after it.

'How about now?' I asked.

'That's perfect.' Chris took another sip. 'What did you add?'

'Grand Marnier and some of this Czech shit. Becherovka.'

'Sweet. What should we call it?'

'How about Monkey Balls?'

We took turns making the most expensive shit mixes imaginable. Behind the bar we found all these cocktail shakers and measuring shots, along with a huge tub of ice. Chris's mom would have been in heaven. It was all hardbar, and it went straight to our heads pretty quick. We didn't screw around or anything, though. We were pretty careful about that. Whenever somebody stopped by for a drink, we acted like bar staff and offered to serve them.

'What can I get for you, miss?'

I said that, super professionally, to the next mannequin who came up – this pretty hot brunette in a strapless black dress.

'Uh... a cocktail, please. Can you make Sex on the Beach?'

'I could, but I'd suggest you try some of this. We call it Monkey Balls.'

'Sure. Okay. Thanks.'

She didn't know what the hell to make of us. Nobody did – but none of them had the guts to say anything. They just assumed we were meant to be there. It was pretty hilarious, actually. Monkey Balls was a huge hit. Within five or ten minutes other mannequins started coming up to ask for it specifically. I couldn't really remember how I'd made it, though, and by the fourth or fifth batch we started running out of Grand Marnier.

'Dude – we should probably get while the getting's good.'

'All right, you go-getter.'

We each poured half a twixer of Grey Goose into a pint glass and went to stand in the corner of the living room. We figured we could do the least amount of damage that way.

'Just think,' I said. I waved my hand in a big, sweeping gesture that took in the whole room – like a salesman presenting his goods. 'One day, this could all be yours.'

We gazed together at the crystal chandelier, the hardwood floors, the monster fireplace, the widescreen TV. Chris didn't say anything. He just shook his head.

'What would you do if you had this much money?' I asked.

'Burn it all.'

'Give it the old bonfire of the vanities, huh?'

'Yep. The straight up bonhomme de feu.'

We sank down onto this recliner – one of us on either arm. All that classy booze was weighing pretty heavy in our brains. We'd sampled a lot of Monkey Balls ourselves.

'You know what's crazy?' Chris said.

'What?'

'Say life is a game. Take a look around. These are the winners.'

I stared at all the mannequins in their super pricey outfits, chatting and smiling and drinking and going through the motions of having a good time. I tried to imagine being like that. I couldn't. I just started laughing.

'Shit,' I said. 'I'm glad I'm a bit of loser.'

Chris grinned. 'You're a bit of a boozer, all right.'

'A real bulldoozer.'

Half an hour later Julian came looking for us. He had a huge frown on his face so I knew right away that something was up. I thought maybe somebody had ratted us out for drinking and shit-mixing all that expensive hardbar.

'What's up, guys?' he said.

'Not much, gigolo.'

Jules leaned closer, drawing us into a huddle and lowering his voice. 'Tim's house is a bit overcrowded. He's asking people to leave.' He shoulder-checked, getting all anxious. 'Don't worry. Just play it cool. If he comes up, let me do the talking.'

It was pretty funny. He kept telling us to play it cool when he was obviously shitting himself. We could see Tim across the room: this beefy, dark-haired guy, swaggering around and acting like a complete gearbox. He had his bouncer trailing along in his wake. All the girls smiled at him, and all the guys gave him a little nod. Totally smarmy. Every so often he'd stop and talk to somebody. If he laughed and joked around, it was all right. But if he acted super serious, you knew the person was about to be kicked out. When the killing blow came, they always looked heartbroken, but none of them put up a fight.

'Okay,' Julian whispered. 'Here he comes.'

He spotted us from across the room. Me and Chris were hard to miss in our shitty shirts. I stood quietly, trying to look as sober and casual as possible. I don't even know why. The last thing I wanted to do was spend another minute at that party. But sometimes, in the middle of things, you don't really think straight, and I didn't want to be one of the ones sent away. As Tim came up, Julian held out his hand and they shook.

'Tim – how's it going?'

'Pretty good, Julian. Pretty good.' He looked at me and Chris – this very significant look. 'I don't think I've met your friends, here.'

'They're my buddies from way back.' Jules looped his arms around our necks to show how tight we all were. 'Chris and Razor. Razor and Chris.'

I smiled. Chris just stared at him. Tim didn't even break stride. He was all ready to launch into his little spiel. He started by holding up his hands in apology. Then he took a deep breath, as if he really didn't want to say what he was about to say.

'I'm sorry, boys. I'm going to have to ask you to leave. It's getting a little crowded in here.' He spoke in this pretty loud voice, so everybody around us could hear. 'No hard feelings, okay? I just didn't expect so many guests. I take it you can see yourselves out.'

He nodded and patted me on the shoulder. All done. He was so used to being obeyed that he'd already started walking away when Chris said, 'What happens if we don't?'

Tim froze. His big bouncer stepped up and crossed his arms.

'You got no choice in the matter, buddy boy.'

I don't think I've ever wanted Chris to clock a guy as badly as I did right then. Even more than Crazy Dan. He would have, too, if Karen hadn't turned up all of a sudden.

'Hey guys,' she said. 'What's going on?'

That was when Chris remembered the promise he'd made about not getting in any fights. He'd almost forgotten. He never broke promises, but he did forget them occasionally. He looked from Karen, to Tim, and back to Karen. It was one of the hardest decisions he'd ever had to make in his life.

'We're going,' he muttered.

'Just you two,' Tim said. 'Her and Julian can stay.'

Chris looked at him. He could say a lot with a look. Somehow he managed to say, 'You're lucky she's here or you would be so fucking dead right now.' Then he took Karen by the arm and led her out. Me and Julian followed. At the door, as we were getting our shoes on, I saw that chick again. Linda. She waved from across the room to get my attention, then mouthed something to me across the room. I couldn't really make it out, but I think it was something like, 'Don't leave me here on my own!' Whatever it was, I laughed and waved back. She was pretty cool, actually. It must be weird for her, a normal girl living among all those mannequins. She'll probably end up killing herself or drinking herself to death. Either that, or she'll get tons of plastic surgery and become one of them.

Growing up in West Van, you don't have a lot of options.

Outside, as we walked to the car, Jules kicked the bumper of this super expensive Landrover and set off the alarm. It was pretty sweet. Not like him at all.

'That guy thinks he's such a bigshot.'

'Yeah,' Karen said. 'What a poser.'

Chris and I didn't say anything.

'Whatever.' Jules spat on the ground. He was more pissed off than any of us. He'd obviously been looking forward to that party for a long time. 'After the Crazy Dan show we'll be famous. Then he'll be begging us to come to his stupid parties.'

In a way, saving Mrs Reever had already made us famous.

I didn't bother pointing that out, though. I assumed he meant we'd be even more famous.

'One day,' Chris said, 'I'm going to break that fucking guy's jaw.'

The weird part is, both those things turned out to be true.


## 29

'Kids these days. Let me tell you. They're really something. They're always doing the craziest things. I'm Crazy Dan Oswald and I'm not half as crazy as most kids I meet. I heard about these kids the other day who lit themselves on fire for a home video. Talk about crazy! Maybe they're trying to put me out of a job!'

Everybody laughed like they thought he was hilarious.

The three of us had to wait backstage, where it was dark. If you stood a certain way you could see the studio audience: row after row of shadowy figures just past the lights. This guy dressed all in black kept an eye on us. He wore a fancy headset that had a built-in microphone so he could talk to all the other stagehands. He was supposed to tell us when to go on. We stood with him and listened to Crazy Dan make lame jokes that weren't even lame enough to be funny. The only reason everybody reacted was because there was a sign above the stage – this stupid sign that lit up and told them when to laugh or applaud or whatever.

If we'd known his show would be so shitty, we would never have gone on it in the first place. The thing is, they'd asked us when Mrs Reever was still alive. Jules was the most stoked, obviously. Chris was fairly indifferent to the whole idea, but at the time I'll admit I thought it might be pretty sweet to go on TV. So we agreed to do it.

Then she died, and by that point it was too late to back out.

The guy with headset turned to us. 'You watch Crazy Dan's show?' he asked.

'Uh, sometimes,' Jules said.

'You like it?'

'He's okay.'

'He's a real dickweed.'

That made us laugh. I hadn't heard anybody say 'dickweed' for about ten years. This guy with the headphones seemed all right. He had a pot belly and kept blowing huge bubbles with his gum. The whole scene was pretty surreal, actually. The backstage area was dirty and dark and smelled like the stairwell of a parkade. I kept bumping into things: rickety pieces of scaffolding, sandbags, light stands – you name it. Out on stage it was clean and bright and slick for the cameras, but back there it was like a shantytown.

'I've told you about my son,' Crazy Dan said. I could tell this joke was going to be the lamest of all. 'He just turned twelve, and now he thinks he's Crazy Dan Junior. Every time I talk about my next stunt, he just yawns. He says, "Dad – that's so played out, man." Doesn't that kill you? Played out. I'm telling you.'

The sign lit up and everybody laughed again. Totally fake. What they really wanted to see was the stunt. At the end of every episode, Crazy Dan did a stunt. He'd started on late night doing stunts for other people's shows, and when they gave him his own show he kept up the tradition. People loved it. They couldn't get enough of those stunts, but I'd always been a little dubious about them. I mean, they weren't even real. He just used a dummy dressed up like himself. He'd put the dummy in a cannon and blast it halfway across a cornfield. Or he'd drop the dummy from a plane without a proper parachute. Then he'd film it and put his voice overtop, pretending it was him. The dummy would hit the ground or blow up or get smashed by a boulder and then he'd say something incredibly lame, something like: 'Oh, man – I need an aspirin. My head is killing me.'

I have no idea why people liked that stuff, but they did. His show was super popular. He had a thirty minute slot on primetime. Aside from his stunts, he filled the half hour with B-list celebrity interviews, variety acts, and these cheesy 'local hero' awards. That week, his celebrity was a soap opera actress and the variety act was this double-jointed gymnast.

We were the local heroes.

'Yep. Kids are crazy. But tonight I've got a couple of great kids on the show. Crazy, maybe, but crazy in the best possible way. They stuck their necks out for somebody they didn't even know....'

The guy with the headphones nodded at us and held up his hand.

'That's why, this week, they're our local heroes!'

The guy blew a bubble and motioned us through this fake doorway that opened onto the stage. Jules went first, then Chris, then me. People were clapping, and when they saw us they clapped louder. After the darkness backstage, the glaring lights stabbed straight into my eyes. I couldn't see the audience. All I could see was the set. Crazy Dan had red leather couches out there, and a big oak desk. He rose from behind his desk and shook each of our hands in turn. His assistant had walked us through all of this ahead of time, so we knew exactly what to expect. We were supposed to sit on the couches and tell our story.

'Crazy Dan doesn't like surprises,' she'd told us.

He shook my hand last. I had the impression of a thin guy with a freakishly large smile, like a cartoon shark. On set, he always wore his stunt jumpsuit – this white jumpsuit with blue stripes running down the sides and a Crazy Dan crest on the front. That day, he was also wearing his crash helmet. It looked like a dirtbike helmet with a flip-up visor.

'Have a seat, boys. Have a seat.'

We sat on the couches, just like we'd rehearsed.

'Welcome to the Crazy Dan Oswald Show!'

Once the applause died down, the interview started. Jules did most of the talking. He looked slick, like always. He'd worn a green polo shirt and gelled his hair up in neat little spikes, like a magazine model. Me and Chris just sat and nodded and added a few details. It was pretty intense. The audience actually wanted to listen. The only one who didn't listen was Crazy Dan. He kept cutting Jules off, trying to make more of his lame jokes.

'That sounds crazy! So who had to break the window?'

'I did,' Chris answered. 'I cut up my hand.'

'You're lucky you didn't end up in the hospital along with her!'

This time, the laughter sounded forced. The audience, at least, could tell we didn't like him joking about it. The less they laughed, though, the more he tried. He just wouldn't quit. It was only a matter of time before he stuck his foot in his big, fat, mouth.

'Are you saying you had to resuscitate her?'

'Chris did, yeah.'

'You gave her mouth-to-mouth? Honestly?'

I looked at Chris. His face was blank and his eyes were half-closed, like the lids had grown heavy. That happened, sometimes – when he was on the verge of losing it.

'That's right,' he said.

'Oh, boy. You're a better man than I am. That must have been crazy!'

A few diehards in the audience chuckled and coughed. Chris didn't say anything.

'Sooooo,' Crazy Dan said, totally oblivious, 'have you seen her since?'

We looked at each other. I asked, 'Seen who since?'

'Mrs Reever.'

I don't know who'd forgotten to tell him. It was a pretty big mistake to make.

'She died in the hospital,' Jules muttered.

When he said that, the whole place went totally silent – like a movie theatre just before the curtains open. Anybody else would have known to let it go. Not Crazy Dan. It was as if he didn't even have a brain beneath that helmet. He was just an oversized doll in a white jumpsuit, a doll programmemed to make lame jokes and laugh at itself.

'Hey,' he called, as if he was talking to somebody backstage. 'We got the wrong heroes out here. You didn't tell me she died!'

Nobody laughed, except him. I remember thinking how badly I wanted to smash that stupid smile off his face. I wanted to smash it with a fist or a foot or a chair or anything. Even as I thought that, from the corner of my eye I saw Chris push himself out of his seat. He was wearing his jeans – the pair that he'd slashed up for Halloween. His eyes were half-closed, almost sleepy. I remember thinking: *If this happens, it's going to be the craziest thing ever...*

Afterwards, tons and tons of people crowded onto the stage. First came these security guards – two huge guys with shaved heads and matching bomber jackets. They sort of stormed around the set, looking tough, but neither of them really knew what was happening or what they were supposed to do. Crazy Dan's assistant rushed out after them. She had a first aid kit and made a big fuss over his bloody nose – stuffing cotton up his nostril and patting down his face with a towel wipe. At the same time, about eight hundred audience members stood up and gathered at the front, ridiculously excited. There were a bunch of reporters, too. They'd been sent to do another article on us. You know – a follow-up article about how great it was that Crazy Dan had put us on his stupid show.

Like always, most of what they wrote was total crap.

Chris didn't punch him, for one thing. That's what they wrote, but it was a lie. He slapped him, two or three times, across the face. That's different from punching him. Plus, they didn't hear what he said. I heard. I was right there so I know exactly what he said.

He said, 'Hey – shut the fuck up, okay?'

And that was all. He said it after he slapped him, or maybe just before. I can't really remember. But he definitely didn't say anything else. He just walked off stage. I did, too. I mean, I didn't want to hang around with Crazy Dan and all those treats. So I went to find Chris. Not Julian. He stayed out there and tried to smooth things over for us.

'Don't mind him,' he said. 'He's always been volatile.'

That was the first time I heard that word – the word

everybody started using. It sounded pretty bizarre, coming from Jules like that. I don't know if he was defending Chris, or blaming him, or what. I just know that he spent about half an hour trying to convince Crazy Dan to keep going with the interview. It didn't work, though. Crazy Dan was finished with us. They couldn't air the show, and Chris almost got charged with assault. That's what the cops said, at least. They phoned up his mom and laid it all out. Actually, they phoned our house, too. Not that I cared. My dad told me those network execs would rather swallow their own vomit than take a couple of kids to court. I mean, that kind of thing isn't exactly great publicity. This way, they came across as the good guys. That's how the papers wrote it up, anyways. Crazy Dan was this super tolerant guy who'd let us off the hook. Nobody mentioned all the stupid jokes he'd been making about Mrs Reever. They didn't mention what happened backstage, either – in the darkness that smelled like dirt and piss. That's where I found Chris, standing with that pot-bellied guy who chewed bubblegum.

'That was radical, man,' the guy said. 'Totally radical.'

He clapped Chris on the back, like they'd known each other for years. Then a frizzy-haired lady walked over, and a little runt with wire-rimmed glasses. They came out of nowhere – all these people who worked the lights and operated the cameras and assembled the backdrop and mopped the stage and flushed the toilet when Crazy Dan took a dump. There were dozens of them, and they all said the same thing.

'You don't know how long we've been waiting for somebody to do that.'

To those people, we really were heroes.

## 30

'It's how you cash out that matters. More than anything.'

The smoke was everywhere, like a thick fog rolling in off the ocean. We'd locked ourselves in Karen's basement suite. That's where we smoked up at her house. Her parents hardly ever came down there, so we pretty much had free reign. I don't know how she explained the smell. Maybe she covered it up with that perfume of hers. Or maybe her parents refused to believe that their little princess liked getting high. It's hard to say. But basically, we were blazing in her basement when Chris started getting super philosophical.

'When I die,' he said, 'there's going to be some fucking fireworks.'

Karen giggled. She loved hearing him say shit like that.

Jules said, 'What's that supposed to mean?'

Whenever Julian got too fried, his face turned white and he became totally paranoid. All night I'd been keeping an eye on him – sitting in his beanbag chair, smoking joint after joint, growing paler and paler. I knew he was getting close because every so often he ran his tongue over his lips, like a scared little lizard.

'Fireworks, man. Fireworks for my dad to see. Fireworks so the whole world knows I don't give a shit whether I live or die.'

He was messing with us, obviously. At the same time, I could tell he sort of meant it.

Jules laughed. 'Why don't you kill yourself, then?'

'Maybe I will.'

Karen reached over and passed the joint to Jules. For a second, I saw a sliver of brown belly as her shirt pulled up above her waist. Then she flopped back to the floor and sprawled out in a starfish position.

She asked Chris, 'Did you really slap Crazy Dan in the face?'

'Sure. I slapped him a bunch of times.'

Jules inhaled, held it, and coughed on his exhale. I caught him looking from Karen to Chris and back to Karen. He knew she loved how tough he was. He couldn't stand it.

He said, 'If you killed yourself you'd go straight to hell.'

'I don't believe in hell, or heaven, or any of that bullshit.'

'That's your problem.'

'No, it's yours.'

Jules licked his lips – totally paranoid – and handed the joint to me. The end was wet with spit from being passed around. I pinched it between my thumb and finger and toked as hard as I could. The smoke filled my chest, filled my head, filled the room. I could hardly see through all that smoke. It was like being in a steam bath. The others were just vague lumps amidst the haze. I stretched out beside Karen. The carpet in her basement was thick and soft – a little cloud that had settled to earth. I floated on the cloud, totally at peace.

'This is heaven,' I said.

'No,' Chris said. 'It's hell.'

We thought about that.

'It can't be heaven,' Jules said. 'There aren't any angels.'

Chris pointed at Karen. 'I see an angel.'

'She's not an angel.'

'Sure she is. Show him, Karen. Show him you're an angel.'

Karen giggled and stood up. She flapped her arms and pranced around the room, moving on her tiptoes. At the same time, she started humming this weird music, the kind of music they sing in church choirs. It was eerie. She actually did remind me of an angel.

'What's an angel without wings?' I asked.

'A whore,' Chris said.

Karen swooped over and slapped him, playfully, on the shoulder.

'Bastard.'

'Okay, you're an angel.'

'She's not an angel!' Jules said. I'd never seen him so stoned. He'd gone completely white and completely paranoid. Also, he was starting to sweat. 'Real angels are invisible!'

'Shut up about your angels,' Chris said. 'You're just like that goddamned minister. All he talked about was angels. What angels? The only reason they invented angels is so God can have somebody to suck him off.'

'You shouldn't say that stuff, man.'

'Why not?'

Jules took another hit, a super big hit – almost inhaling the entire joint. In some ways, I actually understood why he was so upset. I mean, it's one thing not to believe in God. It's another to badmouth him like that. I don't have the guts to do it. I always worry God might hear, even though he doesn't exist. He'll hear and hit me with a bolt of lightning, or flood our house, or make my heart explode like a water balloon.

'It's just not cool,' Jules said.

Chris started giggling. 'Sure it is. There's God, and all these angels kneeling in front of him. I bet God has a huge dick. Bigger than all of ours put together.'

'Shut up, man. I'm serious.'

'Or what?'

Chris stared at him, waiting. Jules didn't say anything. Instead he passed the joint off to Karen and started playing with his watch, pressing all these buttons and adjusting the dials. It was like their conversation hadn't even happened. Meanwhile, the joint kept going around: from Karen to Chris to me to Jules and back to Karen. Pretty soon it felt like the whole room was turning around with it – as if we were on that ride at the amusement park that spins faster and faster until the floor drops out. It was arguably the most baked I've ever been.

'I don't believe in angels,' Karen announced. 'I believe in reincarnation.'

'What?'

'You die, and you come back as somebody else. My mom has all these books on it. She's already decided what she's going to be in her next life and everything.'

'Yeah. She'll be a hooker.'

'You can be such an asshole, Chris.'

He could be, especially to her. It wasn't totally one-sided, though. She had her tricks, too. One of them was Julian. After Chris said that, she rolled away from him and started talking to Jules. They discussed what they'd been in their previous lives. Jules had never believed in that stuff but for her he'd believe in anything.

'I was a soldier in the First World War. I died at Vimy Ridge.'

'I lived in England. I had a castle, and hundreds of handmaids.'

'I sailed around the world on big, wooden ships.'

'I danced for the National Ballet.'

They went on and on like that, enough to make you puke. I ignored them and stared at the ceiling, trying to shake the spins. There were patterns in the plaster – yellow ripples that sort of looked like sand dunes. The dunes were endless, stretching on and on and on.

'That's crazy,' I mumbled.

'What's crazy, Razor?'

'I can see a desert up there.'

Julian snickered. 'Razor's shrewing out.'

'Shut up, Jules,' Chris said. Then he asked, 'What kind of desert?'

'The biggest desert you've ever seen. It goes on forever. The sun is super bright, like an exploding star. There's no snakes or cactuses. Nothing can survive except a few weeds.'

'Am I there?'

'I don't know.' I sat up and started plucking at the carpet. I could still picture the desert in my head, though. 'There's this one set of footprints. Maybe that's you.'

Julian and Karen were both giggling, like they'd never heard anything so funny.

I glared at them. 'Whatever. I was only messing around, anyways.'

That made them laugh even louder. Not Chris. He was rolling a joint, looking super thoughtful. He said, 'Just because you were messing around doesn't mean it's not true.'

That night she gave Chris gummers for the first time.

Jules and I left early. We had to go early because our parents cared about us. Chris could stay because his dad was dead and his mom didn't give a shit when he came home.

Some guys have all the luck.

Karen had a funny look in her eye when we left. I suspected something would happen. I knew what was going on between them, obviously. Jules didn't. In front of us, they just acted like

144

friends. She didn't treat him any different than Jules or I. Not really different, anyways. I mean, it wasn't as if they kissed or held hands or anything. Then again, they didn't have to. It was like animals in the wild. All the wolves know who's the leader of the pack, because he can take on any of the other wolves. It's only natural that he also gets the she-wolf. That's just how it is in the wild. Everybody knows that.

Everybody but Julian.

'Do you think they're doing anything?' I asked him.

We were walking along the parkway. The air was super muggy and I started burning out, big time. I felt pretty miserable, actually – otherwise I wouldn't have even mentioned it to him.

'What do you mean?' he said.

'You know. Chris and Karen.'

Jules stopped dead, like he'd run into a wall.

'What are you talking about, man? They're just friends.'

I looked at him without saying anything.

'We're all just friends, okay? It's not like that between them. Not at all.'

'All right.'

We started walking again. Jules was breathing hard.

Later on, Chris filled me in. I phoned him, actually – at about midnight. I wasn't perving out or anything. I just wanted to know what had happened.

'First she put some music on. Pretty loud.'

'What type of music?'

'This chick singer with a super high voice.'

I guess she wanted to set the mood or something. Until then he'd been sitting on the couch, but he told me she got

145

him to stand up and take off his shirt. I'm not sure why. It wasn't really necessary for what she had in mind. On the other hand, maybe she liked having him half-naked like that.

'Then she started kissing my chest, and my stomach.'

'She probably likes your six-pack.'

'Maybe.'

'And after that she gave you gummers?'

'Uh-huh.'

I don't know if she took off his belt or just undid his fly or what. Chris didn't go into that. But according to him, she knew exactly what she was doing. He said it felt sort of wet and weird at first. Then it felt awesome. Ten times better than pulling your goalie.

'What about the end?'

'What about it?'

Even I know you're supposed to warn the girl when you're almost ready. You know – to finish off or whatever. So he did. But apparently she didn't care.

'What do you mean she didn't care?'

'She just told me to go ahead. She was a bit annoyed I'd even mentioned it.'

'Jesus.'

I stood there, thinking about that. The phone felt hot against my ear.

'Razor?' I could hear him yawning. 'I got to get some sleep, man.'

'Okay. Sure. Thanks for telling me.'

We hung up and I sat back on my bed. Then I stood up again. I couldn't believe Karen had said that. What a harsh chick. I kept picturing her kneeling in front of him, like an angel. Except without the wings, obviously.

## 31

We hated the Avalon, but didn't have any other options. It's the only bar on the North Shore that serves to minors. Or it did. Apparently they've decided to gut the building and turn it into a fancy grill and steakhouse. But back when we went, they didn't even bother to check your ID. I mean, there was a bouncer at the door, but his main job was to break up fights. Chris fought him, two or three times, and he lost every time. Chris hardly ever lost fights but this bouncer was some kind of professional. He held his fists like a boxer and always took off his shirt to fight. He was a bit crazy like that. The funny thing is, after all those scraps he'd grown to like us a little – especially Chris. He was one of those guys who'd beat the shit out of you and then do something super bizarre, like help you up and buy you a beer.

But basically, he never checked our ID.

'You kids nineteen?'

'Yessir. You got it.'

'All right. Have a good time.'

There were two sections to the Avalon. He guarded the back. Nobody guarded the front. The front was this raunchy restaurant where you only went if you wanted to get food poisoning. Julian made the mistake of eating there one time, and he found a fingernail in his soup. No joke. So for obvious reasons we steered clear of the front.

The actual bar, where all the underage kids went, was around back. The only thing holding up the ceiling were these wooden beams that had gone all black and rotten, like an old man's teeth. By the time we started drinking there, I'm pretty sure it had already been condemned. There was a bar at one end, a dance floor in the middle, and a bunch of rickety tables strewn along the walls. Also, it was dark. It was so dark you could hardly see anything. I mean, you could see some things – beefcakes boozing at the bar, dirty old men huddled around the tables, and girls shaking it on the dance floor – but you couldn't see any of it too clearly. It was like being underwater in a fishtank that hadn't been cleaned for months and months. Come to think of it, it kind of smelled like a fishtank, too.

Anyways, that's where we went to get hammered.

A night at the Avalon was always the same.

We'd find a table close to the dance floor and start drinking. Karen drank Canadian Club, usually with ginger ale. Me and Chris guzzled pitchers of watered-down Kokanee. Jules didn't drink much. We always made him drive and like I said, he was super responsible about drinking and driving. So he'd stick to pop – Coke or Sprite or whatever. Nothing else.

'This is awesome, man,' Jules shouted.

I looked around at the aggro guys and skanky girls, at the beer-soaked floor and sagging ceiling. It wasn't awesome. The Avalon was never awesome. But we kept hoping that if we said it enough, one day it might actually become awesome.

'Yeah, it's sweet,' I said.

It was too loud in there to talk or joke around much – too loud to do anything but sit and drink, or stagger onto the patio to hack a few darts. We didn't always smoke. We were sort of casual smokers. As in, we'd smoke when we were drunk, or baked, or when we felt like it. And we smoked at the Avalon. Everybody did. It was pretty much a necessity.

After a few minutes Karen would start wiggling around in her chair, as if the music had wormed its way into her body.

'Want to dance?'

Sooner or later she always asked that, and our answer was always the same.

'No.'

She knew we hated dancing. We were all terrible dancers, especially Julian. He'd tried it, once, and these three guys had threatened to kick his ass. I think it must have traumatised him because he never tried again. Not in the Avalon, anyway.

Karen blew us a kiss. 'Watch my stuff then, will you?'

We ordered another pitcher. This was all part of our little ritual. We would sit there, drinking our faces off and watching her dance. It was impossible not to watch her. She didn't wear a skirt and heels, like most of the dirties in that place. She wore sandals with dark jeans, frayed at the ankles. Super sexy. As soon as she got out there, people noticed her. That's the kind of dancer she was. She said that music was her favourite drug. Maybe that sounds lame but coming from her it didn't sound lame at all. She'd taken ballet as a kid and she still moved like a ballerina: light on her feet and totally confident.

'That cocksucker better watch himself.'

'Which cocksucker?'

'That one.' Chris pointed him out to me. 'Right there.'

'Hey,' I said. 'Isn't that what's his face? From West Van?'

Julian stood up to get a better look. 'Yeah. That's Tim.'

Guys couldn't help hitting on her. It was like somebody had planted a poisonous flower in the middle of the Avalon and all the insects just found the temptation impossible to resist. She looked so lush and sweaty it was only natural to want to touch her. It was always the same. One guy would start circling, like a suicidal fly. He'd get closer and closer, until he was so close she couldn't ignore him any longer. Then he'd say something too stupid to imagine. That night he said, 'Remember me, baby? You came to my party. Tim Williams.'

'Yeah – whatever.'

'Come on. Want to dance?'

'Get lost.'

No matter what she said, they always heard 'yes'. Tim was no different. He wrapped an arm around her waist and started grinding against her. Karen tried to slip away but he held on tight, like a horny little dog she couldn't shake loose. He didn't realise he'd fallen into a trap until Chris came up and tapped him on the shoulder. Chris had seven words for him – the usual seven words. He said them all at once without stopping, as if he'd been saving them for this moment ever since Tim had kicked us out of that stupid party.

'Fuck you outside right now let's go.'

We waited for him in the parking lot.

Karen said, 'You don't have to do this Chris. We can just leave.'

That was part of the routine, too. She'd try to convince him to walk away, and he'd ignore her. Chris had never walked away from a fight in his life. She knew that. She would have been as shocked as any of us if he'd actually listened to her for a change.

'What's taking him so long?'

That was Julian. You could tell he was getting ready to wet the bed.

'Maybe he pussied out,' I suggested.

Then the doors swung open. It was our guy, all right, but he wasn't alone. He had a bunch of his buddies with him. He walked out and they followed him one by one. They all looked just like him – this endless line of clones. Each of them wore dark slacks with a collared shirt. Even their haircuts were identical: short and spiked up with gel. That's the thing about the Avalon. Since it's right near the border of North and West Van, there's always dozens of beefcake mannequins hanging around, ready to team up on you.

Jules said, 'Oh, crap.'

There were six of them, including Tim. Inside he'd been timid as a poodle, but now that they outnumbered us two to one he thought he was pretty hot shit.

He pointed at Chris. 'That's the punk.'

Then he started over, swaggering and rolling his shoulders.

'You're a dead man, you know that? I'm going to tear you a new asshole. I'm going to kick your goddamned head off in front of your whore girlfriend...'

He kept talking like that, coming closer. Chris didn't say anything. He waited until Tim was within range, then took a short step and hammered him in the face. Tim let out a strange noise – this sort of croaking noise – and dropped straight to the ground.

Then it was on.

The other five rushed him. Chris grabbed one guy and started to pound him, but a second came in from the side and tagged Chris with a right hook that split open his eyebrow. Blood started leaking down his face. It got in his eye, too. For a few seconds, he couldn't see shit. He stumbled around, getting hit again and again. They had him surrounded, like a pack of hyenas. That was the moment. Even Chris couldn't fight five guys on his own. Somebody had to help, and Jules wasn't about to do anything. Not a chance. That left me.

I said, 'Fuck it.'

I ran in there and tried something super nuts. I pulled

one of my kung fu moves – this flying sidekick. It wasn't much of a kick but my momentum knocked the guy over. Then I grabbed a second guy by the neck. I had no idea what I was doing. It was nuts. I just grabbed him and kind of hung on. Somebody else punched me three or four times in the ribs, from behind. After that I let go of the neck and started swinging wildly. A face would appear and I'd punch at it. Sometimes I connected, sometimes I didn't. All the faces looked the same to me and I just kept swinging away. Even Karen was in there, screaming at them.

'Leave them alone – you bastards. You stupid bastards!'

At one point, I got nailed right on the jaw. It didn't really hurt, but my legs went soft and I sort of sank to my knees. I thought we were finished. We would have been, too, if that bouncer hadn't showed up. Somebody must have tipped him off.

'Hey – what the fuck's going on out here?'

He didn't really expect an answer. I mean, it was obvious what was going on. We were having an eight-man rumble in the parking lot. He just said that to announce his arrival. The next thing he did was take off his shirt. No joke. He took off his shirt and got right in there, throwing those very crisp and professional punches of his.

'All right, boys. Break it up. Break it up.'

That was how he broke up fights: by kicking everybody's ass. Chris and I knew enough not to mess with him, but Tim's friends were clueless. They made the mistake of fighting back. That was when he really laid into them – tossing people around, busting out these crazy knee and elbow strikes. He even tried a body slam at one point. The guy was a monster. A ninja monster. With him on our side those clones didn't stand a chance.

They knew it, too.

'Come on – screw this!'

'These guys are fags, anyway.'

They backed away, leaving Tim where he'd fallen. The bouncer followed them halfway down the street, just to make sure they actually left. I didn't pay much attention to all that. I was watching Chris. He walked over to Tim, who was moaning and rolling around and cradling his jaw, which had gone all loose and weird. Chris calmly put a knee on his chest and started punching him in the face. His fist rose and fell like a piston and Tim screamed every time it landed. Luckily we were there to pull him away, or he might have killed him. I'm not exaggerating, either. That was another thing about Chris. It wasn't really his fault. He just couldn't help it. In a fight, once he got going, he didn't stop.

White hot rage. That's how he described it to me. When he fought, the whole world turned white like overexposed film. All he could see was the other guy, and all he wanted to do was hit him again and again and again, until there was nothing left. Even I was a little afraid of him when he got like that. In the car, after the Avalon, he was still furious that we'd put a stop to it.

'You pussies. You shouldn't have pulled me off that cocksucker.'

'It was done, man. He was finished.'

'No he fucking wasn't.'

Jules said, 'You want to go to jail or what?'

'Fuck off, Jules. You didn't do shit.'

Julian couldn't argue. He'd stood there like a pylon while it all went down.

I said, 'You showed him, man. Relax.'

He didn't relax, though. I could see him in the side mirror, sitting on the backseat with Karen. His whole body quivered with rage, ready to erupt. Streaks of blood had dried like warpaint all down his cheek. Karen leaned over. She kissed him on the neck and whispered something in his ear. He pushed her away but she came back, and the second time he didn't push her away.

'He called you a whore.'

'Shhhh. I don't care, Chris. It's okay, now.'

It was. She was the only one who could make it okay. He stopped trembling and his breathing slowed down. He was himself again. He caught me watching them in the mirror.

'How does it feel, Razor?'

'Huh?'

'Your first fight.' He grinned, showing bloody teeth. 'I saw that kung fu bullshit.'

'That was my insane crane attack.'

Everybody laughed, even Jules. Nobody really cared that he'd pussied out.

'Let me see your knuckles.'

I turned around and held them up for Chris. They were bruised and swollen.

'Feel good?'

'Yeah, man. It does.'

Later, when I got home, I stood in front of my mirror. I had a shiner on my cheek and my lip was split. I took off my shirt and stared at myself. I didn't have much of a body. My muscles were just kind of soft and pale and shapeless. But I looked tough, all right.

Not as tough as Chris, but pretty damn tough.

## 32

In the week leading up to the riot, Chris got in a fight nearly every night. Karen was just too fucking hot. Insanely hot. That was the problem. Guys hit on her constantly, and Chris couldn't help how he reacted. She loved it, too. Like most girls, she pretended she didn't but underneath all that – where it counted – she couldn't get enough of it. She loved the fighting and she loved calming him down afterwards.

She also loved teasing him.

'How many girlfriends have you had, Chris?'

Karen asked him that on the way back from Esplanade. She was driving us for a change. We'd all gone to see a movie – this movie about a bunch of scientists who create some super smart sharks. Then the sharks escape and eat the scientists. Totally lame.

Chris shrugged. 'None, really.'

She knew he hadn't had any – she'd just wanted to hear him say it.

'What about you two? Any girlfriends?'

Me and Jules looked at each other. We couldn't lie. Neither of us had ever had a real girlfriend. We were kind of losers, in that way. In a lot of ways, I guess.

'Huh,' Karen said. 'I bet you're all virgins, too. What a lucky girl I am. I get to chauffer around a carload of virgins.'

We didn't say anything. She had us right where she wanted us.

'Don't worry, boys. It'll happen soon. And then everything will be different.'

When she said that, she was kind of smirking. Later I found out why. She'd decided it was about time her and Chris got around to doing it. He would never have made the first move, so she had to take matters into her own hands. When we got back to the Cove, she dropped off Julian at his house, then drove me to mine. Chris was supposed to get dropped off last.

'Bye, Razor.'

'Yeah – see you guys tomorrow.'

I shut the door and watched them pull away. Karen was driving her dad's Jeep – this sleek blue Cherokee that would probably cost most people their liver. Karen's parents trusted her completely. Her dad was a real estate agent and her mom was a nurse, and she was their little princess who made the honour roll and acted in all the school plays. She would ask if she could use the Jeep and her dad would say, 'Princess is taking her carriage out tonight.'

If only they knew what went on in that carriage.

Instead of driving Chris home, she headed towards Parkgate. When he asked where they were going, she just said, 'You'll see.' The way he explained it was pretty funny – as if she was kidnapping him. She drove straight to the lookout near the top of Mount Seymour. That was the same place he'd told her about the fireball, actually. It was totally deserted. Karen parked, yanked on the handbrake, and told him to get in the backseat.

I heard about all this the next morning.

'Did you use a condom?'

'No. It was pretty casual.'

I was in the shower when he called me. I had to run to get the phone. Normally I wouldn't have bothered, but I had this feeling it would be him. And I was glad I did. If I hadn't he might have forgotten to tell me entirely. It wasn't like he was dying to get it off his chest. I think he only phoned because he knew how excited I'd be to hear about it.

'Were you nervous?'

He was. Actually, he was terrified. I mean, he didn't hesitate when it came to fighting or cliff jumping or assaulting a talk show host, but sex was something else entirely. Karen didn't mind, though. She liked teaching him. To start with, she pulled up her skirt and got him to finger her. I'm pretty sure they'd done that before, but this was the first time I'd heard about it. He said it was sort of slippery and clinging at the same time. Like damp silk.

'But it's awesome, right?'

'Pretty awesome. It smells a bit weird.'

'I heard it smells like tuna.'

'No. That's bullshit. It's not bad or anything. Just weird.'

'Oh. Then what happened?'

'She told me to take off my pants.'

By that point, he was pretty turned on. He said his dick was so hard it hurt. She had to guide him into place and line him up. Then he slipped right in there.

'And how did it go?'

'Okay, I guess.'

There was a big puddle of water at my feet. I hadn't even bothered to get a towel when I jumped out of the shower. I was just standing there starkers, holding the phone.

'If you didn't use a condom, she might be pregnant.'

'That's true.'

After he died, for a while I kept hoping Karen would be. You know – so at least there'd be a little Chris coming back into the world. But that didn't happen. I guess it's harder than you think to get a chick pregnant.

A few days later I found out more. She told me some of it,

actually. Like how, the first time, he came in about three seconds – so quick it didn't even really count as having sex, except in a purely technical sense. Karen said he got a little angry after that, mostly at himself, but she knew how to handle him. She calmed him down and after a bit they went at it again.

'So how many times did you guys do it?'

'Twice. He did better the second time.'

I'd gone over to her house, just to check up on her. I did that occasionally, if Chris was busy. I was sort of like his stand-in. Karen and I would head up to her room and talk about him. He was the one thing we had in common. Her room was mostly pink. Pink bed, pink carpet, pink wallpaper. Pink everything. The only part that wasn't pink was her poster – this black and white poster of a bird soaring way up in the clouds. It said: *Spread your wings. Believe you can fly.* I guess it was supposed to be inspirational or something.

I asked, 'Where does this pair go?'

'Right at the back. Beside my sandals.'

That afternoon her mom had told her to clean her closet, and she got me to help her. We started by organising all her shoes. She had tons of shoes – like at least twenty or twenty-five pairs. Maybe more. So it took a while.

As we worked, she filled me in on the details. Some of them, anyway.

'I'd say he lasted for ten, maybe fifteen minutes. The second time.'

I nodded, trying to keep it casual. Karen didn't mind talking about it, but for me it wasn't exactly easy. 'That's pretty decent, right?'

'Uh-huh.'

'And was it, like, good and everything?'

'Well, he made me come if that's what you mean.'

I picked up a pair of runners – these pink runners – and carefully dusted them off. Then I placed them back with the other sets. I took a long time lining them up. Not because I cared about the shoes, but because I didn't want her to see how badly I was blushing.

I was too chicken to ask her anything else.

I got the rest of it out of him eventually. We were down in the Cove, waiting for a pizza. They make awesome pizza in the Cove – ten times better than the soggy crap they sell on Lonsdale. We'd sat on top of the picnic table out front, with our feet on the bench.

That's when I asked him about her orgasm.

'It was pretty harsh.'

'Harsh like how?'

He told me that she opened her mouth in a silent scream and bucked up off the seat. Her entire body went completely rigid, as if she was being electrocuted. Then she shuddered and closed her eyes and collapsed. For a second Chris thought she'd had some kind of fit.

'Shit. That must have been freaky.'

'It was kind of freaky, and kind of hot at the same time.'

Afterwards they just lay there, all tangled up and slippery with sweat. He said he probably would have fallen asleep except it was way, way too hot in the Jeep.

'And we talked for a bit.'

'I get you. Like pillow talk.'

'Sure. Except there weren't any pillows.'

I don't know exactly what they talked about, but I know she asked him what it had been like for him. You know –

his first time and everything. But he couldn't explain it. He couldn't even really explain it to me.

'Was it like jerking off with shampoo in the shower?'

'No.'

'Better or worse?'

'Better. Way better.'

I glanced around, then lowered my voice a little. 'Was it like sticking your dick in a cantaloupe?'

I don't know why I asked him that. It's not like either of us had tried it.

'No.'

'Was it like a wet dream?'

'No, man.'

'What was it like, then?'

He stood up. The guy in the shop was signalling that our pizza was ready.

'I don't know. It wasn't like anything.'

'How can it be like nothing?'

'It just was, okay? I put it in her and we fucked and then my whole body sort of exploded and for a second I wasn't even me any more. I was nothing. I was gone.'

'Oh.'

That wasn't really what I expected – but it still sounded awesome.


## 33

'Well, you caught me in the act. You might as well have one, too.'

I went back to see my shrink about a week later. It was

a Tuesday, I think. Or maybe a Wednesday. I can't really remember. But basically, since she didn't have a secretary or anything, I walked right in without knocking. And there she was, sitting at her desk, pouring rum into a highball glass. I was embarassed, for obvious reasons. We both were. But she played it pretty cool. She just got out another glass and offered some to me. Normally I don't even like dark rum, but this tasted nice and smooth. It was Havana Club – a special reserve or something. She drank the good stuff, all right. My psychiatrist was pure class.

'What happened to your face?' she asked.

I was still sporting a shiner and split lip from our brawl at the Avalon.

'Chris and I got in a fight.'

'With each other?'

'With six guys.'

I was glad she'd asked. Everybody asked. It felt good to say it, especially to her. I had these wounds on my face and this rum in my hand and now she knew how tough I was.

'Did you win?'

'It was sort of a draw.'

'Your father must have been pleased about that.'

I laughed. My dad was convinced I'd stepped on a rollercoaster ride to hell. First I'd broken a bottle on my head and now I'd gotten in a brawl. He blamed himself. He thought he was failing me as a father. There was no convincing him otherwise.

'He's decided you're my last chance,' I told her.

She smiled. 'We better get started then.'

I sat in the same chair. She came around the desk, bringing her glass with her. I listened to the swish of her skirt and watched her feet moving across the carpet. When she sat still, her ankles were gorgeous. But when she walked they were almost mesmerising.

As she passed the window she paused to gaze out.

'When was the last time it rained?' she asked.

'I don't remember.'

The summer seemed to have gone on forever: hot and dry and merciless.

'God it's like a wasteland out there.'

She took another sip of rum. She had her back to me and all I could see was her silhouette against the window – which was so bright it didn't even look like a window. It looked more like a square of white-hot metal somebody had hung on her wall. Just staring at it made me sweat.

'There's supposed to be a water shortage,' I said.

'I don't doubt it.' She raised her glass and swirled the liquor around. I was surprised to see it was almost empty. 'Luckily there's enough of this to get by on.'

She went back to top herself up. I put my glass down on the desk and slid it towards her – nice and casual. She glanced at me, surprised, then sort of smirked.

'All right,' she said, pouring me another, 'but let's keep this between us, shall we?'

As far as I could tell, she was the greatest psychiatrist in history. First it had been the cigarettes and now it was this rum. It didn't kick me in the head like the cheap rum we usually drank. It made me all friendly and feisty and warm. The first thing I did was tell her about our scrap. I don't remember everything I said but I remember talking loudly and making huge gestures with my hands. I even hopped up to show her my flying sidekick. I really got into it.

'Would you mind doing that again?'

'The kick?'

'Please.'

I ran across the room and, leaping into the air, snapped out my foot. She jotted something in her notebook. She was unravelling the mysteries of my flying sidekick.

'Do you like fighting?' she asked.

I sunk back into my chair, a little breathless. I had to think about that. I remembered the whirlwind of violence and the hitting and being hit and the sharp fear in my gut, like shrapnel.

'No. But it felt good afterwards, knowing I'd done it.'

'Knowing you weren't scared?'

'I was scared. I did it anyway.'

She found that interesting. I could tell because she wrote a couple more notes down. She had one leg crossed over the other, and her shoe had come half off. It had fallen away from the heel and just sort of dangled from her toe. Super sexy. I wanted to get down on my knees and kiss it. Not the shoe. The foot. And the ankle, of course. The ankle was the best.

'Does Chris like fighting?'

'I don't think he cares. He just does it.'

'To impress Karen?'

'No. He doesn't care about that, either.'

She put aside her notebook and sighed. You know – totally exasperated.

'Is there anything Chris does care about?'

It was a good question. We both sat there in the dark safety of her office, trying to think of an answer. Meanwhile, outside, the sun hammered the city into submission. I imagined it as an apocalypse. Car tyres melted and trees burst into flame and people boiled in their skins. It felt as if we were the only ones left. When we finished our drinks she stood up and reached for the bottle. This time she filled mine right to the top, just like hers. We'd drunk half the twixer without chasing and I was feeling pretty loose.

'Listen,' she said.

Under the hum of her air conditioner I heard this soft rattling noise.

'Do you hear it?'

'I think so.'

'My air conditioner's breaking down.'

It was the most depressing sound I'd ever heard. It was only a matter of time before all that heat found its way in here. Then we'd be finished, and we both knew it.

'How about some music?' she asked.

She had a Discman and some portable speakers in her desk. All her CDs were in the wrong cases. She had to open every single one before she found what she was looking for.

'You like John Lennon?'

'Yeah. My dad plays all that old hippy stuff.'

'Lennon was more than a hippy. He was a martyr – the only Christ we deserve.'

I had no idea what she meant by that. I just nodded and drank as she fiddled with her Discman. The speakers were the kind that make CDs sound tinny and faint, like music on an old transistor radio. She turned them up all the way, which wasn't very loud. It was Lennon, all right. He was singing: *They hurt you at home and they hit you at school...* She sang along with him. She knew all the words and everything.

'God I love this tune.'

*They hate you if you're clever and they despise a fool...* She slipped off her shoes and leaned back in her chair, still humming the tune. *Till you're so fucking crazy you can't follow their rules...*

'Come on,' she said. 'Sing with me. You're making me self-conscious.'

I laughed and tried to join in, but I didn't know any of the lyrics and ended up sounding like a bit of a treat. After a while I tapered off, and instead just sat there sipping rum and sneaking glances at her ankles and feet. She wasn't wearing any nail polish. She didn't have to. Her feet were hot enough as it was – even hotter than Karen's elbows.

When the song ended, she said, 'You know, my daughter once asked me how I wanted to die. She was six. What kind of question is that for a six-year-old to ask?'

'What did you tell her?'

'That I didn't know. I wasn't lying. I honestly don't know. Do you?'

'No.'

We sat there, trying to think of the best way.

I said, 'Chris wants fireworks when he dies. You know – like a big bang.'

She gave me a funny look. 'Do you wish you were more like Chris?'

I shrugged. 'Well, it would be cool to be that tough.'

'And he has Karen.' She picked a bit of fluff off her skirt. 'You like her, don't you?'

'Sure. I mean, she's pretty unique.'

'You dream about her. Do you fantasise about her, too?'

I nodded and didn't say anything.

'About both of them?'

I looked away, out the window.

My dad's a bit of a bloodhound about booze. Come to think of it, he actually looks like a bloodhound. He's got those drawn eyes and saggy cheeks and a pair of middle-aged jowls. And whenever he picks me up from parties, he sort of sniffs the air. Totally suspicious. Then he'll say something super sarcastic, something like, 'God you smell like a brewery.' He doesn't get furious, either. He just goes all quiet and looks disappointed, as if I've let him down in the worst possible way. It drives me absolutely insane, so for obvious reasons I was pretty nervous when he picked me up from my shrink's office. He was driving his Civic – the silver one he got a year or two ago. I rolled down the window, straight away, and made sure to breathe out the side of my mouth. Also, I got him talking. That's the best way to avoid his wrath. Just get him talking and act extremely interested in whatever he says.

'Hey pops – why was Lennon so awesome?'

'Lenin the communist or Lennon the Beatle?'

'The Beatle.'

'Well,' he said, and sort of shifted around in his seat. I could tell he was getting ready to do some serious talking. 'He was one of those people who became more than a person, for whatever reason. The hippies wanted an icon and Lennon fit the mould. So we put him up on a pedestal. And for a while he actually seemed to stand for something.'

I burped – this hideous rum burp – and blew it straight out the window.

Then I asked, 'Like what?'

'Oh, you know. Peace and love. Freedom. All that counter-culture crap. Whether or not he really embodied those values didn't matter – people needed to believe in something.'

He kept talking and I nodded along, trying to look attentive.

The only problem was that I felt harsh sick. My dad's a pretty aggressive driver and zigzagging through traffic was making me queasy. Robson Street is packed with tons of fancy restaurants, and with the window open I could smell the fish and seafood rotting in the dumpsters. The stench practically strangled me. All that rum simmered away in my belly, threatening to boil over. I clutched at the armrest, terrified that I was going to hurl.

'I remember the day he got shot,' my dad was saying. 'Your mother and I were down near Puerto Limón in Costa Rica, camping in our Volks.'

'Um, dad?'

'It came on the radio and your mother just burst into tears.'

'I think you better…'

'It was like all those things he'd stood for had died with him.'

'Dad!'

'What?'

But I didn't have time to ask him to pull over. I just stuck my head out the window and started puking. It was weird puke – super explosive. It rushed out in a single spurt, like a short burst from a firehose. It splashed onto the road and rolled away behind us. I hardly even got any on the car door. Then I sat back and wiped at my mouth, trembling all over.

'Jesus,' my dad said. 'Where did that come from?'

'Uh… my shrink gave me some leftover sushi. It tasted a bit funny.'

It was the only thing I could come up with. I thought I was busted for sure, but all he said was, 'Oh. Did you have tuna?'

'A couple pieces of sashimi.'

'Maybe it had gone off.'

And that was it. He must have suspected something, but

I guess the notion of me getting plastered with my psychiatrist was just too far-fetched for him to believe.

'How'd it go today, aside from the sushi?'

'Pretty good, I guess,' I said.

He slugged me, playfully, in the shoulder.

'Think you can stay out of trouble for a while?'

I nodded. I could tell he didn't believe me, though. That's another thing my dad's got a sixth sense about. Trouble, I mean. It was only two days later that we started the riot.

And it was all downhill from there.

## 34

It was just like my dream.

The water shifted and shimmered, shimmered and shifted, as if a huge strip of sequinned fabric had been stretched all the way across the Cove. And Karen was sitting right beside me, dangling her feet off the edge of the dock. Waves slurped at the pilings and sunlight lashed me in the face and a warm breeze tickled the back of my neck. Chris and Jules weren't there. They hadn't gone to go get ice cream, though. That part was different from the dream. I think they were trying to find us some weed, actually. Or maybe some nachos. I can't really remember. But basically, I had Karen all to myself for a change.

'God it's so hot, today,' I said.

'Mm-hmm. For sure.'

I always turned into a bit of a gearbox when we were alone. Don't ask me why. I was just too aware of her to act normal. I mean, let's face it: a bikini doesn't cover much. There was plenty to look at. I could have studied any part of her for hours. I loved noticing all the little differences, all the little changes. That day she had a sunburn on her nose and a hickey on her neck and a new bracelet around her wrist. It was one of those candy bracelets that you can eat, and she nibbled at the sugary circles as she flipped through her magazine. Meanwhile I just sat there, trying my hardest to look relaxed.

'How hot do you think it is?' I asked.

As soon as I said it, I wished I'd said something else. Anything else. I mean, Karen didn't want to talk about how hot it was, for Christ's sake. That's like standing in the middle of a swimming pool and talking about how wet the water is.

She shrugged. 'Oh, about thirty I guess.'

I felt so shitty that I decided to stop talking entirely. I'd give her the silent treatment. It worked for Chris so maybe it would work for me, too. I flopped back onto the dock, crossed my arms, and shut my mouth. Also, I closed my eyes. That way I couldn't see her and get all distracted. I lay like that for a few minutes, trying to forget she even existed.

Eventually she asked, 'What are we doing tonight?'

I didn't answer. I just grunted.

'Are we hitting the Avalon or what?'

I grunted again.

'But we're partying, right?'

The third time I didn't even bother to grunt. I just lay there with one arm draped over my eyes. Totally indifferent. It was pretty hilarious, actually. After a while, Karen started moving around and rustling the pages of her magazine. When that didn't work, she sighed in this super obvious way – like a spoiled little kid trying to show me how bored she was.

'What's up?' I asked, acting all innocent.

'I need help with this quiz. You're a guy. You should know.'

'Okay.'

'When will a man ejaculate the most: when he's been drinking, when it's been a while since his last orgasm, when he gets a lot of foreplay, or all of the above?'

I tried to look as if I talked about that kind of stuff all the time.

'Um,' I said, 'if you haven't come for a while you're carrying around a bigger load.'

'What about the other two?'

I had to think about it. 'When you're drunk it's bigger, yeah.'

'So all of the above?'

I couldn't comment on the foreplay. I hadn't gotten that far with anybody yet.

'Sure – I guess.'

She leaned over and pecked me on the cheek. 'Thanks, babe.'

Karen hardly ever flirted with me like that. I knew it was only because Chris and Julian weren't around, but it still felt pretty awesome. I sat there in a giddy little daze while she finished her quiz. Then she rolled up the magazine and popped it in her beach bag.

'Want to go swimming?'

When she said that, I harsh tripped out. It was like déjà vu, except way crazier because I'd heard those exact words in about a hundred dreams. I almost said, 'We don't have our bathing suits.' But this wasn't the dream, and we did, so I just said, 'Okay.'

Karen adjusted her bikini straps, pulled off her bracelet, and slipped into the water. I followed, shoving off with my arms and letting myself sink straight down. Five feet below the surface the temperature dropped suddenly, and I shot back up.

'Careful,' Karen said. 'There's a red jellyfish over there.'

'Where?'

'Right there.'

Then I saw. It was only a few yards away.

'I hate those goddamned things. I got one on my face, once.'

Karen started giggling. 'On your face?'

'Yeah. Right on my face. Like this.'

I demonstrated with my hand, palming my face like a basketball. Karen giggled even harder. She swam over to the jellyfish, which was floating on the surface, pulsating.

'It's so beautiful,' she said, 'like a flower.'

'But it hurts, like love.'

I said it super melodramatically, so she'd know I was messing with her.

'You are such a geek.'

But she liked it. I could tell because as soon as we got out of the water, she asked me to rub tanning oil on her back. That was a privilege usually reserved for Chris. I sat cross-legged, directly behind her, so close I could see the wispy strands of hair that grew at the nape of her neck. She held the rest of her hair to one side. The oil was hot and runny and dripped over my hands, splattering onto the dock.

'Careful. That stuff's expensive, you know.'

I almost apologised, but caught myself just in time.

'Quit your moaning.'

That was a better thing to say. That's what Chris would have said. It worked, too. She didn't argue and I began to rub her down. My hands slid smooth and greasy over her shoulders, her back, her spine. I took my time. I was polishing

171

a work of art. I was worshipping her body. The scent was sweet and pungent in the heat – almost like coconut milk. It smelled even better than her perfume. Better than anything.

'Are you going to Julian's party?'

She knew I was. She only asked because the silence had become strange.

'Yeah,' I said.

'Me, too.'

A while ago, I did something that makes me sound like a real nutcase. I don't even like to admit it, but I went to buy a bottle of that tanning oil. Sometimes I still get it out, just to smell it – just to remember what it was like to be that close to her.

## 35

It was like having acid tossed in your face. It stung my eyes and burned my cheeks and sizzled up into my sinuses. I started crying straight away. I couldn't help it. It was worse than being punched in the nose, worse than getting kicked in the balls. Way worse. I could barely breathe. I just kept choking. My throat felt raw and ragged, as if my tonsils were bleeding.

Basically, it was nuts.

I must have fallen over. Or maybe I got pushed. It's hard to say, but the next thing I remember is being on the floor. People were stepping on me and I couldn't see a goddamn thing. I harsh freaked out. I yanked off my ghost costume and crawled around in circles for a while, crying my eyes out. Somehow, I managed to crawl my way into the bathroom.

I could hear sobbing. Another person was in there.

'Are you okay?' I said.

'It's the pepper spray.'

'They got me, too. Can you see?'

'No.'

It was a girl. I didn't recognise her voice, but it stopped me from crying. Like I said, I don't cry in front of girls, even if I've been maced. Especially if I've been maced, actually.

'Here,' I said.

I guided her to the tap and cupped handfuls of water over her face. She made a little sound – like a whimper at the back of her throat.

'It hurts.'

'Yeah. Goddamned pigs.'

'Let me do it.'

We took turns splashing water into our eyes. Outside, people were kicking and punching and screaming and swearing, and we'd found this peaceful little hiding place. Secretly, I was kind of hoping to make out with her. Not in a sleazy way, but in a super romantic way. You know – I'd kiss her on the forehead and then maybe stroke her hair if she'd let me. It didn't happen, obviously. But it would have been awesome if it did.

'Are there any towels?' she asked.

'They're around here somewhere.'

Then I remembered – Jules kept them on the shower door. I handed one to her and used another to pat at my face. The skin surrounding my eyes was all puffy and tender, almost blistered. I could see a little better, though. The first thing I saw was this blue, blurry shape standing in front of me. For a second I thought that she was just a girl who really liked the colour blue. You know, blue jeans and blue shirts and stuff. Then I saw the little gold badge glittering on her chest. I started laughing. I mean, it was impossible not to laugh.

'What?'

'You're a cop!'

'Yeah.'

She sounded almost embarrassed. Of all the cops I've ever met, she had the best personality by a mile. Also, she was the best looking. Seriously. Her face looked funny because she was squinting and grimacing at the same time, but you could tell that on a good day – like on a day when she hadn't been hit right in the eyes with pepper spray – she would have been a fox. A cop fox.

'I've always wanted to be maced,' I said.

She laughed, a little nervously. Neither of us really knew how the hell to act. We just stood there blinking over and over at each other, as if we were trying to communicate with our eyes. No matter how many times we blinked, the tears kept streaming down our cheeks.

Eventually I said, 'Guess we should go back out there, huh?'

'I suppose so.'

We turned to face the door. Neither of us wanted to open it. I mean, we could hear what was happening outside. The sounds of the riot came through all muted and subdued, like a violent action movie playing on low volume. But we couldn't stay in there all night.

'See you on the other side,' I said.

And I opened the door into chaos.

Jules decided to throw this toga party. Don't ask me why. I think he'd watched too many of those stupid college comedies. You know – the kind where the frat guys throw a huge toga party and everybody gets laid, instantly. That's what Jules imagined, I'm pretty sure. Somebody forgot to tell him that high school toga parties are the lamest thing ever, next to turtlenecks and breath-holding competitions. But summer vacation was almost over and his parents were away at a sports conference and Jules wanted to have his party.

I was a little dubious, right from the start.

It's not like I'm completely against toga parties, either. I love a good toga party under the right circumstances. But a toga party has to be casual. It's impossible to act casual in Julian's house. The walls are stark and white, the ceilings are way too high, and the rooms are filled with pricey artefacts – like a museum. There's boomerangs and oil paintings and tribal masks and ebony carvings and all kinds of cultured shit. Super trendy. His house would be perfect for, say, a yuppie dinner party. But a toga party? Not even.

On top of that, I look harsh butt in a toga. To wear a toga, you need a body like Chris. He reminded me of Julius Caesar. I'm serious. Even Jules, with his puffy pecs and inflated biceps, looked better than me. The problem is my muscle tone. I've got no definition. I also have a few wispy hairs sprouting around my nipples. Really lame hairs, like an old man's beard growing out of my chest. That's why I didn't even wear a toga. I just draped a sheet over my head and cut out two holes for eyes. On the front of the sheet I wrote in permanent marker: This is my first ghost party. Everybody loved it. Everybody but Jules.

'It's a toga party, man – a toga party!'

Jules took his party seriously. His toga wasn't just a sheet. He'd gone to the trouble of renting an entire toga costume. He even had a crown of laurels around his head. I felt a little sorry for him, actually. He'd been acting pretty neurotic, lately. He pretended he didn't know about Chris and Karen, but he knew. He had to know. When it came down to it, that's what his toga party was really about: him and Chris and Karen. It was his attempt at a coup.

Jules wanted to be Caesar.

*Hero's Party Turns Nasty.* That was the headline in the *North Shore News.* The others were just as bad. The way they wrote it, you'd think Chris started the riot single-handedly. Technically I guess he did start it. I mean, he was the one who slammed the door in their face. Also, he threw the most punches and ended up in jail. I ended up in jail, too – even though I didn't really do anything. But whatever. All I'm saying is that a riot can't just be started by one person, like a fire. Everybody played a part. Jules and Karen and Bates and the party mannequins and all those cops. Everybody. Even Julian's parents helped out. They were the ones who supplied the booze and left the house empty. They pretended they didn't know about what was going on, but it was pretty obvious that they were in it up to their eyeballs.

At that toga party, nobody was innocent.

Jules wasn't. Not even close. The thing about Jules is that he doesn't know when to stop. When he decided to eat protein powder, he didn't stop until his muscles were all huge and doughy. And when he decided to have a party, he didn't stop filling the house until it was so cramped you could hardly move. He invited people from all over the North Shore, and they came. They came from the Cove and they came from Blueridge. They came from Lynn Valley and from West Van and they even came from Horseshoe Bay. Jules welcomed them all in, smiling and handing out punch.

He asked me, 'What do you think of the party, man?'

'It's cool, Jules.'

I was lying, for his sake. I hated it, actually. The four of us had created our own little world for most of the summer. Now there were these people everywhere, laughing and shouting and dancing and swearing and wrestling in their togas.

'I'll be right back,' I told him.

I fought my way through the heaving, sweaty mass, looking for familiar faces. I couldn't find any. Who the hell were these people? They were just another exhibit in the museum of Julian's house. He'd called in about eight hundred mannequins to impress Karen. It was like they'd come straight from the beach, with their fake tans and fake muscles and fake girlfriends. It was even worse than that party in West Van. Since they'd all worn togas, it was impossible to tell them apart. There were mannequins splashing in the pool and lounging around the jacuzzi. There were mannequins drinking at the kitchen table and making out on the sofas. Everywhere I looked I saw dozens and dozens of mannequins.

They'd overrun the place. For mannequins, they were getting pretty aggressive, too.

'Hey – watch yourself, bitch.'

I'd bumped into some guy near the toilet. It was hard to see in that ghost costume.

'Whatever, man,' I said.

I brushed past before he did anything. It was typical bullshit. I mean, I don't know what Jules expected. Cramming that many drunken assholes into one space is like building a homemade bomb.

He provided the gunpowder, too.

A giant punchbowl dominated one corner of the living room. The punch was neon orange and tasted like Kool-Aid mixed with gasoline. Jules must have dumped at least five litres of vodka in there. I wouldn't be surprised if his parents had gone out and bought all that booze specifically for the party. I mean, who keeps that much Smirnoff in their liquor closet? Nobody – that's who. Except maybe Chris's mom.

Beside the bowl stood stacks of cheap plastic cups. Most people drank from those. Not me. I needed something that would get the job done. In Julian's cupboard I found his dad's beer stein – this classy pewter mug he'd brought back from Prague. It was worth a dozen plastic cups. I grabbed it and jostled my way to the punchbowl.

'Hey – check out this fag.'

'Nice costume, buddy.'

There were a bunch of clowns standing around the table, making stupid comments like that. I ignored them. I filled up the stein and went to sit by myself in a corner, huddling under my ghost sheet. It was like being in a super tiny tent for one person. I peered out at the world, at all the mannequins, sucking back as much vodka as I could as quickly as I could. When I ran out I went back for more. Those guys could laugh at me and make fun of me all they wanted. I didn't care. I felt pretty superior, actually. None of them knew what I'd guessed as soon as I walked in the door: that this party was destined for disaster.

Bates was as guilty as any of us.

The first time he came to the door, I happened to answer. I wasn't even that surprised to see him. It was like that lame old saying – the one about somebody being a bad penny. Bates was our bad penny. Since he always hassled us, it seemed natural that he'd be the one to show up at our party. This time he had another cop with him – a big Asian guy with smooth cheeks and a chin that went right into his neck.

'What's going on here?'

That was Bates. He seemed a little put off by my ghost costume.

'We're having a toga party.'

'That's not a toga.'

I pointed at my chest. 'I thought it was a ghost party.'

The Asian guy laughed. He seemed okay, actually. He had nice, straight teeth.

Bates said, 'Take that goddamn thing off when you're talking to me.'

I started trying to get out of my sheet. It was a bit of an ordeal.

'Wait a minute,' Bates said. 'Is this your house?'

'No.'

'Forget the sheet. Get me the owner.'

I turned around. Jules was standing with a bunch of mannequins.

'Jules,' I shouted, 'it's the cops!'

That got his attention, and everybody else's, too. Somebody had the sense to turn down the music, and Jules came over. Bates hadn't recognised me because of my sheet but he recognised Julian, all right. 'What do you know?' he said. 'It's my hero.' He snorted and turned to his partner. 'This is one of the guys who got kicked off the Crazy Dan show.'

'Oh yeah?'

'Yeah. These kids are trouble.'

That cracked me up. He said it like we weren't even there.

Jules asked, 'Is there a problem, Officer Bates?'

'We've had a couple of noise complaints.' Bates waved a hand in the direction of the party, as if he was fanning away a bad odour. 'You keep it down, or we'll shut it down.'

I'd bet five hundred bucks he rehearsed lines like that in his mirror.

'I understand, officer.'

'This is a verbal warning.'

'Okay, officer.'

Bates still didn't seem satisfied. He lingered on the porch but couldn't think of anything else to say. It was obvious how badly he wanted to shut the party down. But he had nothing to stand on. Not yet. The two of them turned and went back to their squad car. Jules closed the door. We watched through the window, waiting for them to drive away.

Then Jules shouted, 'Let's party!'

Karen wasn't innocent, either. It's impossible to be innocent when you look like Karen. She knew exactly how to wear her toga. She had it looped low across her chest, so you could see tons of cleavage. That was bad enough. But she also had it parted around her left thigh, like one of those classy dresses that have a long slit up the side. She didn't even look like a normal human being any more. She'd transformed into this Roman goddess.

'How's my ghost with the most?'

She sidled up to me and sat right on my lap, draping a sweaty arm around my neck for balance. She had a cup in each hand and some of the punch slopped onto my ghost costume. I didn't care. She was sitting right on my lap. It was awesome. It was better than awesome.

'There's a lot of cute girls here, huh?' she asked.

'Yeah. I guess.'

She took a swig of punch. 'You don't think so?'

'None as cute as you.'

I wasn't lying, either. She made all those Barbie doll clones look harsh skanky.

'Thanks, babe.'

She turned her head and kissed me, right on the mouth. My costume completely covered my face so it wasn't like our lips touched or anything, but it was the next best thing.

'Having fun?' she asked.

'Not really. Where's Chris?'

One of her cups was empty, now. She peered into it and frowned.

'He's ignoring me. He's acting weird.'

'Oh.'

She finished off the other cup, then held them both up.

'Time to reload.'

I watched her go. Wherever she went, mannequins trailed after her. It wasn't her fault, really. She couldn't help that most guys are aggro perverts who walk around with a permanent hard-on. Later on Chris had to deck this one guy. There were tons of other scraps, too. That's the problem with toga parties. If you get a bunch of drunken assholes together with all these half-naked girls, there's obviously going to be problems. The whole place started to spark and crackle with this crazy violent energy. Jules had built the bomb, and the girls acted like a sort of primer. The only thing missing was the detonator.

I'm not saying Chris was entirely innocent. A mob needs a leader. Everybody knows that. But the leader can't take all the blame for the mob. I mean, how could one guy fight two dozen cops and tear a house apart all by himself? Not even Chris could do that. It's pretty obvious that he had plenty of help. The only difference was that none of the help got arrested. A handful of them got thrown in the drunk tank, but just long enough to sober up. Not us. We were stuck in there all night. Bates must have loved that. I'm pretty sure he wanted them to pin the whole thing on Chris – the usual suspect. It almost worked, too.

Halfway through the party I found Chris standing alone on the back porch. He was hunched over the balcony rail, staring into the darkness.

I snuck up behind him in my ghost costume.

'Boo.'

He didn't even smile.

'What's up man?' I asked.

'I'm sick of this.'

'Me, too. Let's blow this pop stand.'

'There's nowhere to go that's any better.'

Then he puked. It wasn't much – barely more than a gag. I guess he'd had too much punch. Or maybe the party was actually nauseating him. Either way, this mouthful of orange vomit spattered onto the patio below us. There were a bunch of mannequins down there.

One of them looked up.

'Nice shot, buddy.'

'Shut the fuck up or I'll kill you.'

I winced. I thought we were in for a fight, but the guy decided to play it safe and avoid a beat down. Him and his buddies sidled away. Chris didn't relax, even once they were out of sight. He clenched and unclenched his fist, as if he were crushing a tennis ball. He'd already punched out that treat for perving on Karen and I knew more fighting was on the way. I just didn't know how much more.

## 36

Jules got a bit weird in the week before his party.

Come to think of it, Jules has always been a bit weird. When we were younger, one thing he used to do was buy Chris's clothes off him. Seriously. His parents gave him all this super expensive clothing, but he only wanted to wear Chris's old jeans and hoodies and t-shirts. He'd pay twenty bucks for an outfit. Chris didn't mind. Most of his clothes he got at second-hand shops, anyway. I found the whole thing pretty bizarre. I mean, me and Chris had pretty similar taste, but I wouldn't have wanted to wear his clothes.

But basically, Julian had a tendency to get all obsessive like that, and Karen brought it out in him.

'Hey, sex-kitten. Are you in bed?'

It was after the funeral that he started phoning her.

'Julian?'

'That's right, gorgeous.'

He phoned her every night. I called her occasionally, too, but I only called when I wanted her opinion on something. You know – like the weather. He called her for no reason at all. The phone would ring and Jules would be on the other end, talking in this low, sultry voice.

'What does he talk about?' I asked her.

'Nothing. That's the problem.'

I grinned. 'Maybe he's after midnight taps.'

She hit me, playfully. 'Don't ever tell Chris, okay?'

I wouldn't have, if Jules had left it at that. But he took it too far, like always. He showed up at her house with a bouquet of flowers. He did that twice. He also texted little poems to her. They weren't cute poems, either. They were creepy. I know, because she showed me one. It went: *I am the bee, fast and strong. You are the flower, soft and delicate. I will pollinate you, little flower.* Me and Julian had been friends for a long time, and I'd always thought that he was an okay guy. But when I read that, I had to admit that he was a bit of a nutball.

Occasionally, Karen caught him following her. She'd be over at Park Royal, or in Pacific Centre, and all of a sudden Jules would be there. He always acted surprised that they'd run into each other. Who knows? Maybe he really was surprised. Maybe they just happened to frequent the same shops. But it seemed pretty damned suspicious to me. He usually ended up offering her a ride home. She accepted once or twice, too. Just for kicks. She told me all about it. In the car, he rolled down the windows and played his dad's Frank Sinatra CD for her. No fucking joke. I bet he thought that was super romantic.

'Doesn't it creep you out?' I asked her.

'Oh, he's harmless. I think it's kind of cute.'

He was about as cute as a sex maniac, or a serial killer. Him and his bees and his fucking Frank Sinatra music. I'd had enough. That afternoon, I told Chris everything.

'Are you shitting me?'

'No, man. She didn't tell you because she thought you'd kill him.'

He laughed. We were down in the Cove, fishing off the government dock.

'Are you?'

'Am I what?'

'Going to kill him?'

Chris checked his line and squinted at the water. 'That would be too easy.'

I snickered, like an evil little sidekick. He was right, of course. There'd be no point in giving Julian a beat down. At the same time, this was too bizarre to let slide. Chris had to do something, and he did. The next time the four of us were together, he clarified things for Jules. We were in my basement, watching a movie. It was a stupid creature feature about killer leeches. None of us were into that kind of stuff any more – it just seemed boring.

Halfway through I heard this wet noise, like a cat licking milk. I looked over. Chris and Karen were kissing. They had their mouths open and I could see their tongues. I could see that and I could see Jules. He had a sick expression on his face, as if he'd been punched in the stomach. Before the movie even ended, he made an excuse and went home. I didn't. Chris and Karen kept kissing. It was almost like they'd forgotten I was there. I sat back and watched. It was ten times better than the movie.

## 37

Bates came back with the sole intention of shutting the party down. That much was obvious. Otherwise he wouldn't have brought a dozen cops with him. If there had only been a few people in the house he still would have broken it up. Of course, there weren't just a few.

There were at least a hundred – maybe more.

'Jules!' somebody yelled. 'Those fucking cops are back!'

A bunch of us herded towards the door. Something was going to happen. You could feel it. Julian jostled his way to the front. He could barely stand. His toga was in tatters and his laurel crown sat at a funny angle on his head. Chris and I followed, keeping him upright.

People pressed against the windows.

'Jesus – there's six squad cars out there.'

'Here they come!'

Knock-knock.

'Who is it?' Jules said.

We all snickered. He could barely talk.

'It's the police!' The voice was muted, weak. 'Open up!'

Jules did. There was a cluster of them on the porch. Bates stood at the front, with a smug little smile on his face. You could tell he'd been waiting for this all night. On his coffee break, he'd probably snuck into the toilet to pull his goalie and fantasise about it.

Jules grinned. 'What's up, Batesy?'

'We're shutting this party down. Clear everybody out.'

'What?'

'You heard me.'

Jules was dumbstruck. You could see it in his face. This was his big night, his coup. He honestly couldn't believe they were breaking up his party. He didn't know what to say.

Chris did.

He said, 'Fuck you, pig.'

And slammed the door in his face. Boom.


Somebody brought a camera to the toga party – one of those

little digital video cameras. If it weren't for that, we wouldn't really know what happened that night. But I saw the footage, and the camera caught it all. When Chris locks them out, everybody cheers. A second later, the cops break down the door – they kick it right off its hinges. I've never seen anything like it. The door goes flying and they pour in, this blue wave that crashes against the group of us gathered in the hall. They pull out their nightsticks and start hitting at random. When you study the tape, it's pretty obvious that those cops had absolutely no plan. They just assumed that if they thumped a few people and busted a few heads, then that would be the end of it.

It wasn't. People started fighting back.

On the video, Chris is at the very front, swinging his fists in a windmill. Then the windmill connects with the face of this one cop who's wearing glasses. Bam. The glasses go flying, like a frightened grasshopper jumping off his face. I'm in the frame, too – stumbling around in my ghost costume. I look pretty hilarious, actually. You can tell that I can't see a goddamn thing. I walk straight into this scrawny cop, who grabs me for no reason.

I remember that part pretty well, but I didn't know it was a cop at the time. I just thought he was some gearbox trying to fight me. We wrestled for a bit and around us everybody else was doing the same thing. That was when the cops totally wet the bed. In the middle of that madness they busted out their mace and started spraying it everywhere. I'm not exaggerating, either. They really did spray it everywhere: all over us, all over the house. They even managed to get each other. Basically, the whole thing was one giant fuck up.

Looking back, it's a miracle that nobody got shot.

## 38

'Come on – let's see who can hold their breath the longest.'

That was another thing about Julian. He loved having stupid competitions.

'Fuck off, Jules.'

Chris, Karen and I were lying around Julian's pool, letting the sun pound us flat against the stone patio. But Jules couldn't relax. He kept standing up and sitting down, standing up and sitting down. Also, he was drinking from this giant water bottle. He must have guzzled at least a litre of water before he mustered up the courage to whip off his shirt. Normally he did that sort of discreetly, because of his birthmark, but just then he was dying to show off his overblown muscles. He flexed them for us as he paraded back and forth across the patio. He'd been working on his fake tan, too. I don't know if he'd been popping pills or hitting the tanning salon or what, but either way his skin was getting pretty orange.

'You're chicken,' he said to Chris.

'Fuck off, Jules.'

'You think I'll beat you.'

'Fuck off, Jules.'

There was no way he'd convince Chris. Not a chance.

Karen said, 'Would you guys quit bickering?'

We were just like a family. A dysfunctional family on the verge of breaking down.

'You guys are such pussies,' Jules said.

He still couldn't get over them kissing. I bet he'd been awake all night thinking about it. The only response he could come up with was this competition. Obviously, it meant a lot to him.

I stood up. 'Fine. You go first.'

'Right on, man.' He clapped me on the back. 'You can use my watch to time me.'

His watch looked like something out of a science fiction movie. There were dials and levers and about six hundred buttons. He showed me which button to press for the timer. Then he eased himself into the water. His birthmark looked darker underwater, almost like blood.

'All right,' I said, starting the clock, 'go!'

'I'm not ready, yet.'

I reset the clock while Jules took these deep breaths. He breathed in and out for about a minute, closing his eyes on every exhale. I didn't think he'd ever stop.

'Tell me when you're going, man.'

'Okay. Now.'

He went under. I started the clock a little late but I didn't tell him that. It was his own fault for having so many buttons on his stupid watch. He didn't need the extra time, anyway. He held his breath for over two minutes. Even I was impressed. The thing is, I'm pretty sure he'd spent weeks practising, waiting for the chance to show off to Karen. That would have been just like him. At the end he popped up, heaving and spluttering.

He ran a hand through his hair.

'Time?'

'Two minutes six seconds.'

Karen applauded, clapping with her fingers spread like a little kid. Jules hauled his soaking bulk out of the pool and took the watch from me, acting all casual.

'Now it's your turn,' he said.

I had no hope of beating him, but I didn't care. Now that

189

he'd shown Karen how long he could hold his breath maybe we could relax again. I slipped into the water, feeling it all tingly against my skin.

'Ready?'

'Ready.'

I took a few breaths and went under, plugging my nose. I kind of enjoyed being down there, actually. It reminded me of sitting in my shrink's office: quiet and cool and safe. Water surrounded me like chilled jello, deflecting the sun, dampening sound, draining my warmth. It would have been perfect – except for the fact that I couldn't breathe. My head started throbbing and the pressure slowly expanded in my chest, like a balloon getting bigger and bigger and bigger. It pushed little bubbles out my nostrils. I squirmed and writhed, then scrunched up into a ball, fighting the urge to give in. But I couldn't. I was done.

I stood up. All the air exploded from my lungs.

'One minute and fourteen seconds,' Jules announced.

'Good one, Razor.'

I sloshed to the edge of the pool and rested my elbows against the deck. My head felt empty and weightless, and white spots drifted across my vision like balls of cotton. The grass in Julian's yard looked a little too green, and the sky looked a little too blue. It was as if the whole world had turned into a digital photograph. For about ten seconds everything seemed clearer and brighter and more real.

'That's so trippy,' I said.

Nobody paid me much attention.

Jules said, 'You're up, Chris.'

'Screw that.'

'Are you scared?' Karen said, tickling his foot. 'Is little

Chris scared?'

'Fuck off.' He swatted her hand away. 'Leave me alone.'

I dragged myself from the pool and sprawled out on the patio. The water dripping off me made the sun-dried stones pop and sizzle. I felt like a fresh fish thrown on the barbecue.

'You should try it, man,' I said. 'It gives you a weird head rush.'

'Yeah?'

'Yeah. You'll like it.'

I had my eyes closed against the glare of the sun, but I heard the deckchair creak as Chris stood up and the little splash as he hopped into the water. Karen started making a drum roll noise. She tried, anyways. It sounded more like a machine gun misfiring – but we got the idea.

'You'll never beat two minutes,' Jules said.

'We'll see.'

I sat up. Chris took a single breath, filling his lungs, and went under. His head stayed near the surface, the hair spreading out like tangles of brown seaweed. None of us said anything. We all knew there was no way he'd beat Jules. Aside from fighting, Chris didn't work out at all – he never jogged or ran or hit the gym or anything. Jules still couldn't help worrying, though. He looked from his watch to Chris and back to his watch. Time oozed by.

'How long?' I asked.

'A minute and a half,' Jules said.

There were no ripples in the water and Chris didn't move. He just hung suspended like a dummy or a doll. Or a corpse. I leaned forward. It didn't seem possible that he could hold his breath this long.

'Time?'

'Two minutes.' Jules waited. Then he added, 'Two minutes seven.'

He tossed his watch aside and crossed his arms. Chris still didn't come up. Small bubbles were popping next to his ear. Then larger bubbles. He had to come up. He had to.

He didn't.

'Is he okay?' Karen asked.

'How long, Jules?'

'I don't know.'

'Check your fucking watch!'

Reluctantly, Jules picked up the watch and said, 'Almost three minutes.'

'Fuck this.'

I jumped in the water and turned Chris over. He was limp in my arms. As soon as his head cleared the surface he started gagging. It was totally insane. I dragged him to the edge of the pool. Jules and Karen stood there and stared. I don't think they could quite believe it.

'Come on! Give me a hand!'

We got him onto the pool deck. He choked up water and lay there, dry heaving.

'Oh my God!' Karen said. 'Is he okay?'

'Chris? Can you hear me, man?'

I slapped his face. His eyes were vacant and glassy, but he smiled at me.

'You were right, man,' he said. 'It's awesome down there.'

Karen and I burst out laughing. We were just so fucking relieved. Unlike Jules. He was too busy sulking to care. He sat and fiddled with his watch until Chris had recovered and we were all lounging around the pool again. That was when he came out with it, like a revelation.

'I think I'm going to have a toga party.'

'Fuck off, Jules.'

Everything was back to normal.

## 39

Total chaos.

That's how one of the cops they interviewed described it. Normally it would have harsh pissed me off. I mean, people use that phrase without even stopping to think what total chaos would actually look like. But in this case, the cop was right.

That party was total chaos.

'Leave us alone, you pigs!'

'You fascist cocksuckers!'

They realised pretty quick that twelve cops wasn't going to be enough. They called for back-up, and the back-up called for more back-up. At least, I'm assuming that's what happened. All I know for sure is that cops kept arriving. There were cops from North Van and West Van and a few cops from Burnaby. Eventually it got so bad that they brought in the riot police from downtown. It was nuts. They came with their helmets and shields and body armour and everything. They looked pretty sweet, actually. Also, they were thirty times more professional than the regular cops. They didn't just attack everybody. They didn't use pepper spray, either. They had a pretty basic strategy. They marched through the house, flushing out the rooms one by one – kind of like shepherds driving sheep from a barn.

Extremely violent sheep.

As soon as I left the bathroom, I got separated from the cop fox. We didn't have much choice in the matter. Sweaty, bodies jostled and pushed up against each other. People were screaming and the stereo was still blaring and the whole house felt like one giant mosh pit. Somehow I ended up in the living room, which was less packed. The punch bowl had been knocked over in the brawling. A sticky puddle covered the carpet, and slices of orange lay scattered around like dead goldfish. Luckily, people had left half-filled cups all over the place: on tables, armrests, bookshelves, wherever. I downed a couple of the fullest ones to get my buzz going again, then headed back into the fray. Most of the action was near the front of the house, but I didn't see Chris anywhere. I didn't see Jules or Karen, either. The only person I saw who I recognised was a policeman, the same one who'd been there when Bates gave us those stupid tickets for not wearing bike helmets. You know – the one with the super big moustache.

'Officer Moustache!'

I shouted that and shoved my way towards him. He was standing by the front door, arms crossed, dressed in a scruffy blue hoody and this Canucks hat. I don't think he was even on duty. He didn't look like he was on duty, anyway. He just looked awesome.

'Hey officer – what's up, man?'

As I said that, I stumbled right into him. He had to catch me in his arms and sort of prop me up against the wall.

'How you doing, kid?'

I don't know if he recognised me or what, I hope he did.

'Pretty shitty.'

A beer bottle smashed on the doorframe next to me, showering us with bits of glass. Somebody screamed: 'Go to hell, copper!'

Moustache sighed and shook his head, then dusted the shards off his hoody. 'Looks like things got a little out of hand here.'

'Yeah,' I said, 'the pigs... I mean the cops tried to shut it down. Then we slammed the door in their face and they started beating people up and macing everybody.'

'What a gong show.'

I didn't know what a gong show was at the time, so I just nodded. Later I asked my dad about it, and he said they had gong shows on TV back in the seventies. All these variety acts would come on stage, and if the judges didn't like something, they'd bang a gong to finish that act off. So when Moustache said something was a gong show, he meant that it was all chaotic and ridiculous and pretty fucked up.

In other words, this was the biggest gong show of all time.

He said, 'You should probably go home, kid.'

'For sure. I just got to find my friend first.'

At that point, this cop in riot gear rushed up. He didn't have the full shield but he had a helmet and a nightstick. He pointed it at my face. 'Is this one bothering you, lieutenant?'

Moustache frowned and waved him away, making it clear he thought the guy was a total marzipan. Then he shook my hand – just to show how tight we were and everything.

'Time to get a move on, kid,' he told me.

'All right, lieutenant. No worries.'

He strolled off, keeping it real. I was stoked to find out that he'd made lieutenant. If anybody deserved a promotion, it was him. He was the kind of cop that probably drank a lot, and hacked tons of darts. Also, there was that moustache. You can always trust a guy with a huge moustache, especially one that hasn't been trimmed or waxed or anything.

Anyways, a few minutes later I finally found Chris.

'Get the fuck off me!'

I heard him scream that as soon as I stepped outside. I couldn't see him, though. By that point the house was nearly empty, but nobody had actually gone home. All the bodies had just spilled out onto the street. The front yard was covered with cops and people in togas. I climbed up on the fence to get a better view. Things were settling down, but among the crowd little bubbles of violence kept popping up. A few die-hards were still fighting cops and each other and pretty much anything they came across. One guy was even fighting a lamppost. No joke. He was kicking it and smashing it with a plastic deckchair. That was pretty crazy, but not as crazy as what was happening to Chris.

'Get him down!'

Three cops struggled with him on the lawn, yanking on his toga and trying to pin him. A handful of others hovered nearby, including Bates. I'd never seen him so excited.

'Stay still you little shit!'

Bates said that, then rushed in and booted Chris in the ribs – quick and vicious, like he was kicking a rabid dog. Even the other cops were a little surprised. I saw one hold up her hand, as if to tell Bates to stop. He didn't, though. He just kept kicking away.

I jumped off the porch and ran over there.

'Leave him alone! This is bullshit!'

I must have looked like a big baby. My eyes were still red and watery from all that pepper spray. I ran straight for Bates and shoved him away from Chris. That was a mistake. Another cop tackled me from the side. My face smeared across the grass and I got a mouthful of dirt. They wrenched both arms behind my back and cuffed me before I even knew what the hell was happening.

'Take these two down to the station,' Bates said. 'They're the ones who started it.'

That's how we ended up in the squad car.

On television, they always show the criminals in the back of the car just before it pulls away. This was the opposite. We were on the inside looking out. We couldn't hear much but we could see everything through the windshield. We saw cops clearing stragglers off the lawn, and neighbours watching from their driveways, and drunks being loaded into the paddy wagon across the street. Then we saw Karen, wandering in circles. Her toga was torn at the shoulder and one of her breasts had nearly popped out. She tottered back and forth like a pendulum – absolutely wasted. Chris's window was open about six inches, and he called to her through the gap.

'Karen!'

She staggered over and sort of slumped against the car door.

'Chris – what's going on?'

'Me and Razor got arrested.'

'What?'

'Yeah. I punched a bunch of cops.'

Karen sobbed – this choking little sob.

'Chris, I'm scared.'

'What's there to be scared of?'

'Kiss me, please?'

He tilted his head up against the roof so they could kiss. Karen started crying. She was crying and kissing him at the same time. It was the most romantic thing I'd ever seen. Then our driver came back. He got in the front and told Karen to step away from the vehicle. She didn't, though – not even when he started the engine. As we drove off I turned around in my seat to watch her. She stood totally still, shivering and holding herself, getting smaller and smaller. Just before we rounded the corner, I spotted Jules crossing the yard towards her. She turned to meet him and he wrapped an arm around her shoulder, comforting her.

The fucking Judas.

## 40

It took Chris a while to get a feel for the car.

As we drove along Dollarton, he would accelerate, then brake, then swerve back and forth in the lane. Just testing. Around Raven Woods he hit the gas – really flooring it – and we roared down that stretch of road that leads to the Reservation. The speed limit there is lower than anywhere else in the city. That's just how the Natives like it. So Chris slowed down – not because he was afraid of getting a ticket, but because he had this enormous respect for Natives.

I asked, 'What's the plan?'

He'd been concentrating pretty hard on his driving. He gave this little jerk and glanced over at me, wide-eyed, as if he hadn't quite heard. Also, his nostrils were sort of quivering. He looked exactly like a caged animal, like a cougar or a wolf or a tiger. You know – something that should never have been locked up in the first place.

'Plan?' he asked.

Obviously, he didn't have one. Then again, I guess he didn't really need one.

## 41

It seemed like the middle of the night when Chris called me. It was probably only about one o'clock, though. Since I didn't have anything to do I'd gone to bed early. Then, all of a sudden, our phone was ringing. I fumbled around in the dark before managing to find it.

'Razor?'

'Dude – what's going on?'

'Not much. Can you come pick us up?'

'Now? Like in a car?'

I didn't even have my licence. I had my learner's, but I hadn't learned very much. We never practised because dad was super worried that I'd crash his Civic. Actually, a few weeks ago I did crash his Civic – so he was probably right to be worried.

'Yeah. Some fucking guy pulled a gun on Karen and we missed the seabus. Julian won't come down because he's being a total pussy.'

For a split second, after he said that, I thought I was dreaming. I thought I'd created this fantasy where they'd gotten into trouble, and I'd have to come to their rescue and save the day. I sort of sat up and looked around.

'Are you serious?'

'Yeah, man. I'll tell you later. Karen's running out of credit. Will you come?'

In the background I heard Karen say, 'Pretty please, Razor?'

She didn't really sound distraught. She sounded like she was enjoying herself.

'Can't you take a cab? My old man will murder me.'

'None of them will pick me up. I'm covered in blood and shit.'

This was nuts. They really were in trouble.

'All right. Where are you?'

'Oppenheimer Park.'

'What are you doing in Oppenheimer Park?'

Before he had time to answer, the line went dead.

We hardly ever went downtown.

To begin with, Julian hated downtown. When he was twelve he got jumped by these two huge skinheads who stole his wallet, his cellphone, and his sweater. No joke. After that, he avoided going downtown whenever possible – and without his car, it was a huge ordeal for me and Chris to get over there. We had to take the seabus, which only goes about once every nine hours. But a week before the toga party Chris wanted to do something special with Karen. You know – like a date. He didn't call it a date but that's what it was.

'Where are you going to take her, man?'

'I don't know. What do you think?'

We split a couple of Kokanees at my house before the date. He had to come over, anyway, to borrow some of my dad's old clothes. My dad was cool about it. He let us root around in his closet and drawers. We picked out this dark green polo shirt and a pretty sweet pair of khakis. The khakis were a little long, but Chris still looked ten times better than the night we'd gone to that West Van party. He'd even combed his hair – probably the first and only time he did that in his entire life.

'How about Brandy's?' I suggested.

Brandy's is this super classy peeler bar where all the Vancouver Canucks go.

'Brandy's sounds pretty randy.'

'Like stealing candy from a dandy.'

Neither of us could take it seriously. He still hadn't decided where he was taking her by the time Karen showed up. She didn't knock. Nobody knocked at my house. It was everybody's second home. We heard the back door open and then her feet appeared at the top of the stairs.

'Hello?'

'We're down here.'

We stood up. It was just like a scene in an old movie, when the guy's date arrives for prom. There was Chris, in his polo shirt, and there was Karen, in her dress. I'd never seen her wear a dress before. She'd chosen this red summer dress, strapless and patterned with white flowers. It hugged her breasts pretty tight. Not skanky or anything. Just nice. She floated down the stairs and came to perch on the arm of our sofa – the one that leaks stuffing.

Then she smiled – this very shy smile.

'Hi, Chris.'

He smiled back, and for a split second, it was like I didn't exist. I'd disappeared. The only thing that mattered was the two of them and their smiles. Then she noticed me and leaned over to tousle my hair, like I was her brother.

'What are you doing tonight, Razor?'

I yawned. 'Oh, I've got a party to go to. In Whistler.'

Chris asked, 'What kind of party?'

'A huge party. With tons of chicks and weed and free booze. It's too bad you guys can't come, actually. But maybe I'll send you a postcard or something.'

They both laughed politely. I didn't want them to feel bad about ditching me. At the same time, I kind of did want them to feel bad. But just to show there were no hard feelings, I gave them a few bottles of Kokanee for the road.

Karen stuffed them in her purse.

'Maybe we can meet up later,' Chris suggested.

'Yeah. Okay.'

That cheered me up. Not a lot, but a little. As soon as I heard the door shut, I did something pretty weak. I ran to the window and peered out, like a kid who's been left behind with the babysitter. Luckily, they didn't notice me as they got into Karen's Jeep. I watched them drive off, and kept watching until the Jeep rounded the corner. Then I went and sat on my bed. It was early. I didn't know what the hell to do. I phoned Jules, but he'd gone to a tennis match at the winter club. I think I ended up watching a nature programme with my dad. Later on, in bed, I kept imagining where they were, what they were doing.

It helped pass the time, at least.


'What was the restaurant like?'

We talked about it a few days after all the shit that went down that night. I think we were getting ready for Julian's toga party, actually.

'Pretty stuffy.'

'Nothing but stuffing on the menu, eh?'

'Like being stuffed in a straitjacket.'

They left her Jeep at Lonsdale Quay and took the seabus to Gastown. Chris still hadn't decided on a restaurant, so Karen suggested one – this place overlooking the water. It was called the Orange Tree, or the Lemon Tree, or some kind of fruit tree. Whatever it was called, it's not called anything now. It's gone. I know because I went down there to retrace their steps. I found the building, but the windows were covered up and half the sign had been painted over. The only word left was 'Tree.' It looked like a pretty fancy sign, though. Chris said it was fancy, too. Probably the fanciest place he'd ever been. There were little tea lights flickering on all the tables, and classical music floating around in the background.

'What did you have to eat?'

'I don't know. A steak. A French steak.'

He meant the filet mignon. Karen told me. She had to help him order, since he didn't recognise most of the stuff on the menu. The food was crazy expensive, too. Chris barely had enough cash – and he'd been saving up for weeks. Karen seemed to enjoy it, at least. But he told me he would rather have lit himself on fire than go back to a place like that.

For one thing, the waiter was wearing a turtleneck.

'You're shitting me. A full-on ninja turtle?'

'A total Donatello.'

I just wish he could have lived long enough to see it close down. Actually, there's a lot of stuff I wish he could have seen. Then again, there's also tons of stuff I'm glad he never had to witness. Like his own funeral, for instance. Or Karen's new hairstyle. He would have hated what she's done to her hair. It's harsh butt.

Anyways, after dinner they went looking for a bar that would let them in.

They tried a bunch of different ones, and kept getting denied. Somehow they ended up at the Roxy – this high-end club on Granville Street that charges about twenty bucks in cover. I don't think they really expected to get into it. On the other hand, they didn't really expect some guy to pull a gun on them, either. I mean, in Vancouver, that kind of thing hardly ever happens – but obviously their first date was an exception.

Oppenheimer Park is pretty much the sketchiest place in the entire city. My dad calls it 'Opium Park' because of all the junkies who hang out there. It's a dirty no-man's land of cardboard boxes and used needles and rotting condoms and broken glass shards. There aren't any trees or shrubs or bushes or anything nice like that. The entire block is covered in dirt and grass, with a baseball diamond shoved in one corner. I don't know why Chris and Karen chose that spot. I guess they'd walked down from Granville, to hide out or whatever.

But basically, that's where I went to pick them up.

For obvious reasons, I didn't ask my dad if I could borrow his car. I just took the keys from his coat pocket and went for it. He didn't catch me, either. I mean, it's not like he's one of those assholes who keeps track of the exact mileage. I made sure not to drive too fast, or too slow. In movies, guys always get pulled over for going too slow. Everybody knows that. So I drove at exactly fifty klicks the whole time, over the Second Narrows and down along Powell. At the park I spotted them right away – sitting on the bleachers behind home plate. Chris was drinking a can of beer and Karen was wearing his hoody. I parked, got out and sauntered over, trying to keep it fairly casual.

The thing is, they weren't alone.

As I came up, I saw a bunch of people sitting with them. The one closest to me was this guy all wrapped in garbage bags, with a giant gash across his cheek. There were tons of others, too – like this girl with sores on her arms and some dude wearing super dark sunglasses and a Chinese lady who had no front teeth. I asked Chris later but he didn't know who they were or where they'd come from. It was kind of like when I went looking for him backstage at the Crazy Dan show. All these people who you hardly ever notice or pay attention to had just appeared and gathered around him.

'Hey, guys,' I said. 'What's up?'

'Not much, Razor. Just chilling.' Chris grinned at me. He was bleeding, too. There was blood caked in his hair, and down the front of his shirt. 'Thanks for coming, man.'

All the weirdos were looking at me, wide-eyed and open-mouthed.

'Say hi to Razor, everybody.'

'Hel-lo, Ra-zor.'

They chanted it together, like a classroom of students. I perched on the edge of the bleachers, trying to remember if I'd locked my car. So much for rescuing him and Karen. I'd expected them to rush into the street and flag me down. But Karen was just leaning against Chris, stroking his arm. She smiled and twiddled her fingers at me. Perfectly content. He had just saved her life, after all – so I guess she was feeling pretty invincible.

'Do you guys want to get going?'

'Let me finish this beer first.'

So we waited there. The weirdos and junkies weren't actually talking, or communicating in any way. They just wanted to congregate, I guess. I don't really know. But they all seemed to like Chris. It might have been the beer. He'd bought a six-pack of Wildcat and shared it with them. He also rolled a joint and passed it around. I took a couple of tokes – making sure not to put my mouth on it. I mean, those people seemed all right, but some of them were harsh nasty.

'Okay, Razor – let's cruise.'

When we stood up to leave, all the weirdos stood up, too. They shuffled along and followed us back towards the car. It wasn't creepy or anything. It was just pretty sad.

They trailed a little way behind us, trying to keep Chris in sight – almost like they thought he could take them away, or lead them someplace better.

On the ride back, I got the whole story.

'This guy had been kicked out of the Roxy,' Karen said.

'So he pulled a gun – in front of about a hundred people.'

They didn't know what type of gun it was. Chris had never seen a real gun. Neither had Karen. But it was a handgun, apparently. A pistol.

'And he said, "I'll fucking shoot you, man. I'll shoot all you fucking Canadians!"'

First he pointed the gun at the bouncer who had kicked him out. Then he started pointing it everywhere, at anyone. He was super thin, with a neat little goatee and these red leather shoes. He didn't look that harsh, but he was wired on something – coke or maybe meth. That's what Chris thought, anyhow. He knew right away that a guy in that condition, wearing those shoes, was capable of anything.

'What did the bouncer do?'

'Oh – he was shitting himself.'

We were driving along Georgia towards Stanley Park, with Chris riding shotgun and Karen in the back. I'd decided to take the Lions Gate Bridge across to the North Shore, since there'd be less chance of hitting a police road check.

'Everybody freaked out,' Karen said. 'Screaming and crying. Some just ran.'

'Only the smart ones. The stupid ones dropped to the ground and covered their heads – like they thought the sky was falling.'

'Like chicken little, eh?'

'They got a little chicken, all right.'

I guess I couldn't really blame them. I mean, it's the kind of situation nothing can prepare you for. There's no telling how somebody will react. Like Karen. When she gets scared – and I mean really terrified – she starts laughing hysterically. She did it in the woods the night we told her about the paperbag killer, and apparently she did the same thing outside the Roxy – so loud that everybody heard. Including the guy with the gun. He thought she was mocking him, I guess. Or maybe that she didn't believe it was for real. I don't know.

But basically, he raised the gun and pointed it right at her head.

Somebody must have reported it, because the incident got mentioned in the *Sun* – just a little article on page four. The thing is, they didn't even know who Chris was. Or the guy, for that matter. They assumed he was American, partly because of the gun, but also because he'd said. 'You fucking Canadians'. It would have been a pretty bizarre thing for a Canadian to say. Other than that, though, they got most of the facts wrong – like always. To begin with, they called it 'an altercation involving a firearm'. That's the most idiotic thing I ever heard. A guy points a gun at Karen, for no reason, and they call it 'an altercation'. Plus, they missed out the best part, as far as I'm concerned. I don't know how. I mean, there were tons of witnesses and I'm sure some of them must have seen what Chris did.

'All of a sudden I was on the sidewalk.' Karen leaned forward into the front seat, talking super fast. She was dying to fill me in. 'And I heard this weird popping sound. At first I didn't know what had happened. I thought I'd been shot. I thought I was dead.'

'That's crazy.'

What had actually happened was even crazier. Chris had shoved her out of the way – sort of down and to the ground. Then he broke a beer bottle on his own head. I doubt anybody knew what he was doing. Even he didn't know what he was doing. In situations like that, Chris didn't think. He just reacted, even if his reaction was totally insane. Afterwards, he stood there dripping beer and blood, holding out the broken bottle like a sword. A very small glass sword.

'Holy shit, man,' I said. 'You actually stared him down?'

Chris shrugged. 'I just told him not to point his shitty gun at my girlfriend.'

I'm pretty sure that was the only time he ever called Karen his girlfriend. Of course, the fucking papers missed all that out. But they got the last part right, at least. They said the guy with the gun fired two shots in the air, then took off. He did, too. He backed down, like a total bed-wetter. And that was it. Chris and Karen walked away. The end.

'You must have been terrified, man.'

I said that to him, later – after we'd snuck into the aquarium. That was the last thing the three of us did on their date. It wasn't planned or anything. It just sort of happened.

'Yeah,' he said, 'I was.'

'Really?'

Hardly anything terrified Chris, but guns were an exception.

'Sure.'

Karen said, 'But you didn't look that terrified.'

'Fear's like pain. If you ignore it, you can make it go away.'

That was arguably the greatest thing he ever said.

## 42

Dollarton isn't really a highway. They just call it a highway, even though it's only got two lanes. Don't ask me why. But near the bridge it connects with the real highway – The Upper Levels – and that's where we headed. We flew up the cut, between that long corridor of pines, then swooped like a dive-bomber towards Lonsdale. It was the hottest day of the year. They said that later, on the news. It was like Judgement Day out there. Old people started dying in their apartments. Kids came home with bright red blisters on their necks and shoulders, as if they'd caught some strange disease. Also, this black dog over at Ambleside went crazy with heat exhaustion and bit a baby.

In other words, it was hot.

Chris said, 'Mrs Reever's funeral was a shitshow.'

He flicked his cigarette out the window. The rushing air snatched it back and it landed on the highway behind us, skittering sparks. On the radio the Chinese DJ was jabbering excitedly about something or other – probably about the insanely high temperatures.

'There's got to be a better way to do it.'

'I heard about this guy,' I said. 'I think he made fireworks or something. But he was sweet. He got himself cremated, then had them pack all his ashes into this one firework – the biggest firework he'd ever made – and shot it right over English Bay. Boom.'

Chris grinned. 'No shit?'

'No shit.'

The police radio crackled for a bit. Then a woman started talking. She didn't say anything interesting, though. She just announced a bunch of numbers, and an address over in Kitsilano. We were a long way from Kits. We were a long way from anywhere. Chris blew by the Cap Mall exit and traffic started falling off. Wind rushed past our windows. It poured into the cab, tugging at our shirts and sucking things off the dashboard: receipts, parking passes, napkins, candy wrappers. It kept us cool, at least. Outside the whole world was melting but we were going so fast nothing could catch us – not even the heat.

'Keep talking,' Chris said.

'Yeah?'

'Yeah.'

'I heard about another guy.' I hadn't, but I made it up. 'He didn't have a funeral. He just got his kids to bury him in the middle of the forest, with a tree planted in his belly. Then as he rotted the tree sucked up all his nutrients. It was like he became part of the tree.'

'Did the tree ever die?'

'Yeah, but not for a long time – not until his kids were dead and even his grandkids. Then this family cut the tree down and used it to build their dinner table.'

'That's nuts.'

He swung wide around a turn. The tyres screamed and we fishtailed into the next lane. I braced myself against the door, waiting for an impact that never came.

Chris said, 'Promise me you won't go to my funeral.'

I promised him. I kept my promise, too. I didn't go. Nobody understood why.

## 43

We threw them together.

They sailed into the air, bright gold against blue sky. The red and white ribbons stretched out behind, like little comet tails. There was a moment – just a moment – when they reached the peak of their arc and hung there, as if all the clocks in the world had stopped at exactly the same time. Then the medals started falling. They streaked towards the water, getting faster and faster and faster. Just before they hit one of them caught the sun, flashing out a mysterious signal. A second later we heard two little plops and they were gone.

'How's it feel?' I asked.

'The same.'

The sea was flat and still and glaring, like a giant piece of sheet metal. Two kayakers crept across the surface in the distance.

Chris said, 'Let's drink those brews.'

He pulled two Kokanees out of his backpack. We sat on a piece of driftwood and sipped them without talking. Chris hadn't been talking much, lately. Not since he'd found out about Jules and Karen. Not since he'd beat the shit out of Jules. The noise from the public beach at Cates was softened by distance. I could hear splashing and shouting and laughing but it was like the sounds weren't real. Or we weren't real. It was hard to say.

'Hey, check it out.'

A fluorescent green circle floated near shore, bobbing in the surf. I went to pick it up. The edge was cracked but other than that it looked like it might fly.

'Want to play?'

I assumed he'd say no. Chris hadn't played frisbee in his entire life.

'Let's shotgun, first,' he said.

Our beers were almost empty. We drained them and got out two more. Chris turned the cans upside down and used his dad's knife to puncture holes in the sides. I took mine, keeping it level so the beer didn't spill, and got my forefinger beneath the pull-tab.

'Ready?'

'Ready.'

We turned the cans upright and fastened our mouths over the holes, pulling the tabs at the same time. The beer rushed out and I started swallowing, but Chris finished first. He threw his can down in the sand. I never beat him at shotgunning. He had this way of opening his throat and guzzling ridiculously fast. It was another one of his super abilities – like his extra hard skull. I finished a few seconds after him and we both burped two or three times in a row. My eyes started watering and I could feel all that beer bubbling in my brain.

We were ready to play some frisbee.

'Come on, man. This'll be awesome.'

'Hell yeah!' Chris said. 'Toss that bitch over here.'

I did. It wobbled a little in flight but other than that it flew pretty straight. Chris snagged it easily. I didn't think he would but he managed it. Then he waved me back.

'Go long, Razor. Go long.'

I ran away from him, turning to look over my shoulder. His first throw wasn't so hot. The frisbee tilted on its side and curved out across the water. I went for it, anyways. I ran into the shallows and tried this awesome catch – stretching myself out like a wide receiver diving for the football. I caught it and landed right in the water. Splash. Then I popped up, holding the frisbee above my head so Chris could see I'd made the grab.

'That's genius,' he shouted. 'Give me one.'

I whipped the frisbee back at him, aiming it straight and low along the shore. His catch wasn't quite as cool as mine, but it was still pretty cool. He reached for the frisbee and bobbled it a little before gathering it into his chest. Then he spun around and fell over backwards into the water. He came out sputtering and choking and laughing his ass off. He hadn't laughed for weeks and now it all poured out.

'Keep it coming!' I called.

He fired the frisbee back. It went on like that, with us flopping around in the water and making these super dramatic catches.

'Frisbee rocks, man.'

'It rocks the Casbah, all right.'

'We're rocking like Casper the ghost out here.'

I don't know how long we played for. Hours, maybe. We played until we were dying of thirst, and then we played one-handed while we swilled more beer. And after the last beer was gone we still kept playing. It was as if the smooth, spinning disc had hypnotised us, and for a while nothing else seemed to matter – not Karen or Jules or Bates or anything. Whoever had had left that frisbee there was the biggest idiot on the entire planet. It wasn't an ordinary frisbee. Actually, it was the least ordinary frisbee I'd ever seen.

'This thing's magic.'

That's what Chris said, just before he threw it away. By then we were so tired we could barely stand up. We staggered onto the beach, dizzy and gasping and waterlogged, and he whipped the frisbee out across the waves. It flew straight, rising on the wind, and eventually settled flat like a spaceship coming in to land. At the last second, I lost it in the glare of the water – way out there – so I didn't actually see it touch down.

'Man, I'm beat.'

'You look like a bit of a beatnik.'

'Yeah, a hardcore beanbag trick.'

After that, morning became afternoon. A hot wind scorched along Indian Arm, stirring the water. It smelled of rotten seaweed and dead fish. The tide sucked itself out, leaving warm puddles of brine among the rocks, and the sun got brighter and brighter, like a bomb going off in the sky. There was nothing to do but stretch out in the shade. We lay there for a while and then these two kids flew by on skateboards, barrelling down the path that led back towards the public beach and concession. They were racing, I think. Or maybe they were just trying to go as fast as they could. Either way, it made me super sad.

'I want to be a kid again.'

Chris made a sound in his throat, like a growl.

We closed our eyes and listened to the waves as the heat cooked seawater off our skin, leaving us all salty. He'd never been as calm as he was right then. I could sense that something had changed in him, that he was ready. All the fury and rage had melted away. It was just like in a samurai film, when the old master makes his apprentice complete a bunch of impossible tasks – like walking on hot coals and breaking bricks with his hands and balancing on tree stumps. Then, once he's done all that, he's ready for the final showdown: ready to fight, ready to kill, and ready to die.

That's how ready Chris was.

'Do you love her?'

I asked him that, just before we drifted off. He didn't answer for a long time.

Then he said, 'Not any more.'

We fell asleep.

It wasn't a light sleep, either. We konked right out and started dreaming. I did, at least. Chris never got the chance to tell me if he did, too. But I think he did. I think he had the exact same dream as me. You know – almost like we were in each other's dreams. A shared dream. I don't know if that's even possible and I don't care, either. Basically, we had this dream. There was water in the dream, water that looked too still – as if it had been frozen in a photograph, or one of my dad's old slides. There were no waves in the water. Not even a ripple. There were no swimmers or boats or buoys or gulls or fish or seaweed, either. There was nothing in the water and nothing in the sky above the water.

'There's nowhere left to go.'

That was Chris. He stood beside me, naked. I was naked, too, but neither of us cared about our nakedness. It was as if we'd never worn clothes before. I could see the desert stretching away behind him. Two sets of footprints led back across the sand. Our footprints. I'd followed him into the desert. I'd tracked him for miles and found him standing here. Somehow in the dream I knew all that, just like I knew that he was right: there was nowhere left to go.

'We could stay here,' I suggested.

'No. Let's go in.'

'Now?'

'There's no point waiting around.'

He took a step forward and I followed. I expected the water

to be cold, but it wasn't. It wasn't warm, either. It was the exact same temperature as my body. We took another step, and another. The water rose up to our knees, then our waists. Once a part of you submerged, it was gone. You couldn't see anything beneath the surface. It was dark and sort of solid-looking, like blue oil paint. But Chris never hesitated. Pretty soon it rose to our chests, then our necks. On the next step, my foot didn't touch the ground. We swam a little ways, just dog-paddling.

'Take a deep breath,' Chris said. 'We won't be coming up.'

I looked back towards the desert. There wasn't much to say goodbye to, really.

'Ready?'

'Ready.'

It was just like that day at Julian's pool. We took a breath and submerged. Once we were beneath the surface, the water seemed impossibly clear. It went on and on and on, like a void. I could see forever, but there was nothing to see – not even a bottom. Chris led me straight down. We kicked along, frog-style, as the pressure built up in our lungs. After a while I started to panic. I mean, I needed air. I wanted to breathe. But I didn't even consider returning to the surface. Somehow I just understood that it wasn't an option.

Then Chris tapped me on the shoulder.

He was pointing straight ahead, to this dark shape in the water. It came closer and closer, getting bigger and bigger. Then there was more than one of them. Sharks. We were surrounded by sharks, naked, and out of breath. We were fucked, obviously. I looked over at Chris, hoping he'd know what to do. But I'd never seen him look so helpless.

That was when Bates woke us up.

# 44

We almost hit this lady near Taylor Way.

Something must have happened to her car, because she'd pulled over and popped her hood. We saw all that as we tore around the corner. Also, we saw her step onto the highway. She was this middle-aged lady with a huge ass and tight clothes. I guess she just had no idea how fast we were going. She stood in the middle of the road, waving her arms back and forth over her head to flag us down. There was no way Chris could stop. He didn't even have time to slow down. He swung wide into the other lane and blasted straight past her. She screamed, I think. Then she fell down. We didn't hit her or anything – it was more like we'd blown her right off her feet. I felt a little sorry for her, actually. That's the surreal thing about driving around in a police car. People see one and instantly assume help is on the way.

But in this case, obviously, help was going to be a long time coming.

Just after that, the highway straightened out and became perfectly flat. A layer of fresh asphalt had been laid down, rich and dark as dirt. The yellow centre lines were brand new, and you could see tracks where drivers had changed lanes while the paint was still wet. It was so smooth it felt like we weren't even moving. I mean, the wheels kept turning, and the landscape flowed by in an endless stream, but there was no sense of motion. It reminded me of those old films they always show on late night TV. You know – where two people are driving along and the background is projected onto a screen behind them.

'Fuck Julian,' Chris said. 'Fuck him and his heaven. Even if it existed, I wouldn't want to go.'

'Why not?'

'Think about it. There's no sex in heaven, or beer, or fighting. There's no oceans and no rivers and no swimming and no pot. There's none of the things we like to do.'

'Yeah. My dad says we're hedonists.'

'What are those?'

'Like we just want to chill out and get high and drunk all the time.'

'Totally. And you can't do any of that shit in heaven. In heaven, all you do is stand around trying on different turtlenecks. It's a rule. Everybody has to wear one.'

'Even God?'

'God wears the biggest turtleneck of them all.'

I snickered, imagining it. 'Then why are people so stoked to go there?'

'No choice.' Chris cleared his throat and hawked out the window. 'It's like when all the bars close downtown. The only thing left open is this one super expensive club. People will do anything to get in: throw cash at the bouncer, sneak in the back doors, pull a gun, whatever. But once you're inside, you see how shitty it actually is. Then you wish you'd never come in the first place. All you want to do is go home. But you can't.'

'That sounds lame.'

'It is. But don't worry – they wouldn't let us into club heaven. We don't even believe in God for Christ's sake.'

'I'd rather go to hell, anyway,' I said.

'Me, too.' Chris changed lanes to blow past this grey Toyota van – one of those ancient snub-nosed models. Then he said, 'Tell me what hell would be like, Razor.'

'The thing about hell,' I said, 'is that it's not even hot. It's actually super cold. All the walls are frosty, and all the floors are ice. The whole place is tinted sort of blue, too.'

I wasn't really making it all up. I'd seen a version of hell like that in some movie. I think it was *A Christmas Carol* – this fairly old-school version of it.

Chris said, 'That doesn't sound so bad.'

'They don't torture people or poke them with pitchforks, either.'

'How can it be hell, then?'

'I don't know.' I tried to remember. 'I guess because there's nothing to do.'

'Whatever. We could just bust out some skates and start a pick-up hockey game.'

I grinned. 'For sure. Me and you would play up front, and we'd hire a couple of real hellbenders to play defence for us.'

'Yeah. Like Bob Probert and Jack the Ripper.'

We both thought about that. It sounded pretty sweet.

'Too bad it's not real,' he said. 'Too bad we can't actually go to hell.'

'Where are we going, man?' I asked.

Chris didn't answer. By then, he knew where he was going, I'm pretty sure. The only thing he didn't know was whether or not I was coming with him.


## 45


'They won't catch us. Trust me.'

He'd climbed up onto this brick wall – about eight feet high and two feet thick. Lying flat on his stomach, he reached down and offered her his hand. Karen didn't take risks. She'd never broken a law in her life – except for smoking weed. And that's not even really illegal any more in Canada. At least in BC, anyways. So obviously this was going to be a bigger deal for her than for either of us. But when he said that, because of what he'd done at the Roxy, and the look on his face, she believed him.

She took his hand.

It was the last thing they did on their date – after the shitty dinner, after the guy with the gun, after chilling with those junkies in Opium Park, after I'd driven down to pick them up. Chris got it in his head that he wanted to break into the Vancouver Aquarium. Don't ask me why. We went there together, back when we were little, and Chris had hated the place. The killer whale was super sick that day, but the trainers still forced her to come out. She flapped feebly around her tank while they urged her on with this shrill whistle and a bucket of herring. She didn't want to do any tricks or stunts. She just wanted to be left alone. It was arguably the most depressing thing we'd ever seen. I think she died pretty soon after that.

But basically, it wasn't like Chris was an aquarium fanatic or anything. The idea just kind of occurred to him while I was driving them back to the North Shore.

'Do you guys want to check out the aquarium?'

We were cruising through Stanley Park. That's where the aquarium is – in the park.

'I'm pretty sure it's closed, man.'

'We can break in.'

Karen was looking out the window, nibbling on her nail. 'I don't think so, Chris.'

'Sure. It'll be easy.'

He was right. It wasn't hard to break in at all. The hard part was actually finding the aquarium. At night, in the dark, it's super easy to get lost in Stanley Park. I cruised in circles like a demented goldfish for at least an hour. Maybe longer. But once we finally got there, we saw that the only thing standing in our way was that brick wall. And Karen.

She sort of got cold feet at the last minute.

'Let's forget it. We should go pick up my Jeep and go home.'

'We'll do that later. This'll be awesome.'

'I don't know, Chris.'

'They won't catch us. Trust me.'

And she did. She trusted him more than anybody, and he trusted her just as much. He trusted her to keep him calm, and to help him understand all the shitty things in the world that didn't seem to make any sense – like filet mignon. That's part of being in love, I guess.

Then again, betrayal is part of being in love, too.


On the other side of the wall, there were no sensors or lights or security guards or cameras or anything. There was just this series of connecting pools and tanks, each with a different kind of sea animal. We crept past the seals, who were sleeping, and the sea lions, who weren't, and at the aquatic petting zoo Chris stopped to touch the sea anemone.

'Hey,' he said, 'it sort of feels like pussy.'

'Chris! That's gross.'

'Razor, touch this thing.'

I did. It was all soft and wet and slippery.

'Now you know.'

Even Karen agreed with him – apparently it really did feel like one. After that we stole some nachos and pop from one of the concession stands, then tiptoed over to the beluga whale tank. I hung a bit to the back, not really saying anything. I mean, I didn't want to intrude. It was their date, after all. I was just kind of along for the ride. And to drive.

'Wow,' Karen said.

'Shhh.'

He wasn't scared of being caught. He was just worried about disturbing the whales. At least five of them were visible in the darkness – these fat white shapes that looked like giant ghosts. Chris and Karen forgot all about their nachos and pop. Instead they stood together and watched the whales, while I stood by myself and watched the two of them.

'Can they breathe underwater?' Karen asked him.

'No.' Chris shook his head. He knew tons about whales. Not as much as me, but still a lot – mainly from all the nature programmes my dad showed him when he stayed with us. 'They're mammals. They've got to breathe air. But they can hold their breath for a super long time, and they live mostly underwater. They eat and screw and play and die and even give birth underwater.'

'That must be amazing.'

Chris pulled out a joint. He always had a joint on him somewhere or other – behind his ear or up his sleeve or tucked into his sock. He was like a marijuana magician.

'Want to smoke this?'

'Sure.'

He took the first couple of drags to get it going. They didn't really offer me any, and I didn't really ask. I'd started to pretend I was more like their bodyguard. You know – the kind who doesn't ever talk and is almost invisible, until danger looms. Then, suddenly, he springs into action and kicks the bad guy right in the face and saves the day.

'Check it out.'

The whales must have noticed us or something, because one of them broke away from the pod and drifted over. I'd forgotten how weird beluga whales look up close. Their skin is slick and smooth and totally white, like bleached rubber, and the dome of their forehead sticks up in this super strange way. As it cruised by, it rolled onto its side and sort of ogled them with one eye.

'Chris – it's staring right at us!'

'I know.'

Pretty soon another whale came over to check us out. And another. They cruised past one by one. I guess they weren't used to people being around at night. Whales are curious like that. After Chris and Karen had finished the joint, the first whale circled back to say goodbye. This time, it raised a flipper out of the water and hung half-upside down – like a capsized boat. The flipper was close enough to touch, so that's exactly what Chris did. He reached out and stroked the tip with the palm of his hand. The whale didn't mind at all. It rolled back over and blasted a big fountain of water out its blowhole – spraying the three of us – before fading away into the dark.

Chris tucked the roach in his pocket, and leaned over to kiss Karen.

'I told you this would be awesome,' he whispered.

Afterwards, we got back in the car and drove to the Lions Gate Bridge. It took about half an hour, because of the one-way system. Stanley Park is just so fucking huge. Supposedly, tons of gay guys go there at night to bang in the bushes, but we didn't see any. We didn't see a single person. There weren't any joggers

223

or cyclists or rollerbladers or shitty people walking their dogs, and for a few minutes, when we first reached the bridge, there weren't even any other cars. It was just like Chris's favourite movie – that one where everybody on earth suddenly disappears for no reason at all, except for these two guys and a girl.

At the centre of the bridge, Chris told me to pull over. He wanted to look down at the water, so him and Karen got out. I put the hazard lights on and stayed in the car, just keeping it fairly casual. At first I switched on the radio and put one foot up on the dashboard. Then I saw that they were talking, so I opened the window a little bit. I wasn't eavesdropping on them or anything. I was just trying to hear what they were saying. I could, too. Barely.

Karen said, 'That's got to be bullshit.'

'No – I swear.'

Chris was telling her about this tourist who fell off the bridge trying to take a photo – this seventy-year-old Japanese guy. He lived, too. Nobody knows how, but he lived. He must have been quite small and spry and light. Like a Japanese feather hitting the water.

Chris said, 'So many people jump off here to kill themselves. Then this guy falls off by accident and totally survives. Trippy, huh?'

'When I'm a bird,' Karen said, 'I'll be able to jump off whenever I want. I'll dive straight down and wait until the very last minute before swooping up and away.'

Chris laughed. 'You're never going to be a bird, Karen.'

He hated hearing her talk like that. Normally, he couldn't even be bothered to discuss it. But that night, for once, I could tell he felt differently. He was so content that nothing could phase him – not even her and her reincarnation.

'Yes I am.' She reached out to hold his hand. 'I'm going to come back as a beautiful bald eagle, a girl eagle, with white feathers.'

'That's such bullshit.'

'Oh, yeah? So what happens when you die, then?'

'What do you think happens? Nothing.'

She thought about that, but not for very long.

'Okay. But let's just say you believe in reincarnation. What would you want to be?'

'You mean if I had no other choice?

'Yeah.'

Chris muttered something that I couldn't hear. I assumed he'd told her to forget about it or whatever, but later Karen told me what he'd actually said. I don't think she realised how much that meant. It was the same as if he'd told her that he loved her. Maybe, on some level, she understood that. I hope she did – because that was as good as it got between them.

Within a week, it all went to shit.


# 46


Those holding cells were cold and cramped, like tombs.

We were too drunk to sleep so we stayed up all night talking. It was just like the sleepovers we'd had as kids – except we were hammered and in jail. Also, we weren't in the same room. Chris was in one cell and I was in another across from him. We had to talk to each other through these little sliding panels at the base of the doors. They kind of looked like cat flaps, actually. The cops are supposed to use them to feed the prisoners.

They never fed us, though.

When we first got to the station, they fingerprinted us and took our photos and made us fill out forms and did all the stuff you'd expect. They also did some stuff you wouldn't expect – like take our shoes. And give us bracelets. No joke. We each got a little plastic wrist band, with a number and barcode and the words 'North Vancouver RCMP' printed on it. I guess it's how they keep track of prisoners or something. Then they dragged us down a hallway and shoved us in those cells. Chris hated it. He hated being locked up, especially in a space that was all confined like that. In some ways, it's pretty lucky that he died when he did. If they'd caught him, he never would have been able to handle juvie.

'Fuck this! Fuck you goddamned cop pigs!'

I heard him throw himself against the door. Then I heard him kicking it. He kicked it maybe a dozen times, barefoot. The echoes rang out all along the hallway – these deep, booming echoes. It reminded me of this eighties horror movie we rented one time, about an old man who finds out his house is haunted by some kid who got murdered in the bathtub. As he drowned he kicked the side of the tub again and again. That's what the old guy keeps hearing, and that's exactly what it sounded like in jail when Chris started booting the door.

'Chris!' I shouted.

He kicked the door once more for good measure. Then he stopped and opened his catflap. His face appeared at the tiny square.

'Yeah?'

'I've got to take a leak.'

There weren't even any toilets in those cells. They were really crappy cells.

'Screw it, man. Use the drain.'

I hadn't seen it, but there was this drain in one corner. I leaned over it and tried to aim straight down, but it was impossible to go in one place. All that punch was catching up to me and I swayed back and forth, spattering piss in wild patterns. The stench caught in my throat. First it made me gag, and then it made me puke. No joke. I ended up puking and pissing at the same time, like some kind of crazed animal with a degenerative brain disease. No wonder they'd locked me away. I was obviously unfit for human society.

'Razor!'

'Huh?'

'You okay?'

'I'm puking my guts out over here.'

'Duking it out, huh?'

'I'm the duke of puke, all right.'

I fell against the door and slid down to the ground. Sometimes puking helps a guy. Not this time. Whenever I opened my eyes the whole room spun around me in slow circles. Also, the lights in my cell were broken and wouldn't stop flickering. It was like being trapped in the very worst section of a funhouse. The only thing that made me feel better was closing my eyes and lying absolutely still. I didn't move more than a few inches the entire night. I didn't sleep, either. Like I said, all we did was talk. It was pretty awesome, actually. We talked about a lot of stuff we'd never talked about before, and some stuff we'd never get the chance to talk about again.

'What do you think that guy meant?' Chris asked. 'That guy at the funeral.'

This was one of the things we'd never mentioned.

'About Mrs Reever?'

'Yeah.'

227

'I don't know, man. He was pretty drunk.'

'But what do you think he was saying?'

I tried to remember. It seemed like the funeral had been a long time ago.

'He said that she was crazy,' I said. 'That's all.'

'I thought he was saying something else.'

'He was saying a lot of stuff.'

'I thought he said she was better off dead.'

'Yeah. He did.' I rolled over to spit on the floor. I couldn't get the taste of vomit out of my mouth. 'But I don't know if he meant it, you know, literally and shit.'

'What does that mean?'

'Like I don't know if he actually meant it.'

'Fuck it,' Chris said. 'It doesn't matter, anyway. Maybe she was crazy. Maybe she wasn't. She's still just straight up dead. People pretend death is this big deal, but whatever. Being dead isn't much different from never being born.'

'Except if you've never been born, you don't know what living is like.'

'It's all the same when you're dead. Dead people can't remember that shit.'

I was too drunk to get my head around that. It just seemed so bizarre.

I said, 'My shrink told me dying is like having an orgasm.'

'Not even.'

'That's what French people think, anyway.'

'French people are awesome.'

'I wish I was French.'

'Me, too. Then we could fuck each other to death.'

We both cracked up. Our laughter sounded super weird – partly because of the eerie echoes in those cells, and partly

228

because I hadn't heard Chris laugh like that for a long time. Now that I think about it, I'm pretty sure he didn't laugh again until the day he died.

In the morning a bald cop I hadn't seen before came to get us. He led us back to the room where they'd checked us in and taken our fingerprints. It was a pretty basic room, with three or four desks and some storage lockers lined up against one wall. There were a bunch of other cops in there, too – including Bates. I couldn't believe he was still around. He must have stayed at the station all night, waiting to see if we'd be charged. Luckily he didn't get to deal with us in any way. He just stood on the opposite side of the room, arms crossed, sort of staring us down and at the same time trying to pretend he didn't give a shit.

'All right,' the bald cop said, 'you kids are free to go.'

They let us keep the bracelets, which was pretty cool, and they gave us back our shoes. They also gave us a speech about respecting authority and staying away from booze. Nobody made it clear why they decided not to press charges. I mean, I know my dad had a hand in it, but he didn't bother to explain what he'd actually said or done. That's the thing about my dad. He's a super savvy lawyer. He knows all these loopholes – these legal loopholes – and he's not afraid to use them. Plus, I guess they figured that a night in jail was enough to make us think twice about fighting any more cops.

They know better, now.

My dad was waiting for us on the front steps of the station. They'd called him in the middle of the night and he'd driven over. They didn't call Chris's mom. On the forms we had to fill out, Chris put down my dad as his legal guardian.

It wasn't exactly true, but it worked. Which meant my old man was the one we had to face.

'That's him.'

'Where?'

'Over there.'

We shuffled down the steps in the morning sunshine, nursing the worst hangovers of our lives. The funniest part was that Chris was still wearing his toga. My dad watched us approach with this deadpan expression on his face – the expression he uses when I've done something totally unforgivable.

'Are you two insane?' he asked.

My dad loves that word. Insane. He loves it so much he asked us the same question over and over. Considering how pissed off he was, Chris and I were both pretty surprised by what he did. He drove us straight over to this restaurant on Upper Lonsdale and bought us breakfast. It was a fifties diner, with red plastic booths and old movie posters all over the walls. They even had one of James Dean in his leather jacket, hacking a dart and looking pretty awesome. We mopped up poached eggs with fatty bacon and scraps of burnt toast while Elvis crooned on the jukebox. The waitress didn't know what to make of Chris in his toga. She didn't mention it, though. The mood at our table wasn't exactly sociable. After we finished, me and Chris sat there waiting for my dad to give us a lecture that never came.

'Feel better?' he asked.

We nodded. We actually did feel a lot better.

'Let's get you home, then.'

The whole drive back he seemed pretty distracted. He drummed his fingers on the steering wheel and kept fiddling with the radio. He was obviously having some kind of anxiety attack. At the same time, I have to give him credit.

Throughout all the shit that happened, he didn't once try to pin it on Chris. That's what Julian's parents did. And Karen's. After the fallout from the toga party, they didn't want her to go anywhere near him. That was fine, because he didn't want to go anywhere near her, either.

When we dropped Chris off my dad said, 'Chris, if you ever need to talk – about anything – you know I'm around, right?'

That's my dad, all right. I mean, he's hopelessly out of touch – Chris would never have taken him up on an offer like that – but at least he was trying. It's important to try, for Christ's sake. At the same time, I'm not saying my dad was totally cool about it or anything. He still gave me that lecture, after we got home. He dropped it on me in the kitchen.

'Look,' he said, 'I know Chris is your best friend. I know he's had a raw deal, and you've got to look out for him. But these were police officers. These were officers of the law. Chris slammed the door in their face. Do you think that was an intelligent thing to do?'

This speech was really taking its toll on him. I could tell how badly he wanted a beer and I felt like saying, 'Hey pops – why don't we both grab a couple of cold ones and forget about the whole thing?' I didn't, though. Instead I sort of hung my head and said, 'I guess not.'

'Just because you're friends with Chris doesn't mean you have to get involved in situations like that. If he's going to do something foolish, you don't have to do the same.' He squeezed my bicep, as if he wanted me to respond. 'Okay?'

I nodded. It was funny. For the first time ever, I felt a little older than my dad. You know – like I was humouring him. I understood what he was trying to say, but things had gone way, way beyond that. There was no use even talking about it, really. I might as well have been on a runaway train, listening to him give me advice through a radio.

## 47

Karen told me everything. Don't ask me why. I guess she had to tell somebody, and she was too scared to tell Chris, so she decided to tell me. As soon as she started she couldn't stop. It came out all at once, like a spurt of vomit. We were on the phone. Usually I phoned her but this time she'd phoned me. I was happy about that, until I found out why.

'We got arrested,' I said, trying to show off. 'We spent the night in jail.'

'I have to tell you something.'

'Sure. What's up?'

I was sprawled on my belly in our basement. Her first words stabbed me right in the spine, nailing me to the floor. After that I couldn't move. I felt like a butterfly being pinned into an insect collection. Each sentence twisted the pin a little deeper. It pierced my lungs and speared my heart and burst through my chest. I started crying – I couldn't help it.

I asked her: 'Why?'

'I was drunk,' she said, sobbing, 'I was so drunk.'

She had been. I'd seen her. But it was no excuse. Not unless he'd raped her.

'Did he rape you?'

'No.'

After that neither of us said anything for about thirty seconds. The telephone receiver felt hot as a blow dryer against my ear. I listened as she choked on her tears, trying to bring herself under control. I wasn't crying like that. I was crying in this completely bizarre way. My face felt all twisted and these shudders were wracking my body, but I was wasn't making any sounds. I don't think Karen even knew I was crying. Through the window, I could see two birds pecking happily at our lawn. One of them came up with a worm and flew off.

'What's going to happen?' Karen whispered.

'He won't ever talk to you again.'

'Don't say that.'

'He'll hate you forever.'

'You're lying!'

I wasn't, though, and she knew it. This was the end of everything. Outside, houses crumbled and bridges collapsed and skyscrapers toppled. It was like a miracle. Actually, it was more like the exact opposite of a miracle. A catastrophe, I guess. Or an apocalypse. Jules had stuck his dick inside her, and the whole world just fell apart.

'You tell him or I will,' I said, and hung up.

I've imagined it so many times it's like I actually saw them. Julian is always on top. His eyes are closed and he's grimacing in this really disgusting way – almost like it's hurting him. Sometimes he's still wearing that stupid laurel crown. Other times he's totally naked. Either way, he doesn't know what he's doing. His movements are jerky and mechanical, like a giant robot gigolo that's only programmed to screw. He throws himself into her again and again and again, gritting his teeth and making these strange little pig sounds. He's not paying any attention to her. He could be banging away at anything, but she doesn't care. She's too drunk to care. She spreads out wide as a starfish, receptive and exposed. And once they're really going at it, once he's really giving it to her, she starts moaning and running her hands all over his bloated muscles. She even leans forward to lick his big birthmark. You know – just sort of lapping at it with her tongue. Jules loves that. That pushes him over the edge.

Somehow, his coup had succeeded.

Once I recovered from the shock, it didn't seem that improbable. It just seemed pathetic. And cheap. I don't know. The whole thing is so shitty I don't even like thinking about it. Or talking about it. Karen wanted to talk about it. She phoned me a bunch of times, after he died, but I kept hanging up on her. It's not that I blame her for his death. Not really. I just don't see the point. It's impossible for her to understand how important she was to him. I mean, I don't think he ever told her. He never even told me. He didn't have to, though. It was obvious. She was this soothing spring he'd found in the middle of the desert.

Then she vanished, like a mirage.

## 48

We came up behind this Volkswagen van, lumbering along like a fat drunk on a bicycle. They hadn't finished repaving that part of the highway – which meant there was only one lane going each way. A bus ploughed past in the opposite direction, followed by a long line of cars. Chris couldn't overtake. We dropped down to sixty, waiting for a break in traffic.

'Smell that?' Chris asked.

A magic, smoky scent drifted in through the open windows, tickling my nostrils. The hippy driving the van was obviously burning a fat one. Until then, I'd totally forgotten about our bag of weed. At the beach I'd picked it up without thinking. Now I knew why. I'd picked it up so I could reach into my pocket and hold it out, super casually, like a gambler who's just drawn the exact card he needs.

'Check this out.'

Chris glanced over, then did a little double take.

'What the hell?'

'I took it when Bates dropped it.'

'You genius. Let's hotbox this thing.'

We both rolled up our windows. I opened the bag and pulled out our pipe and carefully broke up bits of bud with my fingernails. It smelled so rich and green I wanted to eat it. I worked carefully, almost solemnly. This was going to be the most important bowl we'd ever smoked so I had to make it a good one. I added pinches of weed to the pipe and tapped it down with my thumb. Then I sparked the lighter and worked the valve as I inhaled. The first hoot went straight to my brain, spinning me off into giddiness.

I offered up the pipe. 'Here, man. It's going good.'

Chris took it in his right hand and drove with his left. Sweet smoke filled the cab, wrapping us up like silk. We passed the pipe back and forth, back and forth. I'd packed it pretty tight and it burned for ages. By the end my fingers felt all fat and useless, like baby sausages, which only happens when I'm absolutely fried. I started experimenting with them. I flexed them and wiggled them and pressed them against each other.

'How you feeling, Razor?'

Chris couldn't keep a straight face. He knew all about me and my fat fingers.

'I'm rocking and rolling, man.'

'Rocking and reeling, huh?'

'Yep. Keeping it real, all right.'

'Hey,' Chris said, 'how the hell do you work the siren on this thing?'

'Beats me.'

'Come on. We need the siren to scare the shit out of these stupid hippies.'

I said, 'But I like hippies.'

'Hippies are dinosaurs.'

We both started fiddling with all the buttons and switches on the dash. We got the windshield wipers and fluid going, then the signal and hazard lights. Chris even honked the horn a couple of times. By that point we were both laughing our asses off, but it took another five minutes to find that stupid siren. I don't even know which one of us hit the button. All of a sudden it just came on, out of nowhere. The red and blue lights started flashing, too.

The Volkswagen van dropped down to about twenty klicks, guilty as anything. Chris didn't even give them time to stop. He swung across the centre line and gunned it, overtaking. I stared at them as we roared past. The driver was this guy in a straw hat with a scruffy beard. His girlfriend had tiny breasts and huge sunglasses. In a lot of ways, they reminded me of my parents in those old slides from South America. At first, they looked terrified. Then they saw Chris grinning at the wheel and me holding the pipe in my hands. After that their faces went totally blank, as if they'd both been hit on the head at exactly the same time. They'd seen us, all right, but they couldn't really believe what they'd seen.

For that reason, I'm pretty sure they didn't rat us out.

Chris switched the siren off but left the windows up. We

rocketed along in our cocoon of smoke and music. It didn't seem so bright out any more. It was as if a veil had been draped over our car. Everything outside looked murky and dim and strange. Just then, when we were more seared than we'd ever been, when we were going faster than we'd ever gone, the police radio crackled and dispatch started talking. That had happened before, but this was the first time the woman actually seemed to be speaking to us.

'Dispatch calling car twenty-six. Come in, over.'

We stared at the speaker, like a couple of cavemen who'd never seen a radio before.

'Repeat, car twenty-six, come in, over.'

Chris picked up the receiver. It worked just like the ones on television. There was a little button on the side. All he had to do was press the button and speak into the mouthpiece.

'This is car twenty-six, over. What's your problem?'

'You didn't check in, two-six. Just making sure everything's okay.'

Chris wiped his face with the back of his arm. He wasn't messing around, either. He took it super seriously, like somebody talking to God.

'No,' he said. 'Not really. Nothing's okay.'

'Could you repeat, two-six?'

'I said nothing's okay. Everything's totally fucked.'

There was a pause. Then, 'Officer Bates? What's going on, over?'

'Bates isn't here. We left him at the beach.'

This time, the pause was longer.

'Who is this? You know it's illegal to mess around on the police band?'

Chris glanced at me, almost like he was asking my

237

permission to say what he said next. 'What about beating the shit out of a cop and stealing his car – is that illegal, over?'

He didn't wait for a reply. He just yanked on the mouthpiece, snapping the cord. Then he tried to huck it outside, only he forgot that his window was closed. The receiver cracked against the glass and bounced back into his lap. He stared at it for a second, sort of surprised – as if a giant insect had flown in and landed on his thigh.

We burned out faster than usual. Maybe it was something to do with the heat, or how insane the day had been. But pretty soon the smoky haze dissolved into a dark gloom. We opened the windows but even that didn't help. Nothing helped. The murk surrounded us, thick and heavy as swamp water. I felt like I wanted to die, and I'm pretty sure Chris felt even worse.

'Do you think she sucked him off?' he asked.

'I don't know, man.'

'Do you think she got on top?'

'I don't know, man.'

'Do you think they used a condom?'

'I don't know.'

'I hate her. I thought I loved her but really I hated her all along.'

'Don't say that.'

'I hate her,' he said, just to fuck with me. 'I hate her I hate her I hate her.'

Then something happened that I almost couldn't believe. Chris cried. He didn't cry for very long and he didn't cry like a normal person. There was no sobbing or shaking or anything like that. There were just a few tears, streaming down his cheeks. He blinked over and over, trying to see.

Then he gripped the steering wheel like he wanted to choke it and sort of threw his body back and forth against the seat.

'FUCK!' he screamed.

After that we drove in silence, the tears drying on his face. I smelled something rank and sick blowing from up ahead. It must have been a piece of road kill, rotting in the heat.

'You know what I think?' he said. 'I think she did it on purpose.'

At first, I wasn't sure who he meant.

'She popped the clutch and drove right into the sea. She was tired of all the bullshit. And a little insane – like that guy at the funeral said. I guess that makes me insane, too.'

I shook my head. 'It's everybody else who's insane.'

For a second he didn't say anything. Then he smiled – this super sad smile – and came out with something that nearly made me cry.

'Yeah,' he said softly, 'they're insane in the brain, all right.'

'Riding the old brain train.'

'Just one big chain gang.'

We looked at each other. That was when he decided to drop me off. At least, that was when he took his foot off the gas. The speedometer crept down past one-forty, one-thirty, then one-twenty. It was like being on a roller coaster that's finally coming to a stop. Partly you're relieved, but partly you just wish the operator would crank it up and let you go around again.


## 49


Julian wasn't there the night it got a bit weird. He was at a tennis tournament in the Okanagan. It was just the three of us. We stole two bottles of red wine from Chris's mom and walked around the Cove, getting wasted. For some reason we ended up at the dirt bike track in the woods near Myrtle Park, the same park where Pat Shaw kicked my ass on Halloween. We usually avoided the track because of what happened. You know – with the paper bag killer and shit. Karen hadn't heard about him, so we told her.

'He hid out here and killed little girls.'

'He raped them and then he killed them.'

'With this paper bag on his head.'

'Shut up, you guys.' Karen giggled and took a swill of wine. 'That's total crap.'

'No,' Chris said. 'We got warned about him in school and everything.'

'He dragged them down here. Right here. This is where it happened.'

It was dark as a cave in those woods. Karen and Chris were just shadows hovering on either side of me. We heard all sorts of strange noises, noises that might have been anything.

Karen asked, 'What happened to him?'

'They never caught him.'

'Are you kidding me?'

'No.'

'You mean he could still be around?'

'Sure. He probably is.'

Obviously, we were trying to scare her. And we did. I know because she started giggling hysterically, in that way of hers. For about thirty seconds she couldn't even talk.

'Let's get out of here,' she finally managed to say. 'I hate this place.'

'Relax.' Chris took the wine from her. 'He's not around.

He wouldn't do shit if he was. I'd kill him, first.' He started pacing. He hated the paper bag killer almost as much as he hated turtlenecks. 'He's a piece of shit. And the cops are pieces of shit for letting him get away. They'd rather hassle us than stop a pervert like that from killing little girls.'

He thrust the wine into my hand and turned to face the forest.

'Come out and fight me you paper bag piece of shit!'

Then he started storming around, breaking branches and kicking treetrunks. He did stuff like that occasionally, as a way of blowing off steam. It wasn't like he wanted to hurt the forest in any way. He just had a lot of anger – especially towards the paper bag killer.

'Chris – it's okay.'

That was Karen. I saw their two shadows merge in the dark and knew she was holding him. She whispered something I couldn't hear. It was like listening to a trainer talk down a horse that's gone berserk. Eventually she managed to pacify him.

Then she said, 'Let's go drink at my house.'

That was where it started to get all weird.

'Your turn. Time to give me a kiss.'

I froze. Karen was on her hands and knees, crawling towards me. Her face was flushed and sweaty, like a rain-drenched rose. It had started as a joke, but not quite a joke. It was more of a dare. She'd dared us to play spin the bottle – just me and Chris and her.

Now this was happening.

'Don't you want to?' she said, acting all coy.

'Go on Razor, kiss her.'

'Yeah, kiss me.'

I felt Chris's hands on my shoulders, urging me forward. First it had been him and her, and then the bottle had pointed to me. We'd locked ourselves in Karen's basement. It was super dark and quiet down there. Totally intimate. We hadn't even put any music on.

'You have to kiss me.'

'Those are the rules.'

Her face was only inches from mine. I saw all the little details that you can't normally see. I saw the pores in her skin and the fur on her upper lip and the mascara flecks around her eyelashes. I saw all that and fell towards it, touching my mouth to hers. It wasn't much of a kiss. The first one was short and quick – like kissing your grandma, or your aunt.

'He's so cute,' she said, and stroked my cheek. 'Like a little boy.'

'How was that, Razor?'

I was still a bit dazed. 'Nice. I liked it.'

'Good – that means you're not queer.'

We all laughed. The wine came around and I poured some down my throat. It was a cheap red that stained our teeth, making us look like rabid vampires. While I drank, Chris spun the empty bottle again. It went around and around and bumped up against Karen's knee. He kissed her and after that I kissed her again. Our second kiss lasted longer and I felt the tip of her tongue touch my lips. It was pretty crazy, actually. She went back and forth between us, the kisses getting longer and longer. We forgot about spinning the bottle. We forgot about everything except the next drink and the next kiss. It was her lips that did it. Karen's lips were magic lips. They could do anything and say anything.

They said: 'Now you guys kiss. I want to see you kiss.'

Chris and I looked at each other. We were too drunk to be nervous, or scared.

'Come on. If you kiss we can do some other stuff.'

'What stuff?'

'Stuff. You'll see.'

You couldn't say no to her lips. They knew we wanted to try it. We were sitting right next to each other. I kind of turned to face him, and Chris leaned in. It wasn't a short kiss and it wasn't a long kiss. It just felt very natural – like kissing your reflection in the mirror. Afterwards, we sat and stared at each other for about a minute. It was as if we were talking without moving our mouths or making any sound at all. We were talking with our minds.

My mind asked, *Is this cool?*

And his mind answered, *Yeah. It's cool.*

*What happens next?*

*I don't know.*

Karen did. 'Come on,' she said, shoving the bottle at me. 'Just a few more rounds before the other stuff.'

I took one more sip. That fatal sip.

'What's wrong, Razor?'

'I don't feel so good.'

'Seriously?'

'Yeah. But don't worry – I'm not gonna puke or anything.'

The problem with red wine is that it doesn't just get me drunk. It also makes me incredibly sleepy. So I lay back to rest for a second. They kept playing, but the sounds they made drifted further and further away. At one point I think somebody started stroking my head, and I remember Karen saying, 'Aw, little Razor's going to sleep through the best part.'

And I did. I passed right out, like a complete gearbox.

Later, when I woke up and realised what I'd missed, I wanted to cut off my own balls. No joke. I wanted to castrate myself and become a monk for the rest of my life. A neutered monk. Eventually, though, I sort of came to terms with it. I mean, I don't know if I could have handled that kind of thing, anyways. But at least I kissed her. And him. That's got to count for something.

## 50

'What are you going to do, man?'

'We'll see.'

Julian played tennis at the North Shore Winter Club. He took lessons from a pro. The pro taught him how to look good as he grunted and sweated and smashed little yellow balls. It was the one sport Jules was super good at. Every Saturday he went down to the club and spent the whole afternoon working on his strokes. That was where Chris finally caught up with him. Jules had been avoiding him ever since the toga party, but we both knew he'd never skip his tennis lesson. I went along, mostly because I thought I might be able to keep Chris from killing him.

'You spot him?'

'No. Not yet.'

There are dozens of courts down there. Some are on the roof, in the sun, and others are indoors, where it's air conditioned. That day, every single court was full. It was like entering the mannequin training ground. The place was swarming with them. All the guys had the standard muscles and fake tans, and all the girls wore white skirts that matched their designer headbands and bleached blonde hair. They raced around the courts in singles or pairs, hitting the ball with the same perfect strokes. Jules had finally found his route in. He'd been eating his protein powder and going to the gym and taking his tanning pills. He'd even managed to lose his virginity. Pretty soon he'd be a full-fledged mannequin.

If he survived that long.

'Maybe he's not here,' I suggested.

'He's here all right.'

He wasn't on the outdoor courts, so Chris tried inside. We circled the perimeter, slouching along in our jams and sandals like a couple of bums hunting for loose change. Tennis balls flew past on all sides, popping off the clay floors and cement walls. There were no windows. The only light came from rows of those fluorescent tubes – the kind that turn everything sort of sick and pallid.

'There he is. Over there.'

Jules was playing in the far corner, swatting serves at his pro. Chris didn't waste any time. He walked straight onto the court and called him out.

'So I hear you fucked that little whore.'

Jules laughed, pretending he hadn't heard. 'What are you doing here, Chris?'

'Karen. The slut. You fucked her. She told me.'

Jules opened his mouth, shut it, and opened it again. He looked like a fish trying to breathe out of water. Then the pro came hustling up. He was the head mannequin: slick and tanned and chiselled. He was what all the other guys wanted to be some day.

'Is everything okay, Julian?'

'Shut up,' Chris said. 'He just fucked a whore and I want

to hear him say it.'

The pro said, 'Whoah – I don't think that language is necessary.'

'She's not a whore!' Jules said. 'Don't call her that!'

'She's a fucking whore and so are you!'

It went back and forth like that. People started to notice. They drifted over from the other courts, lured by the commotion. A semicircle formed around us. The fluorescent lights stripped away skin tones and sucked the colours out of clothing, so that everybody looked drained and lifeless and even more artificial than usual.

'Shut up, Chris! Just shut up!'

'She's a slut, a whore, a skank, a bitch!'

Nobody stepped in. Just like on that day at the beach, all the mannequins had short-circuited. Instead of stopping it they stood there waiting for the bloodshed to erupt. I wasn't much better. I kept saying really feeble things like, 'Come on, guys,' and, 'You don't have to do this.' I actually broke down a bit and started sobbing, probably the only time I've ever cried in front of that many girls. Nobody paid me any attention – for obvious reasons.

'Did you eat her out?' Chris said. 'I bet you did – you shitty man-whore!'

'Fuck you, Chris,' Jules screamed, raising his racquet, 'I love her!'

Then he smashed it on Chris's head.

Let's face it. We weren't exactly the three musketeers. We were more like the two musketeers with a spare musketeer who had a car and wanted to play frisbee. All the same, I was pretty shocked when Jules did that. I'd never seen anything like it. In movies, when people get things broken on their heads – chairs, pool cues, bats, whatever – it always looks and sounds totally fake, like it wouldn't hurt at all. This was ten times crazier. The top of the racquet splintered into a dozen pieces, making a brutal crunching sound. All the mannequins gasped. Chris staggered back, bent at the waist and clutching his skull. Even Jules was a little stunned. Instead of following up the attack he stood there with this queasy expression on his face, cradling what remained of his racquet. It didn't even look like a racquet any more. With all the strings and splintered fragments jutting out, it looked more like some kind of broken musical instrument. A harp, maybe. Little cupid holding his broken harp.

'Get out of here, Jules,' I told him. 'Get going, man.'

To his credit, Julian didn't listen to me. Maybe he realised it was going to happen sooner or later, whatever he did. Or maybe he actually believed he had a chance against Chris. Either way, he didn't run – not even when Chris straightened up, and raised his fists. Blood had soaked through his hair. A single drop trickled down his cheek, like a red tear. Jules let go of his racquet, preparing himself.

He did a little better than Bates, I guess.

Karen called Chris up that night. She called him over and over and over, but he only answered the first time.

'Chris, I'm sorry,' she sobbed. 'I'm so sorry.'

'Don't ever call me again, you whore.'

## 51

'How deep do you think it is?'

That was Karen. She looked straight down as she said it, as if she hoped to see the bottom. I did the same – we all did – but I could only see my bare feet, beating in circles to keep me afloat. They looked white and fat and seemed bent at impossible angles.

I said: 'Deep.'

Jules said: 'A couple hundred feet, at least.'

And Chris said: 'Maybe deeper.'

All three of us were talking shit. Obviously.

'Sure.' Karen swept the surface with her hand, making a little wave. 'But how deep is that? Is it as deep as a really tall tree, or a skyscraper, or the Lions Gate Bridge, or what?'

I pointed at Mount Seymour, looming above the Cove like a moss-covered monster.

'As deep as that peak, in reverse.'

'Really?'

I didn't answer because I didn't know. I'd only said that to impress her.

Chris said, 'One thing's for sure.'

We all looked at him.

'It's deep enough to drown in.'

Back before Chris kicked the shit out of Bates, before Jules smashed that racquet on Chris's head, before Karen fucked Jules and even before she'd fucked Chris, we smoked up and went swimming. There's nothing – absolutely nothing – better than going for a swim when you're high. We were so seared it didn't even feel like swimming. It was more like flying through the water. We fluttered past the marina and flapped way out into

Indian Arm. Nobody took the lead and nobody trailed behind. We just soared along together and stopped, all at the same time, like a pod of dolphins. By then we were right in the middle of the Arm. For once, there were no motorboats or kayaks around. There was nothing but the sun-glazed water, so bright and blinding that you could barely see the shoreline in the distance.

We treaded water while we talked.

'Think about it,' Karen said. 'There's nothing between us and all that water. If we stopped kicking we'd sink down and down like stones and never stop.'

We thought about it. We were baked enough to think about it for hours.

'Guys dive this deep,' Jules said. 'Without scuba tanks or wetsuits or anything.'

Chris snorted. 'Bullshit.'

'I'm serious, man. They use weights to drag themselves down so they can catch shellfish and crap. They hold their breath for like four or five minutes. Crazy, huh?'

Chris didn't say anything. I knew what he was thinking because I was thinking the same thing: weights had dragged his dad down, too – only he hadn't come back up.

'They don't live very long.' That was Jules again. He just wouldn't let it drop. 'Their bodies get all messed up from the bends.'

Karen said, '*The Bends*? I love that album. It's a classic.'

'It happens when you go really deep and come up too fast.'

Karen started singing: 'Green plastic watering can...'

She sang a few lines, then sort of tapered off as she forgot the words. Out on the open ocean her voice sounded almost supernatural. When she finished I could still hear the tune, floating around in the watery silence.

'Look,' Chris said.

He pointed back towards the Cove. Between the waves I spotted a shiny-wet head and two dark, round eyes. It was maybe twenty yards off, watching us curiously as it swam.

'Is it a seal?' Karen asked.

'Sea otter. Let's see how close we can get.'

We paddled forward, pulling ourselves along as quietly as we could. Usually sea otters don't like you getting anywhere near them. Not this one. It waited and watched us approach, until we were close enough to see its trembling whiskers and quivering nose. We were so close it seemed impolite to get any closer, so we stopped and stared. It stared back. Then, very casually, it ducked beneath the surface like a gopher dropping back into its hole.

I didn't think anything could be better than the sea otter. I thought the day was over.

Then Karen asked, 'Do you guys know how to be starfish?'

We didn't, so she showed us. To be a starfish you took a deep lungful of air, then lay on your back with your eyes closed and your limbs spread out. In the salt water you could float like that forever, breathing gently, while the sun baked moisture off your belly and cheeks. Being a starfish was the greatest thing ever. You didn't have to think or worry about anything. All you did was float around, sucking up sun and hanging out with other starfish.

'Open your eyes,' Karen instructed. 'Pretend you're looking down, not up.'

We did. We gazed down at a stark blue plain littered with strips of cotton.

'Hold your breath. You're not allowed to breathe until I tell you.'

I inflated my chest and closed my mouth, feeling the air tight against my ribs. Karen waited. Blood slowly filled up my head, making it ache with dizziness.

'Now you're falling upwards. Can you feel it?'

At first I couldn't. Then the water surged beneath my back, buoying me up. Each swell pushed me a little higher, a little higher, until I didn't need to be pushed any more and I felt myself sort of drifting towards the sky, a free-falling starfish, and there was no longer an up or a down or a left or a right – we were just a cluster of bodies floating through space.

'Okay, breathe!' Karen gasped.

We deflated together. White spots flickered against the sky and I could hear the heavy panting of Chris and Jules trying to catch their breath. For a long time after that, we lay totally still and silent in a pod formation, our fingertips almost touching, with Karen in the centre and the three of us surrounding her. At that moment, it felt like all the land on the entire planet had sunk beneath the ocean. Every single person had drowned and every single animal, too. We were the only ones left. Us and the sea otter.

It couldn't last forever.

We burned out, big time. Nobody said anything. Nobody had to. We just started swimming back because we knew. By the time we reached the wharf, I had a killer headache and super bad pasties – like my mouth was full of ash. It didn't help that the wharf was crowded with powerboats and houseboats and pretty much every kind of boat you could imagine. Also, there were tons of kids around, screeching and screaming. We gathered our clothes and towels. All we wanted was to get out of there.

'Hey – hold on.'

'What?'

'It's Bates.'

He was parked in the little cul-de-sac overlooking the water. We couldn't see him but we knew his car. He was the only cop who ever bothered coming down to the Cove.

'What's he doing?'

'Looking for us, probably.'

Instead of going up the stairs to the shops we took the long way around, following the water. We'd learned it was better just to avoid Bates, whenever possible. Chris and I found a stone and started kicking it back and forth along the path. Then he booted it, super hard.

'One of these days he's going to arrest us.'

At the time, I didn't think he actually meant it. The idea of Bates arresting us was just too far-fetched. Not any more, obviously. Considering all the other shit we went through, it almost seems sort of tame.

## 52

I got out somewhere between Cypress Bowl and Horseshoe Bay. There was nothing to do but walk back along the highway. The vicious heat of the day caught up to me. With Chris at the wheel we'd been able to outrun it, but now I was alone among whining motors and sickening exhaust and thrashing rays of sun. I trudged for about three miles without looking up once. What I needed was one of those cone-shaped collars that a dog wears on its head when it's got stitches – the kind that stops it from eating itself. That way I wouldn't have been able to see or hear anything. I could have blotted it all out.

I turned off the highway at the next exit. It didn't make any difference. There was nowhere I could go that wasn't just as hot, just as bright, just as noisy, just as nauseating. Somehow I found my way to Marine Drive, then caught a bus that went past Park Royal and the Avalon. It got me to Lonsdale Quay. From there I followed the low road next to the railway yards. On my right, rotting shacks and sagging warehouses leaned against each other for support, looking dry and brittle in the heat. It wouldn't take much to start a blaze down there. A single match would do it. Even the sun could do it. Pretty soon the fire would spread to Lonsdale, and eventually an inferno would engulf the entire city. Everything would be consumed, nothing would be spared. I imagined the earth becoming a great ball of fire and when the fire died out only a desert was left. I wandered alone through the desert, leaving footprints in the sand. Sweat stung my eyes and trickled down my cheeks. My neck and arms slowly seared to a bright, lobster pink. There was nothing in the desert. Nothing but sand and heat and time and a hungry wind blowing from somewhere up ahead.

I thought I heard Chris calling my name.

It took me four hours to get home.

I stumbled through the back door, panting and trembling like a brain-fried junkie. A slick layer of grime coated my face and arms. The sun had fried my retinas and I could hardly see. I wandered through the murk of our basement, blinking back spots and trying to get my bearings. Nothing felt familiar. Actually, nothing even felt real. All the furniture looked flimsy and artificial, as if our whole house was one gigantic stage set. At any moment the show would end and that would be it.

'Pops?'

I followed the murmur of the television upstairs, to our den. My dad was sprawled on the couch, watching one of his nature shows and drinking beer. He didn't say anything when I sat down, but I think he sort of grunted. You know – just to acknowledge me or whatever. Other than that I don't remember much except staring at the TV for about twenty minutes. It showed some dirty boat in the middle of the ocean, with all these bearded guys standing on deck. They were hunting a whale with a harpoon the size of a rocket. I don't know what kind of whale, but you could see it playing in the water on the horizon. Then, bam, they speared it right in the head. Afterwards they hauled it onboard and made a big deal of standing beside the carcass, taking photos of each other. The whale was still breathing.

They were grinning their stupid faces off, too.

'I'd like to kill those fuckers.'

My dad sat up straight, like I'd poked him with a pin. 'What?'

'How'd they like to get harpooned in the head? The shitfucks.'

'Hey – are you okay?'

I didn't say anything. Before I could, somebody rang our doorbell.

'You better get it,' I said.

Normally my dad would have made me answer it, but he didn't argue. I guess he saw something in my face.

'All right.'

He heaved himself off the sofa and walked to the front hall. I heard the click of the lock being turned and then I heard him say, 'Yes? Is there a problem?' I went to the window and looked out. There was a cop on the porch. A short cop, holding her hat in her hands. My dad stepped outside and half-shut the door behind him. I could hear their voices but not what they were saying – not until the end, when my dad said, 'No, I'd prefer to tell him myself.' I moved away from the window. A few seconds later my dad came back.

He looked about a hundred years old.

Under the right circumstances, my dad can talk and talk and talk. He can talk about the feeding habits of Australian wombats or how evolution happened or why Lennon was a musical genius. He can talk about anything, so long as it doesn't really mean anything. But give him a tough topic – like having to explain how my best friend drove a squad car through a police barricade and off a cliff into Howe Sound – and he really clams up. You'd think somebody had stuck a spoon in his brain and stirred it around. He stood there holding his beer and fiddling with the pull-tab like a Chinese finger puzzle.

'That was the police,' he said.

That was as far as he got. Then he sobbed. I'd never really seen my dad cry before. I mean, I'd seen him get a little emotional at the end of sad movies – especially Casablanca – but this was something else entirely. The tears came next – big and fat and rolling down his cheeks. He dropped the can and gathered me in his arms. I don't think he'd had a shower that morning, because he smelled like old sheets. He squeezed me and since he was crying I started crying, too. He kept trying to explain, but all he managed to say was, 'I have some bad news...' He never got past those five words. He just couldn't do it. He couldn't tell me.

## 53

A media circus. That's what my dad called it. I'd heard that term before but I never really understood it. I mean, by this point we'd been in the papers a bunch of times: first for saving Mrs Reever, and then when Chris slapped Crazy Dan around, and again after the toga party riot. All that was nothing compared to this. Chris got his fireworks, that's for sure. Front page headlines, six o'clock news, editorials, whatever. Everybody was scrambling for a piece of the action. But I'm glad he wasn't around to see it. Beneath the excitement it all came across as cheap and fake. They took his story and blew it way, way out of proportion, filling it up with all kinds of stupid assumptions, until even I wasn't quite sure how or why it had happened. It reminded me of being at a party where everybody's talking shit about the person who's just left the room – but only because they know he can't hear them.

They interviewed Bates on City-TV.

His big, fleshy face filled the screen, all bruised and bloody from the beating Chris had given him. He had two black eyes and a massive bandage across his nose – this super lame bandage that practically covered his entire face. Also, his lips were puffed out as if he'd overdosed on botox. You could tell he'd lost a fight, all right. He looked like a loser. That didn't stop the media from turning him into a hero. They played him up as the victim, this totally innocent victim. According to them, Bates was just a poor cop trying to do his job – a real working class hero. That's the main reason he got his promotion, I'm pretty sure. He's a lieutenant over in West Van, now. Or maybe a sergeant. I don't really know. But basically, thanks to those jerk-offs running the media, Bates doesn't have to bother hassling kids any more. He can just shoot them whenever he wants like all the other West Van cops.

In return, he told the reporters exactly what they wanted to hear.

'Let's get one thing straight: this kid was dangerous. Unstable. It was only a matter of time before something like this happened. I'm just glad he didn't hurt anybody else.'

I bet that was a big relief to everybody. They can all sleep better at night, knowing that 'it was only a matter of time'. Chris was volatile, unstable, a lone wolf, a rotten apple, a bad seed. Parents love hearing phrases like that. It helps convince them that this kind of thing could never happen to their kid. Anybody who beats up a cop and steals a squad car has it coming to them.

They forgot to mention his fucking medal.

Not all the reporters were total marzipans. Some of them wanted to show how compassionate they were by telling Chris's side of the story. They were the ones who wrote about his home life, about his dad's accident and his mom hitting the bottle. You know – the ones who decided he was 'troubled'. That wasn't much better, though. Their version was still just as stupid and simple. That's the problem with the news. You can't cram somebody's life into a shitty little article, or a two-minute broadcast. They can say whatever the fuck they want, but Chris wasn't a nutcase and he wasn't some dysfunctional loser. To me he was just Chris. It would be almost impossible to explain what he was actually like. That's why I didn't bother giving any interviews. Jules and Karen did, but not me. The shit they came up with was pretty nauseating, too. Their parents must have told them what to say ahead of time, because it all sounded harsh rehearsed. Karen's was the worst. They made her pretend that she hardly knew him, that he was just some crazed stalker chasing after their little princess.

And of course everybody assumed it was true.

It wasn't as if I didn't get the chance to do interviews, either. After the cops released me, reporters were practically bashing down our door – especially when they found out I'd been in the car with him that day. Some of them even offered me cash to sell my story. I didn't take it, though. I didn't talk to a single one of them. I would have, if I thought they'd listen to me. But I knew they wouldn't. Not really. I mean, the last thing they wanted to hear was the truth. I'd rather tell it my own way, including all the bizarre stuff that happened to us last summer. That's what nobody understands – it all started that day at the water.

It ended at the water, too.


## 54


Chris pulled over into the shade on the shoulder of the highway. I opened my door. Falling from the trees were hundreds of those tiny helicopter seeds that twirl around and around and around. They landed on the hood and all over the windshield. One even spun right in the window and stuck to my arm. We sat there looking at each other. The Chinese radio station was playing this mournful acoustic song. Neither of us said anything. I mean, what was there to say? He just held up his hand, palm out, like an Indian Chief in an old Western movie saying hello. Except, in this case, he was saying goodbye. Then my feet found the pavement and I shut the door behind me. He put the car in gear, stomped the gas, and spun back onto the highway, tyres smoking and squealing like pigs being grilled alive. I stood and watched until I was alone, and then I knew that he was alone, too.

After I got out, he called Karen from Bates's phone. He was lonely, I guess. Or maybe he just wanted resolution. It's hard to say. But either way, he called her – which is how she got dragged into it. By then the police knew he'd stolen the car, and they'd started monitoring the line. They even recorded the conversation. When I first heard about that, I thought my dad might be able to get me a copy of the recording. You know – using one of those legal loopholes of his. He tried, too. But apparently those jokers didn't have to reveal any of it.

So I asked Karen instead.

I hadn't seen her interview on TV, yet – the one where she totally sold him out by pretending not to know him. If I had, I doubt I would have been able to bring myself to do it.

'Karen?'

'Razor!'

She sounded so relieved to hear from me. Relieved and surprised. I mean, I'd been hanging up on her whenever she called, and now I was phoning her for a change.

'How are you?' she asked.

'Pretty shitty. What about you?'

'Not so good. I can't really eat.'

'Yeah. Eating's hard.'

At first it felt good to be talking to her. Then I felt guilty about feeling good, so I decided to keep things fairly formal.

'I heard he called you. From the car.'

'Uh-huh.' She paused. 'But I'm not really supposed to talk about that stuff.'

I could tell she was dying to fill me in, though. I knew her too well.

'It's me, Karen. Nobody else will know.'

She took a deep breath – as if it was an incredibly hard decision for her. 'All right. But we didn't talk long. And his voice was really crackly – so sometimes it was hard to hear.'

'Yeah – but what did he say?'

'Hold on.' I heard some shuffling, and a sound like a door closing, before she started talking again. 'Okay – first he told me he'd beaten up Jules. But I already knew that. Then he told me about Bates, and stealing the police car. That was when I realised things had gotten, like, totally out of hand.'

I could imagine the way he'd said it, too. Not bragging at all. Just kind of filling her in so she knew where they stood.

'Then what?' I asked.

'I told him I wanted to see him, but he just laughed. I was worried he'd get mad at me and hang up, so I didn't say anything for a bit. Neither did he. I don't think so, anyway.'

'You don't think so?'

'I can't remember exactly.'

'How can you not remember?' I was trying super hard not to freak out at her. It wasn't easy. 'This is important, Karen. These are the last things he ever said. To anyone.'

It took a moment for that to sink in. Maybe it hadn't really occurred to her. 'Well, I know he said something funny, like, "It's over for us. But what the hell maybe you were just super drunk after all." Something along those lines, anyways.'

I closed my eyes. For whatever reason, that made me ridiculously happy.

Karen said, 'I guess he meant...'

'Yeah. He was trying to forgive you.'

We were both quiet. I could hear her breathing. It sounded shaky.

She said, 'I keep having dreams about him.'

'Me, too.'

I wasn't lying, either. I still have them. All the time. In most of my dreams, I don't even know Chris is dead. We're usually just chilling out – biking or swimming or whatever. It's pretty awesome, actually. For a little while I'm okay again. Until I wake up.

'What do you think it means?' she asked.

'That we miss him, I guess.'

It was a relief to be able to talk about it. The only person I'd discussed it with was my dad, and he gets a little awkward when it comes to emotional stuff.

Then Karen had to go and ruin it, of course.

'You know what's really weird?' she said. She'd started whispering, as if we were conspiring together. 'I'm pretty sure the call came after they said he was supposed to have crashed the car. Isn't that creepy? It's almost like he called me, you know...'

I frowned. What was I supposed to say to that?

'I've heard that can happen,' she said. 'When somebody dies they'll contact the person they love the most. Do you think it's possible? That it was his ghost?'

'No, Karen. I don't think it was his ghost. At all.'

Partly I was mad because it sounded so stupid. But partly I was mad because I wished his ghost had called me instead. It must have known I wouldn't have been home. I mean, I was still walking back along the highway at that point.

Karen sniffled. She might have been crying a little. It was hard to tell. 'It's nice talking to you again,' she said. 'We should hang out some time – if you ever want to.'

'I don't know, Karen. Maybe.'

We never did, though. The next day I saw that interview she gave. In a way, it was worse than what she'd done with Jules. To have been that close to Chris, then turn around and lie like that. I doubt she realised it, but that was the moment she really betrayed him.


## 55


I've thought about it tons since that day. It's all I think about, really. I've followed the route he took, too. A bunch of times. That's where I crashed my dad's Civic. Not a big crash. A shitty little crash, into the meridian. I was going too fast or something. I wanted to know what it would have been like for him, after I got out. And if you head west along that stretch of highway, in mid-afternoon, the glare of the sun catches you full-on. It was the hottest time of the day on the hottest day of the year – maybe the hottest day ever. In Vancouver, at least. And I'd left him all alone to die.

'I'm sweating like a pig in here, Razor,' he said.

I like to think he said that to me, even though I wasn't there. *Me, too. Like the three little pigs.*

I mean, I'd followed him for so long he must have felt a little lost without me. So he imagined us talking in his head – like on that night we'd played spin the bottle.

'All three, eh?'

*I'm harsh pigging out.*

'What's your favourite fairy tale, little piggy?'

*The Little Mermaid. Mostly because of Ariel.*

'Ariel's pretty hot, all right. I wouldn't mind tapping that tail.'

For a few seconds, he had trouble thinking of what I would have said next.

*I'm sorry I sold you out, man.*

'You didn't. You got out – that's not the same as selling me out.'

*It isn't?*

'Not even, man. Don't ever think that.'

I hope that's what we said to each other, anyway.


Not all the dreams I have are good. Sometimes I dream about him behind the wheel, blazing down that stretch of highway. Except the landscape isn't the same. The pine trees have gone totally grey and lost their needles, and the ground is parched to shit. The ditches are filled with all these rusty cars, like the shells of prehistoric insects, and you can tell that he's been driving for years. The heatwave hasn't ended – it's just gone on and on and on. Chris is the last one left, still keeping it pretty real, racing alone through that wasteland. The engine is screaming and the doors are shuddering and the whole car looks ready to fly apart.

I'm never in the dream with him. It's more like I'm invisible, watching everything happen. And then, out of nowhere, I'll be in the driver's seat, gripping the wheel – as if I've sort of become him. I can't actually control the car, but just before I wake up the dead trees along the roadside start bursting into flame. They crackle and roar and become this long tunnel of raging fire. That's all that happens in the dream – there isn't any crash or big finale. I don't know what it means, either. Probably nothing, I guess. It's pretty fucked, though.

## 56

There's one thing the media never found out. They found out almost everything else, by digging around in his life like rabid little gophers. They were relentless. It was as if they wanted to put together a jigsaw puzzle of Chris, to find out why he did what he did. The problem was that none of them had ever met him, so they had no idea what the puzzle was supposed to look like. And if they'd known about this, they would have instantly assumed it was a super important piece – the missing piece they'd all been looking for. They didn't, though. The only other people who knew about it were me and Julian.

'Let's not tell anybody, okay?'

'Yeah. Fuck that.'

'Nobody needs to know.'

I didn't even tell my dad. He would have wanted to find those guys and prosecute them. There's no way I could have handled that. The same went for Chris. And Julian. It wasn't exactly the kind of thing we felt like talking about in a courtroom, in front of eight hundred strangers. I mean, I would rather have poked out my own eyes than tell anybody.

So we kept it secret, for obvious reasons.

The three of us were playing road hockey one night, a few years back. I think it was the summer between grade seven and eight, between elementary school and high school – a little while after Chris's dad died. We weren't quite teenagers but we weren't really kids any more, either. That was an important summer. We'd only just started drinking and smoking weed. Julian hadn't eaten any protein powder and Chris hadn't been kicked out of any schools, yet. Basically, we were still pretty young.

'Over here, Razor – to the point!'

'Take a shot, man.'

We played in the lacrosse box near my house, down in Myrtle Park. Chris and I didn't have any equipment. Jules did. He had his own net and this full goalie outfit that looked like it had been sent to him through an eighties time warp. The pads were purple and yellow, and the facemask was marked up with these fake stitches – just like the ones that old goalie from Boston had on his mask. Totally butt. We loved peppering Jules with shots. We didn't even care about scoring goals. We just wanted to knock that stupid mask off his face.

*'Time-out! Time-out!'*

Julian was always calling time-outs. He had this little water bottle he kept on top of the net. He'd call time-out and prop his mask up on his forehead, as if he thought he was a real goalie. Then he'd squirt water all over his face and in his mouth and spit it out.

'Okay – game on.'

During the summer, we usually played until about eight or nine o'clock. That night we played a little later than usual. They had floodlights installed above the lacrosse box, so you could still see even after it got dark. Just as we finished, at about ten o'clock, these three older guys showed up with a few shitty wooden sticks and two cases of beer. They challenged us to a game. If we played, they said they'd give us some beer.

'Come on – us against you. Three on three.'

'Okay. But just for a while.'

We only fell for it because we happened to know one of them. His name was Rick Larkin. He was this pretty harsh kid who'd gone to our elementary school for a year or two. Chris had always been down with him, so we didn't think anything would happen. We'd never met the two other guys before. One of them was a fat Chinese kid named Kimchee – like the noodles. The other was a monster they called Punch-out. Looking back, it was pretty obvious that these guys were trouble. But like I said, at the time we were still kind of young.

Not to mention naïve.

'We'll play first to five. Crossbars and goalposts.'

'Okay,' Jules said. 'Who's taking the face-off?'

'There's no face-off. Give us the puck, shithead.'

They were older than us and bigger than us, but they couldn't play hockey worth shit. I mean, Kimchee was okay. He at least looked like he'd stick-handled once or twice in his life. But Rick was pathetic, and Punch-out couldn't even shoot properly. He lumbered up and down the court, hacking at the puck like some kind of brain-dead zombie.

'I think that was high-sticking, dude.'

'No it fucking wasn't.'

They had to cheat super bad to even up the odds. Near the end they started body-checking us and running us into the boards, but we still managed to beat them. At least, we were ahead when the game ended. It didn't end because we'd scored five goals, though. It ended because Kimchee decided to pull out that knife.

'All right, fuckers,' Punch-out said, 'get in the penalty box.'

At first, I thought it was a joke. Then, when I realised it wasn't, I nearly pissed my pants. It wasn't a big knife or anything – but it was a knife and in the Cove you don't see that kind of shit very often. I think it was a butterfly knife, actually. Kimchee flicked it around in front of our faces. He was pretty good with it, too. Not super good, but pretty good.

Chris said, 'Rick – what's going on, man?'

'You heard what he said.'

They herded us over to the penalty box, out of the light and into the shadows. Myrtle Park usually isn't so deserted, but that night there was nobody around, and nobody to hear if we'd called for help. Not that I had the guts to do that, anyways.

Punch-out said, 'Give us your money.'

Kimchee flicked the knife for emphasis. It was weird. He had the knife, but Punch-out did all the talking. They made a pretty intimidating combination. We didn't even think about arguing. We just emptied our pockets and gave them all the money we had, which was only about ten bucks, mostly in loose change. They didn't find Julian's cellphone – he kept it on top of the net with his water bottle – so all they got was the cash.

'That's it? Ten fucking bucks?'

'Sorry, man,' I said, 'we don't have any more.'

'Shut the fuck up.' Punch-out grabbed me by the shirt and slammed me against the boards. Then he started pacing back and forth in front of us. He had harsh bad body odour, actually. Kind of like rotten cabbage. 'All right. Take off your fucking clothes, then.'

'Our clothes?'

'What are you, deaf or something? Fucking take them off!'

Me and Jules obeyed. We stepped out of our shoes, and pulled off our socks. Then came our shirts and shorts.

'What's this kid's problem?'

I looked over. Chris was standing there. Not moving.

'Come on, Rick,' he said. 'This is bullshit.'

'Do what he says, Chris.'

'Fuck that. I'm not taking off my clothes.'

Everybody froze. Punch-out didn't expect that at all. The four of us looked from him, to Chris, and back to him. Even his own guys didn't know what he would do. Slowly, he reached out and took the knife from Kimchee's hand. Then he went over to Chris. Punch-out towered over him by a good five or six inches. To stare him down, Chris had to look almost straight up. He did it, though. They stood facing each other like two rams squaring off. Then Punch-out grabbed him and shoved the knife right up against his throat.

'Strip, bitch,' he said.

Julian started to cry. I was too freaked out to cry. I thought he was going to kill Chris. Maybe he would have, too. You never know how far a guy that stupid will go.

'Fuck it, Chris,' I said. 'It's just clothes, man.'

Chris glanced over at me, still weighing his options, and nodded. Punch-out released him, then stood there holding the knife as Chris stripped down to his underwear.

'And your boxers. Take off your fucking boxers.'

We did. All three of us. We stood there as they gathered up our clothes. Me and Chris clasped our hands over our dicks. Julian cupped one hand on his dick, and the other across his birthmark – almost like he was more embarrassed by that than his dick. He'd stopped crying. All the tears had dried on his face and he just stared at a point in front of him on the ground. It was weird – like he'd completely zoned out.

'Look at these little bitches, huh? These naked little bitches.'

Punch-out said a bunch of stuff like that, but you could

tell he didn't really know what else to do with us. For about five or ten minutes, the three of them hit us and shoved us around and taunted us with the knife. Also, they made fun of our dicks and kept trying to pull our hands away and poke us there with the hockey sticks. It was pretty fucked up, actually. When they finally got bored, they put our clothes in a pile and pissed all over them – except for Julian's belt, which they kept. Then they left. To them, it was nothing. They probably talked about it and joked about it for a few days, and then totally forgot about it.

I think they broke our hockey sticks, too.

My house was the closest. Our shirts and shorts were soaked in piss, so I stuffed them in the wash and got out some fresh clothes for the three of us. Then we sat around the basement, not saying anything. I felt as if we were still naked. In a lot of ways, it was kind of like being raped – only not quite as bad, obviously.

'Let's not tell anybody, okay?'

It was Chris's idea, but me and Jules felt exactly the same way. We didn't make a pact or anything, but we all agreed. After that, Chris got up and went to the bathroom. Julian just sat there, looking miserable. Miserable and feeble. Within a week or two, he'd started buying protein powder and going to the gym. I guess he figured that if he got big enough, nobody would ever mug him and strip him naked again. It wasn't as stupid as it sounds, actually. I mean, at least he didn't decide to join kung fu and try to become a ninja.

That was how I reacted.

'What a bunch of shitheads,' Jules muttered.

'They were cocksuckers, all right.'

Neither of us sounded really angry. We were still too scared to be angry.

'What if people find out?'

'They won't,' I said. 'Those guys won't tell.'

A second later, something smashed in the bathroom.

Me and Jules looked at each other, then sprang up and rushed over. I pulled open the bathroom door. The first thing I noticed was the vanity mirror above our sink. It was gone. Shattered. Chris stood in front of the empty frame, surrounded by glass shards. I could see tiny versions of him reflected in all the fragments, almost like in a kaleidoscope. He held up his fist and inspected the knuckles. They were cut to the bone. Blood drizzled down his wrist and forearm and dripped off his elbow in a steady stream, pattering onto the floor. As we stood there, staring, he turned on the tap and ran cold water over the wound.

'Are you okay, man?'

He didn't look at me. Every muscle in his body seemed to be taut and trembling, like wires stretched to the breaking point. It was the first time I remember him looking that way.

He said, 'Nobody's ever going to do that to me again.'

That was it. From then on, he didn't take shit from anybody, whether they had a knife or a nightstick or a badge or a gun. It was like the part in a comic book where the hero first discovers his super power. Obviously, Chris had other powers – like shotgunning beer and an extra-hard skull – but this was his most important power. He couldn't be scared or intimidated or bullied or beaten. He never backed down, and he never gave up.

## 57

After I got out of the car, the road started winding. It wound its way between ridges and along cliffs and up hills and down slopes. At one point it even seemed to wind back in on itself, like a snake biting its own tail. That's the Sea to Sky Highway, for you. It's a pretty bizarre name for a highway but, on the other hand, it's also a pretty bizarre highway. People die on that stretch of road all the time. Usually teenagers. They crash their cars into oncoming traffic or spin out into ditches or drop right off the sides of cliffs. More kids kill themselves on that road than in Lynn Canyon and Seymour River combined. But basically, that's the road Chris took – and somehow they found out.

The cops from Squamish and Whistler put up a roadblock, just like something out of a bad TV movie. They parked two squad cars sideways across the highway and laid down a few wooden sawhorses – those yellow and black sawhorses they use for roadworks. At that point they didn't really know what they were dealing with. I mean, the cops up there aren't exactly world class. They'd heard a squad car had been stolen, so they set up a roadblock.

At the time, it wasn't such a big deal. There weren't even any reporters around. There were just a few bystanders who pulled over after being waved through – to see what was going on. A roadblock isn't a big deal if it works. It only became a big deal because it didn't work at all. To begin with, they'd chosen about the worst place for a roadblock you can imagine – right in front of a cliff overlooking Howe Sound. Secondly, none of them knew what I knew about Chris.

Once he got going, it was nearly impossible to stop him.

The press only showed up afterwards – like a flock of vultures.

There were all these shitty reporters and photographers and cameramen fluttering around outside the police cordon. Even the CBC decided it was newsworthy. I mean, this was big time. The RCMP had to bring in investigators, and a bunch of weird specialists to piece together what the hell had actually happened. Plus, they had to get the squad car out of the ocean, somehow. The only person who didn't bother coming was Lieutenant Moustache. He was probably off by himself someplace, wearing his Canucks hat and hacking a dart. To him, the whole thing would have seemed like an even bigger gong show than our toga party.

The CBC must have had a news helicopter, because a lot of the footage was shot from overhead. It showed this long stretch of road, streaked with tyre marks and strewn with pieces of metal and glass and all kinds of debris. It was like a spaceship had crash-landed in the middle of the highway. Some of the brush at the roadside had caught fire and in places it was still smouldering. Also, the guardrail on the corner was broken and twisted. I've never seen so many cops and reporters and cameras in one place. I bet the West Van police wanted to kill themselves when they saw what they'd missed out on. The only thing they like more than shooting kids is getting tons of publicity. Bates will fit in perfectly with them. Actually, I wouldn't be surprised if a few of those jokers drove up there after the fact. You know – just so they could claim that they'd been in on it. Of course, by the time everybody got their shit together and realised something completely insane had happened, it was already over, finished, done. Chris was dead. The end.

## 58

I went to see my shrink, one last time.

As soon as I entered her office, I sensed the difference. To begin with, the window was wide open. I mean, her window was never open. It was supposed to stay shut to keep in all that cool, soothing air. But it was open, all right. Sunlight had leaked inside, spilling across the floor beneath the windowsill. Harsh traffic sounds – honking and shrieking and squealing – clamoured up from the street. I started sweating before I'd even closed the door.

'Your air conditioner's broken.'

It sat on its side beneath the windowsill, lifeless and silent.

'It was only a matter of time,' she said.

There was something different about her, too. Actually, there were a few things different about her. She sat slouched behind her desk, one hand gripping a bottle of rum as if it was glued to her palm. Her blouse was damp and wrinkled. Tiny pinpricks of sweat showed through her layers of make-up.

In other words, she looked terrible.

'What's with the boxes?' I asked.

There were boxes stacked on her desk, and more boxes piled up behind the door. There were boxes everywhere, half-filled with books and folders and loose sheets of paper.

'I'm all done with this.'

Her gesture took in the desk, the office, the boiling bright world outside.

'Why?'

'As you may have noticed, lately I haven't been practising what you'd call an orthodox form of psychiatry. In fact, I don't think I've treated you very fairly. I've referred most of my other patients on to colleagues, and I imagine I should do the same for you.'

'I'd rather talk to you than those jokers.'

She smiled. 'We have something in common, don't we?'

Then she took a long drink, straight from the bottle. I sat in my usual chair, angling it towards her so we were face to face. The hot leather cover clung to me like plastic wrap.

She said, 'I heard about Chris.'

'On the news?'

'Mm-hmm. On the news. I saw your friends Karen and Julian, too. It was quite surreal – seeing and hearing these people, after listening to you talk about them. That's a first for me, as a psychiatrist. Typically my patients aren't headline material.'

I smiled, this super fake smile. What I really wanted to do was cry. But I'd already cried in front of a bunch of girls recently – on the day Chris beat up Jules – and I wasn't about to do the same with my psychiatrist. She didn't need to see that.

'You were the other teenager in the car, weren't you?'

I nodded.

She pushed the twixer towards me across her desk. I reached out mechanically and dumped rum down my throat. It didn't taste as good as it had before. There was lipstick all over the bottlemouth that gave it a bitter cherry flavour. Also, the rum was warm and oily, as if it had been simmering away on a stove. Super nasty. After one swig I dropped the bottle back on her desk, as far from me as possible.

'How long have you known him?'

'My whole life. Since preschool.'

She felt around beneath all the papers on her desk until she found her ashtray and cigarettes. The ashtray was loaded with old butts – all mashed together like a pile of dead maggots. She had two smokes left: one for her and one for me. We leaned together and lit them over her lighter.

She asked, 'What are your favourite memories of him?'

I puffed on my cigarette, but didn't bother to inhale. I just wasn't into it.

'Hanging out, I guess,' I said. 'We rode our bikes around and rented movies. This one time we got high on nutmeg and saw the Northern Lights. We messed around with my dad's video camera a lot, too. Making skits and films and stuff. That was cool. And we never got in fights. Not with each other, at least.' I trailed off. I mean, there was no way I could put all my memories into words. It just sounded lame. 'We went swimming, too. We swam all the time. In the river, in the ocean, in Julian's pool. I don't know why.'

'Sounds like you were water babies.'

'Sure. I guess.'

'My daughter loved to swim, too. I think that made it even more of a shock, the way she died. I imagine it constantly. It's difficult not to. She was a tremendous swimmer for her age but she didn't have much chance.' She reached for the rum again. She could really suck it back when she got going. 'I can't decide if it was a good way to go or not.'

I thought of Mrs Reever, and Chris's dad, and the long, cool drinks they'd taken.

'Drowning's okay,' I said. 'Better than almost any other way.'

'Do you really think so?'

'I didn't used to. Sleeping pills always seemed pretty nice. Or doing that thing with the running car and the exhaust pipe. As far as suicide goes, I mean. I wouldn't hang myself, or cut my wrists. It's too sick and melodramatic. People who pull that shit mostly just do it for the attention, anyways. I'd hate it. The only thing worse would be to die in a super lame household accident – like slipping in the shower or electrocuting yourself changing a light bulb. Dying that way would harsh suck. Dying any way would harsh suck, actually.' I took a nervous little drag on my cigarette. I got pretty worked up talking about this stuff. 'But if I had to go, like Chris, and if I really had the choice – like if somebody came up and asked me how I want to die – I'm pretty sure I'd say drowning. Actually, I know that's what I'd say.'

As I finished, she leaned forward to pick up the picture frame from her desk – the one with the photo of her daughter in it. She didn't say anything for a while. She just sat there, tracing her daughter's features through the glass, as careful as a blind person reading brail.

She said, 'You've obviously thought about it a lot.'

'Haven't you?'

She smiled and put the picture down, making sure to get it at the proper angle. The rest of her desk was a mess of pens and papers and cigarette ash and spilled booze, but she was intent on getting that frame just right.

'Do you think Chris wanted to die?' she asked.

'No.' I sat up, because my back was getting all sweaty in that chair. It was hideous. 'He wasn't suicidal or anything. I just don't think it was a big deal to him.'

'Hmm.'

She rested her hands behind her head and stretched both legs out on the desk. Her ankles were right there, directly in front of me, and she wasn't wearing shoes or socks. Normally that would have made my day. There was one problem, though. Her soles. I'd never seen the soles of her feet before. They were rough and calloused and dry. Also, she had a wart on her heel. It was like finding out that your favourite piece of pottery – a mug or a bowl or whatever – has a chip. Her feet were chipped pottery. I couldn't believe it.

'What's wrong?' she asked.

She must have seen my face – but I pretended I didn't know what she meant.

'Well,' I said, looking away, 'my best friend is dead, and now I don't feel like doing anything. I don't feel like eating or sleeping or getting up in the morning or even breathing.'

She leaned forward, reaching past her toes to pick up a pen and pad of paper from her desk. Then she settled back, pen ready, and started scribbling down notes.

'That's perfectly understandable. Chris's death has made you realise that life is futile, that nothing really matters, that it's all pretty pointless, etc. Sound about right?'

'I guess so.'

'You could find religion. That's what my husband did. My ex-husband.'

'You left him?'

'It was a little more complicated than that. People handle their grief differently.' She tossed her notepad on the desk, and I saw that she'd sketched a cartoon picture of me – like the ones street artists do for money. It was pretty good, too. 'My husband handled his by going to church and praying for our little girl. It's a natural psychological reaction, but not one I was willing to deal with. You're welcome to give it a shot.'

I tried to imagine myself, kneeling in some boiling hot church.

'I don't think that's for me.'

'Fall in love, then. Or pick a career. Whatever you do, don't think too much. That's the best advice I can give you. And listen to music. Say, how about some Lennon?'

'Sure,' I said, even though I wasn't that stoked. 'Put that guy on.'

She brought her feet down and tugged open her top drawer. Her movements were all slow and deliberate, like a diver working underwater – but eventually she got the Discman started. It was that same song again. I guess it was her favourite or something.

'Lennon's the best, man,' she said. 'The absolute best.'

She snapped her fingers to the beat, totally into it.

'Yeah,' I said. 'Too bad he got capped.'

'Did you know his killer sat down to wait for the police? Wanted to be famous.'

'What a treat.'

She nodded. 'He was carrying *The Catcher in the Rye* in his pocket, too.'

'What's *The Catcher in the Rye*?'

'A book you'll read one day.'

A little while ago, I found a copy in the library. I liked it so much I didn't take it back. I just told them I lost it. I mean, I could have bought my own copy but what the hell.

'Listen,' she said. 'Listen to this.'

*Keep you doped with religion and sex and TV...*

'Isn't that a great line?'

'Yeah. Sure.'

We kept listening, but I had a hard time paying attention. It was too hot and bright in there and I was getting a super bad headache. I couldn't think of anything else to say, and I guess she couldn't either. After a bit, I started hearing these strange, nasal sounds beneath the music. She was snoring. Her head sank to one side, flopping against her shoulder. I stared at the sweaty mask of her face and the longer I stared the worse I felt. She was one of the best I'd met and all she had to offer me was booze and smokes and music, and a few witty words. I butted out my cigarette in her ashtray and got up, then crept over to the door. I only looked back once. She hadn't moved. The light from the window stretched across her desk but couldn't reach her.

I shut the door.

## 59

Somebody filmed the crash.

It must have been a bystander, because it's shot entirely handheld, and the quality is pretty bad. Of course, none of the networks screened it. Not CBC or City-TV, or even Global – and those guys love broadcasting sensationalist shit. I guess they weren't allowed. I mean, you can't put something like that on television. Maybe in the States, but not here. I managed to see it, anyways. I downloaded it from a website – one of those websites that are full of real accidents and shootings and bizarre deaths. I saw clips of this Colombian drug dealer being executed and a pizza guy getting hit by a truck and some kid falling off a five story building.

And I saw how Chris died.

It's all shot in one take. First you see the barricade by the cliff, and the cops scurrying around to get in position. There's no sound. At least, there wasn't any sound in the file I downloaded. The camera holds on the roadblock and zooms in a bit, before swinging over to the left, way down the road. That's when you see the car, snaking back and forth around all these tight curves, coming right at you. The windows are

279

bright with white-hot sunlight, almost like the cab is burning up. You can see a figure behind the wheel but you can't make out Chris's expression or anything like that. There's this one moment, though, when the car rounds the last curve and slows down – as if he's seen what's waiting for him. It's hard to say what he was thinking. Actually, I doubt he was thinking of anything right then, or anybody. He just needed a second to figure out what the hell was going on.

Then he decided: 'Fuck it.'

He starts accelerating, and the camera zooms out, until the car and barricade are in the same shot. Next comes the moment when all the cops realise that he's not going to stop, and the lady filming realises the same thing. I know it's a lady because the footage goes all jerky as she backs up, trying to get out of the way, and for a few seconds you can see her feet and sandals. But she doesn't panic. She just retreats about ten yards and keeps rolling.

That's when the cops open fire.

First they shoot into the air, and when that doesn't work they try to take him out. If you pause it, at a certain point, you can see the windshield go. They claim they got him but that's total crap. I mean, maybe they shot him and shit, but that's not the same as getting him. It's not like they actually stopped him or anything. In the video, he just keeps going faster and faster and faster, like a plane about to take off. At the last second, the cops give up with the guns and scramble away from the barricade like dozens of blue cockroaches.

Then he hits it.

I watched that clip almost a hundred times. To see how it actually happened, I had to slow it down and play it frame by frame. The sawhorses are the first to go. They just disintegrate into splinters of wood. Then the two cars blocking the road jerk back like a pair of pinball bumpers. The weirdest part is how the back half of Chris's car bursts into flame – not the front. I guess one of the bullets hit the gas tank or something. But even that doesn't stop him. He keeps going – right through the guardrail, right over the edge. For a second the car hangs in mid-air, burning like a meteorite. Then it drops out of sight.

The footage goes all jerky again as the lady rushes to the side of the cliff. By the time she gets there he's already hit the water. The whole car goes under but doesn't stay under – not at first. It bobs back up, then sinks down a second time, more slowly. The camera zooms in, super tight, as the hood disappears, and the roof, and the police lights. For a few seconds you can still see the white shape beneath the water, like a miniature submarine. Then all these air bubbles burst on the surface. After that you can't see anything, but the camera holds on the water for a long time, almost like she's expecting him to come back up.

He doesn't, of course.

Later on, that forensics expert in the turtleneck confirmed it: they'd shot him all right. They'd hit him twice in the chest and once in the arm. But the bullets didn't kill him. Neither did the flames, or the impact. They figured that out because his lungs were full of water and bits of seaweed and crap. He'd drowned after all.

## 60

Like I said, Chris got his fireworks.

Each paper wrote the story differently, and each managed

to screw it up in some totally pointless way. The headlines were the worst of all. There was the one in the *Province* that read: *'Hero' Loses Control*. That was bad enough, but the *Sun* was even worse: *Delinquent Driven To The Edge*. If there's one thing I can't stand about newspapers, it's the stupid puns they put in their headlines. These days, whenever I see them playing around with words like that, I want to buy up every single copy and burn them in my backyard. I did that, too, with some of the articles they wrote about Chris. I burned as many as I could get my hands on except for this one small-press paper, the only one that tried to tell it straight. They ran a pretty simple headline, something like: *Teen Dies After Stealing Squad Car.* That didn't piss me off so much. I mean, he had stolen a squad car. Also, he'd died. So at least that much was true. Those guys were the only ones who actually printed a picture of Chris, too. All the other rags went with photos of the roadblock, or the car being dragged out of the water. None of them cared about what he'd looked like when he was alive.

The hilarious thing is, the most recent picture this paper could find was a copy of his school yearbook photo – from the time he decided to dress up as a sweet seventies porn star. At Keith Lynn, they don't give a shit what you look like on photo day, so long as you bother to show up. I tried the same thing at Seycove and the photographer made me take off my wig and change my jacket. Chris got away with it, though, and he looked awesome. In the picture he's wearing one of my dad's old shirts, unbuttoned to the chest, with the collar flipped up to his ears. A super fake gold chain dangles around his neck and his eyes are covered by a huge pair of aviator glasses – those ones with reflective lenses. It's hard to say whether he's supposed to be a porn star or a cop or a pimp. I laughed so fucking hard when I saw that in the paper. Anybody who bought a copy must have assumed he was a harsh nutcase. I remember thinking how badly I wanted to show him, and that was when it really hit me. That he was dead, I mean.

They've repaired the guardrail he went through.

I saw it when I was driving around up there – this new bend of bright and shiny steel. Somebody had hung a bouquet of flowers on it. I have no idea who. His mom, maybe. Or one of his relatives. I guess it might have even been Karen. Either way it doesn't matter, because the flowers aren't there any more. I tore them down and threw them over the edge. I mean, Chris would have hated that crap.

It's the same with the website they've put up – this website in his memory.

The school district sponsored it, apparently. Kicking him out of all those schools wasn't enough. They had to get in on the action, too. So they created this site with a few photos of him, and a wall that any idiot can write on. Now, out of nowhere, all these treats are leaving messages like 'Miss you, bud', and 'He was such a cool guy', and talking about how they were in the same English class as him. It's the most fucked up thing I've ever seen. I can't look at it any more. Actually, I'm not allowed to look at it any more. I got in tons of trouble for writing threats on the wall to anybody who tried to post something. I said I'd track them down using my computer and firebomb all their houses. I wouldn't, obviously. I hardly even know how to use my computer, let alone track people down with it. But they didn't realise that. It was pretty sweet. For about a week the wall was totally blank. I'd completely scared the shit out of all those posers.

Then somebody reported it and I got banned. They phoned our house and tried to make me apologise and shit, but I wouldn't. Now you need a password to get on, and for obvious reasons they won't give it to me. It's pretty hilarious, actually. I'm the only one who really knew him, and I'm the only one not allowed to visit the stupid website set up in his memory. Not that I care.

## 61

I'm lucky I didn't end up in juvie. I mean, my dad said they could have charged me with a lot of things. As in, even though I didn't touch Bates they could have prosecuted me as an accessory, or an accomplice, or something like that. You know – just for being there and shit. Also, I got in the car with Chris. For some reason that was a huge deal. The way they saw it, it didn't even matter who was driving. We were both in the car so we'd both stolen the car. That's the bizarre thing about the law. They can always cook up some half-baked offence to pin on you. They probably would have, too, if it weren't for my dad. Instead they just kept me locked up for a couple of days. They questioned me a bunch of times, too.

'What if there'd been an accident?'

'You and your pal might have killed somebody.'

It was always those same two guys: Tweedledee and Tweedledum. Apparently they could talk to me alone since I hadn't officially been arrested or charged with anything.

'Hear that, bud? Somebody could have died.'

'There was an accident,' I pointed out, 'and somebody did die. Chris.'

That stopped them. Whenever you said something they didn't expect, they took a couple seconds to get over it. It was like they had super slow processors in their brains.

'Don't get lippy, bud.'

'Yeah – we're not talking about that.'

'We're talking about innocent people.'

'A little boy, or a pregnant mother.'

'Anybody could have been killed.'

'Your pal didn't even have a licence.'

'Didn't know the first thing about driving.'

They loved to finish and repeat each other's sentences, talking in circles. It wasn't like I didn't tell them anything, either. I answered all of their stupid questions, but they weren't really interested in my story. They just wanted to confuse me and trip me up.

'Maybe you should think about getting a lawyer, bud.'

'Yeah – a lawyer will probably come in handy.'

'I've got a lawyer.'

That was kind of a lie, but I figured my dad counted as my lawyer.

'Good for you, bud.'

'If we charge you, you'll need your lawyer.'

'He'll have to be present for your statement.'

They waited, as if they expected that to really shake me up. I shrugged.

'It might not come to that if you tell us what you were doing at the beach.'

'You were looking for Officer Bates, right?'

'No.' I shook my head. 'We were playing frisbee.'

'Frisbee, huh?'

'You and your pal liked frisbee?'

'Yeah.' Since they were being complete idiots, I decided to act like one, too. 'Chris loved playing frisbee. His real dream was to go professional and join an ultimate frisbee league. Sometimes, if he didn't get to play enough frisbee, he became incredibly angry.'

They both nodded together, lapping it up. One of them had a notepad. With his pencil, he jotted down the word 'frisbee' and underlined it three times. The most hilarious part was that some of the newspaper articles actually mentioned Chris's frisbee fixation.

Between sessions I was put into a holding cell on my own – just like the ones they'd locked us up in after the riot. I'd been detained, apparently. Every so often food came through the cat flap, but I never ate any. It was always a raunchy microwaveable dinner – stroganoff or lasagne or some shit – and it was always burnt on the outside, frozen in the middle. I'm pretty sure it was all part of their plan. You know – they thought they could sort of starve me into submission and get me to confess. It didn't work, though. I wasn't hungry in the first place. I mean, Chris was gone. The last thing I wanted to do was try and eat something. All I wanted to do was curl up in a corner and die.

Anyways, after forty-eight hours my dad got them to release me.

'Did they treat you all right in there?'

'Yeah. They didn't hit me or anything.'

'Hell, I hope not.'

We were in the Civic, cruising along. I assumed we were heading home, but instead of turning down the Parkway, my dad drove up towards Capilano College.

'What's going to happen?' I asked.

'I convinced them to stay the charges, under the circumstances.' When I didn't say anything, he added, 'It's on your record until you're eighteen, but you don't have to go on trial or risk facing a detention centre, thank God. You might have to do community service.'

'Oh.'

We kept driving, past the college and all the condos up there.

'Where are we going?'

Instead of answering, my dad turned through a set of large, wrought-iron gates. I thought he was taking me someplace to scream his head off at me. Then I saw this sign that read. 'Boal Chapel and Memorial Gardens'. We pulled into a parking lot surrounded by stiff rows of square-cut hedges, looking bright and green as pieces of Lego.

'What is this place?'

'You'll see.' My dad opened his door. 'Come on.'

He led me past a small, pink building with a cross over the door. There was a courtyard out front. From the courtyard all these little paths wound into the surrounding gardens, like a maze. We followed one path around a pond filled with scummy water and dotted with lily pads. Heat waves wriggled above the surface, and flies and mosquitoes were zipping about in manic circles. A dragon statue crouched at the centre of the pond, spitting streams of water from its mouth. It reminded me of the cheap sculptures you see in tourist shops around Chinatown. You know – those fake Buddhist sculptures. Everything looked a bit familiar, as if we'd stepped into a dream I'd totally forgotten about.

'I've been here before,' I said.

'I used to bring you when you were little.'

Then I knew why we'd come. Pretty soon we reached a small alcove beside the path. Dozens of bronze plaques were arranged in a grid across the stone walls. Each of the plaques had a name and date etched on it. Some of them even had little phrases – just like the ones on tombstones. My dad stopped there, in front of a tarnished plaque off to the left. He was sucking wind from our short walk. Beads of sweat had gathered near his hairline.

'Your mother hated the thought of being buried,' he said.

We stood and gazed at the square of shining metal. My mom's engraving didn't include any little quotation or proverb. I guess my dad thought that stuff was too cheesy. Or maybe she'd just wanted it this way. I didn't ask him. But basically, for my dad's sake, I did my best to concentrate super hard. I tried to think of my mom and what it would have been like to actually know her. But the sun was crushing me from above, and all these bugs were biting me on the neck, and staring at the bright bronze plaque made my eyes ache. Also, I hadn't eaten for about two days and felt pretty light-headed. I didn't know what the hell we were doing there. I'm not sure my dad really knew, either. He just stood with his hands clasped in front of him, looking solemn and a little confused. But at least he was still trying.

On the ride home, I cranked the air conditioning way up, so high that we could barely hear ourselves talk. With the heat locked outside again, I started feeling a bit better.

'Are they going to cremate Chris?' I asked.

'That depends on his mom.'

I thought about it for three or four minutes.

'I guess it doesn't matter. Not to him, anyway.'

'No,' my dad said. 'I suppose not.'

We cruised down the Parkway in silence. We passed an old man jogging and a young mother pushing her two kids along in a baby carriage. As we came up to Parkgate Shopping Centre, I started feeling super thirsty. All they'd given me in jail was warm water that tasted like it had been stored in plastic bottles for about fifty-eight years. The liquor store near the corner looked better than an oasis.

'Pops?'

'Uh-huh?'

'How about we pick up a couple of cold beers?'

My dad opened his mouth. I knew what he wanted to say. He wanted to tell me I wasn't old enough and how I shouldn't be drinking and a bunch of other crap like that. But he closed his mouth before any of it could come out. He drove along for a few seconds, tapping the wheel with his wedding ring. The turn was coming up on our left.

He put his blinker on.

'All right,' he said.


## 62


We hadn't seen much of Bates since the riot. I was kind of hoping that he'd finally grown bored of us. I mean, he'd shut down Julian's party and kicked Chris in the guts a bunch of times and got us both arrested, but I guess all that wasn't enough. Maybe he was pissed off that we hadn't been charged with anything for starting the riot. Or maybe he couldn't help himself – maybe he was like a crazed junkie who couldn't resist coming back for one last hit.

Either way, he turned up at the beach. Our bad penny.

'What do you know? It's my little heroes.'

It took me a second to realise what the hell was happening. We'd been having that dream about being underwater, and then, all of a sudden, I was awake. I noticed the heat right away, smothering me like a blanket. My throat was so parched I could barely breathe, and my head felt swollen from all those beers we'd been drinking. There's nothing worse than waking up to a hangover in the middle of a scorching hot afternoon – except maybe having to deal with Bates when you feel that shitty.

'Must be my lucky day, huh?'

I squinted at him. He lurked just out of arm's reach, with one hand resting on his gun as if he expected us to jump up and rush him. When we didn't, he inched closer. He pulled out his nightstick and sort of prodded me in the ribs – like you might poke an animal to check whether it's just playing dead.

'What are you doing, heroes?'

It was obvious what we were doing.

'We're lying here, sleeping.'

'Is that so? What about all these beer cans?'

He picked one up, making a big deal about pinching it between his thumb and forefinger. You know – as if he was afraid of ruining the evidence with his fingerprints.

'They're not ours.'

'Oh, yeah?'

'Yeah.'

I did all the talking. Chris didn't move. He just lay there with one arm draped across his face. At that point, he might have still been asleep for all I know.

'You think you can just come down here, and drink, and

throw your cans all over the beach?' He dropped the can beside me. 'The big heroes think they own the beach, huh?'

'No.'

'Well, that's what it looks like to me.'

I sat and held my head, waiting. Sometimes, if you ignored Bates, you could make him go away. He was like an annoying dog, or a spoiled child – a child with a nightstick and a badge and a gun. He stomped all around us, kicking up sand. His fleshy face slowly reddened and started leaking sweat. Dark patches showed beneath his armpits and down his back. I knew exactly what he was up to. He was looking for a way, any way, to get a rise out of Chris. He couldn't stand the fact that Chris was just lying there, completely ignoring him.

Eventually he noticed the backpack.

'What's in here?'

He picked it up by the shoulder straps and kind of shook it at us. Totally triumphant. That got the reaction he wanted. Chris sat up. He rubbed at his eyes, which had gone all bloodshot and bleary, and hawked in the sand. He looked even more hungover than me. One glance at his face told me everything. I knew what was about to happen, and I knew that I couldn't do anything to stop it. Karen could have, maybe. If she'd been around.

And if she hadn't fucked Jules.

Chris stared at Bates and said, 'That's mine. Leave it alone.'

'You telling me what to do, hero?'

'Just give me my bag.'

'Shut up unless you want to spend another night in the slammer.'

Bates tucked the nightstick beneath his armpit and started rooting through the bag. That was when Chris stood up, like a boxer rising out of his corner. He dusted the sand off his shirt, his shorts, his knees. His movements were calm and casual, as if he was entirely unconcerned. I knew better. I could tell by his eyes. The lids were heavy and weighted.

Ready.

He said, 'Give it back. It's empty.'

'Empty, huh? What's this, then?'

Bates held up a ziplock bag, bursting with fresh green buds. He couldn't believe his luck. He dangled it like a bell, right in front of Chris's face.

'That's a lot of marijuana, hero.'

'It's not ours.'

'Yeah,' I said, and stood up. I didn't want to sit there while it all went down. I wanted to be ready, too. Just in case. 'It's not ours, okay?'

Bates said, 'The same as the beers, huh?'

'That's right.'

'Maybe I don't believe you.' Bates stepped up to Chris, so that their faces were only a couple inches apart. 'Maybe I'll take you down to the station again. How's that sound, hero?'

'Or maybe you'll sit around on your fat ass, doing fuck all while we try and save an old lady from drowning. Maybe you'll do that instead.'

As soon as Chris said that, all the sound drained out of the world. You couldn't hear the wind in the trees or the waves on the shore or the people splashing around further down the beach. There was nothing. It was like a gun had gone off next to my ear. In the silence all I could see was Bates's face. His features clenched up as if he'd bitten something sour, and his jowls started quivering uncontrollably. He threw the sack of weed to the ground.

Then the sound came back.

Bates said, 'You're under arrest.'

Instead of using his nightstick, he grabbed Chris's wrist and tried to jerk it around behind his back. That was a mistake. He didn't even see the other fist coming up. It cracked across his jaw – making this sound like a branch snapping. Bates stumbled back, doing a little cross-step to keep from falling over. It took him a couple of seconds to recover. When he finally straightened up, there was blood dribbling down his chin. He stared at Chris as if he couldn't believe it – as if he couldn't believe a kid had hit him so hard. Then he lurched forward and swung his nightstick in this awkward, overhand motion. Chris saw it coming. He blocked, grabbed Bates by the collar, and stepped in close. His fists started moving, too fast to follow. Bates had no idea what to do. It was like he'd walked into a whirlwind. He threw up his hands and tried to turtle, but Chris just hit him again and again and again.

The whole thing only took about thirty seconds.

## 63

A few months after everything I ran into Karen at the pharmacy. I'd gone down there to buy some of that coconut tanning oil, actually. At first I didn't recognise her because she'd dyed her hair. Blonde. I noticed this hot blonde sniffing all the different perfumes, one by one. I was checking her out when she turned around and nearly bumped into me. It was pretty awkward. We hadn't seen each other since it happened and then, all of a sudden, we were face to face like that. I slipped the tanning oil back onto the shelf. Totally casual.

'Hey,' I said.

'Hey.'

She smiled. I smiled. We were both smiling these super fake smiles.

'What are you doing?' I asked.

'Buying perfume.' She held her arm out to me. 'Do you like this one?'

I sniffed her wrist. It smelled too sweet and sugary. I don't know why she wanted a new perfume. Her old perfume – the one that smelled sort of like citrus fruits – had been better than anything.

'It's okay. Not as good as your other one.'

'Really? I was just about to buy this.'

'Don't bother.'

She thought about it, but decided to buy it anyway. I walked with her to the counter.

'So,' she said, 'do you want to go get coffee or something?'

We went to this coffee shop across from Parkgate called Bean Around the World. It's not there any more. They've torn it down. A lot of the places we used to go are disappearing: the Hippo Club, the Avalon, our camping spot. For a while they were even talking about knocking down our school, but instead they've just fixed it up and made it unrecognisable.

It's like the city I knew is disintegrating.

Even though the café was only a couple blocks from the pharmacy, we both got soaked. There'd been no rain for months and then there was nothing but rain. Vancouver's bizarre like that. It's either a desert or a deluge – nothing in between.

'God is this ever going to stop?'

'I hope not,' I said.

As soon as we got inside, we shook out our jackets and hung

them up to dry. Karen ordered a cappuccino and I ordered hot chocolate. I hate coffee. I'd rather drop acid, or put on a turtleneck, than sit there drinking coffee. I wouldn't have even bothered except that it was Karen. All my instincts still wanted to be around her, and it was impossible to say no. We sat by the window and watched raindrops squiggle down the glass.

'What happened to your face?' she asked.

I touched my cheek. I'd nearly forgotten that it was still all puffy and bruised.

'I got in a fight with these two guys. They were saying stuff about Chris.'

'Oh. Did you win?'

'No. But I tagged them pretty good a couple times.'

She picked at the styrofoam rim of her coffee cup, leaving little marks.

'You didn't come to the funeral,' she said.

'How was it?'

'Oh, okay I guess. His mom was there. And a few relatives I didn't know he had. Jules came, too, with some other guys from your school. It was a nice sermon. Or that's what everybody said. They kept the coffin closed because of how he looked.' She blew on her coffee and took a tiny sip. 'Why didn't you come?'

'I hate funerals.'

'But it was Chris.'

'He hated funerals, too. He hated funerals even more than me. The last thing he ever wanted was to have a funeral. I'm surprised he didn't tell you.'

She looked at me like she thought I might be joking. It wasn't the kind of thing I normally would have said to her, but then nothing about us sitting there felt normal, either.

'I saw you on the news,' I said.

'Was I crying?'

'No – I don't think so.'

'I did a bunch of interviews, but I only cried in one of them. I was trying not to.'

'If you felt like it, you should have cried. But you shouldn't have said what you did.'

'What do you mean?'

'About not knowing him super well.'

She looked away. I took a gulp of my hot chocolate. It was weak and sweet, like boiled water sprinkled with sugar. I was only drinking it because it gave me something to do.

'I think about him a lot, you know,' she said. Then she stopped. Maybe she realised that was kind of a stupid thing to say. 'I think about how nice he could be, when it was just the two of us. And I think about him in his next life. I bet he'll be something really wild and free, you know? He'll be a wolf or one of those big cats that live in exotic places. Or a whale. He said he wouldn't mind coming back as a whale.'

'When did he say that?'

'The night we broke in the aquarium. On the bridge.'

I remembered, but didn't know whether to believe her or not.

I asked, 'Can you come back as an animal?'

'Oh, sure.' She waved her hand at the window. 'You can come back as anything. It depends on what you've done in this life. It can get pretty complicated. I don't understand some of it. My spirit guide knows all the details. He's been really supportive.'

'You've got a spirit guide?'

'Well, he's my mom's spirit guide. But he's sort of mine too, now.'

'Oh.'

I stared into my cup. The hot chocolate was already going cold.

'But anyways,' Karen said, checking her watch, 'he's been totally nice about getting me through it. Did you know that all of us have a familiar – like a little sprite – that we can't see? It just hovers near our shoulder and gives us advice about what to do. Mine got really sick after Chris's death. You have to nurture your familiar, and listen to it. Your familiar helps you make the adjustment in your next life. In my last life, I died in Mexico. I was a villager that got shot. It's all political down there. I've also been a turtle.'

'A turtle?'

'Uh-huh. I want to be a bird in my next life.' She ran a hand through her hair and glanced out the window. I still wasn't used to her new look. It was harsh tripping me out. 'Imagine being able to fly. I'd fly all over the city, watching.' She turned back to me and smiled – almost as if she knew how flaky she sounded. 'What do you want to be?'

'I don't believe in that stuff, Karen.'

'Well, pretend that you do. What would you be?'

'I don't know.' I ran a finger around the rim of my cup. 'A weed.'

'A weed? Why do you want to be a weed?'

'You don't have to worry about anything, or even think.'

Karen laughed. 'I don't know if you can be a plant.'

'You said you can come back as anything.'

'Well, I'd have to check with my spirit guide.'

'Don't bother.' I swallowed a big mouthful of my hot chocolate. Man, did it taste awful. 'If I can't come back as a weed I don't want to come back at all. I'd rather die and just be completely dead. It would be dark and quiet and cool and nobody would bother me.'

'That's so negative.' She tore off a big chunk of styrofoam and began breaking it into smaller and smaller pieces, looking at them instead of me. 'You sound just like Chris. He was always making fun of me for believing in this stuff.'

I didn't say anything for a bit. I was sick of talking about reincarnation. I never thought I'd find Karen boring but right then sitting with her just wasn't the same. She didn't smell the same or look the same or have the same effect on me. She wasn't the same girl.

'That's because it's bullshit, Karen.'

I didn't say it nastily. I just said it. I couldn't be bothered to lie any more.

'No, it's not.'

'It's a bunch of crap people made up so they'd feel better about dying.'

'Julian doesn't think so,' she said, getting all defensive. 'He believes in it.'

I laughed. 'Jules would believe anything to get you naked again.'

We stared at each other. She wasn't sure whether I was insulting her or Julian. Neither was I, for that matter. I was just in a shitty mood from her dyeing her hair and wanting to be a bird and from this watery hot chocolate I was drinking. But in that moment a barrier dropped between us. It felt like I was talking to her through a glass partition – just like the ones they have in jail for speaking with prisoners.

There was only one thing I needed to know.

'Have you seen Jules lately?'

'I saw him at the funeral.' She stared at her hands, as if she were holding something invisible in them. A heart, maybe.

In a quiet voice she added, 'And we've been hanging out a bit since then. He's really upset over the whole thing, too.'

She didn't have to tell me any more than that. I could imagine Jules at the funeral, and her crying on his shoulder. Probably he'd been crying, too. He was there for her, all right. He was there with his poems and his rides and his Frank Sinatra. He'd been waiting in the wings and now that the main event was over he had his chance to shine. The thought of them together, holding hands at the funeral, was enough to make me sick. I honestly thought I was going to puke hot chocolate all over the place: all over the table, all over the café, all over Karen. I crumpled up my cup in my fist. It cracked and squeaked in the way styrofoam does. Then I placed it in the centre of the table, as if it were a valuable piece of art.

I didn't say anything else. I just stood up and walked out. It would have been rad, except I forgot my jacket. I had to wait across the street until Karen left before I could go back and get it. I hid in some bushes. It was still pouring, which meant I got absolutely soaked. Luckily Karen didn't see me. At least, I hope she didn't.

## 64

Me and Julian both switched schools.

I started commuting across town, because I got so sick of the questions everybody kept asking me. I didn't really have friends at Seycove, anyways. My dad thought changing schools would give me a fresh start but within a week all the kids had found out that I was Chris's friend. Now most of them are too terrified to talk to me, and those that do only want to know about Chris. This one dickhead even asked me if Chris had ever stabbed anybody. No joke. That pissed me off so much I wanted to stab him. The only thing Chris ever stabbed was that racoon, to put it out of its misery. But basically, one of the reasons I left my old school was to get away from all the bullshit. That totally backfired. The other reason I left was to avoid seeing Julian. There wasn't much point in that, either, because he changed schools last fall, too. At first, I thought it was for the same reason I had.

That was before I started seeing him around.

Sometimes I see him with Karen, and when he's not with her he's with his new friends. They drive their cars – these super pricey cars with huge tyres – down to Cates beach and park them in a perfectly straight row, like at an auto show. One of them will crank up his stereo until the windows rattle and the frame starts shuddering. Then they just sit there, peering at the world through Oakley sunglasses. I don't know what they talk about. Nothing, probably. Every so often, especially if there's girls around, they'll get out their frisbees. They've got dozens and dozens of frisbees, in all sizes and colours. This one guy even has a trick frisbee for making fingertip catches. I know all this because once in a while I walk down to Cates and sit in the shade where we used to sit. I don't smoke any pot, though. I hardly ever smoke pot these days. It makes me miss him too much. Also, whenever I'm stoned I start crying and wishing I was dead. It's pretty fucked.

But basically, Julian is usually there, playing frisbee and showing off. I spent a whole afternoon watching him. I wanted to know if he was happy. He looked happy. He looks just like the rest of them, now. He's got the fake muscles and the fake tan and, with Karen, he's even got the fake blonde girlfriend.

At one point, their frisbee landed beside me.

'Hey man,' a mannequin said. 'Toss it here, will you?'

'Get it yourself.'

I was in a shitty mood. Come to think of it, I'm almost always in a shitty mood these days. The mannequin came trotting over, flexing every single muscle in his entire body.

'What's your problem, pal?'

'I don't play frisbee.'

'You just watch it, huh? Maybe you're a fag who likes watching guys.'

'That's right. I'm a fag and I'm going to fuck you in the ass.'

Whatever the guy expected me to say, it wasn't that. A couple of his friends came over. One of them was Tim Williams – that guy Chris had almost killed at the Avalon. I saw him and he saw me at the same time. He had this weird grin on his face, and I figured he was ready to pay me back for that night. Jules came, too, hanging a little towards the rear.

'Get this guy,' the first mannequin said. 'He says he's going to fuck me in the ass.'

I stood up. 'First I'll kick your ass, then I'll fuck it.'

I went over to him and stared him down, as crazy as I could, like I wanted to burn a hole through his head with my eyes. I probably would have had to fight him, but Jules stopped it. He stepped between us and pushed the mannequin back.

'Let it go, Steve. I know this guy.'

Tim came forward, too. 'Yeah, man. You don't want to mess with him.'

His voice didn't sound right, almost like he was talking through gritted teeth. He still had that creepy smile on his face, too. It took me a second to realise his jaw was wired shut from when Chris had broken it. Steve looked from him to Julian and back to me. He tried to act tough but you could tell he didn't want to scrap.

'Yeah, well, he should watch his mouth.'

I didn't even bother to answer. Steve and Tim and the rest of the mannequin mob faded away, leaving me and Jules standing alone. We'd seen each other around since the summer, but we'd always managed to brush past without saying much. Now I felt kind of obliged to talk to him, and I could tell he felt the same way.

I asked, 'Why is that guy's jaw still screwed up, anyways?'

'It healed wrong, so they had to re-break it and set it again.'

'Oh. Fuck.'

We stood there. Neither of us knew what the hell to say. The weirdest part was that I noticed Jules didn't have a birthmark on his chest any more. I guess he'd gotten it removed.

He asked, 'So those bastards arrested you, huh?'

'Just for questioning. The charges are being stayed or something.'

'Oh. That's cool.' He scuffed the ground with his foot. 'How's your new school?'

'It's shit. Everybody's an idiot. What about Collingwood?'

Jules had managed to get into that private school in West Van. I'd heard he was even playing on their tennis team. It must have been like a dream come true.

'Oh, you know. Same old thing.'

'Yeah.'

'Anyways, man. I'll see you.'

He trotted back to join the game, clapping his hands to call for the frisbee. Seeing that completely depressed me. He had all these new friends, a new school, a whole new life. I mean, it's not like I wanted to hang out with them or anything, but just having somebody to talk to would have been nice. The problem is, since Chris died I haven't met a single person worth talking to. I'm completely alone: just me, myself, and and my memories.

I guess that's why I wanted to get them all down.

## 65

The last film we ever made – the very last – was about these bank robbers. We used the local bank on the Parkway. They wouldn't let us take fake weapons inside, so instead we filmed the three of us walking towards the doors, holding our guns at waist level. Then we faded to black and added sound effects that make it seem like we're really robbing the place.

It's pretty awesome, actually.

'Get on the floor! We're robbing this joint!'

'Nobody moves, nobody gets hurt.'

We also put in a bunch of screaming and shouting. You know – so it sounds like the customers and tellers are totally freaking out. That's the very start of the film. Next the credits come up, and it cuts to Jules driving our getaway car. It wasn't just the last film we shot – it was also the best. We didn't worry about having a plot or anything stupid like that. Since we only had three characters, we decided the entire film would be us sitting around in our hideout, talking about how great it is to be criminals and how shitty the world is.

'What do you think it's all about, Bahn?'

Bahn was Chris's character. Bahn Scott.

'You know, man. Just hugging and thugging.'

'Hugging and thugging, eh?'

'Hugging your friends and thugging your enemies.'

I've watched that film about a hundred times. I watch all the old movies we made but I watch that one most of all. Chris wasn't the greatest actor ever. None of us were. In that film, though, he's a natural. Somehow he gets completely into character. We bought a twixer of Wiser's and a pack of Old Port cigars and sat around my basement drinking our faces off. Then we set up the camera and started recording. After the intro, it opens on a wide shot of us sitting at the table, looking awesome. We're wearing these super classy suits, which are way too big for us because we borrowed them from my dad. The table is covered in stacks of Monopoly money. Julian is counting it into little bundles while Chris puffs on a cigar and plays with his gun. For some reason we decided to give my character this sweet comb-over hairstyle. You know – so that all my hair is plastered to one side of my head.

'How you gonna spend your cut, Bahn?'

'I'm gonna buy me a hut down in Mexico. Just me and a little señorita. Someplace where they got tequila on tap and the heat won't ever find me.'

There was no script, but he kept coming up with bizarre lines like that, as if he really had been a criminal all his life. At one point, my character gets up and goes to the toilet. That was an excuse to get me off-screen so I could change the angle. There's a cut – a pretty awkward cut – and you can hear me say 'action' to start the next bit of the scene. This time the shot is of Chris and Jules facing each other over the table. The frame is tighter, so you only see their upper bodies. Chris pours them both a shot and they down it. Julian gasps, grimaces, and wipes his mouth with the back of his hand. Totally dramatic.

Then he says, 'Johnny Bananas told me the heat knows we're holed up here.'

Julian's pretty good in this film, too. We're all good in it. It was our masterpiece.

'Bring it on, man.' Chris holds up his gun – one of the cap guns we bought at the dollar store – and sort of brandishes it. 'We got enough ammo to fight them off for weeks.'

'But shouldn't we get out of here while we can?'

'You go ahead. I been fighting my whole life. I ain't gonna start running, now.'

At that point, it cuts to the wide shot again and I come back into the frame. We planned this next bit out. There's a big argument. Julian wants to grab the money and run, but Chris thinks we should stay and shoot it out with the cops. Finally, Jules takes his share of the loot and leaves with no hard feelings. We had to get somebody off-screen because we needed the police to arrive. In the final shot, me and Chris are sitting side by side facing the door. We've each got a gun in one hand and a glass of whiskey in the other.

Julian is filming.

Chris says, 'Here they come.'

I added some siren sound effects, and cars screeching to a halt.

'This is it, man,' I say. 'I'm going to miss planning heists with you.'

'Same here. You're like a brother to me.'

Right then, somebody bangs on the door. Really it's Jules banging on the table with one hand while he holds the camera with the other – but basically, it sounds like somebody banging on the door. Also, he muffles his voice and pretends to be a cop shouting off-screen.

'This is the police! Come out with your hands up!'

Chris tosses back his whiskey and I do the same.

'You ready to die, man?' I ask.

The camera zooms in on Chris, until only his face fills the frame.

He sort of laughs and says, 'As ready as I'll ever be.'

## 66

'Why did they give us these, anyway?' I asked.

We were standing on the beach at Cates, staring across the plain of burning water. Chris lifted his medal, dangling it by the ribbon like a hypnotist holding up his watch.

'Because they didn't know any better,' he said.

It seemed as good an explanation as any. I stared at my own medal, rubbing my thumb over the engraving. *Hero of the Week.* The funny thing is, for about a week, we really had been heroes. Then she'd died and everything had gotten super screwed up.

'Fuck it,' Chris said. 'Ready?'

'Yeah.'

Together, we stepped back and threw them out over the waves – as hard as we could.

After everything, I went back to Cates and tried to find them.

Nothing had changed down there. It was still super hot, people were still playing on the public beach, and the water still flashed and dazzled like a mirror that the sun had shattered into about a hundred thousand pieces. By then it was supposed to be autumn but it didn't feel like autumn at all. Everything was exactly the same as on the day we'd thrown away those medals. Except Chris was dead, of course. That was different.

But then, that's always going to be different.

I spent the whole morning diving. I even had a pair of old swimming goggles that I'd brought along. I developed this super professional routine. I'd fill my lungs with air and kick down to the bottom, then sift around in the gravel and sand. The only problem was the goggles. The seals kept leaking water, which made it impossible to see anything. By lunchtime I started freaking out. My arms felt weak and rubbery, my eyes stung with saltwater, the heat was boiling my brain, and I still hadn't found those shitty medals.

It made me go a little insane.

I picked up this giant rock – a rock so big I had to cradle it in my arms like a baby – and walked straight into the ocean. When the water reached my head I took a breath and kept going. I wasn't even looking for the medals any more. I just slogged along through the murk until my lungs were burning and my ears were aching, and then I sat down on the sea floor with the rock in my lap. The water at the bottom was cool and quiet and comforting. Overhead, I could see sunlight flickering on the surface. I didn't want to go back up. I wanted to sit like that until the pain went away. I'd never have to face the heat again. I'd never have to think about anything, or do anything.

I'd just be this piece of seaweed in a dark well.

As an experiment, I let a little bit of water in my mouth and tried to inhale. That was a huge mistake. I started choking, obviously. I coughed all the air out of my lungs, dropped the rock, and kicked off the bottom. It was nuts. The surface was miles away, shifting and shimmering. I pawed through the water like a frantic little squirrel. My chest felt as if it was splitting open and white blotches appeared at the edge of my vision. Other than that, though, nothing very abnormal happened. I mean, I didn't have hallucinations about Chris or my mom, or flashbacks to important parts of my life. All I could think about was getting one breath of air. That's all I wanted. Just one.

And I got it.

When I broke the surface, I shot straight up and nearly cleared the water – like some kind of giant man-fish. Then I thrashed around in a panic, heaving and gagging up foam. I don't even know how I made it to shore. I just remember the feeling of sharp shells beneath my knees and palms as I crawled up the beach. When I tried to stand, my legs gave out and I collapsed back into the sand, shuddering and gasping and retching and crying. I cried so hard it was like my entire face was melting. Luckily nobody saw me. I mean, when you almost die like that the last thing you want is for some joker to come up and ask if you're okay.

I lay there for at least fifteen minutes, maybe longer. It's hard to say. But once the shock wore off, the first thing I noticed was how uncomfortable I felt. I had sand in my hair and on my face and all over my chest and forearms. I think I even had sand up my nose. Plus, a sticky layer of brine coated my entire body. The sun latched onto me and started sucking sweat from my back and shoulders. It was terrible. I felt like a shipwreck victim washed up on some super shitty island – an island as big and empty as the entire world.

But I was alive, at least.

## Acknowledgements

This manuscript passed through several sets of hands before going to press, and I'm grateful for the feedback and advice of all those readers: Nai, Dave, Emma, Rupert, Matthew, and Lucy. Without you this wouldn't have been the same novel. I also owe props to the boys back home for the memories, fact checks, and permissions: R.A., P.C., S.C., R.C., R.G., L.M., M.M., C.O., E.R., P.S., and J.W., among others. Additionally, I'm indebted to those teachers who showed me the way, even if they didn't know it at the time – Mrs Sandberg, Mrs Cook, and my profs at both UBC and Aber – and to my family for their support over the years: Pops for those trips to the Wee Book Inn, Mom for always being impressed, sis for showing me what it takes, and J-hawker for sharpening my edge. Thanks as well to the many editors who've published my stories, both over here and back home. Lastly, I've got to tip my hat to all of Razor's literary predecessors: The Underground Man, Meursault, Holden, Chief Bromden, Ponyboy, Maddy-Monkey and Shrimp. And my apologies to all those frisbee fans out there.

Excerpt from an interview with fellow BYT Susie Wild. With permission of *The Raconteur Magazine*.

## You've been nominated for the Not The Booker Prize, and have recently won the Wales Book of the Year People's Prize for your debut novel *Fireball*. How does it feel?

It feels good. It's been great to get some recognition. The Wales' Book of the Year People's Prize, in particular, was a big boost for me – partly because it was so unexpected. There were some well-known names on that long-list, and I assumed the larger publishers would dominate the voting. But readers rallied around *Fireball*. I've always been grateful for the support my work has received in Wales, and this was another example of that.

## Where did the idea for *Fireball* come from?

That's a big question. *Fireball* sort of rose up out of another, abandoned novel I'd been working on. It was this existential thriller set in Prague, full of criminals and Russian gangsters. It had its moments but it also had a false heart. While I worked on it, I found myself jotting down notes about old memories, anecdotes, and urban legends I remembered from growing up. As the Prague novel fell apart, *Fireball* started coming together. Since I was approaching it from a short fiction background, I found myself writing in brief vignettes. At first I thought of it as an interlinking collection of stories, but I was reading a couple of books at the time that made me reassess that. Novels don't have to be as artificially plotted as they used to be. Joyce Carol Oates often breaks up her narratives and plays with time. Her books *Rape* and *Foxfire* were both stylistic influences, as was Spanish/Mexican cinema and literature – guys like Pedro Almodovar, Ray Loriga, and the director who shot *Amores Perros* and *21 Grams*... González Iñárritu. Basically, they showed me that I could adopt a more post-modern approach, and the stories grew into a novel that was fragmented and non-linear. In the end I think that became one of its strengths.

## The story is a coming-of-age tale set during a summer in Vancouver, where you grew up. How much relates to your own teenage experiences?

It helped to have some connection to the material. I did grow up in Vancouver, where the book is set – but it's not meant to be taken as true or autobiographical in any way. I'd be a poser if I claimed to have had a misspent youth. Razor calls himself 'the biggest wimp you'll ever meet' and that's just about how it was with me. I kept my head down, did well at school, tried to be nice to everybody – and was pretty much the same guy you know in Wales. Some of my friends were more rebellious. In all groups, and especially among teenage boys, you have somebody like Chris – somebody who is a natural leader, with a strong personality, that other people are drawn to. In the same group, you'll often find a kid like Razor – the one who's more sensitive, and has a heightened sense of empathy. In *Stand By Me*, which was another influence on *Fireball*, you see it in the character of Gordie. He grows up to become an author, and is narrating the whole tale to the viewer in retrospect. Razor isn't meant to be me, but as a storyteller I can definitely relate to that aspect of him.

## Can you remember your first published piece?

When I started out, I was hugely inspired by the theatre company my wife Naomi worked for at the time, Theatr Powys. They've recently had their funding cut by the Arts Council, which was a real blow to us personally, and also to the kids and communities of mid Wales. We're all a little lost without them, to be honest. It was the members of TP who taught me what it meant to be an artist – their level of dedication was beyond belief. I had nothing else to do while Naomi was devising scripts and touring shows, so I wrote. Looking back, that was when I really learned the craft. I received a big break through a short story contest, the Frome Festival International Story Competition, with a story called 'Mangleface.' At the same time, I was placing a few stories in small press magazines. But my first professional publication was through Francesca Rhydderch, then editor of *New Welsh Review*. I'll always remember that. Those are the debts that can't be repaid. It wasn't just about the recognition, though that was great, obviously. It also gave me a kind of confidence that I never had before. I felt that if I'd done it once, I could do it again – and other publications followed.

### You teach creative writing. Do you believe reading reading reading is a true essential to the writer?

Reading is critical, obviously. I always encourage my students to read, and read consistently myself. However, I also think you can go too far the other way, and scramble-read without absorbing anything. There are so many books out there, and so few years in our lives. But I tell myself I'll never read them all. Instead I try to take my time, absorb a text, and learn from it. I go back to my favourites, too. I'll never get tired of re-reading *The Outsider*. I remember being so grateful when I first discovered it because I had that flash of recognition you get when you find an author who perceives the world like you. That lazy appreciation of life. That sense of going with the flow, and letting things happen. The sun, the water. For Meursault it ends badly but I like the first half of the novel the most, where he's just drifting and existing.

**You have also written numerous short stories, and have a collection due out with Parthian. How does the process differ for you writing long and short fiction?**

For me, short stories can almost come in a burst of inspiration. You get the idea, you see the whole thing in your head, and if you have a few spare days or a week you can complete a first draft. It's nice because you get a kind of creative gratification, instantly. Novel writing is nothing like that. Even when a novel is going well, you can't ride a single burst of inspiration. Instead, it's like going on a long trek. You need to keep yourself in good shape, mentally and physically. You need some good companion authors to keep you company on the way. When you get where you're going, it's not going to be where you expected. The whole process can be daunting. You can become lost, confused, disheartened, distracted. You can get blindsided by something you didn't see coming – some other aspect of your life that crashes headlong into the creative process and messes it all up. You need to work hard, and get lucky, to stay on track and see it through.

An excerpt from Tyler's forthcoming short story collection (Parthian 2013)...

### Snares

As usual, Roger's up before me – looking for his ducks. When I cross the breezeway from the bunkhouse to the cabin, I find him standing at the window with his back straight and his legs apart, like a sentry on duty. He's even got a pair of binoculars trained on the stretch of river between our barge and the shore. The morning sun has already hit the water, setting off crescent-shaped flickers. I know what he's doing, but I also know he doesn't like me to directly mention the ducks, so instead I ask, 'See anything out there?'

He grunts. 'No – not yet.'

I walk over to stand beside him, shoulder to shoulder. I'm six-one and he's still got an inch on me. He's got the weight, too – all top heavy like an old bulldog. Muscled arms and thick, scarred fingers. Nine of them. He lost the other one in a net, during his days on the seine boats.

'Here, you have a look. You got younger eyes than me.'

I accept the binoculars, which are heavier than I expect, and peer through the lenses. The eyepieces feel cool. It takes me a moment to find the place to look – among the reeds and bullrushes and murky water swirling past our dock. There's no movement, though. No ducks. I study it awhile longer, listening to Roger breathe beside me, before I give up.

'Nothing doing,' I say.

'Ah, well – it's still early, yet.'

He means in the season, not in the day. The truth is, though, we usually see the ducks by mid-April, and it's getting close to May, now. He takes the binoculars back from me and starts to

317

fiddle with them, as if he's hoping they might be broken or faulty in some way.

'Better get some starter fluid in you, greenhorn,' he says.

I head into the galley, where the coffee pot is warbling steam, and pour myself half a mug. Roger makes it strong and bitter as crude oil, and I always top mine up with milk to mellow it out. I'm in the process of putting the milk away when Dorothy breezes into the galley, her brown dressing gown flapping about her like the wings of a bat. A grey nightie underneath. Pink curlers in her hair. Varicose veins bulging on the backs of her calves.

'You boys sit down,' she says, yanking open cupboards. 'I'll fix you some grub.'

'Get some clothes on, woman!' Roger says. 'You can't go wandering around like that. You're likely to scare this poor boy to death.'

He always says this, and Dorothy always gives the same answer: 'Oh – Alex is family, now.'

During the season, she would never have appeared in the galley half-dressed. Her cook's uniform of jeans and blouse and apron was as standard and consistent as my deckhand's coveralls. But it's different now that the others are gone, and it's just the three of us. The curlers and nightie are simply part of the routine – the same as the ducks, the coffee. The same as the scrambled eggs Dorothy whips up for us. We sit down at the table together, Roger and Dorothy on either end and me in the middle. I only take a spoonful of egg, and smear it across one piece of toast. This early in the morning I never have much of an appetite, which is something Roger doesn't understand.

'Better eat more,' he tells me. 'We got work to do.'

Roger makes sure that there's always work to do on the barge, even at the end of season: swabbing the decks or scrubbing the walls or cleaning the engine or replacing pipes in the ice-making machines. Today the two of us will be shovelling out the ice bins. It's a job I don't like, because of the rakes – but I've never told Roger this and I never will.

'Don't push Alex too hard, now,' Dorothy says, 'or he might not come back next year.' She's smiling as she says it, and I chuckle politely – as if the idea of me not coming back is crazy, absurd. Totally ridiculous. 'By the way, do you think you boys could finish by two o'clock today?'

Roger stares at her like she's asked him to scuttle the barge. 'We got a full day to put in.'

Dorothy purses her lips. 'Well, I'm only asking because Beverly's stopping by with little Josh, and I thought it might be nice for us all to have coffee and cake together.'

She says this carefully, letting the significance of the words sink in. Roger considers her proposal while lathering butter on a piece of toast. 'Suppose we could skip lunch, grab a sandwich on the go instead.' He glances over. 'That sound okay to you, Alex?'

'Sure. Sounds fine.' Beverly is their granddaughter – the one I haven't met. The oldest, I think. 'We should be able to get the first bin done by then.'

Roger nods, having decided, and bites into his toast. He likes it almost black, and as he chews I can hear it crunching between his teeth.

We put on gloves, take two snow shovels from the breezeway, and clomp out onto the back deck. Our barge, the *Glacier King*, is as big as the ferries that chug to and from Horseshoe Bay, except instead of cars and passengers it carries ice. When the season ends we moor up here, at a dock on the Fraser in New Westminster. Across the river I hear the sounds of the timber yard – cracking logs, whining saws, groaning pilings – and in the distance the thin arc of the Port Mann Bridge hums like a superconductor. Roger leads me down the steel stairway to the lower deck, moving heavily, getting slow in his old age. As we descend, he can't help but glance to his right, towards the shore. But there's still no sign of his ducks.

At the bottom of the stairs, he asks, 'Port or starboard?'

'Maybe starboard – we're listing that way so it'll level us out.'

Our barge was built to house the ice bins. There's two of them, about as long as tennis courts, running bow to stern. Each has its own freezer-style door, accessible from the back deck. A safety diagram on the starboard door shows this helpless stick man, all bent and mangled, caught up in the rakes. The warning reads: Do Not Enter Ice Bins Without First Raising Rakes And Shutting Off Power. I'm sure Roger's done this – he's very particular about safety – but that doesn't make me feel any better about stepping inside.

Our boots crunch on the leftover ice resting at the bottom of the bin. It's dense and compressed, about six inches thick. Roger tests it once with his shovel, to make sure it has thawed enough, before going to fetch the wheelbarrow. I'm left alone in the frosty darkness. Alone with the rakes. I can see them glittering overhead – long girders fitted with talon-like steel hooks. During herring season, they rest atop the ice that fills this bin. When we service a boat, the rakes sweep the ice into an auger, which pumps it out our delivery hose. The rasp of rakes across flaked ice is a constant background noise to our weeks at sea. The noise doesn't bother me, but the nightmares do. Night terrors, almost. This recurring dream of being caught in the rakes and dragged towards the auger. It always starts like this – with me standing alone in the bins. Then the door slams shut, and the rakes lurch into motion. As they descend, I batter on the door, scream over the rumble of the generator. There is nothing I can do, except wake in a tangle of sheets and lie there sweating, heaving, waiting for dawn.

'Give me a hand here, will you Alex?'

The wheelbarrow is stuck on the lip of the freezer door. I go over and help Roger lift it clear. We put down a piece of plywood to make crossing the threshold easier. Then we run an extension cord in from outside, plug in a work lamp, and hang it on one of the rakes.

'Well,' he says, 'this ice ain't going to walk out of here.'

He grips his shovel with both hands and drives it straight down. The steel blade crunches into the ice. Levering a chunk free, he dumps it into the wheelbarrow. I walk around to the other side, so we each have room to work. We fall into a steady rhythm of shovelling, lifting, and dumping, like clockwork men keeping time together. When the wheelbarrow gets full, Roger seizes it by the handles and trundles it out on deck. I stand in the doorway to watch him tip it off the starboard side. The ice slides out and hits the water with a satisfying splash.

As he wheels it back he says, 'Best to dump away from shore.'

I nod. The next time the wheelbarrow fills up, it's my turn to empty it, then Roger's, then mine. As we work we pause every so often to lean on our shovels, exhaling clouds of frost. We talk about the season just past, which was bad for herring roe, and we talk about our plans for the summer. Roger's going up to his family cabin in Sicamous, to hunt and fish. I'll be working as a landscaper – cutting lawns and trimming hedges and pruning trees.

'You take to that work?' Roger asks.

'Not like being at sea. But I need the money.' I work the handle of my shovel back and forth, prying loose a piece of ice. 'I got to save if I want to see my girlfriend. Out in Wales.'

Roger makes a sound in his throat. I know he doesn't understand my situation. This situation I've got myself involved in. It's not like in his day, when people stayed close to home, settled down young, got married. There was no such thing as a long-distance relationship. When I used that term around him, he said it was an oxymoron.

'I'd take you out for salmon,' Roger says, 'but you know how it is.'

I nod. He only gets one deckhand for salmon season, and the union would raise hell if he picked me over some of the other guys who have more seniority.

'But next year herring should be good,' he says. 'Make up for the gongshow they made of it this time around.'

'So you'll be going out?'

Roger's sixty-seven, two years past retirement age. He's talked about quitting since my first day on the barge, but each year the company lures him and Dorothy back with a one-off contract. 'Don't rightly know,' he says. 'Man's gotta retire sometime, but I sure ain't gonna let this girl fall into the wrong hands. Besides – we have fun out there, don't we?'

I know I've got to tell him. Tell him there's a chance I might not be back next year. A chance I'll be moving to Wales, if I get this work visa sorted out. I've been meaning to tell him and Dorothy all season, but haven't found a way to bring it up.

So instead I say, 'Sure, Roger. You know it.'

And I listen to him go on about next season, about how it's going to be a big catch since the company didn't make their quota this year. He says he'll bring out his lobster pots for us to fix up and use. He's got a new lathe and scroll saw, too – so we can do woodwork during the lulls. And that's how we while away the morning, one wheelbarrow at a time. Our shovels shearing back the layers of ice, revealing the fibreglass floor beneath.

Just before noon, Dorothy brings us down sandwiches and pop. She's dressed, now – in her trademark jeans and blouse, her grey hair carefully curled and her face grainy with make-up. I go to fetch the tatty lawn chairs from the storage compartment on the back deck. During our nights on watch, we'd sit on these, huddled in parkas and slickers, waiting for a fishing boat to materialize out of the dark. Today we set up the chairs in the sun, facing the shore. This is so we can keep an eye out for the ducks – though of course we don't say that.

Roger and I take off our gloves and unzip the top half of our coveralls, letting them drape down the backs of our chairs like discarded skin. The sun immediately starts steaming sweat from our undershirts. Dorothy has made pastrami, pickle and mustard – our staple – and for a time we sit and chew in silence, listening to waves slap against the side of the barge.

Then Dorothy says, 'Simon called. Wanted to know when payday is.'

Roger chuckles. Simon's one of the other deckhands. Fortyish. Big and blubbery. Likes sleeping in and drinking beer. Even though Roger keeps a dry boat, Simon always hides bottles of Molson beneath his bunk, to suck back in secret.

'He'll be lucky if he ever gets paid,' Roger says, shifting around in his chair. 'The amount of work he done for us.'

Dorothy says, 'We should give his cheque to Alex.'

'That would be fair.'

I crack open my can of pop and say, 'I sure could use it.'

We all laugh, enjoying our bit of mischief. Roger's no dummy. He sussed out Simon the second he set foot on the barge. He told me, 'That fat old hound is sniffing around after my job.' If he'd had a choice, Roger wouldn't have taken him on. But the barge belongs to the company, and they dropped Simon on us like a hunk of ballast at the start of last season.

323

'I'll be damned,' Roger says now, gazing off the port side, 'if I'm going to let him take over this girl. They'll have to crane me off in a coffin, first.'

'Oh, Roger,' Dorothy says.

There's some splashing in the river, which makes us all lean forward. Roger even half-rises out of his chair – that's how excited it makes him. Near the reeds, I spot the dirty grey body and white head, with its hooked black beak.

'Damn,' Roger says. 'Just a herring gull.'

The three of us settle back into our chairs, frowning.

'Don't you worry,' Dorothy says. 'The ducks will turn up.'

It's the first time any of us have mentioned them, and Roger actually winces, like he does when his arthritis is acting up.

'It's not safe out here for them,' he says.

'They're okay. They're survivors.'

'A lot of idiots in motorboats, these days. Not paying attention.'

'Ducks are fast, honey. They can fly.'

'Not the babies.'

'No, not the babies.'

'Then there's the Chinamen,' Roger says, 'with their snares.'

I take a big slug of pop. Roger's convinced that Chinese people from New West set snares in the reeds along the shore, to catch ducks for their restaurants. I don't know if that's true, but I'm anxious about the ducks all the same. Dorothy is, too. At first we only worried because Roger worried. Now, though, it's gone way beyond that. They've been a part of our routine each year, and we've never had to wait this long for them. It's like those oddballs in the States who wait for the groundhog to appear – and if he doesn't, it feels like spring might never come.

After lunch the pastrami is sitting in my belly, weighing heavy, slowing down the motion of my shovel. We're like two prisoners

324

in a chain gang, Roger and I, digging and lifting with sluggish regularity. I can feel the ache in my lower back from stooping, and the burn in my biceps from all this lifting. I don't complain about it, though. I never complain around Roger. I figure I don't have the right, really – with him being nearly three times my age.

As we work, I ask him about this girl we'll be meeting later. His granddaughter.

'How old is Beverly, again?'

'About your age. She's John's daughter.'

John is Roger's youngest. A portly guy with a walrus moustache. He visited us on the barge at the start of last season. He had a habit of fiddling with things: the tools in our gear locker, the dials in our engine room. It drove Roger to distraction, all that fiddling.

'And Josh is her son?'

'That's right,' Roger says, sticking his shovel in.

For a second neither of us says anything. Roger is struggling with this chunk of ice, more solid than the others, that won't come free. He works his shovel back and forth, using it like a crowbar, and finally the ice cracks loose.

Then he says, 'She's not married. Had the baby out of wedlock.' He says it all at once, quiet and defiant, as if he's confessing something. 'This fellow got her in a family way, and then refused to stand by her. Turned yellow-belly and took off some place.'

I didn't know people still said things like 'in a family way' until I met Roger. And I can tell he's worried I might think less of this girl – maybe even of their whole family – just because she's a single mother. Keeping my head down, I scrape up another scoop of ice.

'That must have been tough,' I say.

'Sure was. But you know what the kicker is?' He's scowling

325

now, shovelling faster. Like he needs to get this off his chest. 'After Josh was born, this fellow all of a sudden reappears. He's decided he wants to be "part of the baby's life." That's what he said. Can you believe it? This is a year after the birth, mind you. God knows where he's been in that time. Living down in Mexico, apparently. Smoking dope with his hippy friends.'

'Had a change of heart, eh?'

Roger grunts and brings his shovel down hard – like he's imagining splitting this hippy's head in half. 'Don't you worry,' he says. 'Me and John went down to his place and told him what we thought of that little plan. No way I'm letting my grandson grow up in a dope-house.' Roger grins. 'Haven't seen hide nor hair of him since.'

Imagining the confrontation, I can't help but grin, too. 'Well, it sounds like she's better off without a guy like that.'

'Damn straight. Better off by a mile. If there's one thing I can't abide, it's a man who shirks his responsibilities.' He sighs, shaking his head. 'I just don't know, Alex. I don't know what's going on these days. Everybody seems to be gallivanting around the place. All airy-fairy. Not sure what they want.'

I grunt in agreement. I'm thinking of my girlfriend, and this relationship I have. A voice on the phone. Sporadic emails. Vague and fading memories. Like I'm in love with some kind of ghost. Then I shrug and say, 'It's a different world, I guess.'

'You can say that again.'

So I do say it again – just to rib the old guy. He gets a kick out of that.

By quarter to two we've finished the starboard bin. Rather than tackle the port side, Roger calls it a day. We head upstairs to wash up before our company arrives. There's a decent bathroom in the bunkhouse, with a full shower and toilet and sink. Roger likes to lather his hands in soap and rub them over and over, cupping one inside the other. He can never get them quite clean – the creases in his palms are stained by years of dirt and engine oil.

'I think I might put on a shirt,' he says, stepping aside to dry his hands. 'Tidy myself up a little. It's not every day we have guests, eh?'

I can tell he's suggesting I do the same, so when he goes back across the breezeway I shuck off my coveralls and dig around beneath my bunk. I don't have many fancy clothes, but I've got this one pair of jeans and a collared shirt that I save for when we've got shore leave. I tug that over my head, slap on some deodorant, and run a comb through my hair – wondering why I feel so nervous.

When I cross the breezeway, the galley is empty. The counters are dusted with flour and the air smells fragrant as a bakery. The sound of voices and laughter leads me through to the lounge. Roger and Dorothy are sitting on the couch beside the window that overlooks the river – our duck-watching window. Opposite them, on the smaller couch, is this girl in a red dress. Her dark hair is pulled back behind her ears and pinned in place with barrettes. A baby boy is standing on the floor in front of her. He's not old enough stay up on his own, so she's holding him by the arms to keep him balanced.

The three adults look my way as I come in.

'My,' Dorothy says, 'don't you look like a catch.'

I laugh at that, because I'm expected to. Beverly and I don't get formally introduced. We just skip that part. The only seat is the one next to her on the couch. She shifts down to make room for me but it's still a tight fit. Our knees keep touching, and it's hard to get comfortable. The couch has a dip in the middle that eases us towards each other.

# PARTHIAN

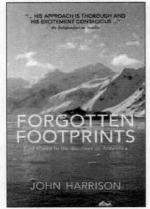

Let us take you there....
www.parthianbooks.com